THE
LAST ONE
OUT

a novel

VICTOR ADAMS

THE LAST ONE OUT
Copyright © 2020 Victor Adams

Published in the United States of America
by Saltwater Press

For information contact:
SALTWATER PRESS
5543 Edmondson Pike #61
Nashville, TN 37211

This is a work of fiction. The characters, incidents, and dialogues are products of the author's imagination and are not to be construed as real. Any resemblance to actual persons, living or dead, is entirely coincidental.

FIRST EDITION

Book design by GKS Creative, Nashville, TN
Cover art by Brian Sheehy, New Orleans, LA

Library of Congress Cataloging-in-Publication Data
Library of Congress Control Number 2020905840
Effective Date of Registration: March 26, 2020
ISBN 978-1-7348314-0-5 Paperback (IS)
ISBN 978-1-7348314-3-6 Paperback (KDP)
ISBN 978-1-7348314-2-9 Ebook (ePub)
ISBN 978-1-7348314-1-2 Ebook (mobi)

PRINTED IN THE UNITED STATES OF AMERICA

To my beloved parents, without whom none of this would be possible.

PROLOGUE

Casa de Nariño (office of the president)
6 months ago
Bogotá, Colombia

Colombian President Alejandro Hernández heard shuffling outside his office door and knew, *just knew*, a former Colombian fashion model was about to ruin his mid-day siesta. He heard her choppy cadence banging toward his office door. He kept his eyes closed and thought, *ten years after her last pageant, and she still walks like she's on a runway.* The siesta hour had ten minutes left.

"Jefe, there is a *tornillo* of North American lawyers on the phone for you."

He imagined her expressive face, framed by short dark hair pinched in at the ends. One hand would be on fisted on her hip while the other held a folder. One eyebrow would be raised in disapproval at the feet on his desk. Her perfect face would be bunched into a false pout.

Lina, his personal assistant, was so gorgeous that even the things she *said* sounded attractive. Well, everything except what she just said.

He opened one eye and rotated it toward her. Fist on hip, raised eyebrow, fake pout. She didn't have a folder, but three out of four wasn't bad.

"Lina, why are you speaking English?"

"I am speaking English because there is a *tornillo* of lawyers on the phone, and they speak just English and..." She paused, obviously trying to remember a word. "English and dumb English."

The president laughed. "You mean *loud* English."

"Yes, this word. Loud. They are always yelling."

"You're yelling." He knew that would get a reaction. He wasn't wrong. The diminutive former model narrowed her eyes and pointed at him with the folderless hand.

"Fine. Put the call through." Colombian women got more dangerous as they decreased in height.

As she spun, somehow, on her 4-inch heel, the president's smile resurfaced as he called out, "Lina, how many lawyers are in a screw of lawyers?"

Without a backward glance she called out in broken English, "It's supposed a *colectivo* of ten. Have fun."

His smile evaporated. *Ten U.S. lawyers?*

Before they even finished yelling their introductions, his feet made their way back onto the desk, and he returned to staring at his eyelids. Then the screw of lawyers rehashed the entire case. Again.

The discussion surrounded what the president referred to as, The Big Case. After his recent election, Hernández announced that his country had located the most sought-after shipwreck in history, the Spanish galleon *San José*. This ship, sunk by the British in 1708, went down in some two thousand feet of water, just off Colombia's coastal city of Cartagena. Legend held that she took nearly four tons of gold to a watery grave. The world searched in vain for three hundred years. A Colombian salvage team discovered the wreck days before Hernández won the election. The day after he took office and announced the wreck's discovery to great fanfare and soaring speeches. The unexpected wind-fall would propel the Colombia to great heights. The nation would spring to the forefront of economic development.

The Americans sued the next day. They claimed half the find belonged to them, and their lawsuit brought the whole thing crashing to a halt.

The case summary, along with the strange version of English the lawyers used, put the president back into siesta mode. It wasn't his fault; he was fluent in English. The words they used made no sense. They talked about *digesting* things that weren't food and *engaging solution protocols*. He still puzzled over that one until he heard his title called out.

"And so, Mr. President, this group out of Seattle has now sued you personally, the government, the country, and basically everything Colombian."

"Everything," he grinned with his eyes still closed. *The North Americans were always so serious.* "What about Shakira? Have they sued Shakira?"

He heard pages flipping.

A voice called into the speaker, "Uhhh…it doesn't appear so, sir. I don't have anything listed." A pause. "No sir, I don't see any Shakiras listed."

Shakiras? Plural? Surely, they understood that he…that she…

"That's not to say, Mr. President," a different dull voice, "that a Shakira wouldn't maintain a degree of liability, if, for example, one were mentioned, either orally or written, in any correspondence regarding the *San José*. We would have to percolate that question through a liability center of excellence to digest the totality of Shakira liability, both to you and the stakeholders of Colombia."

The president remembered reading that the U.S. contained so many lawyers that each state could house thirty thousand.

No wonder that country appeared so unhappy.

If they couldn't take a joke, the president saw no reason to continue the call.

"Gentlemen, twenty billion dollars in Colombian gold sits off the shore of Cartagena. A Colombian city. In Colombian territorial waters. I can't envision a world in which we share that just because they say we should."

Then again, he thought, *five second ago I couldn't envision a world in which people discussed digesting Colombia's biggest pop star. Yet, here we are.*

"We understand, Mr. President. We're pivoting our momentum towards that outcome. As your legal liaison team in the States, do you have any other questions for us?"

"Yes. Is there anyone on this planet not being sued by North Americans?"

Silence on the other end of the line.

Finally, "Sir, to deliver an impactful solution as we crescendo toward a final outcome-"

The president hung up.

Colombian president Alejandro Hernández ran both hands through his thick black hair. Colombian presidents receive one four-year term to make their mark. Twenty billion dollars in gold made a hell of a mark. No way his new administration shared that haul with anyone.

Part I
The Legal Vampires

MONTANA AINSLEY
Present Day
Fort Lauderdale International Airport

Montana Ainsley saw actual faces in the tiny windows of the big Boeing 777 as it rounded the last corner of the runway, revved its engines, and shot down the concrete away from him. He stood less than a football field away. Behind sunglasses, he closed his eyes to the blast of super-heated air. Even through headphones, his eardrums rang from the whine of the GE-90 jet turbofans. He reopened his eyes as the big plane lifted into the sky and another wheeled into the starting blocks. The line of departing planes extended as far as the eye could see.

Montana had never seen a plane take off from this distance. Had anyone? Weren't there rules about things like this? Wasn't it illegal to stand on the airport tarmac?

Oddly, he wasn't standing there alone. A line of passengers from various flights stretched out behind him. The human line appeared nearly as long as the line of departing flights. Montana estimated perhaps six hundred passengers awaiting access to a gray warehouse labeled *Customs Annex*, some thirty yards from where he now stood.

In front of him, one of mankind's greatest inventions thundered up and down the airport highways. Behind him, an endless line queued to enter what looked like a government-run Wal-Mart. The buses, which met them plane-side, *intentionally* deposited him here. This appeared to be by design.

Back home in his *departmento*, the rough equivalent of a U.S. state, they handled about one aircraft a day. People hung out on the tarmac all the time. It was normal. It was also Central America.

Well, he thought, trying to reason through the problem, *I was asleep when we landed. Maybe we diverted to Jamaica? It's certainly hot enough. And this whole warehouse-Customs thing seems on par with the Caribbean. Surely the safety-conscious U.S. isn't dumping civilians onto an active runway.*

Montana pulled off his worn Panama hat, swiped his brow, and turned a 360. He'd stood under the blazing sun for nearly an hour.

This is all too weird.

He looked at the guy in front of him. Khaki shorts, flip flops, baggy t-shirt. Clearly a tourist of some stripe. Surely this guy knew what was up. Montana removed his sunglasses, earphones, and tapped the guy on the shoulder.

When he turned around, Montana nearly laughed out loud. Six feet and three inches of frighteningly sunburned human glared at him through bulging eyes. The burn was so deeply red it actually *looked* hot. Were his eyebrows singed?

Montana mumbled out his question while stifling a laugh.

The man didn't say a word. He just kept staring at Montana.

This set off a yellow flag. Montana's Latino friends warned him about how edgy Americans were these days, and that the slightest misstep sent them into an indignant fury. Montana knew his own appearance didn't help. He didn't possess what people would call, a friendly face.

Montana Ainsley was born in the U.S., although he hadn't stepped foot here since he'd watched the police raid his empty house five year earlier. His skin now held a permanent deep brown color, but the narrow face still held the stress lines of a middle-aged American. He kept his dark hair shaved close. Even behind sunglasses, his stark green eyes permanently squinted against the constant sun. One corner of his mouth was perched slightly higher than the other, giving his face a constant smirk. Life in a non-English speaking country had tamed the North American habit of excessive talking. For the first two years after he fled, he couldn't communicate with the locals even when he had something to say.

Nowadays, Montana was more observer than participant. His silence, coupled with the squinted eyes and smirk, gave the impression of aloof amusement as he watched events unfold before him. He knew it pissed some people off.

Montana rescanned the guy. The sweat stains emanating from his armpits melded together and soaked the entire top half of his shirt. His khakis were sweat-dark around the big waistline. This guy looked like he was either going to explode in rage or collapse on the spot. Montana considered his five-inch disadvantage. Could he…oh, wait a second.

He restated his question, in English.

The guy's posture relaxed, but words exploded out of his mouth, "Yeah buddy, welcome to Ft. Lauderdale," he paused. "So typical." Then he sighed loudly. "Can you believe this? I have a connection to Minneapolis in thirty minutes. Think I'll make that? Yeah, right. I can't believe this. You'd think they would be better prepared to meet arriving passengers."

"Yeah, well I'm sure they'll get it sorted. This is the U.S., after all." Montana overemphasized the point, hoping for confirmation.

Somehow, the guy turned a deeper shade of red. The smirk widened as Montana thought, *indignation red…is that even a color?*

"Sorted? Sorted? Buddy, where do you think you are. Our government couldn't sort a box of pencils." The man extended his arms and sweat droplets flew. "Does this look sorted?"

The guy carried on, but Montana was done. He'd learned what he needed. They *had* landed in the U.S. A sign for energy-infused lunch meat on one of the departing planes confirmed it. Incredible, but facts were facts.

He had bigger concerns than this guy's outrage. As soon as Montana heard the guy say the word *unacceptable*, he put his sunglasses back on and replaced his earphones. The whole world knew that when Americans called something *unacceptable*, a long-winded surrender followed.

As he slid his shades down to signal the conversation was over, he noticed a vendor walking up the line with a wooden box full of mini-sunscreens and water bottles. With the lopsided smile still on his face, Montana pointed at the vendor and said, "You might invest in some of that."

Invest was the right word. The cheery Latina sold three-ounce bottles of SPF 300 for fifteen bucks a pop, credit cards accepted. No wonder she was happy. The guy ahead of him reached for his wallet and raised his hand.

Too late now, buddy.

Thirty minutes later, they made it inside the air-conditioned hanger. It was freezing. The temperature change from the outside had to be over forty degrees. The guy in front of him started shivering almost immediately.

A dozen switchbacks ahead, he saw each passenger get swabbed for DNA. The swabs were walked over to one of three computer terminals. Once the swab was inserted, the terminal hummed for a minute then lit up in one of four colors. Then the swab was taken to the next computer, and the process repeated. Although his own status worried him, the different colors didn't seem to cause the agents any pause. A sample moved from one computer to the next, regardless of what popped up.

Once through the DNA check, the passenger was cleared for a body search, an x-ray, a Scatter Scan, a temperature check, and eventually allowed to approach a table and account for their various items. Most of the carry-ons were hand searched, alongside their owners. The whole warehouse looked like central booking from a *Law and Order* episode.

It appeared that security had been tightened up since he'd last been in the U.S. Tightened up, but completely understaffed. There were only three TSA agents manning the customs search area, and by the time Montana was within sniffing distance, he understood the slowdown much more clearly.

Great. Either there's a glaucoma outbreak, or they finally legalized weed.

To make matters worse, the agents singled out well over half the people for extra scrutiny. It wasn't even subtle. The TSA crew made so much eye contact it looked like they were colluding at a poker tournament. Apparently, anyone scoring above moderately attractive was a national security threat.

Stoned government agents feeling up bodies, searching luggage, and laughing about it. *This is going to take time.*

2

CHRISTIAN RAMÍREZ
Present Day
Northeast Nicaragua Jungle

Jean Christian Ramírez Paolo, *Chris* to his friends, stood on an elevated clearing overlooking his small gold-mining operation. At just over five and a half feet, he needed the hill's help to see down to the river where his crew worked. Despite his twenty-two years, Chris still held the face and frame of a young teenager; he probably weighed a hundred and ten pounds soaking wet. He kept his lush, black hair cut short on the sides and longer in the front. Then he swept the whole mop back and gelled it in place. A few strands poked back over his forehead. After three years of trying, he had finally mastered the look: a baby-faced Clarke Gable.

A Latino Clarke Gable, anyway. Chris had the dark brown skin of his coastal Miskito forefathers. He had an open boyish face, brightened by the gleaming teeth in his smile. Apart from his eyes, he was devastatingly handsome. But the eyes were the problem. The eyes always caught people's attention. They were as dark as shined agates beneath razor thin, pointed eyebrows. His teachers called them *suspicious eyes*, and they changed the nature of his appearance. Little kids, unaccustomed to the notion of tact, said he had the eyes of a thief. Without his constant smile, mothers all over Nicaragua would label him a criminal and ban

7

their daughters from dating him. His grandmother's mother, his *bisabuela*, said that he had the cunning eyes of his Paolo forefathers.

After learning the real history of his family's origin, Chris finally understood what that meant.

A year earlier, he had graduated from university in his dusty, northwestern hometown of Leon, Nicaragua. At the family party celebrating its first graduate, his *bisabuela* pulled him aside for the first real adult conversation of their relationship. While his mother, his *abuela*, and the rest of the family drank Flor de Caña rum in chairs in the front of the house, in the back, the old woman spun out a tale so incredible that Chris still wasn't sure he believed it.

With her third rum in hand, she opened the conversation with a showstopper. "Did I ever tell you that our family once ruled the entire eastern half of Nicaragua?" Her tone was so disinterested, she might have been commenting on a passing cloud.

Chris opened his mouth to respond, but the comment was so enormous he couldn't think of anything to say, so his mouth just hung open. Unlike the North Americans he saw on TV, Nicaraguans didn't question, disrespect, or ignore their elders publicly. His *bisabuela* said it, so it was a fact.

"You are trapping mosquitoes, *amorcito*." Chris closed his mouth. "It's true," the old woman continued nonchalantly. "But before I tell you this story, I want to explain why I am telling you."

His *bisabuela* then went into the long and sordid political history of Nicaragua. The country was a series of near booms, followed by horrific busts dating back to Nashville's William Walker in the nineteenth century. Nicaragua, perhaps more than any nation, proved the axiom that absolute power corrupts absolutely. "I'm telling you this, because another disaster is on the way. Your grandfather," she crossed herself and whispered a prayer, "your grandfather spoke about it often."

She then described how the current president overthrew his predecessor in the 1980's, only to institute the very same policies and repression.

"Your grandfather feared that this dictator would be worse. Unlike his predecessors, he has modern weapons, and he now lacks a common enemy to distract the people. As he has gotten older and sicker, the family has acquired more money and power."

Chris cut in. "I know all this, great grandmother, but what do you mean we're headed for disaster?" The old woman did have a penchant for the melodramatic. "Nicaragua has been the most stable country in Central America for the past decade."

"That's the surface. Underneath, they've stolen everything and bankrupted the country. One financial slip, and we will have another revolution. And that, *amorcito*, is why I am telling you this. You are the first educated male in our family. You have run a business." She pinched his forearm, and he winced inside. "You speak four languages. You understand mathematics. You are one to re-secure the fortunes of this family."

She paused and pointed a withered, bony finger at him, "but you won't do it here. This family has no future in Nicaragua. This country is on the brink of breaking apart, and I fear that prosperity for Nicaragua, and our family, is further away than ever."

The message shocked Chris to his core. He couldn't think of a response with any substance, so he made a joke about her use of the English translation of *amorcito*. "Hey, you're speaking English again?" Chris laughed nervously, but the old woman stared straight through him.

"You are the head of this family, now."

She must have read the incomprehension on his face. For over a hundred years, his family had lived and worked manual labor jobs in Nicaragua's second largest city. The family lived close to poverty, but everyone pitched in whatever money they could, and things had been okay. That would change now that he could earn more with his degree.

"For generations," she said, "the women of the Paolo family line passed along the oral history that I am about to tell you. Because we always seem to fall in love with sweet-natured laborers as husbands, the Paolo women have feared that revealing the truth would be the end of our entire family line. All it would have taken was one man, whether it was your father, grandfather, or his before him. They would have heard this tale and chased off in search of our shared destiny. Even if they found it, none would have known what to do with it.

Mostly likely, it would have killed whomever tried to claim it. In normal circumstances, I would be telling this to your little sister in ten years, but I may not live that long, and unlike every other man in our family, you will know what to do. You have the eyes."

There it was again, Chris thought, the damn eyes. Before he could comment, the old woman carried on.

"Plus, you have a *chele* friend. That American. He's a good man. If you run into trouble, he can help. Between your education, your ancestry, and your father's honesty, you have all the skills you need."

Chris couldn't understand what he was hearing. Leave Nicaragua? Was she drunk? He was considering this when she finally began her bizarre tale.

"Three hundred years ago, our Paolo family was the most powerful family in the Autonomous Caribbean half of this country, and your great-great-great grandfather was the most powerful Miskito tribal chief in Central America."

"Wait, we're not from Leon?"

"No," she said matter-of-factly, "We're not. Decades ago, our family fled the Miskito Coast at the behest of the family elder. The reason is lost to time, but family legend holds that we were once humble fishermen when one of our distant ancestors came across something that transformed our family. Whatever it was, it was so powerful that it elevated the family to wardens of the entire Miskito nation. For reasons I do not know, we were forced to abandon that destiny. Now that there is no hope for a brighter future, I charge you, Jean Christian, to reclaim our birthright. Use it to change this family's future. You want the Nicaraguan Dream for your brother and sister? I am giving you the means. But, you will have to lead the family out of this country first. With this pair in power, corruption is Nicaragua's only future."

"But, you don't even know what this secret is? How can I possibly...what am I supposed to do?" He was at a complete loss for sensible words.

"True. I do not know exactly what it is." She paused with a sly smile on her wrinkled face, "But I do know exactly where it is."

While Chris peppered her with questions, the old woman talked on as she drew a map, filled with her peculiar shorthand of Creole, English, and Spanish. To any outsider, the mix of languages was completely indecipherable. As an

English speaker, Chris could decode the Creole dialect, and her story answered his longstanding question about how his uneducated grandmother's mother maintained fluent command of English.

For weeks after the conversation, Chris wrestled with how to handle the strange charge from his *bisabuela*. It didn't take him long to come up with a working theory. The timeline landed smack in the middle of the Spanish conquests of the Americas. And what could elevate someone from poverty to power in those times? The same thing as now. Chris added *conquistadores* to *money,* divided the sum by *hand-drawn map,* and the answer became obvious: *gold.*

3

LIONEL DEWALT
Present Day
Fort Lauderdale International Airport

ionel scanned the mass of humanity through watery, red eyes and enlarged pupils. The line was endless. Fucking endless.

Lionel had been with the international arrivals TSA crew for seven years. He knew exactly why the lines were endless. They were endless because so many damn lawsuits had been brought against the TSA that their rulebook contained over three thousand pages. They had more procedures to follow than a heart surgeon. Although, he thought, they did ignore most of them. Heart surgeons couldn't do that. That is, they ignored them until someone got caught. Then they got another thirty pages of procedures.

First off, they had to submit each passenger's DNA to three different computers. One was connected to a criminal background check. Standard stuff.

The second was connected to the country's "Legal, Immigration, and Civil Event" database. The LICE database, enacted at the behest of the massive legal lobby in DC, alerted the entire industrial-legal complex of the comings and goings of those with pending civil cases on the books. It didn't raise a notice for immediate action, merely notified the subscribers that a person involved in any type of legal proceedings had entered or left the country.

For an additional fee, GPS tracking, cell service peeking, and personal data streaming were available.

The last computer was connected to the country's National Advertising Database Search[1]. This was a cloud-based data repository which alerted paying retail organizations that potential customers had just entered the country. For an annual subscription paid to the Department of Commerce, companies could advertise to the newcomers. The database came into being as a counterweight to big business' unfair financial advantage over their smaller counterparts. Large tech companies could pay other large tech companies to harvest GPS data on individuals. The smaller players couldn't compete. Enter the Congress and it's NADS.

NADS was designed to level the playing field. Fortunately, Big Tech allowed Congress to maintain the database once they confirmed its hackability. The system was notoriously buggy outside the main coastal cities.

When Lionel first started working with TSA, the processing of inbound passengers was slow. After Congress addressed the problem, things got much worse.

Customs and Immigration gave up on their various attempts to exchange money for a faster customs experience. It turned out that only a fraction of the population was willing to pay the five hundred-dollar program fee and give over their DNA in exchange for faster customs lines. The programs, at various times referred to as Global Pass, Espeed, iCheck, and the very short-lived Top International Traveler, all failed. All had lost billions within months of their launches, and as the agency teetered toward insolvency, Congress stepped in to ensure that everyone got the worst of both worlds.

Since people had paid in, none of the previous programs could be cut. But since not enough people had paid in, the programs couldn't be afforded either. Congress outsourced the problem to a highly overpaid team of business ninjas with logistics black belts. The ninjas attacked the problem; attacked it until they killed it. Now, nothing moved.

---

1   The history of snide acronyms started when Seattle's City Council introduced its newest tram project, *South Lake Union Transit*. Derisively referred to as *SLUT* the very same day, the city council refused a name change, and the race to create the most juvenile database name began.

To manage staffing expenses, TSA teams were cut to three people. The three people processed passengers in the endless regular entry line. The Global Pass/Espeed/iCheck/TIT lane, now collectively known as the *GIT* lane, stayed open, but it wasn't staffed until its line rose above twenty-three people.

The ninjas provided un-sourced data to prove that anything longer than twenty-three people made bad optics.

When a twenty-fourth person stood in the GIT lane, it signaled that special treatment was not being given. So one member of the small TSA crew split off and processed half a dozen GIT lane passengers, reducing the line to acceptable levels, and providing the illusion of a faster customs experience. Wait times soared, but the red ink disappeared. The ninjas returned to their business dojos to contemplate more menacing belt colors. Congress congratulated itself on a job well done.

Despite the increased workload and frustration, TSA employee turnover dropped to virtually zero. Congress took the credit for that, too, though they were at a loss to explain why.

Lionel knew why. So did his fellow employees, but nobody spoke about it out loud.

International arrivals at Fort Lauderdale was like a prison. There was a tense détente among the inmates (numbering in the hundreds) and the guards (numbering less than ten). Most passengers were too scared to complain. The foreigners didn't want to be denied entry, and the locals didn't want to wind up on a mysterious list somewhere. The few passengers who did complain were met with stone silence.

The agents had been trained never to engage irate passengers. Many an un-fire-able agent received a two-week suspension for being filmed abusing passengers. To keep calm, the three-person TSA squads always got high before arriving international flights. It also helped them endure the processing of thousands of frozen, sunburned, and angry passengers, many of whom spoke little English.

The job was, on balance, a pretty good gig. Since drug tests had become obsolete due to conflicting state and federal laws, as long as you didn't have a violent felony on your record, your experience level and attitude meant nothing.

Lionel exploited a tenuous family relationship to get the job, slept through a few de-escalation seminars, tased a few test dummies, and got a lifetime government pension and a license to feel up anyone he thought looked good (providing the wand was set to maximum sensitivity).

But the real reason nobody left the TSA was that you made *real* money here. TSA agents had a mandate to protect the homeland from any object that looked suspicious. Lots of things looked suspicious. Lots of things.

Every item the teams confiscated got tagged, shipped, and resold somewhere. Every month, the cash from the sale got redistributed back to the teams. The weekly item take, *the drag*, was counted, logged, and sent off in large boxes. Lionel didn't know exactly how it worked. He just knew that it worked. It worked a lot.

After seven years, Lionel oversaw the records of the daily *drag*. He logged all the items and submitted the paperwork to the TSA Deputy Director of the airport. That guy's team then took possession of the goods, and at the end of every quarter, the five teams with the largest *drag* received cash payments. Competition was fierce. Since the winning teams and amounts remained a mystery until the final day, they called it a lottery. The TSA lottery.

It was a secret bonus program for the top *draggers*, and the source of massive income bumps for the best crews. All they had to do was confiscate and keep quiet. Most of the teams were low level ex-cons of varying degrees, so silence wasn't a problem.

FLL had three "interview" rooms available for use if the TSA deemed it necessary to detain a passenger. Detentions were up just slightly over three thousand percent from 2001.

One agent managed the door outside the room. One stood next to the seated detainee while the other sat across from them. The luggage was opened on the table in between. The job of the first interview agent was to threaten and distract a passenger while the seated agent slipped one of the passenger's sellable items into a padded pocket concealed under the interview table. So long as they stayed away from phones and computers, most Americans were so stressed they assumed they left their stuff in a cab or a hotel. The foreigners were too scared to lie on their customs forms, which Lionel's team used as a checklist for the *drag.* And nobody could wade through the government morass to make a claim that their property had been seized. The way civil forfeiture worked, they'd have to spend four grand just to pay a lawyer to *try* to recover the property.

Lionel had to hand it to bureaucracy. It sure made it easy to steal.

Any passengers who complained about lost items were put on a special list for extra lifetime harassment. The TSA leaked the list, then denied its existence, thus generating the necessary fear for public compliance.

There was hushed talk of taking The Lottery national, airport versus airport. Although this would up the prize money considerably, inbound customs proved to be the hiccup. International arrivals were prime hunting ground for civil forfeiture, and smaller airports just couldn't compete.

He'd always thought it strange that the civil forfeiture laws that allowed them to steal were the very rules that were keeping the pool from hitting the big time. Who said there wasn't honor among thieves?

Rumor had it that Logan Airport had an MIT graduate close to finding a solution. If the lottery went national, Lionel would retire at fifty-two and buy a house on the beach somewhere affordable, like Mexico.

Damn it. Weed always did this to him. Made him lose his focus. He looked up at the x-ray screen.

"Hey," Lionel called out and switched off the conveyor belt. "Hold up, y'all. Whose bag is this?"

A bald, very sunburned man raised his hand. Goosebumps covered his red skin and dried sweat stains crisscrossed his clothes. He was shivering in the freezing air of the hanger.

Perfect, Lionel thought.

"Okay, listen, I gotta take a closer look. Follow me".

The man's red face lightened to bright pink. "What? Seriously? After melting in the heat for two hours and freezing in this goddamned hanger, now you need to search my bag?"

"Uh," Lionel dropped to a more threatening tone. "I know you didn't just swear at me, did you? I hear you wrong?"

The man's courage evaporated against the full weight of the TSA.

"I…well, I guess not. But I have a connecting flight," he whined.

"Now look here," Lionel said. "We goin' walk into this room and go through this here bag." He kept his voice low, slow, and a tad thug. "There was something on the scanner I didn't understand. I got to pull it out to verify what it is. When I'm satisfied, you proceed to your connecting flight." Calm. Reasonable. Clear.

The man looked around him for support. Out of the corner of his eye, Lionel saw a smartphone start filming. The sun-burned guy followed Lionel's eyes and saw he was being filmed. He stood a bit straighter.

Those damn cameras always give these guys five seconds of courage.

"No," the man shouted as his voice broke. "That's unacceptable. I've been tested, swabbed, and x-rayed already. Enough is enough."

"Sir! I've warned you…"

"This is unacceptable." It was almost a question. The guy was wavering.

"Sir…"

"Damn it, I…"

He never finished. As the guy's eyes rolled up and he started collapsing, Gloria, one of Lionel's crew, deftly caught him with her right arm while re-holstering the taser in her left hand.

Dang, she's like Billy the Kid with that thing, now.

The guy wasn't totally out. Airport tasers were set to administer a "compliance dose". The optics proved better if the passenger didn't completely collapse. It didn't matter anyway. The cuss word he uttered shredded the perception that he was a victim.

Lionel and Gloria loaded the guy onto a TSA PeopleCart 3000. It took less than ten seconds. Unlike the previous models, the 3000 had a drop gate for faster loading. He patted Gloria on the back and mumbled, "nice catch."

She responded at the same low volume. "Maybe I wouldn't have had to tase him if you'd offered to escort him to his connection."

Lionel nodded. That kind of feedback helped teams improve.

He turned back to the line and announced that there would be a short delay while another TSA team arrived. When he finished the announcement, his eyes locked onto the next guy in line, a medium-sized man wearing a panama hat. The guy had a deep tan and the dullest green eyes Lionel had ever seen. The guy didn't even blink, didn't change expression. He didn't look scared or frustrated. Worse, he didn't look down. The dude just looked straight at Lionel. His face was totally slack, like people were tased in front of him all the time. It unsettled Lionel. People were supposed to be shocked. They were supposed to be scared. They were supposed to be as compliant as caged gerbils. They weren't supposed to be cool. Panama Jack looked like he was evaluating a piece of art.

Good thing the suitcase wasn't his.

Calm people caused trouble. There weren't many left, but years of experience had taught Lionel that if they ever got busted, it would be a calm person who busted them.

Since Lionel's team had "caught" one, another TSA crew jumped into place. Lionel watched Panama Jack out of the corner of his eye. The guy snagged a ratty backpack, gave the room a once over with those dead eyes, found the exit, and strolled out like Hannibal Lector following that shrink at the end of *Silence of the Lambs.*

Yeah, that cool dude's got trouble written all over him.

4

TERI BRADSHAW
Present Day
Seattle, Washington

What Lionel and the rest of the TSA agents didn't know was that the TSA lottery shot past "national" some time ago. Several years earlier, the founders brought in professional management and transformed the lottery into a vertically integrated business juggernaut.

The lottery existed in over thirty U.S. airports, transacted business in twenty countries, and employed hundreds of people. There was a non-profit division with a nearly undetectable footprint. The lottery owned rental property on three continents and held investments in countless other businesses.

They didn't call it the TSA lottery. At Seattle HQ, they called it The Bradshaw Group, LLC. On the cover of Time Magazine, they called it, *The Company with a Conscience.* Investors' Business Daily proclaimed the CEO: "The New Face of Capital Consulting" and churned out a five-page cover story about its young, blonde, no-nonsense CEO.

Teri Bradshaw, the CEO in question, viewed the attention as a double-edged sword. First off, she wasn't young, she was forty-one. But the press had done less due diligence on her than they did the company. On the one hand, it was great for business. Once word got out, she had to hire a publicist to manage the interview requests. Her fame attracted investors. Lots of investors.

The extra attention was also the problem. Teri had a lot of balls in the air just now, and the last thing she wanted was a reporter asking questions. So far, none of them had. That was good, because Teri Bradshaw was running out of closets in which to stash skeletons.

*　*　*

Despite her portrayal in Business Daily's *Dollars to Dulce* article, Teri's life hadn't started out this way. She created The Bradshaw Group during a period of sheer, upper-middle-class desperation. Teri was anything but a rags to riches story.

Both she and her then-husband started life as attractive, smart twenty-somethings. Their lives appeared to be on the fast track when he got a plush Regional Director post at his financial services firm. Teri already made good money as an accountant. They got a customized allergy-free dog and rocketed past the joint incomes of their contemporaries. But their lives never quite got out of third gear. He, Paul, always travelled instead of manning a desk and racking up promotions. Meanwhile, Teri struggled to attain top associate billing at her firm.

Their expenses caught up to their income, and by their late 20's the Bradshaws reached their cruising altitude of $190,000 a year. A direct flight, forty years, no stops. They'd start their final descent at age sixty-five and they'd be landing at their destination on the Florida Gulf Coast by age sixty-eight.

At least, that's what Paul wanted. Their lives weren't miserable or unhappy. But Teri was certain that she should attain more. To Teri, more was a partnership. More was the first female CEO of a top three accounting firm. More was a bigger house. More was a second home. More was a better car. More was always moving forward.

After eight years of working inhuman hours, more wasn't happening.

Her mind was completely focused on becoming a partner. That was the top of the food chain. For the first few years, she outworked her counterparts by logging constant eighty-hour weeks. None of her colleagues could keep up.

But her name was never mentioned as an up-and-comer. The next few years saw her living on airplanes to attend to clients across the globe. When she wasn't on a plane, she was officing in executive airport lounges and calling into mind-numbing staff meetings. The partnership didn't appear any closer.

Desperate, she went for a whole life makeover. She jettisoned her starter husband, ignored her pragmatic brain, and gambled that she wasn't embracing the business culture enough. She started peppering her emails with meaningless business slogans. She talked about synergy (*whatever that was*) and leaning-in (*whatever that meant*). She ended nearly every sentence with the word *right*. She got *buy-in* for everything. She thought outside the box (*along with, it appeared, everyone else in the surveyed world*). She hung motivational posters on the walls of her tiny cubicle. The whole façade, so boring and robotic, made her nauseous at the end of every workday. The fake peppy attitude, the endless sentences, struggling to find a *win-win* for every confrontation…it all made her logical mind want to explode.

With Paul out of the picture, she started attending office get-togethers as a single woman, figuring that her single status might help in the male-dominated business. Her stock initially rose, but she just couldn't pull the trigger on bedding any of her coworkers. The attractive ones still liked their wives, while the others were, well…not an option. The single guys were off limits after one experiment. The guy wanted to talk after sex. Teri could suffer the post coital babble, but not the actual language that he used. To Teri, they hadn't just *synergized best in class sex.*

At one final Christmas party, she overheard her boss discussing her with the managing partner. *Medically necessary gastric bypass* described her to *baldness distracting goatee* as a decent accountant, but past her prime.

Decent? Past her prime?

As the shock of the words washed over her, *goatee* chimed in that he'd "still do her".

Still do her?

At those words, a link somewhere inside Teri's brain just snapped. It was like her brain was pulling a trailer at eighty miles per hour one minute, and the chain connecting them just broke free. She felt the chain inside her head whipping around and lashing at her eyes, her ears, and her forehead. The pain staggered her physically. She spent twenty minutes recovering in the bathroom before drove home in a daze.

Then she paced her rented apartment for hours while the liquor wore off. The pain abated a bit, and finally her thoughts came fast and clear. It wasn't that they objectivized her; that door sometimes swung both ways. The women in the office were often much crueler than the men. Apart from each guy's physical shortcomings being their nicknames, the women had a designation for a whole class of partners: "*mauldy*". Married, bald, and paunchy.

It was that they had forced her, *forced her*, to adopt *their* culture in *her* life. They espoused over and over that if she just worked harder, believed more, and bought what they were selling, membership followed. It was all a lie. All the slogans, all the language, all the *leaning in*. They didn't believe a word of it. The difference was that they were in charge. They forced it on everyone, but when the lights went out, they were just as base and average as cavemen.

And the notion that one of these phonies would, graciously, 'still do her'?

That thought triggered her brain pain again.

Her entire career had been decided by life-weary nitwits over a goddamned bourbon. That's what Teri kept coming back to; that they judged her from atop their rum-soaked golf courses, wearing stupid pants and shaving half a dozen chins. Had the rules started this way, she could bare it, she could adapt and overcome. But not this, not the lie. The whole worship of advanced business culture was a sham, and she had fallen for it. Jesus, she'd left her husband for it.

As Teri thought about her shattered marriage, all the hours worked, all the stupid goddamn slogans, she felt a long-term anger bubbling up. Blood-feud anger. Anger that nothing would pacify.

Switching companies was pointless. Three years ago, the top three accounting firms had merged so they could raise and fix hourly accounting prices. When anti-trust regulators sniffed around, they tripled their lobbying donations and franchised back out under different names. The price-fixing stayed, as did the mentality. If you were blackballed at Walsh & Sons, PLC three years ago, you were just as blackballed at the new firms: Count On It, Inc. and AccuStar, LLC, both independently owned subsidiaries of Walsh & Sons, PLC.

So, there she was at thirty years old with no advancement in sight. She cut back hours in favor of yoga. She stopped reading management books. She stopped making verbs out of nouns. She stopped *leaning in*. Her hair faded back to its natural brown, and she traded her contacts for glasses. The pain in her head didn't stop, though. It was muted, but it was always there, reminding her that her life was untethered.

Teri retreated into herself. She wasn't crying for help. She wasn't in depression. Her mind was retrenching. Calculating the next move. She had been deceived and that was part of life. But she vowed never, ever, to let that happen again. Her naivety and math skills had led her into that trap. Her wit and anger would have to lead her out.

She didn't have the money to start her own business. Her divorce wiped out all the savings the former couple had collected. She'd never reflected on it before, but she and Paul only had one property, no kids, and no willingness to fight each other. Their only assets had been $75,000 in savings and $10,000 in home equity. Somehow, the divorce had stretched out for over a year. In the end, they'd divided the last $5500 in savings and sold the house to pay off the new divorce tax[2].

Teri was stuck, and she knew her firm knew it. It felt like a fight she couldn't refuse...or win. It was while searching for the answer to the biggest challenge of her life that Teri took a call from her baby sister. Heather, twelve years Teri's junior, was getting married.

Teri and Heather grew up in vanilla, two-parent suburban bliss. While Teri doted on her baby sister in the living room, their parents battled over cupholders and timeouts in the privacy of the bathroom. Teri's connection to Heather cooled over time as Teri moved into her teen years. Heather was just too young. They were friends, but they weren't close. Now, the years clearly reflected the generational gap between them. Heather led the digitally displayed life of her

---

2   The tax was designed by right wing pro-family groups to dis-incentivize divorce and strengthen households. It was endorsed by legal lobbies who received a facilitation fee. A progressive congress, who wanted the money but not the message, approved the measure. It was positioned as an important support structure for the education of underprivileged children. The tax was spun by all sides as win-win for strengthening the middle class. With the U.S. birthrate at 0.4 children/household, fewer than half of all divorces even involved children.

age bracket, while Teri followed her generation's more conservative approach. In Teri's mind, they might as well have been reared on different planets.

Teri swallowed the idea of Heather's upcoming nuptials like a pre-divorce antibiotic and congratulated her sister on the upcoming wedding.

A four-day engagement? Naturally.

One month, four days, and married. Of course, it *had* to be a destination wedding. Teri didn't give a damn about missing work, but Wall, South Dakota? Seriously?

5

CHRISTIAN RAMÍREZ
Present Day
Northeast Nicaragua Jungle

A year after the conversation with his *bisabuela*, Chris stood in yet another mosquito-infested clearing overlooking a nameless, brown creek that snaked off the Río Escondido in the Eastern Nicaraguan jungle. The day was particularly oppressive since the ocean breeze rarely made it this far inland. The stale air was thick with smoke from a pair of grass fires that his new employees maintained in the camp. The fires smoldered throughout the day, providing an effective anti-bug cover for the workers. For months, they hacked their way up the Río Escondido. A couple weeks ago, they branched off, following a small creek further into the jungle. They chopped their way off a lightly-used animal trail and up the sturdy flow toward the bend shown on Chris' map.

To keep his real mission secret, Chris made them pan for gold sporadically along the river; just another gold prospecting mission. A chance success, finding a strangely twisted piece of gold, kept the enthusiasm going. Nicaraguans are superstitious, and they assumed that Chris, this first-time gold miner, must be lucky, so they eagerly followed his directions.

When they got to the bend marked on Chris's map, he ordered them to clear out a hundred-foot semi-circle on the low bank of the river. With hand machetes, they beat back the overgrowth, chopped down the undergrowth, and ran off some unhappy native reptiles. Now, a week later, he saw three worn-out tents and a couple of grass fires. The surrounding jungle formed a dense barrier hemming them in. The only evidence of their passing was the lightly worn donkey trail they'd hacked upriver.

Monkeys chattered from the trees in all directions, warning each other of the continued human presence. Half a dozen un-named bird breeds squawked at their every move. As dusk descended, dozens of bats started their low, sweeping raids in the fading light. The mining operation looked like the first people to step foot in this part of the river for a thousand years. Two figures in pants and long-sleeved rags lounged by the center bug-fire, using dirty fingers to shovel rice and beans into their mouths from Styrofoam plates. Their eyes tracked a half dozen vultures circling overhead. A third figure, a shockingly obese man nicknamed *Gordo*, squatted in the water, sifting mud from pan to pan.

For the first time, Chris started to worry that his *bisabuela* had lost the plot.

Despite possessing a slight frame, Chris could do, and often did do, manual labor. But on this job, he was strictly management. From his managerial perspective, *operation* was a pretty generous word to describe what he saw. Of the four of them, two were half-asleep and Chris himself wasn't technically working. They were a roughly fifty miles lost, north of the coastal town of Bluefields, in a forgotten jungle, and following a map drawn by a drunk, eighty-year-old woman. Gordo still worked. So that was good.

This crew, hastily assembled in Bluefields two months ago, generally started work at ten in the morning. A two-hour lunch and siesta followed, then a few more hours of work, for a total of about five hours a day on the banks of this brown, bug-infested river. It was over a hundred degrees.

Ramírez, S.A. didn't resemble anything the Western world could call a business. Chris started the business while at University with the help of his one-time Spanish student and part-time business partner, an American who had retired to Nicaragua. Together, they started building libraries in small Nicaraguan towns in the Northwest of the country. They had built three libraries, two small houses, and a baseball field.

Chris had managed to keep the business afloat for the past three years. They rarely worked for money, but instead took whatever contributions the communities could afford. In Nicaragua, contributions could mean the use of a donkey cart, a dozen melons, or a live chicken.

But this? Mining for gold? This was new. Not that it mattered to the Nicaraguan government what a business did. Licensing was only relevant to the government if a business made enough money to be worth extorting.

In every sense of the Nicaraguan version of a business, Ramírez, S.A. was a success. It didn't have hours of operation or an employee manual. It didn't even have paper on which to write an employee manual, let alone an office in which to store paper. In fact, the business had no financial records at all. Not that anyone would ever ask.

Employees didn't work during the two-hour lunch siesta, or on Wednesdays, or most Fridays. Pay ranged from a few dollars to free eggs, a favor, or just a good dinner. In Nicaragua, money had been so hard to come by for so long that most people knew how to get by without it.

To be sure, Ramírez, S.A. wasn't going to IPO on Wall Street anytime soon, but neither was it going to dissolve. More importantly, if Chris could keep the operation going just a bit longer, he could take advantage of the one asset he had in spades. Jean Christian Ramírez Paolo had a secret. The secret of all secrets. And according to his map, he sat right on top of it.

He thought about calling it a day when a shout rose up from Gordo in the river,

"Aquí! Aquí! Mira! Oro! Oro!"

Gold. Old Gordo had found gold.

6

MONTANA AINSLEY
Present Day
Fort Lauderdale International Airport

Montana exited the arrival hall still somewhat surprised this was the United States. Here, in America, they just tased a guy in the middle of the airport. A guy from Minnesota. A badly- sunburned guy from Minnesota. Disappeared, like this was Stalinist Russia.

In Central America, police beatings were pretty much the norm. But here? And should the crowd have been that docile? The only groans emanated because the line stopped inching forward. Within seconds a new TSA crew had manned the perimeter, and business had gotten right back on track. Or off track, depending on your perspective. Between pondering that TSA had just disappeared a citizen and the fact that customs took place on the airport's tarmac, Montana was wandering around outside the airport in a daze when a taxi pulled to within two inches of his foot.

"Sir pleases to tell me the address?" the Indian cabbie shouted through the open passenger window. Montana looked down at his foot, then up at the cabbie, trying to refocus his mind. Did he need a cab?

Well, the customs delay had been long. Why not? He got in and they merged into traffic, barely missing a black Suburban before traffic came to a complete standstill.

"Just the domestic terminal, I need to catch a flight up to Nashville."

"Very good, sir. I am always wishing for longer fares, but I am happy to be servicing you," the cabbie said in thickly Indian accented English.

"What am I gonna owe you?"

"Owe? The sir owes me nothing. This is my job."

"No, the price, man, the price. Sorry, maybe I'm not being clear. I haven't been here for a while." Was Montana's English this bad now?

"I cannot give to you an exact amount. There is very much depending on the traffic and the time it is taking us to travel."

"Yeah, okay, ballpark it. One terminal to another."

"Sir?"

"Estimate."

"I can't."

"Try."

"Twenty-seven dollars, sir."

He stared at the driver in the rearview mirror for a full three count. The cabbie was just bobbing his head and smiling. "Okay, great. Sounds like a bargain…for changing terminals."

"Oh yes, this is a very good price for the sir. I make a special price."

Montana put the disconnected headphones back in. Twenty-seven dollars was a week of eating out where he lived.

While they sat in the twenty minutes of traffic to move terminals, the LICE database pinged offices all over the nation to let them know that Montana Ainsley was back in the country, had entered at Fort Lauderdale, and had checked in for a flight to Nashville, Tennessee. A U.S. cell phone was detected in his baggage, and the number was automatically attached to his file for GPS tracking. One office took particular note of the alert; the Downtown Nashville metropolitan police headquarters. A long sought-after fugitive had finally returned. The duty officer ordered the S.W.A.T. gear cleaned and oiled.

7

LIONEL DEWALT
Present Day
TSA Interview Room 2- FLL International Arrivals

The sunburned man came to a groggy state of awareness in interview room two. Lionel sat across from him. Gloria stood well inside his personal space to the left. The man was left-handed. Studies showed standing close to his dominant arm would make him feel even more powerless. The man's suitcase sat on the table between them. Lionel opened the suitcase and stared at five boxes of Cuban cigars. They weren't even hidden. Lionel did some quick mental math.

A hundred a box, five boxes, not a bad start.

Gloria snatched one of the boxes and stuck it in front of the guy's watery eyes. He stopped moaning and stared at the box. The second his head turned toward Gloria and focused on the illegal contraband, Lionel slipped the solar headphones out of the suitcase and down the concealed hatch.

Four hundred fifty bucks, easy. If they were Apple, a thousand.

He looked up to ensure Gloria still had the guy's attention. She did. At the sight of the prohibited cigars, the guy had gone white. Pale white. Never-seen-the-sun white.

Gloria laughed out loud. "Well, looky here! A few boxes of contraband and you ain't sunburned at all? Lionel, we cure sunburn? We entrepreneurial up in here?"

Lionel winced. *Entrepreneurial?* Gloria's diction still needed work. She had graduated from the University of Virginia with a 3.8 GPA in pharmacology, and Lionel had been working to change Gloria's TSA grammar for weeks. She still had too much banker and not enough unpredictable street hustler.

Well, he figured, *that's what a 3.8 gets you.*

"Wait. Wait. Wait," the guy stammered, "I can explain."

Gloria's eyebrows shot up. "You can explain felony smuggling? I got nothing but ears!" She let out a sarcastic snort.

Better

"You. Wait. Help me. I don't understand." Lionel could tell the guy was coming apart. "I...I didn't know they were prohibited."

Gloria rocked her head back and arched one eyebrow to the sky. "You didn't know Cuban cigars is prohibited since the 1970's?" She shot Lionel a fake, incredulous look. "Maybe he should be smuggling newspapers to educate his-self."

Lionel laughed. He couldn't help it. Gloria definitely didn't sound like someone who scored a 1580 on her SAT. Time to close this out.

"Let me tell you what. I'm prepared to be generous today," Lionel cooed.

Gloria nearly shouted at him, "Help him? You serious? Nah, no way. I got me a felony collar."

Good cop, bad cop.

Tears formed in the guy's eyes as he whimpered to Lionel, "Anything. What can I do? I'm a law-abiding citizen."

Lionel smiled, *I'm counting on it, buddy.*

8

TERI BRADSHAW
6 years Ago
Wall, South Dakota

Teri knew her baby sister to be a little loopy, but who the hell had ever heard of Wall, South Dakota? The place was so remote it sold bumper stickers that said *Where the hell is Wall, South Dakota.*

Teri had a master's degree in accounting. She had a six-figure income. She had a smart apartment and an eco-car. Marriage? Check. Debt? None. Same employer for a decade? Check. Even her checking account earned interest. Teri was an accountant. Accountants wore business suits, took their craft coffee to go, and laughed politely at dinner parties. They didn't log into social media or hang out in coffee shops. They worked. Teri worked. She worked a lot. She worked a lot because accountants were grown-ups.

Teri, the grown-up, stood at the head of a small line of bridesmaids at the Travelers Rest Chapel in Wall, South Dakota.

The chapel was small, essentially an old wood and brick hallway with a dozen wooden church pews on one side and a narrow walkway on the other. A *very* fake smile had been plastered on Teri's lips for hours. Behind her, the priest, dressed as a sheriff from the wild west, yipped in celebration. Ahead of her, her sister and new brother-in-law strolled out of the chapel dressed as Doc Holliday and his longtime sweetheart, Big Nose Kate. Teri wore an Annie Oakley costume. The costume had a bustle. An actual bustle. Teri held a parasol in one hand while firing a cap-gun into the air with the other. Everyone around her did the same. They yelled "yeehaw". Teri did not yell "yeehaw". Teri was a grown-up.

Wall, South Dakota was a peculiar type of small town. The *destination* of this destination wedding was basically an interstate tourist trap made up to look like a wild-west town. The main strip was all wooden buildings on both sides of the street, carefully constructed to give off an old west vibe. There were wax dolls of famous wild west characters everywhere. There were as many old, wooden Indians and goldminers as there were trinket shops. There was an Indian arm-wrestling game where little kids lined up and were unable to move the Indian's wooden arm an inch. There was an old circus Iron Man game complete with anvil. Players smashed a small platform with the anvil. The force of the strike propelled a hockey puck up a tower, labeling the strength of the strike. Middle-aged fathers lined up in droves to embarrass themselves. No matter how hard they swung, nobody's blows rose above the "has-been" strength level. The town saloon, across the street from the drug store, had sawdust on the floor and displayed a thousand signed photos from ancient actors. As tourist traps went, Wall was in a class all its own.

As wedding destinations went, Teri would have preferred the Bahamas.

The main attraction was the Wall Drug Store, a sprawling pharmacy turned tourist mall. The mall led to a warren of shops, vendors, and here; the chapel where her sister just got married.

The small wedding party wore what her grandfather would have described as 'a getup'. All the bridesmaids were Annie Oakley. All the groomsmen were dressed like Buffalo Bill. Her opposite number, the best man, informed her that since all the groomsmen were black, they were actually dressed as Cherokee Bill, an old-west outlaw of African ancestry. Teri feigned interest in the odd bit of history, but she couldn't have cared less. The fact that anyone viewed this as anything but juvenile made her long for airport check-in. She smiled and played her part, for her sister's sake, but she couldn't stop thinking: *You people are adults…or you should be. No wonder this generation is struggling to be taken seriously; they play dress up in their 20s.*

When the wedding ended, most of the party split into two camps. Half went to the saloon across the street to take in Michael Martin Murphy cowboy songs. The other half shopped. Teri holstered her cap-gun and went to the saloon. She ordered a "whiskey", which was just a white wine, and sat down to reflect as the rest of the wedding posse filed in. The words *has-been* on that stupid circus game sent that loose chain in Teri's head whipping around...*has-been...past her prime*, but still *do-able*. The wine helped numb the pain. After a few minutes, her new brother-in-law sidled up and took the stool next to her.

"Howdy, Ma'am," he said in his best old-west accent, wearing a huge, gleaming smile.

"Hey, Mayo," she faked a laugh. "Congratulations again. Great wedding. You guys are very cute." *Barf.*

That sentence constituted the longest conversation they'd managed. They had met for the first time at the airport. Teri knew she was supposed to probe for a little background before her sister committed, but she really didn't care. Out of boredom, she figured she could probe a bit now, just to see who Heather married. With Heather, there was no telling. Her boyfriends had ranged from CEOs to paroled bank robbers. Heather would just as soon dump a millionaire for a convicted felon (check) as long as he *lived his best life*.

Yet, Heather continued to bop through life, constantly posting bikini photos about living *your best life*, being *your best self*, and having *your best hair*. Heather wasn't technically gorgeous. Teri had gotten those looks, but her baby sister still had a twenty-year-old's body, which she constantly posted online, clad in as little fabric as possible. As a general rule, nobody looked at the face of a half-naked body, so Heather owned the "hot sister" title. She described her profession as a social media *Influencer*. Teri eventually learned that an influencer was someone with enough social media followers to supposedly generate sales for a business. Businesses would leverage her platform by offering her free food or a free hotel night in exchange for bikini photos of Heather at their location. The world's first profession that was paid exclusively in-kind. Before he died, their grandfather tried to understand the profession. He'd asked Heather how she got paid to travel around.

She perplexed the old fox by responding, "Not like, you know, in dollars, or in like, a currency, exactly. But I've seen, like, most of the best beaches and hotels in the world. So, I'm like, an experience millionaire, right?"

Teri always wondered if trying to diagram that sentence had initiated the aneurism that killed the old man a week later. Before he died, their grandfather declared her unemployed. Their parents softened the criticism by calling it "an entrepreneurial career". Teri's ex-husband, two generations removed from the cold reality of her grandfather's world, called it "alternative employment." No wonder Teri had divorced his ass. Real jobs paid real wages. Well, it was Mayo's problem now.

Mayo turned out to be a pretty average guy. Lower middle-class parents, a stepbrother, a sister, a dozen cousins, public school, three-fourths of a college degree, and now he sold veterinarian franchises. Some of the cousins sounded a bit dodgy, but the rest of the story was refreshingly bland. Before the conversation got too deep, a big, burly guy draped a big, burly arm around Mayo's shoulders and belted out a "howdy pardners." Mayo introduced him as Lionel, an older cousin from Ft. Lauderdale. Mayo introduced Teri as an accountant and his new sister-in-law. Before Teri could say a word, he flounced off to join a two-step waltz line. Lionel lowered his bulk onto Mayo's old stool and looked right at Teri. Below the cowboy hat but above a moderate gut, a broad smile creased a craggy face from ear to ear. He sported the same old-west getup as the other groomsmen, Buffalo Bill, or Cherokee Bill, or whomever. The guy positively reeked of marijuana.

Are you kidding me? Teri thought and shook her head slightly in disbelief. *My new brother-in-law just set me up for a wedding hook-up?*

Teri figured Mayo saw her as the lonely, older sister who needed a man. After all, this was a wedding and people should be happy at weddings, right? Teri sized up the outlaw in front of her. Late forties, big frame, dark eyes, too many Cheetos, probably due to the weed she smelled. And that absurd costume.

Well, cousin Lionel is about to have a very bad day.

If Mayo didn't think Teri would shoot this shit down, he'd badly miscalculated. The guy even wore a wedding ring. If she had any caps left, she would have shot him. Or Mayo.

But before she could unload her verbal assault, Lionel started talking.

"Did Mayo tell you I'm the one who switched the costumes from Buffalo Bill to Cherokee Bill? Poor Mayo had no idea there were black men in the old west."

Teri gave a tight-lipped smile. Perhaps sensing the impending nuclear attack, the guy quickly moved into a conspiratorial tone.

"You're an accountant, right?"

The question stopped her before she could enter the mental launch codes. That wasn't any pickup line she ever heard. Well, maybe from college frat boy who mistook her for a graduate assistant.

He continued, "Mayo said Heather said that you are super smart about taxes, and I don't know the first thing about it. See, I've got kind of a problem."

When Teri didn't respond, he continued.

"And I was hoping you might help."

Still no response from Teri.

As a final pitch, Lionel said, "I'd be happy to pay you."

Teri sighed. She hadn't seen this coming, and it was certainly better than the alternative. But still.

"Lionel, look, I'm sorry, I'm just not sure how much help I can be. It isn't the money. They pay me pretty well to review hundreds of tax-returns a year. The thought of one more...well, you're catching me at an odd time. Taxes are boring me and I'm thinking of leaving the business."

Despite the rejection, his grin widened. "Boring ain't my problem," he boomed out. Then he paused and thought for a second. "Tell you what. I'll tell you my trouble. Won't take ten minutes. When I'm done, if you don't find my story to be the most interesting tax problem you ever heard, I'll leave you alone."

Teri detected just enough street in Lionel's diction to indicate he hadn't come from great wealth. If he had amassed money, there might be an interesting story there. What the hell, her gun was out of caps anyway. She took a sip of her drink, nodded her ascent, and waved her hand in a *please continue* gesture.

Two minutes into the story, Teri stopped blinking. She was barely breathing by the end of it.

No way. There is absolutely no way this guy is telling the truth.

Terry made him retell it.

Perfect recall.

Incredible as it was, the story was plausible, Teri just couldn't believe it. Cousin Lionel didn't have a tax problem, he had a luck problem. If he was telling the truth, Lionel had stumbled onto the *holy grail* of cons. Not even the legal system could steal this smoothly. Lionel's real problem appeared to be that he was drowning in money. Money that came in so fast and so illegally that only an accountant could hide it.

The two sat in silence for a full minute while Teri's mind whirled. Lionel, to his credit, didn't press her. When Teri finally did speak, it was to order a pair of actual whiskey shots. As the two held up the shot glasses, they locked eyes.

"Yes, Lionel," Teri said, giving him her first genuine smile since that fateful Christmas party. "I am quite sure I can help you."

Clink, drink, slam.

As the whisky burned down Teri's throat, she could feel, physically feel, the chain in her mind stop whipping around. It landed on the floor of her skull with a thud. Slowly, it snaked its way across her brain until she felt it reattach somewhere behind her forehead. Lights flashed inside her head. While some corners of her mind remained pitch black, others lit up like Times Square. Teri Bradshaw had purpose again.

9

CHRISTIAN RAMÍREZ
Present Day
North of Bluefields, Nicaragua

Chris's crew pulled muddy clumps out of the riverbed all morning. So far, they all contained nothing more than weeds and lumps of rock. The morning after Gordo's find, the team crowded around and watched as Chris and Gordo gently cleaned the find with an ammonia-based solvent. When they finished cleaning it, they found themselves staring at a coin. It looked like gold, so they weighed and tested the metal. Sure enough, gold. The edges had been rubbed smooth by the elements, but it was, clearly, a gold coin.

The members of Ramírez S.A. had worked tirelessly from dusk till dawn since. They came up empty for days. Chris had been sitting on the shore, breaking apart the clumps of mud when he heard Juan shout. He looked up and saw Juan was staring into the pan between Gordo's shaking hands. Whatever it was, the two were pretty animated, so he waded into the creek for a look. The closer he got, the more excited he felt. When he could see into the pan, what he saw wasn't a gold nugget like in old movies. It wasn't a tiny, twisted piece like they found weeks before, and it wasn't a muddy coin like they'd found a few days ago. In the old, dented pan, amidst the dirty water, the pebbles, and other river debris, dully gleaming in the half-light under the jungle canopy, sat a fistful of coins. A fistful.

They were dirty, old, and misshapen, but there was no doubting what they were. Coins. Gold coins. Secret. Gold. Coins. The Paolo family's secret gold coins.

Holy shit.

Gordo reached a chubby finger in and flipped one over. It had designs on both sides. Whatever this was, it wasn't naturally occurring.

They all stared in silence. Four guys, in the middle of nowhere, not another human around for a hundred kilometers. Chris could hear the stream trickle by, the buzz of mosquitoes, the warning shouts of the monkeys, and water dripping off their bodies into the stream. He couldn't hear anything else.

All he could think was, *this is…*

"Big trouble," Gordo said, cutting into his thoughts and breaking the spell. "This is big trouble, *jefe.*"

Christian nodded, though he didn't really hear Gordo's words.

"This, this is too much. Too much gold. Too much gold for Nicaragua. See that," the old man pointed a stubby finger at one of the pieces. "That's some kind of writing on there. This isn't gold from the earth. This is gold that someone made."

"All gold is from the earth, you old maid," Juan, the youngest, laughed.

"No. This isn't a find," Gordo repeated emphatically. "This isn't natural gold. This belongs to someone. Someone made this. This isn't for us to find, *jefe.* It belongs to someone else."

Gordo stared at Chris, waiting for a response, but Chris didn't respond. He couldn't respond.

Juan cut back in. "I don't give a damn who it belongs to. We're taking it, fat man. It's ours now."

Brayan, the final crew member, and a distant relatives of Gordo's, chimed in. "Yeah, I don't see anyone else out here covered in bites and wading into this damn river. Juan is right, this is ours now." He turned to Juan, and the two younger diggers slapped hands and started talking excitedly about what they were going to buy.

After a minute, Juan turned to Chris, who was still staring at the pan, and said, "This is a thousand years' worth of money for us. *Jefe*, tell him. This is the reason we're here! You brought us here to find gold. We've found gold!"

When still Chris didn't answer, Brayan started in. "Juan is right, *jefe*, we're not leaving it. Right? Are we?"

Gordo murmured in his guttural Spanish, "This isn't a *find* and you two idiots. This belongs to someone. This is," Gordo dropped his voice to a whisper. "Treasure. Someone will always come looking for their treasure."

And there it was. The word Chris couldn't utter. *Treasure*. The family secret that was so secret, it wasn't a word people seriously used anymore. *Treasure*.

"This is part of a stolen treasure. Some kind of Inca treasure. Or a lost and cursed Spanish one," Gordo carried on.

That comment snapped Chris to the present. "Wait a second," he started, but he was immediately interrupted as the other three started talking over each other.

"This is Conquistador gold. This belongs to our people. The Spanish stole it. It belongs to us."

"Is this enough to be U.S. rich? Are we *gringo* rich?"

"I doubt it."

Gordo interrupted them again. "You idiots, don't you know Bluefields is named for a famous pirate? This is probably his stolen gold, cursed to the end of time."

More babble followed until Juan, caught up in the enthusiasm, blurted out, "I'm getting a yacht and a model with butt implants."

That comment brought the conversation to a much-needed halt.

After a brief pause, Brayan said, "What are you talking about? Why would you want that?" A smile spread across his face, and Juan, reddening, started to mouth a sarcastic response when Gordo cut them off in a quiet, ominous voice.

"It's cursed. And now, so are we."

That shut everyone up. Nicaraguans are superstitious people, and the notion of a curse gave everyone pause. Very slowly, they started arguing again but in more hushed tones. The two younger men didn't necessarily *believe* in curses, but then again...

Chris's mind couldn't catch up to his eyes. He hadn't really expected to find anything. Well, nothing like this. Knowing his *bisabuela*, he expected a jeweled rain stick or some pointless family relic.

But this? A full-blown treasure?

He thought back to her story. The family suddenly went from fishermen to tribal rulers. This had to be it. His family hadn't fought their way to the top, they had bought their way there. But how had his ancestor come into possession of something like this? Had he stolen it like Gordo suggested? Was Chris descended from a thief?

Not that it mattered. The kinds of mental trauma U.S. kids suffered wasn't even on the radar for Nicaraguans. Nicaraguan kids didn't have psychiatrists. God, family, food, community. Mental anguish ranked somewhere below shoelace color.

Surely his ancestor didn't just stumble across gold coins. And to that point, how many were down there, buried in this river? One thing was certain, the back-story needed to stay hidden. If he claimed ownership of the find rather than treating it as random, the crew would blab it across the entire country. They might already be wondering how he led them here so directly. But that could wait. Right now, he needed to focus on the problem at hand. Focus. Calm. Just like his business partner taught him.

"We need to put it back in the river," he heard Gordo say. That snapped him into the present.

"Wait. Stop. Just...everyone just stop!" Christian finally said, some authority returning to his voice.

They quieted and turned to their young boss. The one with the college education. The one who spoke half a dozen languages. The businessman. The one who led them here. The lucky one.

"We are not putting this back in the river." He looked straight at Gordo. Then he looked at Juan and Brayan. "If someone talks, this *will* get around. Then we really *will* have the kind of trouble Gordo is talking about. Somebody gets drunk at a bar and blabs? How long till a whole village shows up? Or worse, forces one of us back up here. People get killed over things like this. This is gold, not a pack of cigarettes that fell off a truck."

The group nodded silently. Reality had started dawning on them.

"We're going to do the only thing we can do. The only thing we know how to do. You're going to stay up here and keep digging for more while I figure out how to get this out of here. I have a friend who can help us."

"Who?" Gordo asked. "Your *gringo* pal? The *chele*?" The other two exchange nervous glances.

"Yes, him."

"*Jefe*," Brayan started, "*gringos* take advantage of Latinos."

Chris cut him off before the objection could build steam.

"Guys, people aren't their governments. Would you want people thinking every Nicaraguan is like our president?" Silent nods of agreement. "My whole family can vouch for him. He's the guy who saved my little sister."

The diggers nodded their heads at that. They'd all heard the story a few weeks back. A couple years ago, Chris's family went to the beach town of Las Peñitas to celebrate Easter week. Their rental house lost power during siesta, a near daily occurrence in Nicaragua, so everyone fell asleep in hammocks on the porch waiting on the power. Instead of sleeping, his little sister wandered onto the beach and into the surf. She got knocked down by one of the thunderous Pacific waves, and the undertow swiftly pulled her forty-pound body out to sea. By the time the family came running onto the beach screaming, she was too far out. Nobody in the family could swim.

They jumped up and down, crying, and begging God to save her. Then they saw a multicolored flash as someone ran into the water, dove under a massive wave, and swam out to rescue the drowning girl. He brought her to shore and pushed the water from her lungs until she started breathing again. Then, he casually walked back to his towel, stretched out, and appeared to fall asleep.

Once the family calmed down, they were incredulous. Thankful, but incredulous. The guy saved her, then just walked away as if nothing had happened. They descended on the tourist, mobbing him with hugs, tears, and heartfelt thanks, while Chris translated it all. Then they forced him into their celebrations for the rest of the week, while he taught them how to swim. The guy had been an honorary Ramírez ever since. It turned out that he wasn't a tourist, but a recent *emigré*. Chris taught him how to speak Spanish, and he taught Chris the basics of business management.

The first lesson? Always remain calm. Whether it's saving a drowning girl or running a business, calmness separated bad bosses from good ones.

"He can help us, trust me. This is the find, guys. This is the find that changes all our lives." He paused then said, "but we're going to need help."

"But *jefe*," old Gordo said, seriously, "I don't need my life to change. I like it as it is."

That quieted everyone for a full minute. Chris had no response to that.

Finally Juan broke the silence, "Well, think of your kids, Gordo, you've got about a dozen." Everyone laughed. "Maybe one of them can go learn to do something besides make more babies."

Even Old Gordo responded with a belly laugh before following up with, "So you know something better than working all day and screwing all night, Juan? Or maybe you just lack the experience of it?" Everyone laughed, except Juan. Chris noticed his face flushed red and his fists clenched.

Old Gordo hit a nerve somewhere, he thought.

"Guys!" Chris cut in. "It's not going back. Gordo, if you don't want any part of it, fine, but I've hired you to help, and at the very least, I now have the money to pay you." More laughter.

"Look, we can't un-find this." Chris looked around to emphasize the point. "Once word gets out, we need to be long gone or we're dead. Let's find out how much is down there before we do anything. Look, this is dangerous, I know. That's why everyone stays here. No going to town. This isn't gossip like whose girlfriend screwed who. We'll find a place to hide it while I figure out how to get it out of here. Agreed?"

The small group discussed the implications for several more minutes. In the end, consensus was reached that the good outweighed the bad. Gordo and Juan would keep digging while Chris and Brayan went off to find a place to hide whatever they were going to find.

As Christian turned away from the group, he couldn't wipe the smile off his face.

Before he could even start calculating a plan, Old Gordo called after him. "*Jefe*, you really think this *chele* can help?"

For the first time since he was a small child, a devious smile, a smile that matched his suspicious eyes, spread across his face. "This guy can. He's part of the *Paolo* side of my family." He turned away as a puzzled look came into Gordo's face. The big man couldn't know the reference to Chris' thieving ancestor.

Walking back to his overlook, Chris pulled out his smartphone and dialed a local number. Voicemail.

"Hey buddy, this is Chris. Give me a call. I need some serious help." He hung up and surveyed the area.

Head of the family, indeed.

10

MONTANA AINSLEY
Present Day
Nashville, Tennessee

Montana had unpacked and was dozing to the sounds of the snarled traffic outside his hotel room on busy West End Avenue. Rush hour started early in Nashville, and the cars were already lined up for miles tracking back to downtown. He thought back on the days when he had a car and had to endure traffic, his hands wrapped tightly on the wheel, constantly swearing, frustrated by every brake light. Then he smiled. He hadn't driven a car for years.

His U.S. phone rang and broke the reverie. The sound surprised him; the phone hadn't made a peep in nearly five years. The thing had been sitting in a drawer in Central America. As soon as he had arrived, he'd inserted a burner sim card, and the phone downloaded a congressional library worth of updates for the next hour. In the end, most of the updates wouldn't load because his operating system was so out of date. The down time gave Montana some leeway to ponder his first seven-dollar cup of Fair-Trade Jamaican coffee. He doubted the boys down at Blue Mountain Coffee in Jamaica saw much of the revenue share. It struck him that Big Coffee tended to change their country-de-jour as soon as the locals figured out that selling their beans at eight cents per pound wasn't a fair trade.

The ringtone coming out of his phone was AC/DC, which meant a lawyer. Montana just couldn't remember which one had been assigned *Hells Bells*.

When he'd left the States, he had so many lawyers on his payroll that he had them numbered and associated with ringtones. The day he'd left the U.S., his phone lost signal, and he hadn't given it another thought. As he picked up the phone, he saw that it already had twelve missed calls, seven messages, and a dozen advertising texts. He touched the answer icon.

"Hello?"

A robotic voice said, "Please hold for Aubrey Langeholt the third." Then the line clicked twice.

Ah, Montana thought, *lawyer number one.*

The hold music was Aubrey's voice reminding the listener of the many injustices that might have been visited upon them. The recording climaxed with Aubrey proclaiming that his expanded firm stood ready to help because *more lawyers means more justice.*

Aubrey Langeholt, III was forged in the same human printing press that churned out lawyers by the thousands. He saw injustice in every action, and he was positive he could wrangle justice, in the form of money, from all wrongdoers. When Montana found him online years earlier, he had a reputation as an above average lawyer handling everything from contracts to business law.

In his forties, Langeholt had an above average amount of dyed brown hair for his age. He was above average in height, slightly trimmer than average, and wore off the rack suits from Brooks Brothers. Average, but at the top end of the range. Aubrey and his wife drove used Lexuses. Average, but again, at the top of the range. If he'd been a baseball player, Aubrey would have hit around .269.

The lawyer once admitted to Montana that he wasn't drawn to the law out of nobility but attended law school due to the fear of facing the real world after college. After three years in the country's largest babysitting program, Aubrey launched into a much more controlled labor market. In the legal world, all the rules were spelled out, and everyone knew what to expect. Lawyers processed cases that higher-ranked lawyers found, and the partners paid them. Law firms had strict rules on who did what. Most importantly, the income was guaranteed.

Associate lawyers received paychecks; they didn't have to go create them. Being an associate lawyer was like spending time in minor league baseball. Everything was laid out. All an associate had to do was follow the rules, work, and receive a paycheck. Once those skills were honed, an associate could get called up to the majors and add the responsibility of putting clients on base, but only after years of practice in a controlled environment. After seeing who could graduate, Montana viewed law school as the path of least resistance.

When he first hired Aubrey, Montana was operating a laundromat in a leased space with a roof that had started to collapse. The building's owner refused to pay for a new roof, despite the lease clearly outlining his responsibility to do so. With little choice, Montana had to shell out thousands of dollars to keep the roof from falling in on his customers and destroying half a million dollars' worth of laundry machines. That was when the building itself was deemed structurally unsound. When the landlord wouldn't acknowledge responsibility to fix the structure in any way, Montana found Aubrey and tried to sue for his money. He closed the business and stopped paying rent while the case wound its way through the courts. It was his first step into the legal world, and it had opened his eyes to the reality of the law.

"Well, well, my favorite missing person just showed up," boomed a voice on the other end. "I knew it. I knew you weren't missing. Hah! I was right. How ya doing buddy, or should I say *amigo*?"

Montana started to ask, "How did you know I was…" but the lawyer's voice plowed over his reply.

"The firm has this new software that shadow-calls your phone twice a day until you shut the program down. It's cutting-edge stuff, and it sliced our collection problems in half. It works off the phone's serial number. We've been pinging your phone for two-and-a-half-years now. It was like the moon landing around here when we realized your phone went active. Once the phone rang through, my administrative director sent the call through. So how are ya? I know you're in the States because I got a ping from the LICE database, as well. Tell me about life south of the border. I knew that was where you'd gone. All those trips down there were a dead giveaway. Oh, and how did you get outta here without border patrol pinging your passport? We can talk about the case later."

Montana knew what *talk about the case* meant.

Aubrey charged $414 an hour for his counsel. He thought coming in under 415 made his fee appear more affordable, like charging $4.99 for a Coke. Aubrey was smooth, but underneath that layer was a shark. Like many lawyers, he charged in fifteen-minute increments regardless of the topic discussed. So, if you talked to him for one minute, you got billed for a quarter of an hour. If you spoke for sixteen minutes, you got billed for thirty. Lawyers only round up.

Any conversation between a lawyer and a client was considered "thinking about the client" and subject to billing. As a result, lawyers loved to talk about a broad array of topics. By the time Montana had left America, he calculated that he had spent over six thousand dollars hearing about his lawyers' vacations. But he wasn't the legal neophyte he once was.

"Am I on the clock, Aubrey? I mean, I just got into the country."

Brief pause.

"No, buddy, of course not. I promise. I just want to catch up with an old client. Besides, you know I farm out the basics to my legal staff to save money for my clients. We aren't talking business. Did you know I made partner while you were away? I'm crazy busy these days. I'm on a whole new chart."

A whole new chart was code for higher billing, which legally appeased the requirement to notify clients. It also meant Aubrey's *less expensive* staff would be billing out at higher rates. The "staff", made up of mostly young lawyers and paralegals, was where the real charges were hidden. They charged less but moved at a glacial pace. Montana always figured they were escapees from *Animal Farm* who had just developed fingers. That, or they worked ten minutes of every hour. He'd once been billed $710 for "translation services" when he accidentally sent an email to the firm in Spanish. When that month's bill arrived, a copy of the translated email was included. Montana had plugged the translation into an online translator and, not surprisingly, found an exact match to the document the firm provided. He'd been billed for seven hours of work. It would have been cheaper for Aubrey to bill him one hour and admit to using the online translator.

"Okay, then I'm great Aubrey. I'm still not working, but I am discovering loads of interesting opportunities down there," he monotoned while eyeballing the clock. 4:03 p.m.

"Hah, that's funny, living the dream, eh? Where exactly are you?"

Montana noted the downshift in enthusiasm as the attorney calculated that additional fees would be tougher to collect if the host wasn't getting regular transfusions of money. "How have you been, Aubrey?"

"Well, great, I just got back from the family vacation, and let me tell you, South America has cornered the market on humidity. We went to…"

Montana sunk his head in his free hand as Aubrey droned on. *A real pro, huh?* he thought. *You rookie moron, never ask them questions.*

Third year law students took two semesters of a class called "Phones I & Advanced Conversations II". The classes were publicly positioned under the guise of keeping the clients talking to uncover lost or forgotten details. In reality, the classes were some kind of vampire bard training. The classes taught each of the money-suckers how to keep draining the precious life blood from the client's accounts by spinning endless tales about various adventures. Every vacation description included a three-to-five minute "scene" that occurred at an airport somewhere. It was maddening.

"…and little Aubrey, Jr. just started baseball…"

4:14 p.m.

Montana almost asked how Aubrey himself could be a *third* while his child was merely a "Jr.", but he knew by now that all the Langeholt kids had odd names in order to spark conversation. The kids' names alone had probably earned ten thousand dollars in conversation billing. Montana couldn't remember the girl's name, but it was something totally outlandish.

"Hey, Aubrey, sorry, I've gotta walk out the door in a sec. What's new with the case?" 4:26 p.m.

"First, you have to tell me about South America. I bet those are some crazy stories."

It was Central America, but Montana wasn't going to bother correcting him. "I'll tell you in person. What's new with the case?"

"Okayyy. All business." Montana noted the fake guilt trip. "So now that we're on the record," meaning, *now that you're being billed,* "as you know, we've had quite an ordeal getting this thing tried. If you recall…"

Aubrey then went on to re-summarize the entire case, a case which Montana had lived through. Recapping the situation was a direct tactic from Advanced

Conversations II, and it usually added ten minutes to each call. Lawyers also intentionally 'forgot' details, knowing that nervous clients would stop them, go back, and insist on adding in the forgotten detail. Every minute counted. Montana stayed silent for the recap. Small victory.

"...so that brings us to the present. They've passed the point of being able to switch attorneys, I think, so I really think we're on for next Wednesday. Your timing is incredible. You don't have to be there, but hey, since you're here."

4.43 p.m.

"I've heard this before, Aubrey. Their fourth different attorney was supposed to be more than the court should allow."

"And that's true, but this all plays into your favor. The judge will look much more favorably because she's gonna recognize the game they're playing. Constantly changing attorneys just to cause delays is unacceptable."

Right, thought Montana, *unacceptably normal. Plus, that's assuming a) a judge even sees this before it settles for $20,000 less than my legal fees and b) there isn't a last second chicken massacre on the highway that prevents the judge from getting to work...again.*

"She? We have a new judge? And what kind of game is this when the fifth time is the last straw?"

"Well, in fairness, it's reasonable for them to switch attorneys. The first guy was really a dunce, plus, who could foresee a chicken truck overturned, plus one delay was..."

Cue the legal magic act that every client endured. As a client, your average case got delayed three to five times. It was irritating. It made you think the system didn't work. But before you could solidify that opinion, your lawyer would make a couple of delays sound reasonable: *They filed a motion so we had to file a counter motion, so the hearing had to get delayed or else we'd have a hearing on a moot point. That made sense, right?* Presto, two or three nonsense delays magically became reasonable. *So, really, Mr. or Mrs. Client, it's really just one to three nonsense delays, and never fear, the 'underhanded' tricks will be exposed once the judge gets a look at everything.*

So, all the money spent on filings and complaints would be well worth it when the judge dropped the hammer, right? Wrong. Virtually all cases got settled before trial, and the tricks went unpunished.

Every judicial delay, every motion, every little thing that postponed your case from being heard pushed money into the legal system. Motions had to be answered, letters of fake outrage had to be exchanged, phone calls made, emails written, and all of this accomplished by an army of legal staff at your expense. Occasionally, the lawyers showed up to court to receive an official delay. Those were the most expensive days. The whole thing made Montana, and probably half the nation, sick.

The judges weren't really any better. They were mostly former lawyers who now made less money, but since they'd made their real money milking the system, they didn't really have an interest in seeing it change. After all, they might return to a private practice one day.

They talked for a few more minutes and planned to meet before court next week.

"Just one last thing, buddy," Aubrey said.

5:04 p.m.

"Yeah? Shoot. What could we have not covered?" Montana was ready to end this call. He'd just dropped about $500, assuming he was grandfathered into the old billing cycle.

"Oh, well...nothing, it's nothing. We can talk about it later."

"Great. Next week." Montana hung up without waiting another second.

Damn it, he thought, *if Aubrey knows I'm here, this means they all know. My phone will never stop ringing.*

Montana had returned to the U.S. to resolve his divorce, not deal with all the other legal woes he abandoned. He planned to slip in and slip back out. That might not work in the current surveillance state.

He had lived, worked, and played in Nashville, Tennessee for decades before he'd left. He'd owned three businesses in the hip southern city. He had married a Nashville local, had no kids, and the couple's dogs had passed away just before he'd left. Between the businesses and renting out his parent's old home, the Ainsley family earned a respectable middle-class income. Not well-off but comfortable enough to buy a four-dollar cup of coffee whenever they wanted.

The marriage had been crumbling when the problems at the laundromat cropped up and he filed his first lawsuit. Enter lawyer number one, Aubrey

Langeholt: case still pending. Sitting with his accountant one day, she mentioned to him that by filing his lawsuit as a person with a little money, he had alerted the system that he was "open" for business. She hadn't been wrong. Within two months, the inevitable divorce got filed. No cheating, no nasty surprises, just two people who had made a mistake. Lawyer number two: divorce still pending. Then his restaurant had been sued, twice. Lawyer number three (twice): both cases dropped after thousands spent on legal fees. Then the tenants at his parent's old house stopped paying rent. He evicted them and installed paying tenants. The former tenant sued him. Lawyer number four: case status unknown. Then his internet business had been sued…twice. The first suit forced them to close the fledgling business. Montana had no idea where the other lawsuit sat now. Technically, that was lawyer number five, but Montana decided to use lawyer three again, just to save time. Status unknown.

The situation had become absurd. Montana would have been convinced he was the target of some sinister conspiracy, except that most business owners he knew were fighting similar battles against the legal system. They all borrowed money to pay legal fees, but the system was voracious, the cases endless, and nothing ever got resolved. His stress level shot through the roof. He developed arthritis in his hands and constantly battled headaches. If he'd dropped all the lawyers, the fees would have stopped accruing, but he would have had to default on all the lawsuits and lose everything. He had sacrificed most of his money, his credit, and his health just to try and resolve the various suits. He had kept up the fight knowing that he was protecting the livelihood of over forty employees, but as he borrowed more money with no increase in revenue to pay it back, he saw the writing on the wall. His life had been sucked into a death spiral. The legal system was really no different than a payday loan-sharking business. Once you got into it, it wouldn't leave you alone until all your assets were wiped out.

It was at that point he started preparing to leave. He'd set up an offshore company with a checking account and poured about half his remaining money into it. He'd planned to leave the other half for his future ex-wife.

When, a few lawsuits later, enough became enough, he'd boarded a bus to the southern border and crossed into Mexico using his old driver's license, which pre-dated the new computerized chip licenses. He'd acted like he had forgotten his passport, paid a thousand-dollar bribe to the official, who couldn't imagine someone trying to get *out* of the U.S., and never looked back. Border bribery worked all the way to Nicaragua. He was going to keep going south, but the Costa Ricans ran a much tighter ship. Nicaragua it was.

Within a year, he was fluent in Spanish. Within two, the arthritis evaporated, the headaches dissolved, and he was reading books and exploring the country. The next two years found him fully engaged with Nicaraguan society and living a new life. He was working with his former Spanish teacher to build libraries throughout the country.

He'd never said a word to his attorneys. He just disappeared. Only the two managers of his restaurant knew he left. They alone had an email account by which they could contact him. That first year, they sent an annual update. They'd been inundated with questions from lawyers and visits from police. The second annual update informed him that he had been labeled a missing person. This year, the fifth year, the update informed him that his wife was engaged to remarry but couldn't because she was never legally divorced. His wife had come by the restaurant begging them to contact Montana if they could.

Montana and his almost-ex-wife were never on bad terms. Neither could figure out why their divorce was so expensive and lengthy. Montana had given no thought to her marital status when he left. Now, knowing that she wanted to move on with her life, just as he had, he couldn't in good conscious leave things as they stood. He traveled to Honduras and took a flight back to the U.S. He had hoped to resolve the divorce without engaging the legal system. The legal system, it appeared, had other plans.

11

TERI BRADSHAW
6 Years Ago
Wall, South Dakota

After Lionel's second telling, Teri switched to coffee. She needed to do some due diligence on Lionel, but if he checked out, maybe Heather's wedding wouldn't have been such a waste of time after all.

At least for her, Teri thought caustically.

Lionel had started out life as a garden variety flunkie in north Birmingham, Alabama. With no family life to speak of, he built himself a rap sheet with a couple of drug charges (which weren't nothing in the deep south back then). When he got popped for a felony B&E, he finally realized he had big trouble. He'd gotten a slap on the wrist for his first misdemeanor possession charge. His second conviction for attempt to distribute was a bit more serious. That plea deal got him six months (out in two weeks), a fine, and community service on the plea deal. Going in front of the court on a third offense, showing a progressive record of delinquent behavior, was a bad idea.

Lionel contacted his young cousin, Mayo, who made decent money selling franchises. Mayo found and paid for a real lawyer to defend Lionel. It was Lionel's first glimpse at an actual lawyer. His guy mopped the floor with the young assistant DA. Since marijuana had been federally legalized, the previous charges would have no bearing on this trial. For legal purposes, this was a first offense. Furthermore, Lionel's lawyer had already filed suit against the city for not expunging the previous marijuana charges (as had been federally mandated, but impossible to carry out within a bankrupt city bureaucracy).

In his attorney's words, the state maintained a fraudulent criminal record on Lionel. This kept Lionel from attaining real work. The city of Birmingham had deprived him of a lifetime of earnings, then arrested him for their own crime. The ADA looked punch drunk as the meeting wrapped. The city agreed to plea down to a misdemeanor if Lionel dropped the lawsuit. The judge wearily ordered time served.

Before the judge released him, he warned Lionel that the next meeting would result in prison time. In a gross breach of decorum, the old man bet Lionel a dollar, that he would see him within two years. The judge had only hoped to scare a young man straight, but instead wound up with a three-month suspension for violating the state's anti-gambling law. Such was the state of legal bureaucracy.

When Teri heard the story the first time, she expected this to be the point where Lionel got in deep. The point where he hooked into a Mexican heroin cartel, got rich, and needed her help to shield the money from machete-wielding MS-13 gang members.

Boy, was she wrong.

The judge's gamble worked. Lionel cleaned up his act, got his GED, and started a training program to become a security guard. He excelled in the program and landed his first full-time job. After a while, a friend of his suggested he apply at the fledgling TSA. It was essentially the same job, just with lush government benefits. He got the job, and they stationed him at the Fort Lauderdale International Airport.

Lionel did well at TSA. He enrolled in night school and received a degree in, of all things, history. After his four-year anniversary with the TSA, his supervisor approached him with a proposition.

Now Lionel was approaching Teri with a proposition, and to paraphrase her initial thoughts, *she couldn't fucking believe what she'd just fucking heard.*

With the exception of a suspended judge somewhere in North Birmingham, everyone, including Teri, had underestimated Lionel since he was a kid. She didn't care that she had, she just cared that she didn't do it again.

Lionel worked as a TSA agent and had a wife and three kids. He had about $125,000 in cash that he kept in a safe in his closet. One of his kids wanted to attend college, but Lionel couldn't put the money in the bank and write a check to the University.

Why? Well, first off, if he showed that he had that much money, there was no way his kid would qualify for any form of tuition reduction[3]. To afford college, a family either had to be Hollywood rich or dirt poor. Lionel's family was in the middle, totally screwed, and totally aware of the fact.

This was a standard middle-class tax problem that Teri faced regularly, so she already had a tax avoidance structure in her head. Then Lionel dropped reason number two. Reason number two was a doozy.

The thing was, Lionel had never paid taxes on the money, so he couldn't just drop it into a bank even if Teri had a structure for it. As part of the endless and all-powerful Patriot Act, banks now communicated directly with a new federal agency to monitor all non-payroll banking deposits over $3000. Anything over thirty bills, and a person could expect an inquiry from the new agency overseeing banking transactions, the Department of Income Checks. The DICs reported suspected fraud activity directly to Chief Directorate of Finance, formerly the IRS. One whiff of a transaction this size, and Lionel would be facing questions he couldn't answer.

Teri asked the same questions the DICs would. No, he wasn't a drug dealer. No, he wasn't robbing banks. He'd gotten the money through his employer, the TSA.

"So, wait," Teri finally asked. "How have you never paid taxes on such a large amount of money received from a government employer?"

---

3   Three years earlier, Congress passed the Free Tuition act. The legislation aimed to "level the playing field" and "close the loopholes" the wealthy exploited in tuition scholarship rules. The sales pitch claimed this would free up billions in tuition grants for underprivileged children throughout the country. Regardless of academic excellence, children of parents earning over $500,000 jointly (or $300,000 for single parent homes) would not qualify for any tuition reduction or scholarship money. But the income requirements dropped over the years to broaden the benefits *for the children*. Currently, children whose parents earn over $100,000 (or maintain over $90,000 in combination of liquid assets and income) pay full freight.

"Well," Lionel responded, "that's kinda the rub."

And so, an adult white woman, dressed like Annie Oakley listened to a middle-aged black man, dressed as Cherokee Bill, describe one of the bigger frauds ever perpetuated *by* a U.S. governmental agency.

In the wake of the 9/11 attacks, the U.S. government formed the Transportation Safety Authority. Among its broad responsibilities, the agency was tasked with ensuring the safety at ports of entry, specifically airports. The days of tearful goodbyes at the boarding gate were gone forever. People had to do their crying in front a rope line that led to the terminal. Henceforth, only ticketed passengers would be allowed into the transit lounges. Additionally, every conceivable item had to be assessed as to its threat level inside an airplane. Initially, the hysteria was so complete that even plastic forks and knives were banned from terminals. In the beginning, virtually everything got confiscated. All the items went unrecovered, unlogged, and were eventually thrown into massive dumpsters and into even more massive landfills.

After a few years, the rules solidified, and the TSA's power was elevated to near absolute. A few agents tested this by committing various infractions of basic human decency. There were brief outcries followed by bureaucratic inaction.

Eventually, an enterprising agent at LAX decided to sell the confiscated items rather than toss them in the garbage. His goal? Pay for his young son's private pre-school. He started by removing only select items from the trash haul. A specialized knife here, a slingshot toy there. Within six months, his resale business was netting him about $1,000 a month, just enough to cover pre-school tuition and supplies. He recruited his TSA team members at LAX, and pretty soon, they were all making an extra few thousand a month. Since the TSA was a new organization, promotions came swiftly to the early employees. The original team found themselves as regional TSA managers at different airports, and the lottery concept was born. They introduced the scheme at select airports, managed it from their regional HQ in L.A., and dispersed the proceeds annually among the teams. The top teams got the most proceeds, the management team skimmed their fee, and everyone was happy.

"At least," Lionel continued, "we were happy for a while. The *drag*, that's what we call the take, is down because people have adjusted to the regulations.

Fewer and fewer confiscate-able items are coming into the airports now."

"So," Teri surmised, "now you've got a slice of employees with a big tax problem."

"You guessed it," he lamented. "They're talking about stopping it. The *drag* is down, and we don't even know how to use this money. Our kids are all college aged now, so we need it. Basically, we need a lot of help."

Teri looked straight into Lionel's eyes and said, "I can help. I know I can help."

"With which part?" Lionel asked.

"All of it."

* * *

The following morning, Teri left South Dakota. She initiated a new LLC, ordered a new credit card, and spent four days prepping a business plan presentation. She professionalized and printed six copies. When the new credit card arrived, she maxed it on a $350 hair cut & color, a $275 makeover, a $1200 power suit, and $4,000 for airfare and hotel accommodations for a week in Los Angeles. She met the lottery management team and walked them through her presentation. In her black suit, with freshly dyed blond hair, and three-inch heels, she exuded power CEO. Her ice blue eyes sparkled as she laid out a three-phase plan to streamline operations, grow the lottery, and tax-shelter the proceeds. She was all business. Precise. Brilliant. Gorgeous.

Once they picked their jaws off the floor at the sight of her, the all-male management team indicated that they needed to discuss the matter among themselves. But Teri saw the hooded glances and grins on their faces.

She knew she had them, but time kills deals, so she cajoled them into a group dinner that night (a little black dress, gold earrings, and a dab of Chanel). Using every ounce of physical and mental talent allotted to her, she got them drunk and envisioning a wealthier future. A future that might include a vacation house, a boat, or even a younger woman (hint, hint). She cracked risky sexual jokes so they'd know she wasn't an uptight feminist. She made visual innuendo with every member of the team. When the marathon dinner was over, all of them, no matter how happy their marriages might be, were aglow with possibilities of a better life—whatever that might mean to each of them.

She slept fitfully that night, recalling her problems at the accounting firm. Regardless of gender, an employee sleeps with a boss, more or less, for advancement. A boss sleeps with employee simply because they can. No way would Teri Bradshaw fall into that trap again. Before she started with these guys, she wanted the upper hand. Either she took over the lottery entirely, or she walked. There would be no "let's see how you do, first" crap. It was Teri's way or the highway.

She needn't have worried. The TSA guys turned out to be more professional than her accountant masters. They loved her ideas, they just needed to ensure Teri displayed a little bit of ethical flexibility. They came away satisfied. She was smart, mathematically literate, and appeared flexible if the situation demanded. Most importantly, no way Teri Bradshaw became a whistleblower.

Late the following day, Teri Bradshaw, CEO of The Bradshaw Group, became lead consultant for the TSA and secret manager of the disjointed but lucrative TSA lottery.

At 9:00 p.m. that night, Teri quit her old life by voicemail from the Beverly Wilshire hotel in Los Angeles.

She never even used her return ticket.

12

MONTANA AINSLEY
Present Day
Nashville, Tennessee

Montana sat in his favorite BBQ joint in Nashville's quaint 12th South District. A friend and former business partner used to own the place, but it was clearly under new management. It still had good food, but the ambiance had gone from authentic to Nashville's new glossy country décor. "Used" guitars lined the walls.

Probably made in China, gritted up in Vietnam, and shipped via Baidu to Nashville. Culture in a box. The Chicagoans who now ran Nashville's restaurant scene would never get it.

Montana had been trying to contact his almost-ex-wife all morning. He called her three times, but he figured the odd phone number from his SIM card meant she was ignoring the calls. Naturally, the voicemail was full; standard tactic to avoid robo-calls.

While he waited, he contemplated one of the lawsuits he was currently ignoring. It had been filed against his now-closed internet endeavor. A few years into his restaurant business, Montana turned the operation over to his two female managers. Both had worked there since it opened. Together they managed the place about 90% as well as he did, so he started on another project. He and another local restaurateur, a Boston native, developed an app that would help drive business to their respective restaurants. It was a neat piece of engineering which relied heavily on the emerging use of social media for advertising. Things hummed along for about nine months when they hit their first snag. The publicly available computer code that they'd used was, it appeared, patented by a company called RiKill, International. RKI owned over 13,000 patents and essentially made their living by suing and settling patent infringement. Since they owned so many patents, someone, somewhere, always violated one.

RiKill demanded a hundred-thousand-dollars to drop their suit. Montana recognized it as just more legal bribery, but neither restaurateur had the money. A patent attorney advised them that the suit would likely require north of seven hundred thousand dollars to litigate. With no real options, the two restaurateurs shut down the app, the business, and let go of their three employees with heartfelt apologies. There was nothing anyone could do. They just didn't have enough money to play ball with the U.S. legal system.

They kept the employees appraised of the lawsuit the whole way, so the shutdown hadn't been a total shock. The business closed as a financial breakeven for the partners, so they both took it as a lesson learned.

Then the other lawsuit rolled in. Not from RiKill, but from one of the terminated employees. The lawsuit claimed that Montana and his partner knowingly infringed on RiKill's patent and enticed the former employee to quit his previous job in order to come to work for them. In short, fraud. In an effort to make the suit more intimidating, and thus encourage a quick settlement, the plaintiff's attorney insinuated that the seed money from the restaurateurs into the "fraudulently conceived business" could be considered wire fraud, and that if the case were litigated, the district attorney's office would be notified for a potential criminal referral.

The business partners split on how to handle the action. Their short-term strategy, over Montana's strenuous objections, was to delay the complaint by claiming difficulties producing all the relevant documents, then filing to have the owners tried separately, then filing to have the action thrown out, and finally filing to suppress depositions. Montana, by now a veteran of half a dozen suits, tried to warn his business partner of the pitfalls of this legal strategy. He'd been living through this same nightmare, albeit in reverse, with his laundromat. But the partner was hell-bent on proving his rightness. A lawyer's dream.

The plaintiff's lawyer kept increasing their costs by filing amended complaints three times and insisting on deposing the restaurateurs twice each: once as the owners of the app business, and once as private individuals. Between that and forcing the defendants to answer constantly re-filed complaints, the legal bills mounted quickly.

The relationship between the two partners soured. They no longer spoke. Their attorney gleefully updated each individually, effectively double billing them. They amassed nearly $60,000 in legal bills in four months.

Then Montana disappeared. He knew that if he just went "missing", this lawsuit wouldn't be allowed to move forward until he was declared dead or found. It would take five years in Tennessee for him to go from "missing" to "dead".

Now, sitting in his former friend's former restaurant five years later, he wondered what had happened. He opened his phone, scrolled to his former business partner's name, and hit send.

The phone picked up after four rings. The first sound Montana heard was someone clearing a flemmy throat, then a voice rasped into his ear.

"Yeah?"

"Jimmy, it's Montana."

There was a five-second pause on the line. "Well, well, well, the prodigal son returns from the dead, eh?" The thick Boston accent hadn't diminished. The rasp made it worse somehow. Jimmy sounded like a two-bit mobster rousted out of bed.

"Yeah, sorry about that. I'll explain, but I just called to see how you are holding up first?"

A wet smokers' cough followed his question. Jimmy hadn't smoked.

"Oh, me? Just fine...*old friend*," the last two words dripped with sarcasm. "I work the graveyard shift as a line cook at a fucking all-night diner on lower broad. I'm fucking peachy." Montana heard a lighter click and the sound of cigarette paper crackling. Lower Broad referred to lower Broadway Avenue, a section of the main drag in downtown Nashville lined with old country honky-tonk bars and endless lines of drunken bridal parties. Unless you grew up working in New Orleans, it was the toughest service-job imaginable.

Montana tread cautiously. "Geez man, I'm sorry to hear that. I don't really know what to say." Before he could finish the sentiment, he heard Jimmy exhale a stream of smoke, and his former friend cut him off.

"You know, I hated you for a long time, man." The words drifted off into space before he repeated, "a long time."

It hit Montana like a gut punch. Somewhere, he had nursed the hope his former friend had softened with time. It appeared he hadn't.

"I know, Jimmy, I know. I just couldn't…"

Jimmy cut him off again. "But you know what? When you disappeared, that fuckin case went into, like, hibernation. They tried to drop you from the suit and just go after me, but that lawyer, he worked some serious magic to keep them from doin' it. Then I look up one day, after about a year, and I notice that my IOU to the lawyer kept going down, not up." He paused for a minute. "Yeah, funny thing is, you disappearing like that? That turned out to be the best way out of that goddamn nightmare." Another intake and long exhale of smoke. "So whatcha doin' now, Montana? You back for good? Do I gotta worry about this all over again?"

"No man, no, I'm not. I'm just here tying up loose ends before I bail out forever. As for the lawsuit, I'm not sure what to say. I gotta be honest. I've got a bad feeling it may resurface. My coming back into the country seems to have triggered some kind of goddamned broadband alert. One lawyer called as I checked into my hotel."

"Yeah. I remember that you had a bunch of other legal problems, too. Did you know I lost my restaurant?"

"Oh man, no." Montana lied. He was sitting in the place, but why rub salt in a wound. "Jesus, I'm so sorry. That's awful."

"Yeah, same thing as happened to you. Lawsuits. You was right, Montana, once you get in that system, it never lets you go. Goddamn blackhole. Two diners got into some kind of political fight at the restaurant, and before we knew it, both sides was suing us. Half the city protested us, the other half cheered us. We never even issued a statement. I tried to fight the lawsuits. You know me.

But in the end, the legal bills and drop in business ruined me. I barely sold it with enough value left to get out. Support local business, huh?"

"Jesus," Montana slowly shook his head. He could viscerally feel Jimmy's pain. To lose everything, not through bad management, bad luck, or bad operations, but to lawyers. That pain hurt so much worse. "I'm so sorry, that's just…what can I say?"

"Nothin' to say. Just don't gloat that you was smart and got out. You know, that lawyer is pretty pissed at you, too. You owe him like thirty grand or something. To tell you the truth, I was pretty happy that you stiffed him. I think you're in the clear on that one, too, lucky bastard. Sorta like you warning me not to engage in the *legal process*," he said, emphasizing the words with disgust. "You was right about that, too. Now I got a tip for you. Don't pay. I had about eight grand left in bills, and I just stopped paying. The lawyer went crazy for a while, but I can't pay what I ain't got. I had to put up with collection calls for a few months, he threatened to sue, garnish my wages, all that. In the end, I just stiffed him and there wasn't nothing he could do about it. He moved outta state a couple years ago, so I doubt he is gonna come looking for you." Jimmy paused and they both sat silently on the phone. Montana heard the burn of cigarette paper.

"He tried, you know." Jimmy said through an exhale. "Yeah, right after you left. He hired a PI to track you down, but you just went poof. No passport, no nothing. The PI didn't even have a place to start lookin'."

"I know, man, I really wanted to tell you what was up, but…something snapped, and I just kind of freaked."

"What was that, something with your divorce? What ever happened with that? Jeez, you walk out on that, too?"

Montana thought of his almost-ex-wife. Five years. He had messed that up badly. Every minute he delayed was a minute more of punishment she didn't deserve.

"No, Jimmy, wasn't anything like that. I was all set to leave, but I hadn't made up my mind. I told Joanna and Nell over at the restaurant, but they were the only people I told. I was never totally sure until…" Montana stopped. He never told anyone this story. Why not. Jimmy had been through hell.

"I came home one night, and as I pulled onto my street, I saw half a dozen cop cars in front of my house. I saw flashlights in my backyard. They were about to raid my house, man. A fucking SWAT team. I figured that lawyer had convinced the district attorney to go after us for wire fraud. You remember how broke we were. If I got arrested, no way I can pay for a defense. So, I freaked, and just hauled ass."

There was silence on the line for at least a solid minute. Finally, Jimmy rasped, "I never knew that. I guess, thinking back to how stressed and miserable our group of friends were, yeah, I can kinda see how that would look. But you ain't gotta worry about that. Whatever was going on at your house, it didn't have nothing to do with us...with our case. They never came after me. There were never any criminal charges filed."

The two talked for about ten more minutes before Montana hung up. The good news: he might have one less lawsuit to deal with now. Maybe.

But if the SWAT team hadn't been after him for wire fraud five years ago, what the hell did they want?

13

TERI BRADSHAW
3 Years Ago
Seattle, Washington

Teri's changes to the lottery system were as legendary as they were lucrative. First off, she needed data. Data on everything. What was taken. How it was handled. How it was transferred, sold, and redistributed; every touch-point from owner to TSA custody. Detailed logs needed to be kept, checked, and over-nighted to her once a month in L.A. The old system had slippage, and if the teams wanted to see more money, that had to stop.

Second, she consolidated and streamlined the resale of items. Everything got centrally collected and sold in bulk on auction sites around the world. In Teri's hands, five-dollar nail clippers became million-dollar contracts. Reselling a pair of nail clippers for ten dollars? Pointless. Selling sets of five thousand to nail salon franchises? Smart. Reselling them to airport convenience stores so that the owners could re-buy them? Genius. Within four months, lottery payouts were up nearly twenty-five percent.

The boldest part of Phase I involved repurposing the millions of water bottles that TSA confiscated every year. First, she got the TSA teams to systematically slow inbound customs processing so badly that the lines were backed up into the main airport. To avoid a safety disaster, TSA's main consultant,

The Bradshaw Group, recommended they move operations outside of the main airport. Passengers had to stand in enormous lines far away from prying eyes, licensed vendors, and the air-conditioned comforts of the main airport.

The millions of water bottles collected by TSA got donated to The Bradshaw Group's new non-profit division. Everything got shipped, in 501(c)3 tax-free containers, to highly bribable, low cost, and stable Nicaragua. There, her sorting facility handled non-U.S. distribution. The resold items shipped out using non-U.S. based carriers. The empty bottles were re-filled, re-sealed, and re-labelled as mountain fresh Nicaraguan Water (courtesy of The Bradshaw Group). The water bottles were imported, tax free, back to the U.S. and resold by immigrants on airport tarmacs starting at eight dollars a bottle. The profit delta was nearly six dollars a bottle.

In Nicaragua, the population had endured decades of economic and social mismanagement. Women still fought over their second-class status, so Teri's five hundred-dollar-a-month (female only) jobs were positioned as a public good. In total, Nicaraguan Operations cost a mere $75,000 a year. Back in the U.S., the airport vendors took a dollar cut of every bottle sold. Since it was on a commission basis, Teri eliminated the variable cost of her sales force. It didn't take the Nicaraguans long to figure out that by owning both ends of the transaction, a family could clear over fifteen hundred dollars a month. A fortune in Nicaragua.

As a result, nearly 80% of the airport sales teams had family members who worked on the distribution side back in Nicaragua. Teri had them on a rotating basis to ensure nobody overstayed their tourist visa. Everybody won. Staff turnover didn't exist, another business victory. Water operations, known colloquially inside the TSA as "Nicaragua Falls", now cleared over forty million dollars annually.

Teri opened the lottery in nearly every major U.S. airport. TSA turnover among participating teams dropped to zero, a statistic for which Congress blindly took the credit.

Phase II of her plan was even more ambitious. It involved the outright bribing of a government official. Now that Customs was managed outside and away from the eyes of airport officials, Teri wanted to open operations to inbound

Customs collection. To start *dragging* items from inbound travelers, Teri was going to need cover from the governmental watchdog group that oversaw all TSA operations. The Nicaragua Falls operation had earned her everybody's trust. Enough trust to move operations from Los Angeles to Seattle, where the head of the Government Accountability Office lived.

The GAO was headquartered in Washington, D.C., but the head of the GAO was a Seattleite whose wife much preferred the scenic Northwest to the concrete jungles and socialite parties of official Washington. As a result, the Seattle campus of the GAO was the de-facto power center.

In Phase II, Teri meant to address the declining monetary value of the items being seized by the TSA. As travelers adapted to the stringent TSA rules, it had become harder and harder to find high value items to *drag*. Teri planned to use her TSA teams to search out, seize, and resell items as they came *into* the country. It was risky, because some of those items were illegal and had to be reported, such as kilos of cocaine, and the GOA ultimately reviewed the job performance and seizure lists of the TSA.

Teri wasn't interested in the illegal items, but if, for example, the TSA seized 100,000 bottles of liquor that came in undeclared last year and only 2,000 this year, the GOA was going to notice. Likewise, she expected the number of passenger complaints to skyrocket once people started missing things. Those complaints all landed on the GAO's desk, so she needed a working relationship with the agency.

And so, three years after founding The Bradshaw Group, Teri was escorted onto the campus of the Government Accountability Office in south Seattle, Washington. She passed through security wearing a $4,000 business suit and carrying a chic leather satchel. The metal detector sounded, but nobody stopped her. A good sign.

Attempting to blend-in thematically with the Pacific Northwest, and with an unlimited budget, the building had been constructed with a nautical theme. The entire exterior was shaped like a pirate ship. She flipped through GAO magazine in the lobby and learned that all the finishes came from wood reclaimed solely from eighteenth century sea vessels (those which weren't in museums).

Well, that's certainly one version of accountability, she thought as her steward led her into the elevator to escort her to the fourth floor.

She stepped out of the elevator and into a Disney ride. The office appeared to be set up like the deck of a ship. A deep lacquered mahogany covered the floors and walls. There were two rows of desks down the center of the massive office suite, and the front of each was shaped and painted like an outward-facing cannon. To the right, a line of distressed mahogany doors led into individual offices. Each wooden door was rough and solid looking with a circular portal window carved at head height. Next to each door hung an old flint lock pistol or a sword. Gaudy chandeliers hung from the ceilings, and the desk-cannons were decorated with a variety of pirate knick-knacks. When she looked to her left, she nearly lost her balance. The wall was actually moving.

She steadied herself and realized that the entire wall was a projection screen showing a live action view over the horizon from a moving ship. Sure enough, she heard water lapping against wood, she saw birds gliding through the air, and the sun sat in about the right position for the time of day. Even the office air smelled faintly of the ocean. Teri almost believed she was outside.

"Jesus," she muttered, "the cost of this place."

Her deck hand led her past the fore-deck, or whatever, and toward the back of the ship. She kept glancing at the moving wall. The moving scene un-nerved her. Teri hadn't even read about things like this.

As she headed aft, she approached a raised, wooden platform with five wooden steps on either side, leading up to it. There was a waist-high, old wooden railing across the front of the platform. It looked, for all the world, like the stern-end of a ship.

She walked up the short steps onto the platform, past a sign that read "Welcome to the Quarterdeck" and to a set of heavy, wooden double doors with curtained windows cut into them. The doors, she assumed, led to the captain's quarters. She noted a wooden parrot on a post. Her guide knocked, announced her, and swiftly departed. As one of the doors swung inward, Teri half expected Jack Sparrow. Instead, a short round man poked his head around the door. He looked to be in his late 50's. He wasn't wearing a sword, but he did have a superman pin on his shirt pocket. Teri groaned inwardly.

Steve Largent's parents obviously named him after the famous Seattle wide receiver. Although the similarity ended there, Teri could appreciate that specific problem. What was it with their parent's generation? Largent had the harried look of a lifelong bureaucrat, right down to the sweaty brow, reversed stomach/butt combination, and short sleeve button-down shirt. He reminded Teri of the senior accountants at her old firm.

The thought of her old firm made her sneer inwardly.

At least women have the good sense to let themselves go in proportion.

In three-inch heels, Teri towered over the man. It clearly made him nervous and his hands constantly fidgeted as he ushered her to a plush leather chair. Steve sat across the reclaimed wooden desk and struggled through the pleasantries. Just as Teri was about to lead him into her sales pitch, Steve took a personal call on his cell phone. He didn't even ask or excuse himself. He just accepted the call.

Wow, thought Teri, *it really doesn't matter to government employees.*

The ensuing conversation appeared very one-sided. Steve mostly listened to the raised voice on the other end.

Teri heard Largent say, "There isn't much I can do." Then she heard, "I'm sorry" half a dozen times.

As Teri watched the conversation, her mind replayed her own arguments with Paul, her ex. Paul had that same hunted look on his face during arguments. Or more properly, when Teri argued and her ex concocted meaningless sentences using action nouns. Like her ex, Steve Largent's head popped back every time the voice in the phone raised an octave. The motion made it look like he was being punched in the face. It gave both men the appearance of a double chin. As with Paul, she found the display weak and unflattering. This guy's wife owned him. She could use that.

Finally, Steve's head jerked away from the phone like it had bitten him on the ear. He looked at the screen. It made an audible beep and went dark. Steve put the phone down and rolled his eyes.

"Are you..." he started and stopped. Tentative. His eyes glanced down to search for a wedding ring. "Are you married Teri?"

"Divorced."

"Oh, so you understand. Nothing is ever easy. Kids?"

"None."

"Ah. Well, we're having a bit of trouble with our twenty-five year old. He's a bright boy. Graduated top of his PLU class, and got an MBA from the UW."

Teri's mind frowned. *Perhaps referring to a twenty-five-year-old as a "boy" was at the heart of the problem, Steve.*

"He's had several good job opportunities, but really, nothing that's been challenging enough to hold his focus. He's a big picture guy, and he just keeps getting inside the box opportunities."

Ahhh, Teri thought, *potential employers won't bring a live-at-home kid on as senior management, big fucking shock.*

She'd interviewed dozens of these cocky MBA grads. They were all "world changers" who really just wanted to be on reality TV shows. Half of them still lived at home. About a quarter had parents wealthy enough to pay their kid's rent...essentially buying their own freedom. Children in suits, the lot of them.

She sighed inwardly as Largent droned on about the virtues of his adult adolescent. As a childless observer, Teri had always placed the blame on the baby boom generation for the softness of their children. They were the ones who complained about participation trophies while constructing bigger display cases to house them. They were the ones who never missed a soccer game, tried to negotiate better grades for their kids, and never accepted "average" as an outcome when, statistically speaking, average had to be the most common outcome. She remembered one parent calling about their Duke MBA grad. The parent complained that The Bradshaw Group hadn't hired their daughter after a second interview. It was the call that sealed the kid's fate.

She even heard that one parent called to renegotiate the employment status of someone they fired for not showing up on their first day. Things had gotten so bad that her hiring manager started "fire-able offense dossiers" the minute employment offers were extended. Really, the outcomes didn't surprise Teri. Their parents taught them they were special, then viscously attacked anyone who tried to hold the kids accountable for their behavior. What did the parents think would happen?

Most of Teri's rank-and-file U.S. employees didn't have four-year college degrees. Those were the adults of the generation. She overpaid them and they repaid her with hard work and loyalty. Much of her staff probably out-earned the MBA types because they had been patient enough to start early, take lower pay, and earn years of raises. Now those years of service were indispensable to the operation. An MBA who came with zero business experience? They were as interchangeable as car tires.

When Teri zoned back in, she hoped his story was close to a conclusion. She didn't give a shit about this idiot's kid.

"...spent some time as a freelance web designer out of college before MBA School. He and his mother are very anxious to source him an appropriate opportunity here. I've been efforting an explanation to her." Teri noted the business babble and it set her teeth on edge.

"There isn't an appropriate fit here at the GAO because of the new nepotism guidelines which are out of my control. It's a perception of integrity thing, but his mom finds the situation unacceptable. Honestly, after two years of this, it's becoming a drag on the family's togetherness quotient."

Teri lived with this verbal crap for a decade in her accounting days. Now that she was in charge, she preferred real English.

"Well, what are you going to do now?" Teri heard herself ask. Did she really just ask that? This idiot's personal life didn't matter to her. Phase II was riding on this.

"I just don't know, Ms. Bradshaw. Dylan is looking to transition more toward your field; investment capital and business consulting. He is committed to making a difference in a field that really powers sustainable change...where the real excitement is nowadays. What do you think?"

Teri's mind slammed into focus. Largent was staring right at her. He was clearly asking her to hire his son. His live-at-home, MBA, unemployed son. A kid who'd probably turned down eighty grand a year because he couldn't wear flip flops on Wednesdays. She had been prepared to break the law and offer a straight-out cash bribe to a government official, but this guy just beat her to the punch.

Wow, they really don't answer to anyone.

"Well," she began cautiously, "I think I can help."

She said it with no real thought behind it and Steve smiled encouragingly. "I might have a job he could do." Steve's face screwed up in puzzlement.

Ah, she remembered, *he only speaks meaningless drivel.*

"I mean, Steve, I might have an expansion opportunity in the near future where our interests align."

The puzzled look disappeared, and he started nodding as she spoke.

"As you may or may not be aware, we have been retained to provide business intelligence to the TSA at several airports, and we're assembling a crack team whose core mission will effort ideating critical problem solutionation." She droned on to the point where even Largent's face slackened. Nobody could obfuscate better than Teri Bradshaw. All those years in corporate America finally went to good use.

"What I haven't sourced yet is a team lead to report directly to me." His face brightened. "I have to warn you, though, it would be a challenging position. The Bradshaw Group is on an exponential hockey-stick growth trajectory, and we are struggling to resource dozens of top-line projects. Those will require a lot of mental shelf space from each team. A team lead is going to have to mindshare across multiple lines. I am really looking for an exceptional world changer here, Steve. As you well know, the TSA isn't an organization that easily adapts to change in their proven methodology. This person would be swimming against the stream."

He nodded vigorously.

Teri thought, *Good thing I didn't say "fighting an uphill battle." That might sound too violent for this tart.*

"That's great. That's great, Ter...err, Ms. Bradshaw. I think Dylan has all the professional metrics to successfully navigate challenging waters and generate consistently positive outcomes." He nearly stumbled over the excessive word usage.

Teri didn't understand a word. "Please, call me Teri."

"Great, Teri. Can I have him contact you directly to ensure he is afforded maximum exposure in the hiring process?"

"Sure, Steve." Teri could hear the sigh in her voice, but this dough-ball didn't seem to notice. "Perhaps if I take a personal hand in his application, it ensures the highest likelihood that we create a win-win."

She was done. She couldn't vomit up any more clichés. She locked eyes with Largent. He was either on board or he wasn't.

Steve Largent nodded solemnly. "Teri, I'm all in." He melodramatically unrolled his hand for a solemn shake. "Let's partner and ensure that The Bradshaw Group facilitates TSA's forward pivot into the next century."

"Steve, if Dylan is even half of what you say he is, that is a foregone conclusion." She smiled, shook hands, and turned to disembark from this ship of fools.

"Oh, and Teri," he said. She turned, noting his face flushed with embarrassment. "Would you, uh, mind calling to let me know…well, um…Dylan sometimes sleeps through his alarm." He paused, then rushed the last sentence like an apology. "Just so I'll know he presented himself in his best possible light."

Jesus, she thought. *Better make sure you set his alarm clock, too, Steve.*

"No problem."

The GOA was now on board. She would bury the kid deep in some out of-the-way department. If he was anything like his father, he could bore someone else with his verb-less sentences. When she needed real work done, she'd hire from a junior college.

14

CHRISTIAN RAMÍREZ
Present Day
North of Bluefields, Nicaragua

At his young age, and in a country on the cusp of transitioning out of poverty, Chris didn't know exactly what he wanted in life. His original plan, to study linguistics and teach Spanish to tourists, wasn't generating the money he hoped. The business had supplemented enough food, money, and goodwill that his family was living better. Like most Nicaraguans, Chris was a pragmatist. Wealth and glamour rarely found their way into the hands of Nicaraguans, but times were changing. Chris held a real hope that one day he would have children of his own, and they would have bedrooms of their own. Maybe even see a bit of the world. Incremental improvement.

But the internet called to him, with its endless images of the wealthy across the globe. Chris didn't think for one second that the future it portrayed was attainable for a Nicaraguan. At least, he *had* thought that.

That was before he stood next to a truckload of...no, this was still Nicaragua. That was before he stood next to a donkey cart full of gold.

And his crew pulled more out by the hour. The proximity to that much wealth sparked a desire in him that he could barely control. Suddenly, incrementalism wasn't the only option. That new life, which he wanted but couldn't define, might be within his reach.

But Chris wasn't looking for the western version of success. He wasn't a North American. The thought of his family in a seaside mansion, with a dozen cars in the driveway, didn't even compute. How would he try to explain to his parents that his new, insta-model girlfriend was bulimic, vegan, and had butt implants.

Oh, yeah, grandma she can't eat your cooking unless you sign a legal guarantee that it's peanut-free. And, mom, you'll be happy to know she's going to throw it up afterward to maintain her bikini body; which she is going to show off, half-naked, on the internet, to a collection of digital friends whom she hasn't met nor wants to marry.

Explaining the concept of the internet would be the easy part.

While he thought of all this, he stared at the phone in his hand. He had been trying his North American friend for days, but the call wouldn't connect. He was getting desperate. He hit redial.

"*Hola*, Chris, how are things in Nicaragua?" the tinny voice sounded out of the phone.

Montana. Thank God.

Enormously relieved, he inquired how Montana's lawyers were doing. He still couldn't believe the stories about lawyers in the U.S. If the U.S. citizens were paying thousands to lawyers just to solve arguments, how much money must they all have? He knew his friend wasn't rich, but he wasn't Nicaraguan poor, either. Plus, he was in the U.S. That meant he had access to goods and services that Christian couldn't get down here. And after what the team had unearthed, he was going to need all the help he could get.

The two chatted for a few minutes about Montana's trip. Chris was nervous and anxious. Since birth, his government had taught him to be mistrustful of *Norteamericanos*. But Chris' generation grew more mistrustful of the government's narrative with each tourist they met and each year Nicaragua remained the second poorest country in the hemisphere. Heck, Montana risked his life for the Ramírez family. Chris's government hadn't done that. Every day for six months, he and Montana took a one-hour bus-ride north to a small pueblo to build a library. They'd had endless conversations about every topic imaginable.

Every day, one of the village dogs waited at the bus stop for Montana. He'd given the dog a piece of bread every morning, and every morning the dog led them to the pueblo. Every night the dog had led them back to the bus stop for another piece of bread. During the day, the dog refused to leave Montana's side. On the last day of their project, the dog hadn't shown up at the bus stop. They'd found it near death in the village. It had been bitten by a snake on the road to the bus stop and had limped back to the village. Chris watched as Montana held the dog in his lap, stroking its head until it died. All the while, this grown man had tears streaming down his cheeks.

No, Chris thought, *our government is wrong. The government of the U.S. might be all those things, but the individual people weren't like that. Not at all.*

"*Chele,* buddy, I have a problem down here. Well, we have a problem down here, since you technically own a portion of this business."

"Me?" His friend laughed through the phone. "I thought you wanted to do this…whatever it is, on your own?"

"Well, I did, but we—" He stopped, struggling for the words. "We sort of found something."

"Wait," Montana said, laughing a little. "Finding stuff is good. That's what you're supposed to do."

Chris didn't laugh. "Yeah, but what we found is a little bit…scary. Maybe even dangerous. I don't know the right word, but I am very worried, Montana. I am very worried." Chris knew that by using his full first name, his friend would know he was concerned. Chris hadn't called him Montana since their first Spanish lesson.

There was a long pause on the line. "Oh. Okay. Well, what'd you find?"

"These things we found…they are…it is…" Chris stopped, collected his thoughts, and restarted. "I am scared to say it over the phone because of your NSA. But, this thing we found, well, if word got out, it would be bad. Dangerous maybe."

"You're worried about word getting out? Just what the heck did you find? No offense, *prix,* but you're in the Nicaraguan jungle. What could you have found? And no, I'm not going to make a donkey joke here."

Chris didn't laugh, but he did smile at his former student's use of the word *prix,* which was Nicaraguan for "dude". He tried to think of how to explain the problem without explaining it.

Montana cut back in. "Hey buddy, you're worrying me now. The donkey joke was funny."

"We found something serious, Montana. Something *very* serious."

Now it was Montana's turn to pause on the line. "Okay. Wow. What can I do? How can I help?"

"We are going to need some excavation equipment. Nothing too complicated. We can build most of what we need, and I can get most of the supplies in Bluefields or Managua, but I'll need some money to do that. And trust me, when you see what we found, paying you back will be the easy part. I'm also going to need some money to pay off the team for a while."

"Pay off the team? With actual money? What are we talking here? A grand?"

"Maybe around that, probably less."

"That's not too bad." Silence on the line. "The excavation stuff answers my initial question, but why pay off the team now? When we do pay them, don't we usually wait till the end of a job?"

"Well, we aren't exactly building libraries out here. To be honest, I want to be able to keep them quiet until we can figure out what to do with what we found."

"Chris, this sounds a little weird. I'm going to try and wrap things up here a bit faster, so I can get back down there. The money is no problem, I know where your parents live," he joked.

When Chris didn't laugh at this old joke between them, the voice carried on. "Hey, Christian, you've got me worried, man. Are you in real danger?"

Chris ignored the question. "I also need a few things that I can't get here. Do you have space to bring down a few smaller items? I will text you a list when we hang up. How long until you're back?"

"Not sure, exactly, but call it two or three weeks. Really, Chris, you're okay, right? You aren't in physical danger?"

"Yes, I am okay. No physical danger. Not yet. I am just...how do you call it when you are in water that is too deep, and you can't swim? Like with my sister?"

"Drowning. The word is drowning. Like you're in over your head. Chris, buddy, this doesn't—"

"Yes, that's it," Chris cut him off. "I am in over my head. I think that I am in over all our heads."

They talked for a few more minutes about logistical matters before hanging up. Christian breathed a sigh of relief. Montana was an older and more experienced guy. In the years Chris had known him, nothing rattled the guy. He would come up with a plan. If nothing else, it made him feel better just to tell someone.

He walked back down the hill, swatting away mosquitoes as he went. When he reached the river, the whole team stood knee deep in the water, sifters in hands. They'd been pulling coins out of the river all day at a ridiculous pace. They washed everything in the dirty river water and laid the items in the donkey cart they'd used to bring up the supplies. The donkey stood unhitched next to the cart, chewing on the low vegetation their machetes hadn't hacked down. The cart itself oozed dirty brown water from between the uneven boards. He lifted the tarp coving the back of the cart. A muddy fortune stared back at him.

No, he thought, *there is no way to keep this secret in Nicaragua. Somehow, this was going to get out, and when it did…*

He replaced the tarp, stripped off his shoes, and waded into the river to help his crew. His mind was much more at ease now. Talking to Montana had calmed his nerves.

Because of his youth, Chris never once considered the nerves of his crew.

15

TERI BRADSHAW
2 Years Ago
Seattle, Washington

Four years in and Teri started to see the strain around her eyes. The more she modernized operations, the more they grew, and the more she fell behind. She now worked ninety-hour weeks. Money poured in so fast she couldn't have stopped it if she tried. Between making it and hiding it, she hadn't had much time to spend it. She had a nice car for those rare occasions when she drove. She had a waterfront condo for those rare occasions when clouds lifted. She even had a designer wardrobe, which had yet to even require dry-cleaning.

Other than that, she didn't really have plans for her money, except that she planned to collect a lot more. Her worth now registered in the tens of millions. She wasn't quite Wall Street rich, but that was fine. Having more of something you didn't know how to use didn't strike them as pointless either.

Phase II proved a smashing success. The TSA provided a limitless source of secondhand goods. The seizure crews at customs were nabbing everything from Cuban cigars to jewelry. They were hauling in goods by the truck-load, shipping them down to central America, selling them on off-brand websites, and drop-shipping them out all over the world. The margins were so far in her favor it was laughable. Most professional jobs in the United

States now required regular air travel, so the airports stayed packed. Flights schedules were so tight that one aircraft going down nearly paralyzed the entire system. At least two Latin American countries were always on the brink of disaster, so countless upper and middle-class Latinos were flooding the southern airports. On the west coast, wealthy Chinese didn't appear the least concerned if entire luggage containers went missing. As long as they had their handheld electronics to stare into, whole suitcases of designer clothing could be snatched. Her airports got busier every month. The lottery paid out more than ever, averaging over $48,000 per agent. Since the crews thought $20,000 had been amazing, Teri was a goddess in their eyes. The tens of millions in payouts amounted to peanuts compared to what was flowing into The Bradshaw Group's shell companies.

The Group pulled in well over $150 million a year. Teri constantly schemed new reinvestment vehicles to shelter the money from prying eyes: commercial real estate, venture capital funds, startups, and anywhere she could tuck a few million to stay off the radar. What Teri needed was help. She was tired. She hadn't sat for a yoga class in nearly a year. She needed help from someone who wouldn't ask questions. Help that was ethically flexible. Help that wasn't smart or interested enough to see beyond the next mile-marker. Teri needed an MBA.

"Alice," she said, buzzing her $70,000 a year personal assistant, "can you find Dylan Largent and send him in here?"

"Right away, Ms. Bradshaw." Teri noted the slight disgust in her personal assistant's voice. She had heard the rumors about the kid, though she hadn't even met him before.

A minute later, Dylan Largent, son of GAO head Steve Largent walked in wearing a black business casual suit with a dark blue button-down. No tie. He was about six feet tall. He had deep green eyes and a mop of unruly brown hair, a cleft chin, and his clothes clung to his young athletic body like a glove. Whatever Dylan Largent might be, it started with stop-traffic gorgeous.

No way that idiot bureaucrat is this kid's dad, Teri thought with amusement. *Mrs. Largent, you were a naughty woman once.* Then she remembered Steve Largent. *Can't say I blame the woman.*

Dylan's college-length hair jostled with the air as he strode into her office. He smelled faintly of tobacco and cherries. The combination distracted her, men her age didn't generally wear cologne.

The Bradshaw Group offered young Dylan a job halfway through his first interview. Teri had no intention of dealing with that dopey father again. After that, the kid got thrown to the wolves restructuring the inbound customs procedures at TSA. He had proven adept at the logistics, and yet clueless as to their purpose. He was also tangentially involved on the real estate investment side, looking for investment opportunities, or creating buyout plans. He never asked why. The perfect candidate for what Teri had in mind. She had completely forgotten about him until a few minutes ago.

Quite surprisingly, the reports on him had been positive: a bit spacey, but he got the job done. Looking at him now, though, Teri suspected that her mostly female management team gave Dylan Largent a lot of slack, which is what lead to the rumors of his womanizing.

"Have a seat, Dylan. How are things going?"

"Uh, thanks, Ter…uh, Ms. Bradshaw. Really good," he said, pausing to collect himself. "Great, actually. Thanks for asking. I literally think I've adapted to the various pressures, and I literally feel comfortable with literally every assignment so far."

Although the kid was obviously nervous, his excessive use of the word *literally* killed the sexual desire rising in her. The corporate speak reminded her of her old life. Him opening his mouth was like a cold shower.

But, damn the kid was hot.

"You do? That's good," she said, just to cover her smirk. "Sorry, my mind has been wandering all day. And it's just Teri, Dylan. You can call me Teri. According to everything I've seen, you're doing an excellent job. I want to talk to you about expanding your role here. Do you think you're at that point?"

"Me? Oh, I'm like literally—"

"Good," Teri cut in, trying to cut him off before he could say literally again.

"To tell you the truth, I'm just completely at capacity. I want to talk to you about business development. I want to get a sense of how you think you could create ROI if I give you a bit of freedom here."

His whole face lit up.

"Wow, well, let me think here. I mean, like, I've got ideas, right? I just…I feel like my stress level just went way up." He half laughed. "I mean, I'm literally on the spot, right?"

Ahhh, Teri thought, *the millennial finally surfaces.*

Maybe this wasn't such a good idea. She considered pulling the plug, but the kid spoke up.

"Well, and you gotta, like, indulge me because I'm literally just thinking of this now, so some of this isn't totally boardroom ready."

Teri eyes narrowed as she tried to process the sentence.

"I guess I'd first re-deploy a part of the organization to be more of a traditional venture fund, like, to attract investors and capture more of the personal wealth space, right? Then, I think we should diversify assets into more traditional real estate. We have commercial spaces, but we have synergies with some business we could move *into* those spaces. Plus, if we repositioned and repurposed on the individual property side, we could like, participate more fully in the gig economy. We could outsource cleaning and management and soak up passive fees, right? I mean, that's pretty cool, passive income on, like, a commercial scale."

Teri held up her hand like a traffic cop and Dylan stopped talking. She needed time translate his bullshit into English: *spin out a VC fund, move their retail businesses into commercial spaces they owned, buy houses and rent them on AirB-nB. All pretty good ideas.*

She waved her hand for him to proceed, thinking that she was going to need one of those *walk/don't walk* signs for their next conversation.

"Well, I also think that we could get more mileage out of the 501(c)3 angle. I mean, the biggest tragedy in the world is indifference, right? So, I feel like we can expand and highlight our impact on the world to tug at some heartstrings. I mean, I know people say Wall Street is coldblooded, but I think deep down people want to do good and—"

Don't walk. "Dylan, the 501(c)3 is off limits." That cut way too close to the heart of the real operation. But, since this cupcake couldn't deal with a "hard" no, so she softened it.

"Dylan, that's kind of my personal baby, and I want to…" she paused, looking for a fuzzy word that meant no. "I want to keep my personal growth vehicle private. I don't want to exploit all that good for personal gain. I hope you can understand."

His face seemed to brighten even further. "Totally, Ms. Bra…Teri. Totally. I wish I could find inner peace—"

Don't walk

"So, look, Dylan," she cut across him before he could build momentum. "I like a lot of what you were saying." When Teri looked up at him, Dylan looked confused.

Oh, she remembered, *the English confuses him.*

She restarted. "Dylan, I think that your initial diagnosis for growth has potential. I'd like you to organize a progress structure that we can discuss, err, ideate over, in a week's time. Let's tentatively plan on Friday. I'm going to consider resourcing thirty million dollars to your efforts. I assume that provides foundation-ing…or whatever." She waived her hand as if shoeing away a fly. She had to end this meeting. Her mouth felt dirty from the felony assault on the English language.

He looked like a statue.

"I think…uh, I think it's amazing."

Whoops, thought Teri with a sardonic smile, *English just slipped through.*

Dylan continued. "First, you're incredible. Thanks so much for faith-funding this natural progression in my career. And second, I can give you a thousand percent assurance that we'll exceed expectation. My team is ready to shrink the world and change lives." He paused for a second. "But I might have some questions on the restructuring side, though. I don't really know how the original Bradshaw Group is structured. I mean, I can't know, right? Should I reach out to legal for that?"

"Maybe, but it might be easier to just call me directly." She handed him her card. "My personal cell is on here, just let me know as things come up."

She knew how millennials worked. Giving him her personal cell number was the equivalent of a first date. He'd start timidly with a few texts to see if she responded. Then the texts would edge into the personal by using stupid text emojis.

Fine. He couldn't handle the face-to-face stuff. Whatever.

She wanted to bed the kid, so she'd play along.

"Wow, this is momentous, Teri. Thank you so much. There is no limit to our accomplishment potential. I feel like this is going be an historic year. We're going to totally change the everything, right?"

"I'm looking forward to it." She giggled in response. It was either laugh or strangle the kid. She couldn't help herself. All that "change the world" stuff. The notion of this kid being anything other than a babbling sex toy made her laugh.

"Oh, and Dylan," she called after him in a motherly tone. "Don't forget to reach out to HR tomorrow to iron out all the paperwork on the job change." Sounding like his mother would keep him a tad off balance.

He looked puzzled. "Job change?"

"Yes, you're going to be my new operations chief." She switched back to a girlie giggle. Now the kid's mind would be completely confused.

"Oh. OH! Well, okay, wow! OMG. I literally didn't...you're totally the best boss of all time. Thank you, thank you, thank you. Hashtag Teri Rules. I swear, anything you need, ever. Day or night. Success never sleeps."

As he exited, Teri knew what her problem would be. How to have sex with him and duct tape his mouth shut. If he said "OMG" after sex, she'd smother him with a pillow. And hashtag Teri rules?

What a moron.

Well, at least she had him where she wanted him – off balance. He wasn't sure whether to speak teenager or business school. She hadn't planned on giving him the title, but it would indebt him to her for years and remove any question of whether she could seduce him. After all, she wasn't thirty anymore.

The job title didn't really matter that much. The Bradshaw Group was privately held, so she could limit his access without issue. Who knew, maybe he'd actually be able to reduce her workload. He'd proven a pleasant surprise so far. Except for the slogans. She'd have to rid him of that disease.

* * *

Eight Weeks Later

Dylan called to Teri from inside the bathroom of her waterfront condo, "don't forget, you have that critical piece with Investor News & Bloomberg Finance today. I feel like this is our first step toward raising your profile." Dylan talked while redressing himself in front of Teri's full-length mirrors.

Teri was luxuriating in her thousand-dollar sheets, looking out over Puget Sound and reflecting how much she hated the word *critical*. Watching him dress after their sex sessions fascinated her. The way his back muscles flexed as he pulled his clothes back on made her want him all over again. All that muscle wasted on someone who started every sentence with the passive aggressive phrase, *I feel*. The tryst wasn't their first, but it was still new enough that neither knew what to expect. She set the ground rules before their first meeting: it was just sex, and he couldn't stay overnight. Regardless of how many action-nouns floated inside that head, like any man, he hadn't heard anything past 'yes'. But when she handed him his clothes right after their first encounter, he looked hurt. Then he did the math: sex and leave versus no sex.

It was 1:00 a.m. and they'd retired here after an expensive business dinner to discuss her upcoming interviews. The interviews would discreetly raise her profile within the business community. Their publication would coincide with The Bradshaw Group's new LLC and venture capital fund launch. They planned to secure $300 million in funding from the profile bump Teri would receive as an icon in female entrepreneurship. Dylan had already secured half of the funding. The press would take care of the rest. These would be Teri's first press interviews, and she wanted to relax beforehand. Dylan relaxed her. Repeatedly.

"Um, Teri," he called again. "You with me?"

"Um, yeah," she snapped irritably, "I got it." Now that she was relaxed, she didn't want him to start talking and ruin it. She softened her tone. "Alice has that matter in hand." Teri rarely spoke after they had sex. She found that her silence had an unsettling effect on the younger man. He never knew what she was thinking, and she liked that power. She figured that so long as he never knew when it would end, he would continue to perform. Teri had seen first-hand that complacent men made sloppy men. And while this kid was just a toy, he might be a dangerous one because he had access to a lot of money at The Bradshaw Group. He clearly wasn't an adult, so she needed to manage him carefully before she was done with him. Even if the affair became public it wouldn't do her any real harm, and she wanted to keep it that way.

He crossed the room, softly touched her cheek, and kissed her on the lips. "I can't wait to see you again." The gesture was so pathetically melodramatic that she almost laughed. Instead, she swatted his ass, hard.

"Me too," she barked out. "See you at the office, you can let yourself out."

His eyes registered surprise, but he walked into the front room. At the condo's front door, he turned back and looked through the living room and into her bedroom. "Teri...be your best *you* today." And with that, he exited.

Teri got up and went into the bathroom to try and wash that sentence from her soul.

16

MONTANA AINSLEY
Present Day
Nashville, Tennessee

Montana spent two days sourcing the items from Christian's list, and now he'd have to check a bag for the return flight. Based on the list, it was clear that Chris had found some type of precious metal that required solvents to clean. The TSA would have a coronary if they started reading those ingredients in a carry-on. But what kind of discovery would have other people looking for it? How could a gold find, if it was gold, scare him? And how could gold even be in Nicaragua? It was briefly known to have had gold, but that had all been mined. An old mine, maybe? And sure, in the States there might be big businesses that would come in and take it over, but in Nicaragua? The place made the wild west look tame. No way someone in Managua would have a clue what was going on in the eastern part of the country. There wasn't even a road connecting it to the capital.

Montana gave up guessing. He couldn't stall anymore. Christian's call allowed him to put off his primary reason for returning. He still hadn't heard from his almost-ex-wife. Out of options, he had to do the unthinkable. He picked up his phone and called lawyer number two, his divorce lawyer.

"Wiley, Mills, Sandberg, Goldwin, Mix, Anderson, Gottleib, Showenweiss, Winston, and Shale." The woman on the other end of the call took a short breath.

"Sandy Sandberg, please. This is Montana Ainsley calling."

"One moment, Mr. Ainsley, let me see if he's in."

Right, thought Montana, *let me look up your name, see if you owe us money, and make sure Sandy isn't busy playing minesweeper.*

The line beeped again, then Sandy's upper-class British accent boomed through the speaker.

"My, my, the world's champion of divorce poker. You've cost me five quid, dear boy. I had exactly four weeks until your state of Tennessee declared you legally dead. My secretary wagered that you'd show." He paused. "I did not. I suppose that she is more familiar with the psyche of your bankrupt culture. Welcome back from the abyss."

Montana loved Sandy's over-the-top Britishness. Sandy's lingering distaste for American culture, mixed with his acidic wit, made for fun conversation. Criminally expensive at $650 an hour, but still fun. Sandy took up lawyering as a second career after retiring from the family furniture business in London. He relocated to Nashville with his American wife to be closer to her aging parents. Sandy still possessed a sharp mind well into his 70s, and the two always spent a few minutes fencing about what Sandy called, "the West's dis-advantaged society."

"What, no reports of my death have been exaggerated quotes, huh?"

"Don't be gauche," Sandy reproached. "We don't misquote American authors in this office. Now I know of your dislike for so-called *small talk,*" he said, pronouncing the words *small talk* separately and with great disdain, "so I'll inform you directly that not much has changed with the disposition of your divorce. Your future ex-betrothed sent me a polite request some months ago—through that frightful attorney of hers. And since I am never sick at sea, even with my most wayward clients, I engaged them in conversation regarding it." Sandy paused for effect. "I'd say say that lightning appears to have stricken her delicate American emotions. Twice. Savannah has found love. Again." Sandy cleared his throat. "Not you, of course. She'd like to bin you so that she can pursue a truer love. The note did seem conciliatory. It would appear she is prepared to move forward on more agreeable terms. I pray you weren't still holding a candle?"

"Not so much, Sandy."

"Just so. I did manage to wrangle an agreement that your parent's home isn't part of our great divorce struggle. You are free to sell to the highest bidder. Our auditors watch the current value like hawks. I'm told it would fetch quite a price on the market. Sadly, Savannah's attorney still insists that the business you owned beforehand is communal, so the true crux of the problem remains. Your future ex doesn't appear quite so keen to fight as her attorney."

"Ah, but she owes, right? So she has no control."

"Precisely. The bloody attorney won't let it go because it's the only way he'll get paid. Should I remind you that in all your future dealings, a prenuptial arrangement would prove a sound investment? Why do Americans persist in the belief that love lasts? The statistics are quite clear."

"We're Americans, Sandy. Everything is sunny-side up. We'd believe Tuesdays were green if someone told us so."

"Indeed. Yes, the prized American optimism. Strange how it often leads you down dark alleys."

"Divorce isn't an American invention, Sandy."

"No, but like so many other aspects of this life, you've managed to perfect the amount of misery it distributes."

"Fair enough. Luckily, we invented the computer, the airplane, and most of the 20th Century to offset it." There wasn't much conviction behind the comment, but Montana knew it would rile his attorney to no end.

"Ah yes," the lawyer intoned with mock sadness. "Sadly, you weren't able to invent nor perfect, decorum. So now the world must hear of your accomplishments with shameful regularity. And let us not forget how fortunate we all are to be living in some version of *stretch pant nation*. It's even infected the home country. Camille and I ventured to St. Basil's in central London for Easter. The cathedral looked like a yoga studio with stained glass windows."

Montana stifled a laugh. "Great news on the house, though. You really think it's worth a lot? That wasn't such a great neighborhood when I left."

"Oh, I should think so," the lawyer intoned sadly. "There's always some construction vulture waiting on his next meal. The area is quite different you know. The miracle of gentrification. In my country, they call it sweeping out the blight."

"Sandy, I'm confused. Is that good or bad?"

"That's in the eye of the beholder. We took the liberty of commissioning an appraisal. The house would 'hit the market', as you *yanks* say, just a whisker under a million of your overvalued dollars. I'd call that good news. It's the land everyone wants, you see. You've stockpiled two acres within a brisk walk of downtown. Not that anyone here walks further than the car to the yoga pants store. The real estate developers are tripping over themselves to build a city the size of Manchester onto your acreage. I can recommend an agent."

"Great, let's do it. How are we on billing, or should I ask?"

"Fear not. You left me an additional $4,000 if my aging memory serves. That is, before you managed to disappear. What a show. Our accountants were apoplectic at being overpaid for once. Afraid of being accused of money laundering, I should think. Your "missing person" status bolloxed up the works quite brilliantly. After the initial shock of you simply not being here, your case fell into the legal equivalent of a bin. There were half a dozen motions from your wife's counsel early on, but in the end, missing is missing. Naturally, they thought I had something to do with it, but whilst I had a sense of your plot, I genuinely didn't know a thing. This must be the longest divorce on record. I'd say congratulations, but I don't want to appear self-serving. I hadn't heard from your wife's attorney in nearly a year before this note a few months ago. On balance, I'd say you probably have about a quarter left thus far."

Wow, Montana thought, *what a pointless paragraph. Sandy must have taken a refresher on Keeping Clients on the Phone, II.*

"Alright. Well, you can reach out and tell them I'm back. See what kind of response you get and let me know. We'll take it from there."

"Right-o. And welcome home, dear boy. Oh, there is another matter that I… well, nothing. It can wait. I suppose a contact number is out of the question?"

"Yes, it is. Why?"

"Well, a smidge of a problem developed whilst you were away. It appears, the grass grew to such an unbearable height at your parent's old home that the city sent your repeated warnings to cut it. It appears your renters merely hacked their way to the front door, rather than chopping it all down."

"Okay, who cares."

"They do, old man. The city. They've begun legal proceedings to repossess the lot from you."

"Over tall weeds?" Montana laughed into the phone. "Wait, Sandy, you're not serious."

"Oh, all too, sad to say. Never fear, your great Uncle Sandy has begun steps to halt the process. However, it's not without cost."

It never is, Montana mused silently.

He thanked Sandy, noted that the call cost him $900, and called Sandy's real estate. They met at a restaurant close to his hotel and signed the papers. The guy said the house would be on the market in twenty-four hours.

Two days later, the real estate agent called to inform him that he had a range of offers. The one Montana liked best was $30,000 below the asking price, but the buyer said they could close in two weeks. The fast close was attractive and he took the night to think about it.

The following morning, the real estate agent called with bad news. All the buyers withdrew their offers, a lien had been placed on the property, and a subsequent lawsuit had been filed against Montana. No, the agent didn't have many details. He did, not surprisingly, possess the name of an excellent real estate attorney.

Montana entered the contact number into his phone, assigned AC/DC's *Highway to Hell* as the ringtone, and typed in *Lawyer 6* as the name.

17

THE DUNAWAY HOUSEHOLD
Present Day
Charlotte, North Carolina

Elaine Dunaway watched her husband, Alan, adjust his power tie and stare into the bathroom mirror. It must be Monday. Monday meant power tie day.

Elaine knew that her husband saw a Porsche Boxer, a seven-figure bank account, and a Zegna suit staring back at him. Elaine saw a guy of average height, with dyed hair, the self-esteem of a teenage boy, and the vicious nature of a cobra.

The marriage wasn't going well.

Elaine quietly padded towards the kitchen in yoga pants and an oversized t-shirt. She would make breakfast, pointlessly offer it to Alan, and then prepare herself for a half-day of accounting work at Alan's law firm. The house felt cold. It always felt cold nowadays.

The trip through the house didn't take long. Their house, one of ten dozen mini-mansions in Charlotte's most exclusive gated enclave, actually covered less square footage than most of the other mansions. Echelon Estates featured a golf course, a grocery store, two banks, half a dozen restaurants, and a small lake. Elaine insisted against the ostentation of a three-story affair with Roman columns. Reluctantly, Alan agreed. That felt like Elaine's last marital victory.

She'd even lost the argument over their daughter's name, conceding to the ridiculous *Anastasia*; a name that meant nothing to either family. But Alan had been adamant that the name could prove vital to his and their family's success. Very few who argued with Alan Dunaway, power-lawyer, ever won.

Elaine loved the house with its "U" shaped design. She loved the pool in the middle and the beautiful garden she had cultivated around it. Not that Alan noticed, but Elaine had probably spent a tenth of the money the rest of the neighbors spent redecorating houses that they had just custom built.

Charlotte, North Carolina was one of those rare American cities which enjoyed a perfect climate for nearly seven months out of the year, so Elaine spent a great deal of time outside. She had turned the five empty bedrooms into a variety of showcase areas. The library was full of used books, purchased over time and at great discounts. The bar (or drawing room as Elaine's old-south mother would have referred to it) showcased Alan's prized decanter collection. Elaine used tapestries to cover large sections of wall rather than purchasing gaudy artwork or massive family portraits. She'd acquired the tapestries on her various pre-Alan travels. Most of their friends couldn't tell a rug from a tapestry, and so everyone agreed that she'd made smart, economic use of her skills.

Their social circle viewed Elain as an excellent matrimonial asset to Alan's estate.

Their social circle. Elaine could live without, too.

In front of the coffeemaker, she reflected on Alan staring into a mirror. She didn't blame him. His life moved from one success to another. He never seemed to lose at anything. Faced with those statistics, she might stare into a mirror all day, as well.

No, probably not, her rational mind conceded.

Alan didn't appear to know frustration, or loss, or, it seemed, empathy. Why would he? Nothing ever went wrong for him.

He should be the poster child for law schools everywhere.

Lately though, the mirror sessions made her sick. With their daughter off in college, Elaine had no more distractions in the marriage. Just Elaine, Alan, and the house. Every day.

Alan had a partnership at the law firm of Alaways, Sinclair, Goldstein, Rogerson, Whitman, Milstone, & Dunaway, attorneys at law.

Even the secretaries couldn't pronounce it without a breath. The original firm, Berstein & Alaways, got rich on class action lawsuits in the lucrative Mississippi markets of the 1990's. As the two partners got wealthier, their needs grew. Specifically, their need for less work and a private plane. Enter Alan Dunaway, a corporate law specialist.

As Alan succeeded, the firm grew. As the firm grew, Alan added the accoutrements of a top tier lawyer. Enter Elaine Sawyer. Now Elaine Sawyer Dunaway. Elaine wasn't sure how much longer she could live with the situation.

* * *

Alan Dunaway marveled at the reflection staring back at him. He saw the image of someone who ate healthily, cussed excessively, and wore expensive clothes; just like the warriors of old.

He got chills just thinking about the toughness in those eyes. Those eyes belonged to a man so successful, he chose his clients and not the other way around. The man in the mirror preferred franchise clients for two reasons. Franchisors had deep pockets and an endless supply of problems. Franchisors had franchisees, and franchisees thought they were *tough*. That was, until they crossed the franchisor. Then they met the man in the mirror. Then they learned what a true alpha-male looked like. A franchisee may risk their entire life savings, but they did it under the umbrella of Alan's client, the franchisor. To Alan, that wasn't *tough*. *Tough* was forcing those people into bankruptcy.

Alan convinced his clients that wayward franchisees weren't just wrong, they were dangerous. They were dangerous because they thought they could supplant the franchise. Those people wanted to take away his clients' livelihoods. This was all part of a speech he delivered to prospective franchisors. The basic theme was that there were no petty slights. It was all out war, all the time. Alan got paid not just to prove people wrong, but to destroy their lives by any legal means necessary.

Alan charged $1,000 an hour.

He finished knotting the power tie, checked the hair one last time, grabbed his overnight suitcase, and walked out of the bathroom headed for work. Like most people in Alan's socioeconomic sphere, he was never really *late* for work. When you are Alan Dunaway, work starts when you arrive. Generally, around 9:00 a.m. He entered the kitchen for the morning kiss, coffee, and goodbye.

It was a painful ritual.

His wife always tried breakfasting together now that Anastasia was away at school, but Alan had no time to waste. He had people to ruin. He entered the kitchen and found Elaine sipping coffee and leisurely packing her own work satchel. A small plate of toast cooled on the breakfast nook.

Well, he thought, *she is slowly getting the message. In this house, we're too busy for breakfast.*

"Well, don't you look nice," she said as he walked into the kitchen, cleaned and coiffed with his suit jacket over his shoulder and a small roller bag behind him.

"Thanks, you too." He looked around. "Where's the dog?"

"Daycare." Chelsea, their something-doodle, usually got picked up later in the morning, so Alan figured his wife planned to head into the office early.

"I forgot to tell you last night that I'm gonna be stuck in Seattle a day longer than I thought," he said, affecting a carefree tone. "Remember that client I told you about, The Bradshaw Group? Well, that trip got extended because of some business hiccup they've got, and as it turns out, there is a continuing education seminar I can catch while I'm up there…save me the hassle of dealing with it when I'm back here and we could be spending time together." Alan liked that, it was good spin. He studied her features for suspicion. Nothing.

"Oh, well that sucks. How much longer? And what's the continuing ed. class?"

"Just another night. It's a three-hour refresher on *blame shifting.* Total bore, but probably not a bad subject to brush up on. Just a bunch of reminders on phrases to hand to clients when they complain about their fees. The usual stuff. 'This is the system, its slow but it works…their lawyer is stalling…the firm won't let me continue…blah, blah.'" He took a sip of coffee. "Word is that they're rolling out a new program. Seems there is a congressman who is putting together a bill to limit legal fees, and the lawyer's association has crafted a message on how to shift blame for the country's economic problems to his political party. That should teach congress who's in charge."

He needed to load her down with details to deflect from the "extra night" part of the trip, so he kept talking.

"The Bradshaw meeting will be interesting, too. That's going to be a retirement caliber client in the end. What's up with the lemonade people? Did you get a chance to finish the review on the financials?"

He could see her mind mentally shifting gears to keep up. *Excellent.*

"I did, and things are looking a bit grim. But I came across this weird thing in The Bradshaw Group's reports. I started going through the stuff the firm provided, and I'm seeing some weird inconsistencies."

The Bradshaw Group was a client assigned to Alan, and by extension, Elaine, as one of the firm's staff accountants. Her title was a subterfuge, but the job was actual accounting. Three years ago, Elaine suggested she quit her job and come to work at Alan's firm. That way, they could discuss cases without breaking any confidentiality rules. Alan readily agreed, since it meant they could gobble up more revenue from clients, and he could double bill them without even leaving the house.

"Hold off for a sec there," Alan said. "One thing at a time. Where do we stand with the lemonade people, Mother's Little Helper? Surely there isn't a financial shortfall there? That franchise is killing it.⁴"

---

4   Mother's Little Helper, LLC was a Delaware Limited Liability Company. The company sold turnkey franchises of lemonade stands to the parents of little kids all across the U.S. For a mere $9000 franchise fee, the families received a carbon-plexi stand, a battery operated audio/video billboard, a proprietary lemonade mix, and a variety of marketing materials (including, but not limited to, cute chalkboard signs, doggie water bowls, and a permanently mounted selfie stick). Despite the infantile nature of the venture, MLH ran the business as ruthlessly as any giant franchisor. The Franchisor received 20% of gross profits, paid weekly, and required monthly Profit and Loss Reports. Annual report and photos of the stand in operation were also required annually. The franchisees received a protected territory (no other franchises within a one-mile diameter), marketing plans, and ongoing business expertise for their franchise fees. MLH positioned the business as the "go-to" method of setting your child apart when it came to middle-school entrance resumes. Their marketing literature boasted that the "life advantage of adolescent entrepreneurship would help create exceptional middle-school applicants." MLH, LLC posted $1.15 billion in gross revenue last year, beating analyst expectations by $0.03 per share.

"No, not grim for them. Grim for the defendants, the Robinsons. They pulled their older daughter out of private school and are now homeschooling her. I imagine that decision went over like a lead balloon. Could you imagine what Ana would have said if we—"

"Anastasia wouldn't have allowed it. Sure, I get that. Wait, so they're having money issues?"

Elaine took a deep, audible breath. "I think so." She made a sad face at him. "Their credit report shows that they've maxed the HELOC on the house, and all their credit cards are maxed. They've made a lot of credit inquiries, but no new accounts have been opened. It looks like they're trying to get access to cash, but they're not having any—"

Bang!

Elaine jumped as Alan's fist slammed down on the table. Coffee splashed out of her cup and onto the table.

Alan grinned. "We got 'em. They're screwed. They'll have to settle now. We'll draw up a brutal agreement today, and I'll have the office ship it out while I'm on the plane to Seattle. Excellent."

"Excellent?" Her voice sounded soft and confused. "Alan, those people could be a week away from living on the street. You understand that, don't you? We've billed Mother's Little Helper over $220,000 just for this suit. I can't imagine a regular family can afford anything close to that. It feels—"

"Like victory," he interrupted her again. "Look, they chose the fight. If they didn't have the resources, they could have settled at any time. Settlement offers have been flying around like mobile homes in Nebraska. They could have backed down after they refinanced the house. No, Elaine, they know what they're doing. I don't buy the 'poor me' act for a second. They're trying to undermine the entire franchise system. The system depends on a franchisor's ability to control their franchisees. That can't break down. Nearly 90% of all U.S. businesses are franchised. It doesn't matter who's wrong. The system would collapse. A franchisee can't just do whatever they like. It's intellectual property theft. It's breach of contract. It's an attack on the American system. I mean, look around Elaine, the world has changed. Our opponents aren't just wrong anymore, they're evil. They're not trying to argue their side of it, they're out to take everything we stand for."

"OKAY," she said, in a placating voice. "I get all that. I'm not disagreeing." She had interrupted his tempo. "And yes, Alan, you've clearly won the case, but this family is decimated. Honey,

we're talking about a lemonade stand here. And didn't YOUR client file the lawsuit[5]?"

"Jesus, Elaine. This is what put braces on Anastasia's teeth and bought your Mercedes. And no," he held up a finger to silence her, "don't tell me you didn't ask for the car. That's beside the point. The point is that we aren't the ones who started this fight. I'm just the lawyer. My responsibility is to my client's case. Should I break that oath? Should we say 'no' we don't want to get paid? Should our daughter suffer because these people got in over their heads? Do you even understand what's going on in the country, Elaine? If we don't make more money this year than we did last year, we fall behind. Within three years, we won't be able to make the mortgage, Elaine. Forget Anastasia's graduate programs, she'll be flipping burgers. This is about money, Elaine. Money and justice. My client seeks justice, and my job is to get it no matter how much money we make."

He expected that to be the end of it. Surely she'd drop this whole conversation in the face of that onslaught.

Instead, she fired back, matching his tone. "Knock it off, Alan, this is me. It isn't like you're taking a moral stance. You'd argue the exact opposite if the Robinson's had hired you."

Alan stopped. He had no response. This was the lawyer's prisoner's dilemma.

---

5   Twelve months earlier, Mother's Little Helper, LLC filed a lawsuit naming Brian and Jane Robinson-as guardians of Maize Robinson -and The Robinson Beverage Company, LLC in a multi-count suit. The Plaintiff alleged breach of contract, intellectual property theft, and false advertising among several other counts outlined in the lawsuit. The lawsuit alleged that the Defendants de-branded from the Mother's Little Helper's franchise and illegally operated a home-made version of a lemonade stand in front of their house in Charlotte, North Carolina. Moreover, they operated said illegal entity utilizing techniques stolen from MLH's operating manual. The lawsuit alleged that the hand painted "Maize's Lemonade" signs were false advertising, and that the company owed back royalties on unreported sales for over a year. The Defendants countered that the franchise had, in fact, violated their contract by selling MLH franchises to three different families within the protected territory operated by the Robinsons. The Franchise had yet to answer those claims as the case had yet to be heard in full. There had been dozens of motions, re-filings, and hearings as the case ground its way through the legal system.

In practice, *legal ethics* got defined by who was paying, and a lawyer's individual morality dictated that one should pay the mortgage first and ask questions later. Alan was trained to hide his argument's shortcomings behind the curtain of *legal ethics*. Elaine didn't seem to be buying that this morning. Her comment infuriated him because he couldn't figure a way around it.

Rather than engage her more fully, he saw an opportunity to close the conversation. As indignantly as possible, Alan turned to storm out of the house. Unfortunately, one of the roller wheels on his suitcase jammed on a wad of non-allergenic dog hair. With only three functioning wheels, the suitcase kept slamming into the wall as he dragged it behind. Alan eventually picked up the whole thing and awkwardly stormed out of the house. It wasn't the dignified exit he had planned, but it didn't matter. The subject of his extended trip went unnoticed. Score one, Alan.

* * *

Elaine watched him pull out of the driveway. The morning had gone pretty much as she'd expected. He told her she looked nice, though she was wearing a t-shirt, yoga pants, and hadn't showered. He made an excuse to skip breakfast, and then treated her like a low-level employee about her job at the firm. Check, check, and check. At least this morning was a bit different. She got to hear his defense of the law pitch, the one meant for prospective clients, not wives.

Elaine knew Alan had pre-planned their fight. She even knew why, and the whole thing just made her sad. That was why she had pulled out her closing argument. Watching his face go red had been worth it.

She was tired of making breakfast and throwing it away. Tired of being kissed on the top of her head. Tired of Alan's excuses. Just tired of the whole charade.

Ever since she had taken a job with Alan's firm, things had gone from bad to worse. She had hoped it would give them some common ground, something to talk about. Alan had become uninterested in anything that wasn't a lawsuit, and since Ana left for college, the house always felt like a tomb.

By working as an accountant on Alan's case files, Elaine circumvented the confidentiality rules. But her clever move backfired. She actually spent her time assessing the financial strengths of the firms' clients and their victims. Watching the firm's opponents go broke depressed her. Watching Alan kick them while they were down made her soul queasy. It wasn't just his desire to accumulate money. Alan took actual pleasure in the destruction he left behind. And Alan wasn't unique. The whole firm operated that way. Jesus, the entire system did.

Then they got a new client, and worse became unbearable. Ever since the firm brought on The Bradshaw Group as clients, Alan's trips to Seattle got "extended" for one reason or another. A year ago, she might have bothered to check on the continuing education seminar. Now, she already knew it didn't exist. She'd paid a private investigator $1,000, using pre-paid visa cards, to track his movements six months ago. The PI confirmed what she already suspected: her husband was sleeping with The Bradshaw Group's CEO.

She wasn't even mad about the infidelity at this point. Alan was what he was. What she married. He hadn't changed, he'd just perfected being the asshole that always lurked there. A person trained to run as fast as possible, for as long as possible. Alan didn't ask where and he didn't ask why. He didn't ask because he didn't really care. In the end, Elaine supposed, that was the problem. Alan needed *more*.

Elaine needed *happy*.

But she'd wait before she ended it. She still had an accountant's mind and that meant a structured exit. Once that plan was assembled, then she would decide if she wanted to leave. And there was always the chance that Alan would come back to her. They'd been married so long. They had so many memories together. She knew his smell. She knew his mood just by the sound of his footfalls as he walked through the house. They could carry on a conversation without even saying a word. Or at least, they used to. They'd slept together nearly every night for so many years…millimeters apart. Could that kind of intimacy really not mean anything to him?

They'd always talked about travel once Ana was out of the house. They had plenty of money, but as the years passed Alan had become focused solely on the acquisition of more and more money. Their life goals had diverged over time, and

Elaine couldn't see a path where they intersected. That was why she wasn't mad about his cheating. Alan just came to grips with the situation before she did.

Could she start over at forty? Could she put a lifetime of memories into a safe and lock them away? She could always open the safe and sift through the memories if she wanted to. But single? At forty?

Ugh.

But how much more time did she have to waste? Alan might be fifteen years older, but he had someone. Or, he thought he did. Elaine's PI earned an extra five hundred dollars for learning that that CEO Teri Bradshaw split her time screwing Elaine's husband and some other young employee at the Bradshaw Group. When the final fight came, Elaine planned to shatter Alan's carefully crafted self-esteem with that little nugget.

But what if her only options were more versions of Alan? Nearly everyone she knew seemed bred to chase "more."

She let out a long breath and grabbed a sponge to clean the spilled coffee off the table. Those thoughts would keep. She'd would work from home today. She wanted another crack at The Bradshaw Group's financial picture, and now she was glad Alan had cut her off earlier. He wouldn't remember her comment about the Group's financial inconsistencies, so she could still gather whatever she needed without raising suspicion.

Something was off about that company. And something was off about the glossy Ms. Teri Bradshaw…besides the fact that she was sleeping with Elaine's husband.

18

Money now flowed from various Caribbean and Central American shell companies to The Bradshaw Group LLC, then into Bradshaw Partners LP, and eventually into the brand-new Earth Ventures Fund. Teri designed the system herself. The clowns at the Securities and Exchange Commission would need a legion of officials just to find a team of forensic accountants to track it all. The amount of money all but assured the success of her fledgling venture capital fund. Normally, VC funds locked up investor money for two years. That kept nervous investors from pulling the financial rug out from underneath new funds. Being so flush with lottery cash, Teri's fund didn't require the hold. That sent a signal to investors that Teri didn't need them, which brought them begging to invest.

Teri backstopped the fund with lottery money. If someone wanted their cash early or if the fund needed to cover losses, Teri could shift over her endless supply of TSA lottery money. The scheme had the added bonus of laundering the lottery cash.

Pure genius, she smiled inwardly.

To clients, everything Earth Ventures invested in seemed to make money. The first round of investors received their initial investment plus a thirty percent return after just eight months, courtesy of the TSA cash. Everybody tripled down after that. Their massive re-investments were then locked up for two years.

If Earth Ventures lost money, *not that it would if Dylan wanted to remain alive*, Teri could use lottery cash to pay out the investors at breakeven. There was a limit to how much she trusted Dylan to run the fund.

But Dylan's strategies proved effective and the fund made money. Unlike the thousands of pyramid schemes out there, Earth Ventures could prove its purchases and investments…at least after Teri had done the books. All she had to do was fudge the ownership percentages if someone asked. Or she could hide the lottery money as investment income from the VC fund. Worse case, she diverted money to the bleeding-heart non-profit, which was secretly snapping up properties by the truckload. By then, everyone was too busy staring at Teri on magazine covers to ask questions.

Teri made sure Dylan kept at least forty percent of the fund's holdings in residential and commercial real estate. That way, she could launder the lottery money as she needed. All she had to do was make up fake renters and book their "rent" payments as income from the property. Teri could easily gin up fake income and rental records as needed. The rest Dylan could invest his precious gig economy or invest in other ways. The Bradshaw Group's tentacles were global. All in all, Dylan had done well. He was young, but he seemed to have great instincts for diversifying the money.

For her part, Teri finally had some free time in her life. She made the gym by 6:00 a.m., the office by 8:30, and spent most nights at home. She got a few touch up surgeries and spent a fortune on hair and makeup. She got herself appointed to local and national business boards. She got involved in various local charities. She didn't much care for any of the causes, but her profile was significant now, and she needed to figure out what to do with it.

And so, a rested, wealthy, and much younger looking Teri Bradshaw attended the weekly management meeting at The Bradshaw Group's HQ. Before the meeting started, Dylan got up and introduced the unknown man sitting next to him as Alan Dunaway, a franchise lawyer from Charlotte, North Carolina.

Not bad looking, Teri thought, *full head of hair, rich lawyer.*

She clocked a wedding ring.

Maybe.

Earth Ventures retained him to advise on several matters, and he was here to address a new business venture that Dylan would outline later in the meeting. Dylan assured everyone that the guy was listed as a "top 50 over 50" lawyer. The lawyer made an insecure remark about not being fifty and everyone laughed politely.

Dylan closed his comments with the phrase, "So he is like, a super lawyer, and we're totally under attorney-client privilege."

The comment made Teri wince. She assumed the entire office knew she slept with the kid on occasion, and when he talked like that, she felt like a statutory rapist. Not that she cared.

After the odd start, she listened to all the department heads give her an update on the current state of their divisions. When it was Dylan's turn, he outlined the staggering revenue figures generated by Earth Ventures' management fees, followed by the mountain of income generated by the fund itself. Although Teri alone knew that a large portion of that *income* was lottery money, the numbers were still impressive.

Dylan then went on to outline the fund's newest initiative. They wanted to get into the brick and mortar service business.

"Hang on a sec," Artie Goldstein interjected, "all businesses have to be franchise businesses[6] to have any hope of success."

Artie headed up *Business Consulting* at the original Bradshaw Group. The haggard veteran's career included every big-name Wall Street firm imaginable. His long experience earned him the most eloquent compliment the MBA crowd could muster: "Artie knows his stuff."

---

6   Three years earlier, congress passed the Business Resource Initiative & Benefit Endeavor to "improve early stage outcomes" for America's small business owners. The crescendo of online complaints, spanning everything from bad meals to sleezy contractors, drove a sharp spike in private lawsuits across the country. The class of lawsuits, known as Expectation Torts, had, in turn, driven business failure rates close to 85%. With insight from the International Franchise Council, BRIBE established a set of guidelines under which new businesses would have to operate. Businesses starting with under thirty employees now faced reporting and taxation so overwhelming that the only realistic option was to open under the protective legal umbrella of a franchise. To sweeten the deal, Congress allocated generous subsidies and favorable banking terms (which was to say, any) to entrepreneurs who agreed to fall in line. The IFC got its pipeline of entrepreneurs. The Plaintiffs' lawyers were happy to sue rich insurance companies instead of bankrupt business owners.

"Are you saying we should buy into a franchise?" he continued, "because I'd have quite a few questions if you are. Seventy percent of franchisees fail in the first six years, and of the remaining thirty, nearly all of those say they would never repeat the decision. Franchisors won't even grant multiple stores anymore to avoid power struggles with their top performers. Dylan, the ongoing fees never justify what the franchisor delivers."

"Art, I'm—"

"And that's not even taking into account that it's essentially legalized serfdom. After the initial franchise contract runs out, you basically have to renew it. Well, you could choose not to renew, but then your iron clad non-compete says you can't operate a similar business for five years. So, after paying millions in fees over ten years, we couldn't even take the businesses private. It's like medical schools saying you have to work at a certain hospital after graduation or else you can't be a doctor." Artie paused to let the example sink in. "You can't seriously be suggesting we get into that racket? Being a franchisee is like declaring bankruptcy."

While Artie was talking, Teri watched Dylan's smile grow bigger and more conniving. Dylan had baited a trap, and the old man was walking right into it. Inside of two years, she'd molded this kid into a fox. Well, maybe just less of a hen. Old Artie must have seen the grin on Dylan's face and realized something was wrong, but he was so intent on showing up the boss' *boytoy* that he couldn't stop himself. Teri waited on Dylan to spring his trap. She was less interested in the content than the drama. This little proxy war ought to remind the old windbag that she was still the master here.

Dylan responded when Artie had finished. "Art, I'm not suggesting we go in as *franchisees*, right? I feel like we go in as *franchisors* for all the reasons you just laid out."

Then Dylan stuck out his balled fist and opened it, miming a "mic drop". Obnoxious as the move may have been, the kid's point brought all objections to a halt. Dylan looked over at Teri. She gave him the *walk* sign, thinking, *this was why people Artie's age hate your generation. No sense of subtlety.*

"Okay, let me start off by saying that this is going to change everything. Period. Full Stop. All of you sitting here, within two years, are going to be viewed as the visionary team that inspired a generation. Your initial reaction is going to be that it's impossible. And that's how we know we're on the right path. History proves, every day, that anything can be done. Every person who tells us we're crazy is a person who wants the status quo. Those people are stagnant. Frozen in time…and it's *time* to pass them by."

He paused and looked around the room, gloating over his turn of phrase. Several people shifted uncomfortably.

Teri interviewed enough MBAs to know they were taught that making managers uncomfortable was a sign of success. In Teri's experience, it was a sign of idiocy, but business schools got paid to tell kids what they wanted to hear. She knew their discomfort would only wind the kid up.

Dylan kept streaming. "Everyone knows that selfies are the central theme of the Millennial generation, right?" He stopped and stared at Artie. "Those are like, photos that you take with your phone facing you".

Even the bags under Artie's eyes looked pissed.

"I feel like everything we do is put online to demonstrate that we achieve more with our time on this earth than the people before us. *Being our best us*—that's what we call it. I mean, it's even in the name, selfie, self-indulgent. Right? And that's inspiring. That self-indulgence drives people to create moments that impact lives and inspire positively in the world. If your friend has a photo teaching the underprivileged to read on a mountain in New Guinea, it makes you feel the need to do your part. There are literally instances of people falling off cliffs while they were positioning themselves to get a selfie. And that's a courageous act of self-sacrifice to inspire others to be better versions of themselves, right? Who wants to grow old and die in a hospital bed? Who gets inspired by that? Nobody. But dying serving a cause inspires."

Teri almost raised her *don't walk* hand so she could try to untangle his bullshit thinking, but the kid plowed on. Obviously, the unicorns had already left the barn.

"Ever been to New Orleans? You literally can't walk a block without being in the background of someone's selfie. Even the dozen malls still in existence have selfie stations. This entire generation, literally, travels the globe just so they can take selfies and inspire their fellow world citizens. Nobody cares about Machu Picchu. But everyone cares about having a photo in front of Machu Picchu, right? And all those photos, and I really mean this, like, capital letters A-L-L of those photos are hash-tagged and put online. Hashtag Eiffel Tower. Hashtag Notre Dame. This generation can't really get nine to five jobs cause the previous generation outsourced them, so they're making up jobs by creating huge digital footprints and collecting followers."

If Terry had been paying attention, she might have pointed out to Dylan that he, in fact, had a nine to five job, but she stopped paying attention after his first "literally." Regardless, the kid kept babbling.

"Getting one hundred thousand followers to like us is like 'entry level position' to your generation. How do you get followers? Images. Photos. Likes. Shares. Basically…content. Everyone with me? Influence matters. Words matter. Thoughts matter. Images matter. Take musicians as an example. They can sway elections with their followers even when they don't know who is running. Actors can wreck a business and drive a dozen people to unemployment just by posting about a cold coffee or a bad experience. Social Media can bring down governments. The Bradshaw Group doesn't have that power right now. We don't have a toe in this space. I feel like this a massive market we need to tap into. I mean, like, Ms. Bradshaw, you have a sister, right? What does she do for a living?"

Teri had been staring at a chipped nail her stylist missed. She considered returning to raise hell with the woman when her mind registered Dylan saying her name. She tried to recall the last actual verb she had heard.

"She is, uh, a social media influencer."

"Right." Dylan pounced, as if his point had been made. "Exactly. This stuff touches everyone on the planet. I mean, like, Ms. Bradshaw is a super CEO, and even *she* has a family member involved. Social Media is literally the future of capital through influence, right?"

Teri's mind was completely scrambled. She couldn't diagram that sentence with a protractor. *Jesus,* she thought, *am I my grandfather now? Am I going to get an embolism trying to understand this nonsense?*

But the kid kept going.

"So now we have to monetize that, right? I feel like we have the unique resources to provide a social media platform destination. Why spend a fortune flying to Egypt to see the pyramids? Not only does it drain your allowance, but it takes time you don't have. It's not like you can fit three vacations into a year. Machu Picchu, The Pyramids, and Big Ben? You'd have to freelance for a decade to save up the money to see those. Not to mention, third-world governments tend to melt down like the polar ice caps, and those countries can be really dangerous. It would take a lifetime to maximize what the world has to offer in order to fully inspire its citizens. What if all that stuff existed in the same place. Everest in the morning, the Great Barrier Reef at lunch, and The Sphinx at dusk. Not only does it economize travel, but there is, like, no way you don't rack up your first million followers with all those photos, right? An entire world can be inspired by our creation. Everyone with me?"

Teri looked around. Everyone was not with him.

"And I'm talking a holistic, economically viable solution to bringing the world's treasures to one location. Hostels, local vendors with local products, and…"

Artie finally interrupted. "Dylan, look, I have no idea what the hell you're even saying."

"Six Flags for selfies," Dylan shot back. "This is the culmination of a generation of change. This is what we've been waiting for. This is our giant leap for mankind."

He finally took a breath and looked around the room. Teri heard the building's air conditioner click on. The Dyson EcoCool 9000, the most unobtrusive central air system ever designed, a system so quiet they used it in the White House Situation Room, sounded like a goddamn thunderclap in the silence.

19

MONTANA AINSLEY
Present Day
Nashville, Tennessee

"So, let me get this straight," Montana mumbled through his hands. "Someone I have never met filed a lawsuit against me alleging that I agreed to sell them my house, on two acres of land, half a mile outside of downtown Nashville, for *forty thousand dollars*? And, they've put a lien on my title so that I can't sell it until the underlying lawsuit has been resolved? Does that about cover it?"

He sat in a house on Music Row, just outside of downtown Nashville. Technically, Music Row occupied two rows, separate one-way streets, lined with old houses that had been converted into record labels and law offices. The record label planted flashy vinyl posters out front, congratulating the various artists who had reached some level of acclaim. The law offices just hung wooden signs from the mailboxes.

The house Montana sat in, a small Victorian, had a wooden sign out front. The lawyer Sandy's real estate agent recommended sat across from him. They conferenced in the living room, which doubled as the board room. Between them, the remains of a Bolton's hot-chicken lunch littered the oak conference table. Montana couldn't eat. It didn't help that Bolton's secret recipe appeared to be coating chicken with liquid magma. With this so much stress induced acid in his stomach already, one bite and he might explode.

The lawyer, number six, alternated between eating and delivering bad news.

"That's the short form, yeah," the guy said through a mouthful of the Chernobyl flavor. He looked around for something to wipe the radioactive sludge off his fingers. Montana pointed to the fire extinguisher.

The lawyer laughed and said, "Look, the system isn't perfect. Obviously, this is a crap case. In their original filing, they said you agreed to sell a year ago. When I mentioned that you'd been designated a missing person and no-one had talked to you for the last few years, they filed an amended complaint claiming you agreed a few days ago and that their original complaint had a typo." He paused and wiped his fingers. "This is obviously nonsense, and any judge is going to see right through it. This is just legal strong-arming. They figure that everyone selling their house is in financial trouble, so these big developers sniff around big land sales. It's worth it for them to drop five or six thousand on a lawsuit. They figure either you'll offer triple to settle, or you don't have the cash and they can swindle the house out from under you. This is all pretty standard stuff, I'm afraid. But have faith in the system. Judges can smell a rat for what it is."

"Assuming the judge doesn't get hit by a chicken bus or retire, right?"

"Huh?"

"Forget it. This sounds more like an investment strategy than a lawsuit?" It wasn't a throw-away comment. Montana wanted to see his reaction-he was testing a new theory.

The guy stopped moving. He stopped breathing. Stopped blinking. He just stared straight at the papers on the desk for a full ten seconds.

Finally, with the fake pomposity of a used-car dealer caught selling a lemon, "Oh, it's nothing like that. I can't imagine how that would make sense. I mean, they're risking too much by losing in court. The one thing I know for sure, we'll beat this, no problem. It may take some time, but in the end, we'll prevail."

Montana thought, *we all know this never sees court. They invested five thousand in a lawsuit figuring I'll pay them twenty to go away. Find me a stock with those kinds of returns.*

Montana said, "Can we prevail faster?"

"Well," the lawyer waggled his hand in a *so-so* motion. "We can file motions for an expedited hearing, but in the end, we have to go through depositions and discovery. There are strategies we could employ to try to hurry it up, but a judge usually won't entertain a motion to dismiss before depositions."

Montana knew this legal tactic, too. Dangle ideas the client wants to hear, ideas that waste their money and accomplish nothing, but make sure to advise against the ideas so that blame-shifting can be placed on your client's own decisions.

Can this really be happening? Again?

Montana pondered his fortunes while the lawyer droned on, "...the system is designed so that every person can have their say in a lawsuit, so large corporations—"

Finally, he had enough. The guys words were meaningless. "Hey, so when this gets dropped, can I sue them for, what, for frivolity or something to get my fees back?"

"Youuu...can. That's an option." Hardly convincing.

"Jesus, I don't have this kind of money sitting around to pay a retainer. What, like thirty grand?"

"About, but I tell you what. How much do you think you can put together now?"

Montana knew this scam, too. It took a million variations, from the spice markets of Istanbul to the vegetable stalls in Guatemala City. Rookies gave an honest answer. Experienced people halved the amount. Montana had been negotiating vegetable prices for five years. He cut his account balance by two-thirds.

"Best case, four-grand, and that leaves me with barely anything leftover."

"Well, I'll redraw an agreement for a $4,000 retainer." Montana noted the attorney's complete lack of concern at leaving his client penniless. "The house is obviously worth a dang fortune, so I know you're good for it. In the meantime, I'll reach out to them and try to hustle this along, maybe push for expedited discovery. They'll want all your electronic communications for the past year. Let's call it a year-and-a-half to be on the safe side."

"Easy. I don't have any," Montana said with a smile.

"Any what?"

"Electronic communications."

"What. Seriously? You don't have email? Texts? Social media accounts?" The lawyer let out a nervous laugh.

"No to all three." He did, in fact, have those things, but they were local and specific to his life in Central America. A U.S. based attorney couldn't find those in a million years.

"What? Seriously? You don't text?"

"No. I don't. I've been missing for five years."

"Ohhh, righttt. I forgot about that. Well, uh, that might be a problem."

"A problem? How? How is that not easier?"

"Well, the thing is, opposing counsel is going to find that suspicious. They're going to go to a judge and say *that's suspicious*, and a judge is going to tend to agree with that. The assumption will be that you're hiding something, so the judge will authorize a subpoena on all your records for the past five years. You get where I'm going with this?"

"Yeah," Montana croaked out. Staring up at the ceiling, he felt something in between vomiting and screaming. "I know exactly where this goes."

20

ELAINE DUNAWAY
Present Day
Charlotte, North Carolina

Elaine spent the whole week tracking the money movements of The Bradshaw Group. Now, she sat in her home office with a glass of viognier, trying to relax her mind on a Friday night. Something didn't add up with The Earth Ventures Fund and its parent company. The Bradshaw Group proved a total black hole for information. But Earth Ventures was a hedge fund that doled out press conferences and prospectuses. She pulled K-1 forms on everyone involved, statements and annual reports from every business that invested, and a dozen other publicly available corporate forms. She backtracked who put in what, then what they declared as income. It wasn't a complete picture, but it wasn't far off.

The fund raised a lot of capital, but still Elaine had suspicions. It wasn't operating like a pyramid scheme—she was sure of that. The underlying investments succeeded, but then again, that might be the problem. They succeeded too much. Plus, there were far too many underlying investments. The fund never seemed to miss. Based on the financial records that Alan's firm required (to ensure that payment would always be made), Earth Ventures owned about 60% more in assets than it should.

She'd never seen anything like it. They received investments, paid out handsome returns, yet still had enough left over for an annual dividend and asset purchases. This was where most pyramid schemes fell apart. They wound up paying out more than they could take in because the top tier of the pyramid skimmed so much profit. Earth Ventures seemed to be the exact opposite. Regardless of how much they paid out, their asset base kept growing. Just a short while ago, they'd purchased over $200 million in commercial and private real estate alone. She found proof of about half that in actual revenue, but when you factored in expenses, there is no way they should be able to afford all the buying.

Hats off to that woman, the accountant in her thought, *those were amazing margins. So amazing they couldn't be real.*

There were additional expenses, but basically, a company with $0 in Net Income had somehow purchased $200 million in real estate. And it wasn't a standard accounting trick of where the investment was booked. Earth Ventures flat out shouldn't have had enough money to make those purchases.

Elaine had checked and re-checked the numbers. They owned the properties, so it wasn't a Savings and Loan scam. If it wasn't the S&L scam, and if it wasn't a pyramid scam, what the hell was it? What new swindle had Teri Bradshaw cooked up?

Then Elaine looked at the non-profit in Nicaragua. There were articles about it in the press. The Bradshaw Group milked it for massive PR value, but the connection seemed bizarre to Elaine. Women like Teri Bradshaw weren't do-gooders. Elaine didn't know her, but she was screwing an older married man and younger employee at the same time. No matter what her public profile looked like, Teri Bradshaw didn't suffer from a crisis of conscience.

Her reverie was interrupted by the sound of Alan arriving home from work. She imagined each element of the routine before he could execute it. Keys and wallet on table. Then, *"I'm home, how about a drink?"* Then a short walk back to the bedroom to remove shoes, jacket, and tie. Then to the bar to pour a scotch. On with the pool light and fountain; groan into a wingback chair, and finally spend an hour staring out at the pool while he finished half a bottle.

Thunk, clang. "Babe, I'm home, how about a drink?" The swish of expensive fabric down the opposite hallway. Clunk, clunk. A sigh. The sound of a silk sliding through cotton. The lighter tap of stockinged feet back up the hallway to the drawing room. The clink of ice in a glass. The flick of a switch. The pool light lit up Elaine's dark office. She could see Alan in his half of the U, looking at her from across the pool in his wingback chair. She saw a look of surprise, and he got up and walked out of the room.

Probably headed over here, she sighed inwardly. She really didn't want to talk. Not to Alan, not to anyone. She just wanted to relax and let her mind unwind.

A few seconds later, he'd walked the length of the home's U and she felt him fill the doorway. "Hey hon, whatcha doing in here? Little late for work. We don't bill you out hourly."

Jesus, a work joke.

"Nothing, I was just finishing up some work on…"

"Take a break. Come have a drink with me. It's been a long week."

"Yeah, it has. Alan, I want to ask you something about The Bradshaw Group." She paused and studied him. He looked nervous and fidgety at her mention of the name Bradshaw. Part of her almost laughed. Watching him squirm sounded like fun on a Friday night. Why not?

"Yeah, so there is a weird financial irregularity I can't square. It looks like…"

"Can't it wait till Monday? I mean, it's a Friday night. We should be relaxing, not digging around client files." His smile was so plastic she couldn't hold in the giggle. They hadn't "hung around" on a Friday night in five years.

"What's so funny about that? I just want to spend some time with my wife."

Surely, she though caustically, *he won't passive-aggressive this back at me.*

"Jeez, Elaine, every time I try to relax with you…"

Yep. He did. He was turning this around on her. She was thinking of a reply in her head, when her mouth opened, and someone else's words came out.

"What, Alan, fucking Teri Bradshaw on Monday didn't relax you?"

It just came out.

It. Just. Flipping. Came. Out.

She didn't yell it. It wasn't accusatory. She hadn't planned it. It just came out, in a monotone, like a statement: *hi Alan, nice shoes, did you wear those to your girlfriend's house before you fucked her?*

The question echoed through the air like they were at the bottom of a canyon, the words repeating more softly as the wind carried them off. All the blood drained out of Alan's face. Elaine arched her eyebrows and produced her nastiest sarcastic face. "What, you didn't think I knew? Like you are some secret agent? Alan Dunaway, the James Bond of adulterers?"

"Lainey, this is…crazy!"

"Lainey? Really, Alan? Lainey? Suddenly we're back to college sweethearts 'cause you got caught? I thought Lainey wasn't serious enough for high-profile, legal society. I thought *Elaine* was more, what did you call it? Polished? Shouldn't we be polished when discussing who else you've slept with?"

"Honey, I never said that. I love that nickname…"

"Jesus! Really? You're trying to spin this conversation away from you screwing one of your clients to my nickname? And I mean really screwing one of your clients, not just financially. Is this you, 'taking control of the narrative'? Fuck you, Alan."

"Wait a second. Now, I…I have never…that's ridiculous. I want you to calm down." He held his arms out, palms down, trying to mime her into calm.

She reached into her bag, withdrew a 3x5 photo, and spun it at him.

It flew through the air like a magic trick. Like Ricky Jay himself had slung it; strait as an arrow, right into Alan's nose. His head jerked back, and he yelped like she'd punched him. After he made sure he wasn't bleeding, he picked it up off the floor and flipped it over. It was a picture of Alan going into Teri Bradshaw's condo.

He froze for a second, processing a lie. "What? Pfttt? Seriously? This doesn't… honey, we had a meeting at her condo. It's outfitted like a command center. We always meet there."

"Always?"

"No, not like that. Everyone meets her team there. Oh my gosh, Lainey. I'm so sorry you got this idea…no, Lainey, this…"

The lie added to her frustration about The Earth Ventures scam and pissed her off more.

"It's time stamped 2:00 a.m., asshole. How can you not even be a good liar? You're a fucking lawyer!"

Alan responded with frozen silence.

Then more silence. She could see his mind working frantically. Finally, he spoke.

"You mean you knew? You knew and you didn't confront me? Why? Why would you let it go on? What's wrong with you? Couldn't you tell it was a cry for help?"

Un-be-fucking-lievable, Elaine thought.

"A cry for...just shut up." She shook her head violently. "Shut the fuck up. I don't even want to hear your passive aggressive crap. Trying to turn it around on me? Is there any Alan in there, or just empty suit lawyer? How the hell do you think this makes me feel?" Elaine could feel herself getting wound up. That wasn't what she had planned.

"You? Think about me? I just got this dumped in my lap?"

"Wow," she dead-panned, and the anger left her in a rush. "Seriously? Is talking about your lap where you wanna go with this?" She narrowed her eyes. "Is there room for both of us there?"

No response. Her lack of anger and heavy sarcasm outflanked him. She moved in for the kill.

"You know what, maybe she has a fat ass and I won't fit on your lap. I'll ask that Dylan Largent kid. You know, the COO? The young hunky guy who works for her. She's been fucking him just as long as she's been fucking you."

She reached back into her bag and flung another photo at him. It didn't fly with the same accuracy, but it landed face up at his feet. It was a picture of Dylan and Teri kissing on the balcony of her condo.

Alan's face completely slackened, and his mouth dropped open. He stared at the photo on the floor. Tried to start a sentence. Couldn't. Tried again.

"I...I think I'm gonna go. I'm going to spend the night in a hotel...maybe let you cool off. I need to...we can discuss this when the moment isn't so charged."

"Need to make a call, Alan? Yeah, you're going to a hotel. That much I know. Don't pack light. I'm gonna need a lot of cooling off."

He physically limped, shock all over his face, as he left to pack a bag. When she heard his car pull away, she took her wineglass and sat with her feet in the pool, staring distractedly at the pool light.

Well, that hadn't gone to plan. The thought put a faint smile on her lips.

But it was done. She had hoped to have the Teri Bradshaw thing nailed down by the time she drew this fight, but The Bradshaw Group proved far more difficult than she had thought.

Damn that woman. Damn that woman. Damn that woman.

She felt the moisture gathering in her eyes. She breathed in the scent of rosemary from the herb garden and looked around at the tranquil scene she had built over half a lifetime. Alan had actually paid for most of this life-she knew that. Alan would be fine without her. Alan drove Alan, and by now he had driven far away from her. Could she say the same about herself?

She felt the first tear escape. It rolled down her cheek and dropped into the pool with a low plop. That sound sent a dozen more cascading off her cheeks. She stared at the water as the teardrops fell from her chin into the pool. Each drop created a circular ripple. More drops. More ripples. Dozens of ripples, slamming into each other, creating a tiny storm on the surface. That was her life now. She fought against the first sob. She gave in once it broke through. Ten seconds. Thirty. A minute.

When her breathing was back under control, she watched the remaining ripples dissipate, and the pool calmed again. The worst was over.

Then she buried her eyes in her palms. Then the gut-wrenching sobs started again. She cried out the twenty years she had just lost. She cried for the grenade she just lobbed into the middle of their lives. She cried for being the kind of wife a husband cheated on. She cried for the decision of a young girl to marry, early and older, to avoid the economic pitfalls of her peers. After about an hour, when the tears had dried up and her breathing came under control, something Alan had said popped into her mind.

He had asked her why she would "let it go on". A lawyer's question. An ambulance chaser's question. It was spin. With Alan, everything was spin. This wasn't her fault. He made the decision. He took that action. He made the damn grenade, and then he pulled the pin. All she did was throw it back at him. This was goddamn blame shifting.

Son of a bitch.

He'd probably ask her to sign a non-disclosure in the divorce. That made her giggle. Then the giggle turned into a laugh. She imagined Alan, squealing after being struck by an index card-sized photo. Some corporate assassin.

Within minutes, she was holding her ribs, trying to contain the pain from her laughter. Alan wasn't tough or scary. He was a lawyer. Almost by definition, he was a coward. How many times had he admitted that he'd attended law school because he was afraid of having to find a job on his own?

This isn't my fault. It's his, the bastard.

She got herself under control, poured the warm wine into the pool, and went back inside. In the coming days, he would drag their daughter in as leverage, then things would get ugly. She needed to think about something other than Alan. Besides, Alan hadn't done this alone. He had help, and that woman had inflicted a mountain of pain on Elaine.

Time to return the favor.

She'd read that Teri Bradshaw started out life as an accountant. Well, it was time to see which accountant was smarter. Elaine would ruin that woman if she had to fly to goddamn Nicaragua to do it.

21

CHRISTIAN RAMÍREZ
Present Day
Managua, Nicaragua

It took Chris two days to go from the campsite to the capital city of Managua. He rode a donkey out of the jungle and hitched a ride to the Caribbean town of Bluefields. The town felt strange. The dusty streets were nearly empty, and the boat dock was completely deserted. Most of the shops he needed hung closed signs. It felt like the town had prepared for a hurricane.

He decided to get out of there on the first river panga the following morning, so he took a room at a cheap hostel. At night, the silence of the town became eerie. Through his room's window, he heard the ocean wind whistling through the streets, but no evidence of life. Restaurants and bars stood empty. Something about the town was off.

He caught the early boat up the Escondido river to the town of Rama. From Rama, a mostly empty bus took him the remaining six hours to Managua. Old Gordo nailed it, Bluefields had been a waste of time. But not for the reasons the old man had thought. Gordo had warned him that the ancient port town was so small, if someone saw him buying mining equipment, there was a good chance they'd follow him back to the camp. But Chris didn't leave Bluefields because someone was watching him, he left because nobody was.

Montana had come through and Chris arrived in Managua to a flush bank account. He set about acquiring what he needed the minute he got into town. The city of two million was uncharacteristically quiet for a Wednesday. Normally, the streets were packed with cars and choked off with exhaust. Not today. His taxi zipped around the city in record time. He even got in and out of the Oriental Market with ease—a feat he'd never managed before. He'd tried to buy a plane ticket back to Bluefields, but the late afternoon flight had cancelled, so he was stuck.

He took a hostel for a night, dropped off his purchases and money, and set out for the central mall, MetroCentro, to grab some food and buy more minutes for his phone. Most Nicaraguans couldn't afford phone plans. Typically, they bought minutes or data by the day or week. Chris's phone had run out of minutes days before. As he approached the street leading to the mall, he heard what sounded like chanting, and as he got closer, he saw hundreds of people streaming along the main road.

They're in the dang road? What the heck?

He took out his phone and checked his Facebook account. No data.

He entered at the southern end of the plaza and joined a throng of people marching up the avenue. People were blowing horns and shouting. Everyone wore the blue and white of Nicaragua. Some draped flags over their shoulders. Nearly everyone waved small Nicaraguan flags.

This has to be a thousand people, he thought in wonder. Chris had never seen so many people at once. They were chanting slogans of varying kinds, but he got the gist; a protest march.

What had Montana always said? In for a penny, in for a pound.

He mingled with the crowd and struck up a conversation with a couple people who were holding hands—an old man and his grandson. The grandson was marching because of the forest fires raging in the indigenous zones down by the southern border. The region had been ablaze for weeks. The Costa Rican government offered to help, but Nicaragua's lifelong dictator claimed it would be an act of war. Instead, the government chose to do nothing.

As a result, thousands of *manzanas* burned out of control. The area was supposed to be protected, indigenous land. The boy suggested that the government was letting the fire burn to displace the residents in favor of the president's grand plan to build a canal across to the Caribbean. It sounded a bit fantastic, but Chris could believe anything from his government at this point. The older man marched to protest the economic "reforms" announced the day before. The government raised the retirement age, raised Social Security taxes, and then cut benefits. That Chris could completely believe. Common gossip held that the President's family used the treasury as their own personal slush fund.

The trio walked about a half mile until they stood across from the mall's entrance. Chris bid the strangers good luck and veered off toward the mall. At the entrance, a thought struck him. He wanted to get a sense of just how big this march had become. He was too short to see over anything and get a sense of the size, but the noise was incredible.

He climbed the built-in service ladder of a light pole just outside the entrance. The view shocked him. Not hundreds. Thousands. Tens of thousands, stacked sidewalk to sidewalk, north to south, as far as his eyes could see. Pride flushed his cheeks at the sight of thousands of his countrymen standing together against corruption.

As he panned back toward the front of the protest, something caught his eye in the McDonald's parking lot across the river of protesters. His pride soured. He was separated from the parking lot by a sea of people, but there was no mistaking what he saw. Dozens and dozens of police in riot gear had formed up. A couple of them pointed at him and spoke into shoulder mics. There had to be over a hundred black armored bodies in the parking lot. They held riot shields in one hand and shotguns in the other. The whole scene, thousands of protesters marching right by a line of armed police, looked like something out of a Hollywood movie...right up until it turned into one. The police formed into two rows, donned helmets with black visors, raised their weapons, and started firing into the crowd.

Bedlam followed.

Chris involuntarily cringed at the first pops of the rifles. He'd never been this close to armed violence. His hands tightened on the ladder rung. People started screaming, and the crowd scattered in all directions. The panic rippled out from the McDonald's parking lot like a growing wave. People slammed into each other, bodies fell, and voices shrieked out in pain.

The riot police moved into the vacated area and separated into north and south rows. Then they jogged down the street, one line in each direction, firing at the fleeing protesters. Chris's body froze. He issued mental commands to climb down, but his limbs wouldn't respond. He watched, paralyzed in fear, as five armor-clad police marched through the smoke towards him. He knew he was in big trouble.

One of the cops ordered him down off the pole. He wanted to comply, but his body wouldn't react. He couldn't even open his mouth to speak. When he didn't respond, an armor-plated arm reached up, grabbed his leg and yanked. The man was so strong, Chris couldn't hang onto the pole. He fell six feet and landed, hard, on his butt. Pain shot through his spine. He arched his back and reached around toward his backside, yelling in pain. The police laughed, and one zip-tied his hands with plastic cuffs. He struggled to his knees, hand behind his back, spine stinging.

Chris had never been handcuffed, and the feeling frightened the hell out of him. He was completely exposed. He couldn't ward off blows. He couldn't even get his balance to stand up.

His mind screamed that he had just been on his way to the mall, but his mouth betrayed him and stayed shut. One of the cops kicked him directly in the stomach. He vomited and fell to his side. He couldn't breathe, and his hands were still locked behind his back. He felt the panic taking over as two more blows landed. His mind couldn't process anything except that he couldn't breathe. Another kick. No pain, But still no breath.

In that moment, he wanted his hands more than anything he had ever wanted in his life, more than air in his lungs. If he just had his hands, he could breathe, he was sure of it. But he didn't have the use of his hands. And he still couldn't breathe.

He was dying. Right here, on this shitty street corner, he was dying.

The blows stopped, and finally, a breath came back into his lungs. His mind registered voices above him. Then another breath. His eyes filled with tears and he couldn't see anything. Another breath, and with it, calm started to return. Whatever happened, the kicks had stopped. The cops must have lost interest in him.

Regular breaths returned. He could just make out the blurry backs of the police armor. A rushing noise filled his ears so he couldn't hear anything, but he could feel the thud of his heart in his ears and neck. It pounded like a jack-hammer.

They've walked away, he thought. *I'm not going to die here. I have lost my breath before. I have been kicked before. I have to calm down. I have to get my hands in front of me.*

In the brief quiet, the pain from the fall and the kicks started to register all over his body. Tears blurred his eyes again, and he still couldn't free his hands. He pulled his legs in to try and slide his arms over them, but the pain in his back forced a yelp from his mouth, and he straightened back out. He smelled vomit on his face and felt pain everywhere.

His hands. That was the worst part. He could endure the pain, but the defenselessness was unbearable. The officers still had their backs to him. He could get away, but he had to go now! He strained to bring his hands around his sides, but they were locked too tightly behind him. He rolled onto his knees, preparing to try and stand up.

The second he was upright, the cops turned back toward him. They hadn't been called away. In the hazy light, through blood and tear-soaked eyes, Chris saw the figures close in. The shiny black armor. The guns, the visors. He couldn't even see their faces above their mouths.

"You one of the leaders?" one yelled. "You were looking up and down it from the light pole like a proud little shit. Are you proud now?"

They circled around him, blurry black-clad robots. His face and chest were unnaturally pushed forward and exposed because of the handcuffs. The fear came back. The helplessness. The panic. He felt a stabbing pain as a boot lodged in his stomach. He vomited again, fell over, and everything went grey.

He heard vague voices and saw a fuzzy outline draw up to kick him again. The figure slid in vomit and Chris felt a hammer blow slam his thigh. Lightning shot through his pelvis, and he cried out. Pain shot through his chest as another blow landed. He felt something crack.

One of the figures stepped forward and started talking. Chris could sense words, but his mind kept slipping in and out. The pain in his groin felt like an electric shock and his vision kept blurring. Then one of the thugs leaned close and whispered to him. He couldn't make out everything, but he heard the words "broom handle" and *El Chipote*." His bladder released, and despair rolled over him like a wave.

El Chipote is, nominally, a prison. In reality it is the state's medieval torture and rape dungeon, rebuilt away from prying eyes. Two girls from his graduating class had once been arrested, raped, and released within seventy-two hours. They were never even charged with a crime. The girls didn't discuss what happened, but their description of the conditions haunted everyone's nightmares. If they took him there, game over. His head started spinning. His body tried to vomit, but nothing came up.

This had happened so fast. A train wreck of events with no way to stop it. He had been on his way to dinner, and now he was going to die in *El Chipote*? What would happen to his mother? His father? His sister? He hadn't talked to them in days. Not since he left for Bluefields.

One of the figures grabbed him by his handcuffed arms and yanked him up roughly. Pain shot through his shoulders in protest of the unnatural angle. A fist hit his eye. He would have fallen, but the other cop held him up. When the cop let go, he was able to stand for less than two second. He heard the guards laughing at him. He felt the piss down his leg, the vomit on his chin, and the tears in his eyes. The shame hurt worse than the pain. Then he thought, *El Chipote*, and his mind shut off. The cops pushed his collapsing body backward to avoid being touched by his vomit and urine-soaked clothes. Instead of falling head-first onto concrete, the shove reversed the fall, and Chris landed butt first into a stand of low-lying bushes. For the next ten minutes, dozens of other armed police marched by without taking notice of him.

* * *

Chris's one good eye slowly opened, and his wallet came into view. It sat on an unfamiliar nightstand. He felt a bed underneath him. His brain hurt. Why wouldn't his other eye open? He gently reached out and touched it. Swollen shut. Then it hit him. Full recall.

He remembered being pulled off the light pole. He remembered their muffled voices, their laughter, and pain. The pain still wracked his body. And his hands. He remembered the feeling that he couldn't use his hands. Chris saw clothes, balled up in the corner of the room. They told the story. Blood. Vomit. Piss. The look and smell of violence.

He recalled the desperate escape back to the hostel, falling over half a dozen times with his arms still locked behind him. The fear. The muted pops of gunfire close-by, car horns, the almond smell of tear gas, the putrid stink of burning rubber, and the hazy glow of sodium lights dimmed by smoke and fog, and bugs. He remembered seeing shadows slipping through the darkness all around him. He wasn't running fast enough. His legs were stuck in molasses. Then he was at the hostel.

It seemed to take the staff forever to open the door. Then he was in. Safe. They hustled him in and cut the zip ties holding his hands. He cried as his limp arms drooped to his sides. He had no control over them. He couldn't raise them. Half a dozen people massaged feeling into his shoulders, bandaged his wounds, and tended to his cuts. Chris cried inconsolably because he couldn't feel his arms. Then, after half an hour, he cried because he could. Then they all cried for what was happening to their country.

Darkness still filled the open window of the bedroom, and he could hear yelling and gunfire in the distance. Close. Although the door to his room sat wide open, his wallet, money, and supplies sat untouched. An older woman came in with a bucket of soapy water and a cloth. She called out to someone in the hallway to come clean Chris's clothes, then she set about re-cleaning his wounds. Nicaraguan households didn't keep an abundance of medical supplies on hand, and Chris knew his care depleted their meager supply. He tried to thank the woman, but she shushed him. While she worked on his face, she recounted stories from the rebellion in the 1980s. The roadblocks, the bullets, and the repression. It sounded chillingly familiar.

"We traded one dictator for another," she told him through tears. "In the morning, you need to get as far away from Managua as you can."

When the woman left, looked up at the ceiling through his one good eye. He knew exactly where to go, but he had a new problem. How exactly could he move a pirate's fortune in gold through a revolution?

22

MONTANA AINSLEY
Present Day
Nashville, TN

One of Montana's eyes slowly opened, and the digital clock came into blurry focus. It read two-something in the morning. As his subconscious dream receded, his conscious mind registered shockwaves, pounding out his name. *Mon-tan-ah. Mon-tan-ah.* He was too far into sleep to make sense of the phenomenon, but trying to reason it out brought him closer to full consciousness. When the tenor of the shock waves changed, the fog in his mind dissipated just enough for him to open his eyes and take in his surroundings. He was in his hotel room, the numbers on the clock said 2:34 a.m. He heard the thumping again.

Thud, thud, thud. Something, something, police, open the door.

That part, *police, open the door,* Montana heard clearly. It didn't make sense, but he couldn't connect why. Groggy and confused, wearing only his boxer shorts, he swung out of bed and stumbled toward the door. He was still unfamiliar with the hotel suite, and he banged his shoulder on the doorframe as he trudged toward the front of the suite. The slight pain brought a bit more consciousness. Did he hear right? The police were at his door? Were they evacuating the hotel? Did they have the wrong room?

With his eyes still only half open, he opened the door to three, black-clad figures in...was that body armor?

"Montana Ainsley?" the tinny voice emanated from one of the black visors. He couldn't tell which one.

"Uh, yeah," he groaned. "Is something wrong with..." he stopped. His eyes shot wide open, and his brain slammed into gear. He flashed back to a scene five years earlier.

Darkness. Flashlights searching through his backyard. An armored figure, just like this one, knocking on his front door. Two other men with shotguns poised and pointed. Unseen dogs barking from the fence line of both neighbors' houses. Police cars filling his driveway, lights flashing.

Before Montana could finish the scene in his head, the armored figure hit him like a tank. A Kevlar-covered shoulder armor slammed into his stomach, and he went down, hard, the breath knocked out of him. His mind blanked. He couldn't breathe. Hands grabbed him everywhere. He felt a punch in his kidney. The pain didn't register, he was too focused on regaining his breath. Rough hands flipped him over, and he felt a knee in his back. Finally, his breath started to return. He heard people shouting "clear" throughout the tiny hotel suite. His arms were pulled back and tight metal cuffs were cinched around his wrists. Only then did the knee come off his back.

"What," breath, "what is going on?"

"You're under arrest."

"Me?" Breath. "Why?"

"They'll take care of all that downtown. We just make the arrests."

"You guys, wait," he took in another breath, "you have the wrong guy." Breath. "Seriously. Stop. Let my hands go. I'm not an escaped felon. I own a restaurant. I'm not a criminal."

Staring into the carpet, he realized how stupid he sounded once the words were out, but he had never been arrested before. He really, really, wanted his hands uncuffed. Having them locked behind his back unnerved him more by the second. When the figures didn't respond to his initial statement, he switched tactics. He hadn't committed a damn crime. What the hell was this?

He turned his head to the side to avoid breathing in more carpet fibers. "Guys, I'm cuffed, I'm in boxers, I'm face down on the floor. I'm not armed. I'm not a threat. I want to understand what is going on. Please. Jesus, I'm half naked and handcuffed. Can I get up at least?"

The figures, satisfied that the threats had all been neutralized, removed their helmets and slapped hands like they had just stormed Little Round Top.

They still didn't answer his question. They read him his rights. "Do you understand?"

"I don't understand what I'm charged with. Don't you need a warrant? Can I put some clothes on?" The speed with which the situation had deteriorated was dizzying to his half-asleep mind.

Two of the cyborgs locked eyes, and the leader nodded cautiously, as if to say to his fellow cyborgs; *be careful, I've seen people break titanium cuffs before.* The third cyborg drew a pistol and aimed it at Montana. The second cyborg grabbed him roughly by his handcuffs and yanked him to his feet. The motion nearly pulled both Montana's shoulders out of their sockets. Suddenly, he could feel the pain from the kidney punch, the obvious broken rib from the tackle, and the Tommy John surgery he would need on both shoulders.

"Yeah," the lead cyborg smirked, "you can get dressed for your ride to the station, and no, I won't uncuff you."

A gun, a 9mm Glock by the look of it, was aimed at his head.

Glocks don't have safety catches, he thought to himself.

Montana couldn't even see the guy's face through the black visor. Not being able to see the eyes felt ominous. His hands were locked behind him. He felt completely powerless. In that exact moment, all he kept thinking was that all of our power as humans is in our hands.

"Hurry up."

Montana edged toward a pile of clothes.

"Slowly."

Montana didn't think it wise to point out the Raising Arizona moment. This was serious. If that guy so much as sneezed, Montana was dead. Not movie "make believe" dead. For real dead. What the hell was happening?

He managed to step into a pair of athletic shorts and awkwardly pull them on. They were backwards, but there was nothing he could do about it. There was no way he was getting a shirt on, and when he asked for help, the second cyborg grunted and yanked a t-shirt off the floor, pulling it over Montana's head. He was marched out of the hotel in front of a line of guests. Three more armor-plated cops escorted him to one of four flashing police cars.

They didn't say a thing. The back seat of the police car was molded plastic and incredibly painful on his bound wrists. He sat there for a half hour while the now vizor-less cop typed into a computer. With no visible guns in sight, Montana's mind started to relax, and he thought it safe to ask a question.

"What's this all about?"

Silence.

"What's this all about?" he repeated.

"I don't know, we're issued paper, we serve the paper...*warrants* as civvies call them. We go heavy at this hour because there is the greatest chance of the perp being at home and in bed. Your being asleep and dazed gives us an edge."

"An edge?"

Silence from the cop.

"And what warrant? I never even saw a warrant..."

"We showed you a warrant, sir." He said it in a very formal tone, like it was being recorded. Montana didn't want to press the point. He was handcuffed in a police car. He was going to jail. Jail. He'd never had so much as a speeding ticket.

It was the cop's referral to Montana and his class of non-cops as "civvies" that had him worried. Did these guys really believe this was humans versus cylons? Worse, if Montana remembered Battlestar Gallactica right, the cylons were the bad guys.

"So, you can't tell me what's going on?"

"No point asking me, sir," he sneered the word *sir*. "I just serve the paper. It doesn't have a description of whatever crime you committed."

"Crime? I don't even have a traffic ticket. You can look it up."

The cop looked at Montana in the rearview mirror. "I did. I see here a California Roll violation, so you wanna try again." He paused to let Montana absorb the words. "What? You're innocent of that, too? Look, the rules of engagement clearly give us the authority to execute a warrant in a manner deemed safest to our personal health. It's not like I went John Wayne on you. I served the *warrant*, subdued you, and read you your rights, textbook knock and lock. Safe for everyone and by the book. We follow the rules, no matter how many times they change and how complicated they get."

Rules of engagement? A California Roll? The cop wasn't making sense. Montana could figure out what a *knock and lock* was. Everything else was just nuts. "This is crazy, I haven't even been in the country…"

"Ohhh, we know," the cop cut him off and turned to look at him through the plexiglass. He wore a malevolent leer. "We know you've been on the run for five years. That ended tonight. Customs alerted us when your passport was registered. Did you see three little computers at customs when you were at the airport? One was connected to the national criminal database. It cleared you and notified us so that we could track you." His radio squawked, and he spoke into it. "Roger, Adam Henry in custody, rolling to the barn."

Jesus, did this asshole think this was a movie?

Montana could tell the guy was getting pissed, so best not to push it. Although he wondered if Adam Henry was the guy they wanted. Montana opened up his mental rolodex. He'd gotten a ticket years ago, but he'd paid it. He couldn't even remember what the ticket was for. Something petty and stupid.

But it was paid, his mind screamed!

He visualized the transaction on his bank statement. Getting answers from this cop was useless. He'd have to wait till he got to the station. He sat in silence as they drove to the downtown booking HQ. Slowly, now that a gun wasn't pointed at him, his shock turned to rage.

Once inside the secure police garage, the cop pulled up to the curb like he was dropping off a pizza. He pulled Montana out, led him through two sets of electronically locking doors, and finally uncuffed him. Relief flooded through Montana. He rubbed his wrists with his now free hands. Whatever was going to happen now, he could handle it. He had his hands back.

He stood in a line of people about seven deep. Most of them looked staggeringly drunk. When Montana got to the counter, an angry woman held out a bag and demanded his personal items. How the hell could he have items when he'd been handcuffed for the past hour.

"Cell phone?" she asked. "I can give you a pen to write down any numbers you may need"

"Uh, no...I think, I don't know?" She must have taken that as a no, and placed his two possessions (wallet, cell phone) in a plastic bag. "Hey," he called, "that's my wallet and cell phone? How the heck? Where did those come from?"

"The officers confiscated them at the scene. They'll be returned to you."

"But, wait..."

"Next," she yelled.

"Wait, I have a question."

A man in a Sheriff's Office windbreaker grabbed him and shoved him roughly forward into a white tiled room with blue plastic chairs bolted to the floor. With nothing else to do, Montana sat. He sat in the blue chair for hours. More arrestees filed in. He sat more. Finally, a loudspeaker shouted his name. The voice directed him to a window where a woman asked him a series of questions about his blood pressure (I don't know), his heart (it seems fine), and if he had frequent fainting spells (no). She was completely uninterested when he tried to explain the pain in his kidney, shoulder, and ribs. The medical bureaucrat pronounced him *not a medical risk* and sent back to his chair. After what felt like hours, he was photographed and fingerprinted. By that point, he was actually excited just to be able to get up and do something. Consider your level of boredom when you're happy to finally get booked into jail.

Eventually, he and his growing contingent of arrestees were shuffled into the main convict waiting room, a cavernous hall surrounded on two sides with glass-fronted cells. Drunks, in various stages of undressed bellicosity, pounded on the glass from inside the cells. The third side housed janitorial offices, which stood open, revealing mops and cleaning supplies. The fourth wall featured half a dozen glassed-in teller windows and, like a bank at Friday lunchtime, most of the windows stood dark. Only two tellers appeared open for convict business. Behind the glass, uniformed police officers shouted instructions to the convicts seated in front of them.

Jesus, even convicts have to do paperwork.

Throughout the hall, dozens more plastic chairs had been bolted to the floor. In the middle of the whole thing sat a huge circular desk, like a circulation desk at a library. But instead of librarians, the desk was manned by enormous, intimidating people wearing Sherriff's Department windbreakers and hip holsters. Just in front of the circular desk, there were several circular pay-phone banks which must have been broken. A couple inmates had tried to use them, only to replace the handle a second later. With nothing else to do, Montana sat in another chair. He watched as person after person approached the circulation desk, only to be shouted away.

Montana sat and stewed. Hours passed. As time passed, his anger melted into disgust. The sheriff's officers were belligerent to the point of absurdity. They alternated between threatening every arrestee who dared to stand up and joking with each other so loudly that it was an obvious attempt to display their brawn and authority. It dawned on Montana that two beers and one bad decision were all that separated the inmates from the employees.

While he waited, lines of actual convicts were led through the waiting area. They hooted and howled at the people in the chairs. He sat more. Eventually, a cart containing rancid bologna sandwiches rolled by. Montana took a pass. A peculiar grin finally crossed his face when he remembered that in a week, two at the most, he would be gone forever.

Meanwhile, he sat, shaking his head at the scene before him.

The huge seven-footer behind the library desk announced that the "lock down" had been lifted and the phones could be used. Within seconds, the line at the phones was twenty people deep. It struck Montana that "lock down" didn't seem that strict since lines of convicts had been marched through the detention center all night...or was it morning? Either way, the sheriffs were obviously just keeping the phones off.

His mind kept repeating; *petty people, petty power, one-way flight. Adios, assholes.*

While he sat and waited, he heard names announced over a loudspeaker. Each time, an inmate rose and staggered to a teller window. They held brief conversations with the tellers, got yelled at, and returned to their chairs. Within ten minutes, an officer arrived to escort them through a doorway marked "Exit/Salida."

He eventually got to one of the phones. He could practically see the viruses coalescing on the phone handle. He looked at a list of bail bondsmen on the wall and called one.

"Hi, I've just been arrested, and I have no idea why."

The Bondsman explained the process to him. He was a little surprised Montana didn't know the reason for the arrest, and even more surprised when he couldn't pull it up in his system.

"How long they had you, buddy?"

"Uh, since two or three this morning, why, what time is it now?"

"Sheesh, they had you over twelve hours? That's rough. Tell you what, normally someone has to come here and pay me your bond amount, but since you don't have an amount, how about we call it $2500. Can you call someone to get over here with cash, check, or a credit card?"

"Fine, but I don't know anyone's phone number? I'm...I don't have anything."

"Didn't they ask you about writing down phone numbers when they took your phone?"

"I think so, but I had no idea what was going on. I've never been arrested. I still don't even know why the fuck I'm here!"

"Okay, relax. But that's gonna be a problem. Listen buddy..."

"Wait. My banker. She can help. She..."

"You got a banker, huh? Well I ain't got a banker, and I been in business for thirty years." Montana clocked the sarcasm.

"Listen man, I am just now realizing how much bullshit you probably hear. It's my first arrest. I'm not a flight risk." Despite the circumstances, Montana's smirk inched up his face. He was the very definition of a flight risk. "Damn it, I can't believe I'm an arrest risk. Google my name, Montana Ainsley, and see what you get. I own two businesses in this town. I'm a regular guy, not a repeat offender."

He heard keys clacking. "Hmmm, yeah, okay. So, call your banker."

"I can't, I don't know the bank's phone. Please, you have to do it for me. Just call Gena Zorento at Promenade Financial Partners. Give her my name. Tell her what happened. She'll iron out the bail. She can wire the money directly to you."

"Ain't you got any friends you can call? Banks are closed, buddy."

A pause.

"She is my friend."

Another pause.

"Banks are closed? What time is it? Wait. Call my restaurant, ask for the manager, Joanna. She can help. She's my manager. She's worked for me for ten years. Please, just call."

"Okay. Sad, but okay. You got one friend, your banker who earns fees for your money, and another who owes her living to you. You gotta get out more. Call me back in twenty minutes."

Back in his chair, Montana pondered the guy's words. They hurt. They hurt because he was right. Business ownership had completely changed the trajectory of his life. Most of his friends had gotten married and lived typical suburban lives. Montana chose to battle daily with customer experience, employee management, cashflow, and the legal system. He didn't have time for friends, his wife, and anything unrelated to running the businesses. To bandage the mental wound, he reminded himself that he no longer had that life. He just had to stay focused on getting back to the new one.

He had left the U.S. because paying his taxes, following the law, and doing the right thing had landed him here. Right here. In jail. He wasn't about to make that mistake again. Flight risk? You better believe it.

About twenty minutes later, he picked up the sticky phone receiver and dialed. "Hey, it's been twenty minutes. Did you get a hold of her?"

"Yeah, buddy, I did. Wow. Your manager sure likes you. She drove down here and handed me $2500 in cash. I get the sense that the restaurant is gonna come up short tonight." He laughed. "But hey, you got a new customer. I never heard of da place. I'm gonna eat there tonight." A little bit of his Boston accent started slipping into his diction. It reminded Montana of his old business partner.

"Great, then this whole arrest was worth it." They both laughed. "Yeah, I'd be lost without her. So, you can get me out?" He was relieved beyond words. There was a light at the end of this dark tunnel.

"Normally, yeah. But, well, that's the thing. I been callin' the jail, and no-body knows nothin' about you. Lemme keep callin'. Try me back in an hour. We can't do nothin' till they find your name. I'm gonna keep harassing them."

Montana sat back down. He'd finally located the clock in the room. Past 6:00 p.m. This was the justice system? This was a joke. No, joke wasn't the right word. This was…the loudspeaker interrupted his thoughts.

"Montana Ainsley, window three."

Montana walked over to window three. The woman behind the glass looked at him and asked in a sympathetic tone, "Hey honey. How long you been here?"

Montana sat down, carefully. There was some unidentified pain starting to register in his stomach. He hadn't eaten any of the rotten sandwiches, so he couldn't quite place the source of the discomfort.

"Sir?" the woman called to him through the glass.

"Oh, sorry, since four this morning I think."

"Oh, my Lord, what the hell is wrong with y'all?" This to her colleagues behind the glass. "This man has been here for twelve hours and y'all ain't even filed a goddamn charge sheet. That's unacceptable." The minute Montana heard the word, he knew it was an act. They'd be laughing as soon as he walked away.

"Your bail bondsman called. He made quite a fuss about why you here. You made bail. Fill out this form and an officer will escort you out the detention center."

Montana walked out of the detention center that night. He wore backwards gym shorts and a t-shirt with flip flops. Tennis shoes had proven too difficult to put on with cuffed hands.

He hailed a cab and headed back to his hotel to brush his teeth for the next hour.

23

TERI BRADSHAW
Present Day
Seattle, WA

Teri entered The Bradshaw Group's downtown Seattle office in a good mood. She'd been to the gym, met her image consultant, and so far, nothing had pissed her off.

Inside the office, she found a party in full swing. People slapped hands and milled about drinking out of plastic champagne flutes. Spontaneous applause broke out when she stepped into the office suite. Dylan approached her with a plastic flute.

"Congratulations, boss, we launched the Wheel of Wonder today! This is what happens when you don't take no for an answer. When you tell critics that they're wrong, and you push ahead with your dreams. Today, we made the world just a bit smaller and more attainable for everyone. We…you, are now historical."

Teri eyed him to see if he was cracking a joke at her expense. He wasn't, so she was momentarily confused. Was this his stupid selfie park? Wheel of Wonder? It launched? She didn't remember hearing that name, but her focus had been far away from The Bradshaw Group for a while. The numbers all looked good, and there weren't any reported problems, so she'd pressed ahead with her personal goals and let the business run itself for the past few months.

But the name. Had she heard that goddamned name right?

She wanted to light into Dylan but realized that the entire staff was staring at her. They were waiting for a rah-rah speech.

These fucking kids, Teri thought, *they might work hard but they seemed to need an enthusiasm infusion every two weeks.*

Out of habit, she conjured up her best business sentences and assembled a meaningless paragraph in her head. The fake smile appeared.

"You guys are the greatest. I certainly didn't expect this. I've been meeting with policy directors to ensure our smooth integration across market segments around the globe, and I'm happy to report that it was thoroughly encouraging." Clapping, hooting.

"I thought that was the pinnacle of execution for the day, until I walked in here." More hooting.

"I feel I need to express my sincerest congratulations to you all." *That was a good one,* she thought. *These kids all started sentences with I feel to avoid committing to an actual position on something.*

"This is our boldest endeavor yet, and you are key strategic stakeholders, not just in The Bradshaw Group's family of companies, but in the future of this planet. It's true that we faced down an army of critics. It's true that everyone said a positive impact business like this couldn't create value." Boos from the audience.

"And today, we proved them all wrong." Thunderous applause.

"Nothing is impossible. Nothing. To acknowledge the word 'no' is to commit to a life devoid of dreaming further. And our dreams are what make us who we are. Our dreams are what have allowed us to change the world." Teri thought she was quoting from a movie, but whatever, it brought the house down.

While the room cheered, she set her smile to auto-pilot and whispered to Dylan, "Be in my fucking office in ten minutes." He was completely taken aback. She saw his face tense. He shot her a sideling glance and took another hit of cider from his flute. "Ten minutes," she reaffirmed.

The minute he strode into her office and closed the soundproof door, she let him have it.

"Wheel of Wonder? Wheel of fucking Wonder! Are you fucking serious? Is it too late? Has that stupid fucking name gone out to press?"

She didn't wait for an answer. "Like as in Wonderwheel? From *The Toy*? *The Fucking Toy,* Dylan? Seriously?"

He looked blank.

"It's a goddamn movie, Dylan. Jesus, you lived at home for thirty fucking years, surely you watched a few movies. Or did Richard Pryor's not *feel* relevant because the movie is older than five fucking minutes. This is a fucking joke. We're a joke. This is going to land like a goddamned lead balloon in the press. If you can't call this back, Dylan…" she left the threat unsaid.

Dylan's face was white. Pale white.

Good, the little bastard.

"No way, Teri, no way. The upside potential of this is a plus two standard deviation event. The shareable value is off the charts. The social value alone will be incalculable. Vacation solutions. Business solutions. Social media expansion solutions…we now own all these spaces, Teri. There is no one else in them."

"Speak fucking English." Actual spit flew from her mouth. "Did it ever occur to you that there is a reason no one is in those spaces? Did it even dawn on you that there *is* something cooler than a picture of Machu Picchu, Dylan? Going to Machu fucking Picchu! Did it ever occur to you that no one markets to the social media crowd because they're completely fucking broke!"

Silence.

Then, sheepishly, "I feel like I hold a different opinion."

"Knock off the *I feel* shit. And one last time, speak fucking English and quit using nouns as fucking verbs."

"Okayyy, well, like, I don't even know what you're talking about with the naming convention? What is The Toy? What is Wonderwheel? I've never even heard of it. And trust me, if I haven't, like, no one under thirty has. Relax."

"Did you just tell me to relax?" He shriveled in the chair. All pretense of flippancy and male ego evaporated. He looked like a little kid. "Don't ever fucking tell me to relax, *like*, especially after you've pissed away $200 million of my dollars on a fucking joke. And I just told you to quit speaking in corporate gibberish. It isn't a naming convention, it's a name. Got it? And a goddamn stupid one. And knock off the 'solution' bullshit. Every goddamn thing isn't a solution. They're business services, not tactical solutions. They're vacations, not vacation fucking solutions. Keep talking that crap and you'll start believing it's real. Then you're no longer just spewing crap, you're fucking full of it, too."

More silence.

Finally, in the voice of a chastened nine-year-old, "I'm sorry you feel this way. I don't...I don't think I presented this to you the right way. I feel, like," he stopped. "Sorry, I mean, if you could just listen to my side, you'll see the opportu...that we have a chance to make some real money. We're providing solut... we've created a new market, filled a missing need. There is money in that."

Teri's anger started to lose steam. She'd burned through her rage, and she was going to need this kid to unscrew this mess. She softened her tone, slightly. "Dylan, I went through the numbers before you came in. We're committed to over half a billion dollars over the next five years. Half a billion. And we bought all the real estate? Next to airports? Where real estate doesn't appreciate? Tell me you can turn this around."

"I won't have to, I promise. We've got pre-commitments for over a dozen franchises in ten different countries. That's nearly twenty million dollars in up-front franchise fees, right? Add to that the millions we're going to pull in from each park, daily. It's like an apartment building. Sure, you sink ten million to build it, but the revenue stream is, like, eternal, right? Even if it takes forty years to get back your ten million, it still shows as a long-term winner on your books. If the name concerns you, I promise, my team and I will meet about it first thing tomorrow. We'll launch a nickname campaign."

She wanted to snap at him for giving her accounting advice, and for using a meaningless term like pre-commitment, but her mind was already in motion.

How do I minimize the reputational damage of releasing Wonderwheel?

Dylan's solution, *correct fucking usage*, to the problem meant spending more money. *Great!* She wanted to light into him for burning more cash, but it wouldn't help. Yelling at him felt good, but it amounted to screaming at your lawn.

"Dylan, your team will meet today. Get out in front of this."

"I see what you mean, but I just feel...like, everyone's head is in a celebratory place and the energy won't be focused, you know?"

"Dylan," she said slowly, "don't feel. Fucking do what I tell you!"

Teri dismissed him and steepled her hands under her chin.

This gaping hole in their financial picture, especially if the rollout was rocky, might well sink her. And would rolling out something called Wheel of Wonder be anything but rocky?

Could she just cut the hedge fund loose? Let Dylan and his team take all the heat? No, The Bradshaw Group was linked with it forever. But if this thing failed, The Bradshaw Group wouldn't have enough money to pour into Earth Ventures to shore up their books.

She envisioned her face, superimposed on Richard Pryor's body, gracing the cover of *Fortune,* below the headline; *Wonderwheel Deflates, Again.*

24

MONTANA AINSLEY
Present Day
Nashville, Tennessee

Montana woke up late on the day following his arrest. His ribs ached. He pulled up his shirt and saw deep purple bruises. Well, if they were cracked, there wasn't much a doctor could do except charge him money and tell him to be careful. He could always hire a lawyer and sue the city for his medical bills. He certainly knew a few lawyers.

He skipped the doctor and the lawsuits. He'd just be careful and save the four thousand in fees. He showered carefully, brushed his teeth for half an hour, and called his manager, Joanna. It was an oddly strained conversation. Joanna had been uncharacteristically reticent on the phone. Was she embarrassed for him? Joanna was no angel, and neither missed the chance poke fun at the other. They'd known each other for over a decade. They'd encouraged each other through separate divorces. The atmosphere was always light and fun between them.

So why in the world would my getting arrested not make her howl with laughter?

He knew she was happy with the money she made, happy with the job, and generally a happy person. Although she was in her thirties, she referred to herself as a girl because she said it made her feel younger. She was feminine, but also tough without being brutish. When guys hit on her, she said it made her feel pretty, not offended. When girls hit on her, she said it made her feel scandalous. If someone had an issue, she used humor to diffuse it. If that didn't work, she either kicked them out of the restaurant or fired them. Montana had never once questioned any of those decisions. Joanna defined someone comfortable in their own skin, so her nervousness concerned him.

Just before he disappeared, so much of him had rubbed off on her that Joanna started making decisions based on how much comedy they could provide. That led to some pretty kooky employees. One twenty-six-year-old girl was afraid to drive without her mother in the car. The poor woman sat in the parking lot for hours reading a book while her daughter, proud owner of a Sociology Master's degree, waited tables inside.

Another employee had no social security number and cited some obscure Naval Law as proof that the government couldn't make him pay taxes. Joanna hired him because it saved 20% on payroll tax and the kid had no legal standing to sue if something went wrong. Funny. Professional. Mathematically defensible.

Joanna never went to college, but instead spent those years developing a keen street sense that turned out to be much more valuable for managing people. At thirty, she was in complete control of a successful restaurant and answered to nobody. By the time Montana secretly announced his departure, Joanna had effectively run the place for years.

She was one of only two people inside the U.S. who had had his contact information.

They met at the restaurant before it opened for the day. Joanna got out of her car looking like what she called a "hot mess", and what Montana called, the hooker look. She wore jean shorts cut off an eighth of an inch below her butt, exposing a fading thigh tattoo. She had on a lime green baseball hat, high on her head, and slightly cocked to one side. Huge Jacki-O sunglasses covered half her face. A cigarette, unlit because she wouldn't smoke in her car, dangled from circus red lips. She had a Starbucks cup in one hand and wore a hot pink cutoff shirt that read "Cure The #RASH". The short shirt exposed a new stomach tattoo Montana didn't remember.

Wobbly three-inch high heels completed the ensemble. Her secret was that she, despite all appearances and public commentary, was surprisingly conservative in a lot of her views. A lifetime of hard work had made her staunchly opposed to taxes after seeing what was done with the money. Half a decade in management made her cynical about the common perception that business owners were all rich. She managed payroll, and she knew exactly how much everyone made. The way she figured it, she made $65,000 a year and worked over 4,000 hours. Thus, she made less than twenty bucks an hour. Although only the political crazies really voted anymore, Montana guessed that she was a closet libertarian. They greeted each other warmly but without physical contact. They were able to maintain a close working relationship exactly because they had strict physical boundaries. She opened the restaurant and they went back to the tiny office to talk. Joanna started making coffee as Montana gingerly sat down.

"Hey, so what's up with the shirt?" he asked her. "What is a *pound-RASH*, and why does it need curing?"

She looked at him, genuinely confused. Then followed his eyes to her t-shirt. "Oh, God, you're so old, and why are your eyes so dead flat? There's almost no color to them. Nobody calls it a pound sign anymore. It's a hash-tag,"

"Okay, what's a hash-tag Rash?"

"Of course, you would ask." She rolled her eyes. "I have no idea about the cause. It's just a super comfortable shirt. A RASH is someone who is Racist, Anti-Islamic, Sexist, and Homophobic."

The look on his face must have conveyed his confusion, because Joanna explained, "You've been gone a while and the country needed an acronym. So many people have been labeled RASH that it got absurd to keep throwing out all the words. It's like, a catch-all people for like that. Some UTV star came up with the acronym to save us all the breath. If you ask me what a UTV star is I'm going to throw coffee at you."

The smirk crept up one side of his face.

"I know. I know what you're going to say. How can you ban something in the name of free speech or whatever? I just love the fabric. The movement people were smart. The shirts are really nice. It could say I hate Joanna and I'd wear it."

"You mean, so all those marketing people who say that "branding matters" are overpaid idiots? Just use soft fabric?"

"I guess so." Normally, Joanna would have made a sarcastic remark about how "smart" he thought he was. And she hadn't even mentioned his arrest. Something was definitely up.

They spent several minutes getting caught up on the business, Joanna's new husband, and life in general. Montana laid out the previous day's disaster, and of course, thanked her for bailing her boss out of prison. She listened, shaking her head the whole time. When he was finished, he gave her back the money she'd used for his bail.

"I don't know what to say. That's just...horrible. Sorta funny, but horrible. I'm really starting to understand why you just left."

"At this point, I don't even care. I'd still like to know why I was arrested, but the one thing that I'm pissed about is that now I have to..."

"Hire a lawyer," she finished his sentence laughing. "Surely you can just re-use one at this point."

"You'd think, but I have to find out why I was arrested first. Then hire a law-yer for that specific charge. There are so many lawsuits now that lawyers can sub-specialize by crime."

He bemoaned the point for a few more minutes, and she started to get fidgety.

"Hey, what's up with the fidgets? I know you. Something's wrong."

She smiled and paused before responding.

"Yeah, there is this thing. Well, two things, but one is going to...you have to promise not to get mad."

Montana laughed, "Okay, fine. Do I ever?"

Joanna ignored him, "Three things, actually. But you still can't get mad."

Montana, still laughing, held up his hands. "Joanna, okay, stop. I just got out of the joint for a crime...for a crime I'm not sure if I committed. Nothing you can say will make me mad."

"Lemme start...first, the restaurant is doing great. This isn't about that."

He just stared at her.

"Okay, okay. The first thing is that I kinda knew you were gonna get arrested. After you left, the cops sniffed around the restaurant for a few months. You know, hiding down the street, coming in for two-hour cups of coffee, stuff like that. They never told me what they wanted, and I would have warned you, I just didn't know you were coming back...ever. Plus, Mike, my new husband, got in a fender bender, and the guy he hit sued us."

"Typical. Whiplash?"

"No, worse. Claimed he had an *expectation* to make it from one place to another and we ruined that. Long story. I got all wrapped up in that, so I kind of forgot about the cops."

Montana just shook his head and smiled. "Expectation law is a new one. Well, no worries, it was customs at the airport who alerted to cops to my presence...wasn't anything you did."

"Well, the other thing isn't so fun."

"Worse than getting arrested, seriously?"

She waved her hand in a so-so gesture and started in. "Two nights ago, we were totally slammed. Ever since the $20 minimum wage went into effect, we had to let go of a ton of people. Since we aren't a franchise or government entity, we just can't afford everyone. So, Nell, she's the co- manager now, she and I do everything to take up the slack."

Montana knew Nell, he'd hired her just after Joanna. "Oh, congrats to Nell. Good call."

Joanna nodded in acknowledgement. "Two of our servers offered to take less money if we hired more people. I'm seriously considering it; legal or not. Anyway, we always wind up running food and stuff like that. So, everyone was totally weeded the other night, and she and I were running food and...stop staring at me."

He laughed. "I'm just waiting for the actual problem to surface before my coffee gets colder."

"Okay, so one customer sends back her vegetable side because it's cold. Nothing Earth-shattering, right?"

Joanna went on to describe a scene that has taken place in a thousand restaurants, a thousand times over:

A side dish slips through quality control on a busy night. Managers are too busy managing an understaffed restaurant to catch it. The kitchen botches the reheat job, and the side dish comes out the same. The diner finishes the meal, except the side dish, and demands a manager. The manager gets berated by the diner; invariably a super important person who has never been treated with such disrespect, and whose important night has been ruined by the experience. Then comes the blackmail, a free meal or a damaging online review.

The part where the story differed was that Joanna ran this restaurant. She maintained a strict policy never to negotiate with restaurant terrorists. Once word got out that a restaurant could be blackmailed, the place would be held hostage by any table that complained, and the kitchen would be working for free until the restaurant closed and sent everyone to the unemployment office. You eat it, you pay for it. There were bigger troubles in the world than cold food.

"Okay," he said when she paused, "I get it. We had a food terrorist, or a foodie, or whatever they're called. I'm sure there is an online review. I'm sure they have a $70K college degree which resulted in using the word *meh* a dozen times. How is this…"

"Yeah, there is a review. Yeah, it says *meh*. Yeah, she is writing her first bad review ever, blah, blah. Nell and I internet stalked her; Master's degree is something useless, volunteers at an animal shelter, part time bartender. Fucking typical. She'll pay a hundred thousand for degrees but wants a free cheeseburger because she wasn't treated like Princess fucking Diana."

"Well, you and I both know she isn't paying for shit. That education money is all borrowed with a 0% chance of being paid back. Okay, so she's a…"

"Oh, it gets better. That night, Nell goes over to her table. Keep in mind, Nell is eight-months preggo, so her bullshit meter is at zero. This girl has already bitched out the server, and rips into Nell in front of the whole place. Nell! Who is, like, only the sweetest girl, ever! So Nell gets pissed and tells her she is gonna call the police if the girl won't pay. Then the boyfriend tried to intervene. Nell said the girl turned on him and told him, quote, 'You shut the fuck up'."

Montana interrupted her to laugh out loud.

"And, Montana, the guy just shuts the fuck up. I mean, totally emasculated. Why even date a guy with no balls? It's not like you can have sex with him?" Joanna laughed and got up to refill her coffee.

"Okay, so he isn't exactly Iron Man. But they eventually paid the fifty bucks. No tip. She wrote her online novella, case closed. We charge too much for her crowd to affect us anyway."

Joanna spilled some of the coffee she was pouring and cursed loudly.

"Joanna? What's going on. What aren't you telling me?"

She put the cup down and let out a long sigh. "She sued us."

There was a long pause.

As Montana breathed in to respond, Joanna plunged ahead of him. "I know. I know how you feel about lawyers. I know you've already had, like, eight billion lawsuits. I just need help. I don't know what to do. I've never dealt with this stuff before. The legal stuff. You never showed me…you just always bitched about lawsuits. I never really saw the inside. Mike is the same way with this fender bender lawsuit. I don't really know how he is handling it. I just know that we're writing checks every month." She paused and took a breath, "and you have no idea what it's like now. We had someone complain once that the water wasn't cold enough. I'm not kidding. The water. And I can never get a hold of you…"

"Whoa. Stop right there, Joanna. Hang on. This isn't an us thing. This isn't our fault. Not yours, not mine. Really, it's not even the girl who sued us. This is how they get away with it."

"Who?"

"The lawyers. The system's bloodsuckers. A shit show this absurd can only be created by lawyers."

"Lawyers? They created people complaining about tepid water? Well, maybe so, but I'm sorry anyway. I didn't mean to sound like it was your fault."

"It's your first lawsuit, I get it. The legal system created this super-highway for outrage: a way to transform cold asparagus into a thousand bucks. A way for the lawyers to pocket $50,000 and our staff to go on unemployment. It's the redistribution of wealth to the legal class. That's who's to blame."

"I just…I don't know. That's kind of above my paygrade. I've never really been involved. I mean, after the divorce, my first husband and I were totally broke, but we didn't have much money to start with, so I didn't give it much thought. I mean, I love you to death, but I always thought you were a bit loony about all this. Now I'm thinking maybe you were right."

He smiled broadly.

She sighed and buried her head in her hand. "I just said you were right, now you're gonna be impossible. Okay, yes, you were right. So how do we kill the lawyers?" They both laughed.

"No, seriously, Joanna, this isn't a you-thing. This is a them-thing. Really, if you want to blame someone, blame parents who sat by as their kids got taught that failure leads to the same place as success. We removed competition as a teaching tool and pacified the whole generation. Since they're not allowed to be mad and they've never known losing, seeking some kind of justice is the only outlet for a perceived wrong. Especially since blame is all that matters. Even the smallest slight requires justice. So, they have two options."

"Obviously, one is setting the social media mob on us." Joanna answered in a dispirited voice.

"Right, that's one way. The other is legal justice, where a legion of lawyers wait to drain everybody's bank accounts in the con of the millennium."

She pressed her bottom lip together with her fingers. "So, you aren't mad?"

"You didn't hear anything I just said, did you?"

"Yeah, I did. It's just that everyone already knows it. The difference is that I don't give them the same pass you do. I don't really care how pissy they are because they just found out they aren't special. I just want them to accept that life is full of shit that goes wrong. We already know that millennial guys are like ten-year-old-girls. That's why the girls run the show in their age bracket. They *are* the guys. The problem for the girls is that being surrounded by weakling guys makes them pissed. They've basically fallen into the same trap men did. That's why Nell and I stuck around for so long. You were the only actual guy we knew." She paused. "But, so, for real, you aren't mad about the lawsuit?"

Montana laughed. "You stuck around because I'm hot, be honest."

Joanna laughed. It was an old joke between them. "Maybe once, but then the continents drifted apart and the ice caps receded. Forget it, you're old now. Besides, we're both married to younger Latino guys." Montana raised an eyebrow at that.

"Yeah, Nell went first, and I snagged the guy's best friend at their wedding. But seriously, you're not mad?

Wow, he thought, *two non-college educated women had perfectly dissected a societal shift that it had taken him years to puzzle out. College was a total waste.*

"Earth to boss? Are. You. Mad?"

Montana shook his head to clear it. "Joanna, at 2:00 a.m. two days ago, a swat team tackled me in my hotel, handcuffed and dragged me off to jail. Someone I've never met is suing me to steal my house twelve hours after I put it on the market. I still have two other unresolved lawsuits rummaging around this country somewhere, and my divorce has stretched on for more than five years. You think this rattles me? If you and Nell had taken her outside and hit her with a tack hammer, maybe I'd be concerned. Remember, I get to leave. You're stuck here."

She frowned at the last sentence, but then sighed and said, "Well, someone has to pick up the fight. Okay, so what do we do? I mean, there is all this stuff on the internet about a two-tiered justice system. Which tier are we?"

"Well, it's more like Neiman Marcus. You can either afford to shop there and you win, or you can't, and you lose."

Joanna nodded, this she understood.

"We carry business insurance which lets us shop there. Our insurance company will basically bribe their lawyer to go away, so the courts never really enter into it. It will take a few months, and our insurance will go up 10x, but that's the basic trajectory."

"Uh…there might be a problem with that. We may not be able to shop there. We kinda aren't covered."

That froze Montana. "Kinda?"

"Yeah. Kinda. One of our customers, it turns out, surprise, surprise, is a lawyer. Well, three dozen of them are, and they all called, but he's the one I liked best. He is how I found out about the lawsuit. He called and told me it had been filed and offered his services. I didn't agree to anything, don't worry. But he did explain about the insurance and why it won't cover the lawsuit."

"It won't? How is that possible?"

In response, Joanna pulled a thick file of bound paper from her handbag. "That's the insurance plan. It's 417 pages. I can't get past the first page-it's one long sentence. I also had to go online and accept their terms of service digitally, so I have no idea what we agreed to with that. The terms of service had over a hundred pages. No, I didn't read it, obviously, nobody could."

"Yeah, I'm not disagreeing with that."

Joanna went on to describe how the insurance industry, after the passage of the BRIBE Act, scrambled to shore up their own legal protection against *Expectation*[7] lawsuits. The Center for Reliable Insurance Methods and Ethics negotiated with the National Trials Lawyers Association (whose name pre-dated the acronym frenzy) to ensure that the insurance companies had protection from the frenzy of new Expectation Tort lawsuits. In exchange for protecting franchises from the BRIBE Act, CRIME redrew all non-franchise insurance contracts. Insurance plans now divided at the sub-atomic level. The only plans that covered Expectation Torts for non-franchised businesses were, not surprisingly, Emerald Plans. Emerald plans had a $65,000 annual premium.

"Okay," Montana said when she concluded, "so we're not covered basically because we aren't a franchise."

"Right," she agreed frowning. "And, she sued us because she had an *expectation* of a properly cooked meal. Those expectation lawsuits are too new to be covered. I'm so sorry."

"Stop apologizing. This isn't your fault. We'll figure it out. I trust their lawyer has been calling constantly."

"Oh my God, he's come here three times looking for you. Here." She handed him half a dozen printed pages from the lawyer's personal social media sites. "We internet stalked him, too."

"Okay. Wife Debbie, one kid, two dogs…Jesus, you think there are enough names on the firm's letterhead? What is that, fourteen lawyers?" he said. He laughed, but Joanna didn't share the joke. "Okay, let me read through all this and let's see what we've got. Lawsuits are basically four pages of allegations and thirty pages of '*heretowiths*'. Essentially, they've been copying and pasting the same one lawsuit since the Roman Senate."

---

7   *Expectation* lawsuits were filed against people for violating another person's right to "the pursuit of happiness". In the restaurant context, one has a right to expect a 5-star meal at a restaurant rated with 5 stars. If a 2-star meal is delivered, a restaurant could be sued for denying the patron their *expected* experience. The *expectation* class of lawsuits extended to nearly every aspect of the human interaction.

Joanna kept staring into her coffee cup, so Montana said, "Hey, this is crap! That was actually funny, you're supposed to laugh."

"So…there is one…" She drifted off and let the words hang there.

"Finally! What? Tell me! I'm dying for you to just spit it out."

"My, well, my parents wanna buy the restaurant." She paused. "Before you say…"

"Done."

Her head rocked back, and her eyes bulged through hooker-thick eyeliner.

"Have them give me a price. Tell them to draw up an agreement. Let's try to get it done early next week."

He watched the face he knew so well migrate from shock to disbelief, then to joy.

"Seriously? You're…you're." She couldn't even finish.

"Joanna, I'm leaving, and I'm not coming back. I just wish they'd offered sooner."

They hammered out the details for twenty more minutes. The place had opened while they'd talked, and they walked out to a half-full restaurant. Montana hugged and shook hands with the staff members he knew and congratulated the co-manager, Nell, on her marriage and pregnancy. Joanna nodded to Nell, and the two hugged fiercely. Nell congratulated her. Apparently, this had been planned. He wasn't surprised.

They all agreed to catch up over dinner.

Montana turned to leave when a clean-cut younger man in a suit walked in carrying a briefcase. Montana heard Nell whisper "oh shit" under her breath. Between Nell's warning and the guy's haughty walk, Montana pegged him as a lawyer before his third step.

The man called to him halfway across the restaurant. "You're Montana Ainsley, the owner of this restaurant. Consider yourself served."

The entire restaurant looked up. The kitchen stopped working. The lawyer strode up to him, confident as a bullfighter *before* the bull enters the ring. He continued in the same loud voice he had used to call across the restaurant.

"My client is seeking justice for the outrage perpetrated on her by this restaurant. My client has never suffered such an indignity, and I'm here to ensure no one gets treated like that again. One of your employees even went so far as to threaten my client with arrest. Since you are not represented by counsel, I demand to speak with you immediately."

Montana paused for just a second. There were two ways to go with this, and it might be the last lesson he could impart to his crew before they took over.

Humor is Joanna's strength, I'll use humor.

"Demand?" Montana half cackled at the same volume. "You don't even shave, let alone rate to demand anything from me. Besides, you're a lawyer. The whole world views your profession as toilet water. Toilet water doesn't get to demand stuff." Hearing laughter from nearby patrons, Montana pressed his attack.

"Your own profession even degrades itself. Do you see a lot of plumbers making plumber jokes? Are there loads of neurosurgeons talking about how sleazy other neurosurgeons are?" Several diners openly laughed.

The lawyer looked around. That people laughed at him seemed to diminish his courage and his volume. He switched to a more reasonable tone.

"Fine. I want, I don't demand. I want to speak with you, and I assure you, when a lawyer wants to speak with you, you need to listen."

"Great," Montana laughed back at him. "Get used to disappointment, kid. Sometimes life doesn't work out. Now get out of here and go play grown-up somewhere else."

The laughter from restaurant patrons ticked up just a bit.

"Unfortunately for you, sir, I'm a—"

"You're an ass clown, now hit-the-door before I have one of these girls take you over their knee." He gestured towards his managers.

"P-pardon me?"

"You heard me," Montana sensed the fear in the kid. "I know you heard me 'cause I'm using the same self-important volume you are. You think you being a lawyer scares me? You're a pissant. Get the hell out or I'll drop you right here." Montana then eyed him up and down. The lawyer took a tentative step back.

Montana faked a lunge toward the lawyer, and the kid stumbled backward, wrenching up his briefcase in defense. The kitchen let out a cheer like they just watched Ali drop Frazier, and the entire restaurant laughed. Some even clapped. Obviously embarrassed, the attorney straightened up and looked around. Montana assumed he'd never been threatened in his entire sheltered life.

"And hey, tell Debbie thanks again for...for...let's call it lunch." Montana smiled as he said it.

The lawyer just stared at him.

"Debbie. You know, your wife, Debbie? Thank her again for me. On second thought, don't worry about it. She said she'll tell you herself."

The lawyer's face splotched red. Montana heard the girls cracking up behind him. Verbally and emotionally defeated, the young attorney headed toward the door. With his hand on the handle, he turned around and announced, in a flimsy, melodramatic voice, "You've made a big mistake. Welcome to the 21st century Mr. Ainsley, bullies are unacceptable here."

"But that's not stopping you and your client, is it?" Montana shot back.

Unable to make even his dramatic closing statement, the lawyer slunk through the front door. The restaurant burst into applause. Loud applause. Sustained applause.

As he looked across the clapping patrons, it occurred to Montana exactly how to deal with his newest lawsuit. There would be no *lawyer number seven*.

"That was so awesome," Nell and Joanna said in unison after the restaurant had settled down. As they re-said goodbye, one of the diners got up, laid some bills on her table, and walked over to the three of them. Montana pegged her in her mid-twenties. She wore a tailored charcoal business suit, enormous glasses, and had her dishwater blonde hair tightly pulled back. She carried a briefcase that looked eerily similar to the one the young lawyer had been carrying. Her face wasn't amused. Montana tensed. Lawyer? The guy's partner?

In a slightly chilled monotone, she addressed Montana without actually looking at him. Her eyes focused on a spot on the floor behind him. "You've uh...you've got no idea how much trouble you're in, do you?"

"Come again?"

"You can't, like, threaten people publicly, it's a prosecutable crime. That's why he called you a bully...so everyone could hear it. He was, literally, labelling you. It's called Legal Marketing. They teach it in third-year. Three months from now, when deposed, the only thing any of these people will remember is that you were kind of funny, and a little bully-ish. Physical and verbal threats are prosecutable. They're considered hate-speech. Well, the threats are hate-speech." Her eyes finally glanced up at him for an instant, then back down. This time, she focused on her phone.

Montana rolled his eyes. "Wait, just a second. This is still a free country. Congress hasn't rescinded the first amendment. I can still say stuff." He looked at Joanna, then Nell, then back to the young lawyer. "Right?"

Still looking at her phone, she responded, "As a matter of reality, Congress doesn't make laws. Lawsuits make laws. That means lawyers make the law in this country. And we've made laws specifically to create a more passive society. When you lunged at him? That can be considered inciting violence, and you can actually be prosecuted as a bully. It's a class C felony. I'm sorry to have to tell you this, but that lawyer wasn't wrong, the country just doesn't have space for dinosaurs like you," she paused, flashed a look up at him, then back down at her phone.

She continued, "I left my card on the table. I do personal defense work. You need me." Her posture suddenly shrunk back like a cornered animal as she raised her eyes to meet Joanna's, then Nell's, then back toward the floor. "I mean professionally, you'll need me professionally...not, like..." she trailed off as her cheeks turned red. She then turned around and walked swiftly out of the restaurant, staring into her phone the whole way.

Montana looked at his two managers. "What the fuck just happened?"

Joanna burst out laughing but Nell, always the more serious of the two, said, "She's socially awkward...but yeah, she's serious. And in truth, boss, she's right. She was actually trying to be nice, but she just doesn't know how to interact with anything that isn't digital. She comes in once or twice a week. We need to get you the heck out of here before you wind up arrested again." Nell paused, then smiled warmly, "But damn, we're so going to miss your attitude."

25

In Elaine's mind, Alan already had an ex-husband. She left Alan a message, written on a legal pad because, of course, everything in their house had to be in hard copy. The offer was simple. They had to sell everything. She would take 30%. End of marriage. No muss, no fuss. She knew Alan could never hope to accomplish more through the courts. If he wanted to fight, they would end up splitting a tenth of that money, fifty-fifty at best. At least, that's what she remembered hearing from her divorced friends.

They all reminded her of car accident survivors. Before their divorces, they had nice cars and full bank accounts. They'd been advised to avoid the legal road, taken it anyway, and *wham*. They woke up two years later, the divorce was final, the car was totaled, the money gone, and no one knew what hit them.

Lainey made certain to indicate in her note to Alan that if he hired a lawyer or mentioned the divorce to anyone, the deal was off. It was a clever play. So long as Alan couldn't advise his law firm of the divorce, she still had access to The Bradshaw Group's files and data. If he did hire a lawyer, she would let his own legal system bankrupt them both. Alan would never choose that option.

This left Elaine free to chase Teri Bradshaw. She was closing in on some concrete facts: cash investments made by The Earth Ventures Fund weren't matching up to declared investments by public company clients (who had to declare such things in annual shareholder filings). So, if investors put $20 million into the fund, how was it spending triple that to buy things. She couldn't figure out where the hell the money was coming from. She had calculated that Earth Ventures spent at least $100 million more than it collected. Donations to the Nicaraguan non-profit were large, but the non-profit claimed publicly it was near bankrupt. It was a Nicaraguan company, so Elaine couldn't verify anything.

When Elaine had done about as much as she could from behind a desk in Charlotte, she hit the road to Atlanta to visit The Ventures Fund's new flagship project. She couldn't remember the exact name, but it was something like Wonderwheel...from from the old Richard Pryor movie, *The Toy*. She wondered if that idiot COO had dreamed that one up. Surely, Teri Bradshaw wouldn't have approved that little oversight. The thought of future headlines made Elaine smile.

She arrived at the Atlanta site, just down Camp Creek Parkway from Atlanta's sprawling Hartsfield International Airport. The site was hidden behind a twenty-foot cement wall, but from up close, she could see astounding sites poking up. She made out the top half of what looked like the Eiffel Tower. Further away, a large grassy knoll overlooked something stone. She couldn't make out the stone structure, but her attention was drawn away by the sight of what appeared to be a massive snowcapped peak rising out of the back part of the park. How in the hell? Was that...no way. Everest?

"Hey, can I help you? You can't be here. This is a restricted site." A very serious man in a hardhat, wearing a holstered pistol approached her. The sight of the gun made Elaine nervous, and she blurted out the first thing that came to mind.

"I'm just an accountant. I'm part of the firm. I'm...I'm Earth Ventures' accountant." Jesus, she sounded like a petrified child.

Technically, it was true, and in the safety of the guard shack, the guy verified her with Alan's law firm. The guard couldn't tell her much. He filled her in on a few facts and things he'd picked up from being on site. The work crews were all licensed, legal, and working insane hours. The guard said they worked for about sixteen hours a day and were planning to open the park within a week. It was called The Wheel of Wonder.

The guard laughed at the look on Elaine's face. "I know, *The Toy*, right? What can you say, you got enough money, you can call it what you want. The overall boss is maybe twenty years old, probably doesn't even know who Richard Pryor was."

The guard explained that the park was rolling out as a franchise, and there were sites set to be opened all over the world in the coming months and years. "Where a kid like that gets the money to buy land like this I'll never know"

"Wait, they bought the land?"

"Hell yeah, no way a landlord would let a tenant do what they've done around here. Plus, all them Mexican workers? The hours they're puttin' in? No way that's going through a unionized contract."

"Huh?" Lainey didn't follow what he was saying.

"Well, not Mexican, but Latinos. From, wait…Nicaragua. Yeah, that's it. Probably 80% of the whole dang workforce is from Nicaragua. Remember them, from the '80's?"

Lainey did remember them, but from much more recently. That was another intersection of The Bradshaw Group and the small Central American country.

She got a bit more out of the guard, thanked him, then went to a coffee shop to get online and pull property records. She was pondering how excessively expensive the Wonderwheel project had to be, times at least three, when she pulled up a copy of the escrow check written for the land purchase. The escrow deposit had been written on a check from a Nicaraguan bank…from a Nicaraguan non-profit.

Gotcha.

She went straight to the Atlanta airport and booked a flight to Nicaragua. While she waited for her flight, she opened up her laptop and typed two short emails. The first she sent to the managing partner of Bernstein, Always, Sinclair, Goldstein, Rogerson, Whitman, Milstone, & Dunaway. It read simply:

To Whom it may concern,

I quit.

Sincerely, Elaine Dunaway.

Her second email contained two sentences and a .jpeg photo attachment. She sent that to Dylan Largent at the Earth Ventures fund.

The PA system called her boarding group. Elaine was exhilarated. Now she had a sense of this whole scheme. The money was being laundered through Nicaragua, somehow. That was what all the do-gooding was about. Teri Bradshaw had something going on down in Nicaragua, the Western Hemisphere's second poorest country. In a country that poor, an operation with this much cash would stick out like a sore thumb. All she had to do was get down there.

26

MONTANA AINSLEY
Present Day
Nashville, Tennessee

Montana left the restaurant in high spirits. Joanna's parents made a very reasonable financial offer, and Montana stunned them by knocking $50,000 off the offer if they could close the deal sooner. They could. Now, Montana sat at a sticky, worn-out lacquered lunch table in Brown's Diner, just down from Vanderbilt University. Brown's is a famous Nashville dive. A burger and beer joint, the restaurant feels like a pair of mobile homes jammed together. One trailer serves food and the other liquor. The food is simple and cheap. Brown's fame derives basically from being Brown's. Not for being anything special. Along the walls, famous faces smiled down through smeared glass frames. Across from Montana sat his two bankers. Their mouths hung open. He had just relayed the story of his arrest.

They met to arrange wiring instruction and codewords that would allow him to access his accounts from Central America, without having to make phone calls. First however, he explained why he'd missed their previous meeting: police intervention.

When he finished, it took both women a minute to speak. "This has got to stop," said Gena, his personal banker for over fifteen years. "Have you told the newspaper?"

"What? Seriously? Like they'd care, and who even reads the news?"

"She's right, Montana, this has to stop." This from Diane, Gena's assistant.

"Well, that was my first kidnapping. I try to wait till the third before I call the press."

"No, I don't just mean you." The two bankers exchanged a wary look. "You aren't the first client of ours to have this happen."

"Are you kidding?" His turn to be shocked.

"No, and all of you guys keep quiet like it's some kind of male ego thing. If you don't speak up, this is going to just keep happening to people."

"Wait, this happens a lot?"

"A lot isn't the right word, but it isn't as rare as it should be," Gena said.

Diane touched a few spots on her phone then set it on the table. She looked pissed. Montana heard ringing through the phone.

"Nashville Police Department, Media Relations."

"Sgt. Nathan Wilson, please, this is Gena and Diana from Promenade Financial."

The cop came on the line within a couple minutes. Through clenched teeth, Diana explained who they were, summarized the bank's financial contributions to the force, and walked the officer through Montana's story.

"Oh man," the cop said. "I'm so sorry that happened to him…to you, Mr. Ainsley. That really shouldn't happen. It's so unfortunate, but it's the system, and we just can't make individual decisions anymore. We've been sued too many times. If we don't follow the rules laid out…"

"Sergeant," Diane cut in, "I appreciate your comments, but we still don't know what he's been charged with. Can you at least help there?"

There was the sound of keys clicking.

"Uh, okay, it looks like he missed a court date and a bench warrant was issued…jeez, nearly five years ago. He got recategorized to flight risk, maximum danger."

"A court date," Montana asked, "for what?"

"Well, it says here driving with a suspended license. It appears you received a citation for running a stop sign. Does that ring a bell?" The cop's tone had shifted just a bit, from apologetic to slightly accusatory.

"Yeah, and I paid the ticket. You guys cashed the check." Montana shot back, much bolder now that he wasn't in handcuffs.

"Yes, I do see that, but there was some sort of communication breakdown and it didn't get put into the system until after the due date. Because of that, your license was suspended, and a court date was issued. A notice was mailed to 417 Elmore Avenue. Is that your address?"

"What? No? I have no idea what that address is. Wait, my license is suspended?" *That was why I couldn't rent a car at the airport,* Montana thought.

"Yes sir, and that's why you couldn't rent a car at the airport last week. We were notified by the rental agency and denied their request to rent you a car. There is no way we can track every rental car reliably." He was downright accusatory now.

"Holy shit…sorry, are you serious? Track rental cars? Track me? I'm not a dang terrorist. My license was suspended because of a computer glitch at your end. It's not like I blew up…I mean…I ran a stupid stop sign."

"Sir, please don't become aggressive with me, or I'll have to fill out a report to supplement the recording of this call and notify the digital cloud of your propensity to aggression."

All three heads at the lunch table lurched back at that. They exchanged dazed looks.

"Okay, let's try to calm this down and sort this out," Gena soothed. "So, he missed a court date for a license suspension that was the result of running a stop sign?"

"That's correct ma'am. By law, we aren't even required to notify him, but as a courtesy, we mailed him notification. And we don't differentiate between arrest warrants once they're issued. Legally, we are not allowed to show bias toward any crimes, irregardless of their severity, according to the Supreme Court."

Irregardless? The misuse of the word set Montana's teeth on edge. "But I've never lived at Elmore Avenue. It isn't really a courtesy to mail something out to the wrong address, is it? Is there even an Elmore Avenue in Nashville?"

"That's our information, sir. Irregardless, we aren't even legally required to notify you."

"You mean you can suspend my license without me knowing? This is insane, you guys black-bagged me because of a computer error on your part. I mean, that's what started all this. No, sorry, running a stop sign did that. Jeez man, this just sounds like a ploy to get everyone's information into your database." He looked up at his bankers, they both had wary looks on their faces; like something horrid had just occurred to them.

"Sir, you elected to miss your duly assigned court date."

"I didn't elect to miss it. I had no idea I had one because I had no idea you failed to process my payment on time. And I had no idea your late processing led to a suspended license, again, your fault. I paid my ticket. I did my part."

The cop completely ignored him and continued. "You were in violation of the law. There was no wrongdoing on the part of the NPD. We are Nashville's guardians. We have the legal authority to apprehend anyone, using appropriate force, that the court deems in violation of the law. If you have further questions, I suggest you hire an attorney and discuss the matter with him or her and avail yourself of the best legal system in the world. We follow the rules laid out for us. If you have problems with that, I suggest that you, as a currently paroled criminal suspect, spend the appropriate amount on a legal defense." The officer hung up.

Montana looked up at his bankers. "Nashville's guardians? When you have to tell people how wonderful you are, doesn't that mean…"

Gena responded first, "Do you have an extra bedroom in your place South of the border?"

"Bunk beds would be fine," Diana chimed in.

27

CHRISTIAN RAMÍREZ
Present Day
North of Bluefields, Nicaragua

Chris's first day back at camp, his guys fussed over him and treated him like glass. They couldn't believe his story. The delicacy gave way to rage and swearing that they would head up to Managua and hunt down the offending cops. It was an empty promise, Chris knew, but as their boss, it made him feel good. It took a full day to assure them he was okay, calm their outbursts, and coax them back to work.

They'd heard about the chaos before Chris's arrival because against their agreement, they'd spent a couple nights in Bluefields. Chris couldn't blame them for that. Nobody, except his dear departed grandfather, could have seen this coming. All three swore up and down that nobody had said a word about what they had found up here in the jungle. Gordo claimed they'd all passed out at the same table drinking, then he launched into a story about the night.

He made a passing mention that Juan had finally bedded Maria, a barmaid who had rebuffed his advances for over a year. Gordo, through bouts of laughter, managed to reduce Juan's love life to nothing more than a cheap Latino novella.

"You should have seen him, *jefe*, he did everything but beg the poor girl. He even did her job. He followed her around the bar after closing. He cleaned all her dishes and wiped down her tables. Then he swept the floor while she sat taking rum shots and shouting orders. It looked like she was numbing herself for the inevitable. And him, half drunk, following her commands like a well-trained pig. Hah, some peacock he turned out to be." The *machista* role reversal had all the Latinos in stiches. All except Juan.

Chris laughed too, despite the pain it caused in his chest, stomach, and heav-ily- bruised face. As the crew slowly started back to work, Chris found it odd that Juan didn't celebrate the loss of his virginity. Had the roles been reversed, he would be smiling for days. But there was something in Juan's face that shouldn't be there. Something was off. Juan didn't look triumphant. He looked worried.

Chris chalked it up to stress. After all, the country appeared to be falling apart, again. And even he felt helpless waiting for Montana while the danger meter ticked up by the second. They needed to get this gold the hell out of here. His *bisabuela* had been right.

28

TERI BRADSHAW
Present Day
Seattle, Washington

Teri pulled into her parking space at Seattle HQ and watched the drizzle dots connect on the windshield. It was a typical cold, wet day in Seattle, and the grey seeped into her mood. She'd been tough on Dylan the other day.

Not that he didn't deserve it...fucking Wonderwheel.

Teri made a mistake taking her eye off him. Big surprise, the son of a clown turned out to be an idiot. But she needed him at the wheel while she caught herself up on this disaster. Then, he'd be roadkill. If Teri couldn't salvage this theme park disaster, The Bradshaw Group may not survive, which meant the TSA lottery...

What Dylan needed was a pep talk. She needed to march in there and remind him of how special he was. She'd even bring him around for sex tonight if she had to. She hadn't done that in...wow, had it been a month?

She stepped into the office and saw that Dylan's office light was off. The entire office was silent, save for the clacking of keys. It appeared the whole place had heard about the row, and they were all scared to death.

Great, now they'd all need a goddamn pep talk. Her mood soured further, and she sighed inwardly.

She'd iron out a few details, then come out on the floor and deliver another *We Are the World* speech. Teri's office phone rang as she sat down. Alice put through a call from Alan Dunaway. Teri occasionally sought Alan's counsel when he was in town on Earth Ventures business. They met mostly in her condo, late at night. It started the night after Dylan introduced him as Earth Ventures' primary attorney. The married lawyer proved a pathetically simple and unsatisfying conquest, but Teri valued the legal insights. He might be a crappy lover, but he possessed a keen legal mind with a who's who of high-end business contacts.

To control him, Teri made sure he knew that their sessions never satisfied her. That reduced the proud lawyer to an obsequious mouse in her presence.

"Alan, good morning. What can I do for you?"

"Wow, that felt a little cold, Teri. I didn't mean to interrupt."

Always so passive aggressive.

"You can always go back to your wife if you don't like my tone, Alan. I've got issues of my own over here. You of all people know that the thing, the Wheel of Wonder, is launching in days, so it's all hands on deck."

"Well, I was hoping to schedule some face time. I wanted to talk over a few... strategies."

"Hmmm, that might be tough right now. When were you thinking? When is your next run through town?"

"Well, I'm actually in town now."

That woke Teri right up. Lawyers didn't fly across the country unless they could bill at least four times the airfare. "Now? What's wrong? Are we being sued?"

"No, no, nothing like that. My situation has changed a bit back in North Carolina, and I wanted to talk over some options with you. I was hoping the past year's um, expertise, would buy me a bit of a favor."

Teri didn't like the sound of this. This didn't sound like a favor. This sounded awfully close to blackmail. Well, two could play at that game. And no one was ever better positioned than Teri Bradshaw. Alan was married. He might even have a kid or two, she couldn't remember. Either way, he was in no position to blackmail her. Lawyers were a dime a dozen.

It wasn't that he wasn't useful, but the relationship was beneficial only in that Teri was able to pick his brain. He represented far too many personal entanglements to seriously entertain the idea of a real relationship.

"Alan, listen, I've got…"

Alan interrupted her. "Elaine and I are getting divorced."

Silence. Alan probably assumed that Teri was absorbing the shock. In truth, Teri was wondering who Elaine was. Was that his wife? Why would Teri care? Was it relevant to Earth Ventures fund? When she didn't speak, Alan tentatively continued.

"So…as you know, or maybe don't know, I'm not sure how informed…"

"Alan. The point?"

"Right." He sniffed. "Sorry. Well, Elaine, my soon to be ex-wife, found out about us."

Again, silence.

Again, Alan sheepishly continued.

"Well, Elaine worked part-time as a bookkeeper for the firm. For me…for my clients…"

"Okayyy." This did get her attention. She didn't like accountants. Accountants could cause trouble. Accountants looked into things. Teri was an accountant, the only accountant she needed. She'd built multiple layers of complexity into The Bradshaw Group's dealings. Nobody could peel the onion around her companies. Nobody except a gifted accountant. Or worse, an accountant with a motive.

Alan was still talking. "…and she was helping with work on The Bradshaw Group's stuff." Alan really didn't have a point to make. Teri could tell he was just talking. She zoned him out and considered the wayward wife. Could she really unravel Teri's scheme? It wasn't until Alan asked to meet with her that Teri zoned him back in.

"Not lunch. I've got a few things to go over first. Can you be here at 12:30?" Her schedule would have to be pushed. She didn't like the sound of this at all.

"Oh, you do have time?"

"Alan, do you want to meet or not?"

"Absolutely. Sorry. I'll pick something up. Talk to you then." He hung up quickly.

Teri chewed over this new problem but realized she didn't have enough data for analysis. She yelled out into the main office, "Alice, can you get Dylan for me?" Immediately, the red light on her phone blinked on.

"Yes."

"Ma'am, it's me, Alice. Can I come in for a quick second?"

Alice tiptoed into the office looking like she'd seen a ghost.

"Uh, ma'am."

"Alice, really? After all these years? It's Teri."

"Okay, yes, ma...err, Teri. The thing is...I think Mr. Largent may have quit. Or, resigned or something."

"Nah. Alice, come on, really? He's probably just taking a safety day or something...you know, to re-center his best self or whatever." Teri smiled at her own joke. Alice didn't.

"Well, I don't know for sure, but he didn't show up today, and his assistant got a really strange text message at two this morning. I mean, she is pretty used to it. He texts everyone at all hours, and about random stuff, too. It's pretty awkward sometimes. Anyway, Maureen, his PA, she usually keeps her phone off 'cause she has a newborn. But the baby woke up in the middle of the night, and while she was up with him, she saw this text."

Teri waved her hand for Alice to speed it up.

"So," Alice continued, "Maureen showed me the text this morning. It said something like, 'Zaijian, the best days are ahead of you and your unique child. She is gonna be a world changer'...or something like that. We looked up Zaiji-an, it means goodbye in Chinese. Does he speak Chinese?"

Teri rolled her eyes, "No, I'm sure he just learned the word from a 'greeting seminar' or something. Okay, Alice, thanks. I'll go check his office and see if he left a note."

When Alice left, Teri's stomach dropped. Obviously, a text that stupid had to come from Dylan. But, *goodbye?* What was that about? Maybe her little tirade had gone too far? If that little shit had, in any way, compromised her business...

She got up and marched toward his office. The entire floor of The Bradshaw Group was silent as her heels slammed down on the fake hardwood floor.

Dylan's office looked like a museum for motivational nonsense. Behind his desk hung a giant poster of a ship and some slogan about ships needing to leave harbor. Glass etchings of motivational sayings lined the few bookshelves that didn't house positive management reinforcement books. She saw trinkets and doodads from two dozen conferences, most of them emphasizing the power of togetherness.

Did this kid do anything besides go to conferences?

The Bradshaw Group employed half a dozen conference management staffers. They conferenced professionally, expensively, and constantly. She didn't pay this kid to do that, too. On the desk she noticed a small khaki-colored envelope with her name written across it.

Son of a bitch.

Teri sat down in Dylan's chair with the envelope in her hand. She took a deep breath. She didn't really care that he'd left. There was nothing Dylan Largent could do that Teri couldn't accomplish with her eyes closed. But he'd passed the goddamn Wonderwheel's expenses right under her nose. What else could he have been up to? His dad was a crooked federal employee. Like father like son?

She pulled out the note. A photo, printed on copy paper, dropped out with it. She put a hand on the photo to keep it in place but read the note first.

Teri, I want to thank U for the excellent opportunity. I don't feel as though I am being appreciated as I deserve and between being yelled at for trying to save the world and learning that you have another man in your life, I just don't feel that this environment is the right fit for my personal growth ☹ I have left all the relevant work documents and computer passwords in the top drawer of the desk, I know that I have signed a variety of legally binding docs, don't sweat it. I would wish U a successful life. But I already know that U will continue to B more successful every second of every day for the rest of your life.

She read it twice trying to parse meaning from the awful grammar. It looked like a ten-year old's first Instagram post. There was even a goddamned frowny face. She looked at the photo, Alan Dunaway going into her condo complex at night.

Boo-hoo. Grow up.

She checked the drawer. Everything was there. All she had to do was box up all his crap and Fed-Ex it to a landfill. She crumpled the letter. That wouldn't make it to HR. She grabbed a zip drive from her pocket and logged into his computer. Nothing was password protected or encrypted. She copied all the files and left the office.

As she exited, she saw two dozen faces staring at her from their computer cubicles. *Shit.* She needed a speech, right now.

"Hey everyone, so...sad but exciting news about Dylan. He's decided to pursue some life goals outside of The Bradshaw Group's iron umbrella of protection." She couldn't resist the subtle reminder of her power and influence.

"I, for one, am excited for him, and I'm sure we'll all be reading about his exploits in the years to come. I've got alternative leadership in mind already, and we're having lunch later today. Dylan was able to complete the project for which he was assigned, and he felt like his job here was done. We'll all miss him. We have a big week ahead of us with a major business launch, so let's all pull together, change the world, and...yes...maybe turn just a teeny-weeny profit." Laughter all around.

"Stay focused on the future. Who says we can't change the world and buy new BMWs, too?" Loud applause, cheers.

When she'd personally thanked each employee face-to-face, she returned to her office to dive through the Wheel of Wonder files. The more she read, the deeper her frown lines dug into the corners of her mouth. She now had two major unknowns: Dylan's father and the financial colossus of Wonderwheel. She was formulating a plan when Alan Dunaway knocked on her open office door.

Great. Three unknowns.

29

As Elaine Dunaway's flight took off for Nicaragua, Montana stood outside of courtroom 4B, on the fourth floor of the downtown criminal justice center in the Tennessee capital. He had been laughing for nearly five minutes straight. His attorney, attorney number one, did not share the joy. Aubrey Langenholt III tried to explain to his client, again, the precise grounds upon which their lawsuit had been delayed, yet again.

The two had arrived in court for 9:00 a.m. roll call, then sat and waited until after 3:00 pm when their case got called. The defense lawyer announced that his clients (the landlords of Montana's laundromat) were considering filing for personal bankruptcy. That they were bequeathed two million dollars in assets a year prior seemed immaterial. Due to the nature of a bankruptcy filing, the new judge agreed that it made no sense for Montana's lawsuit to proceed if, and until, the bankruptcy filing could be adjudicated. If the couple did declare bankruptcy, Montana would either never be able to collect, or worse, be prohibited from proceeding against the Chapter 11 defenses. If the couple was found unable to declare bankruptcy, Montana's lawsuit could continue. The judge gave the defendants three months to adjudicate their bankruptcy. Gavel. Next case.

Total time in front of the judge; four minutes. Total cost of renting his lawyer for the day, $3,000. He figured Aubrey earned nearly double that, since he would doubtless bill all the clients he spoke and texted to while waiting for court. Afterwards, Aubrey had pitched several different legal strategies that Montana could attempt. Each time he spoke, Montana laughed harder.

"So, Aubrey, this is the greatest justice system in the world?"

"Without question," the lawyer said, scoffing as though no other country even had courts. "Look, today was unacceptable. I grant you that. This just isn't a representative outcome. You'll see."

"What does that even mean, a representative outcome? This is the outcome. It represents itself."

The lawyer looked puzzled. "Um, well, this is the system, Montana. You gotta give it time to work through all the motions. Trust me, I've seen this dozens of times. All of this is totally transparent to legal insiders. They've sealed their fate with this one. We have obvious proof that they aren't bankrupt. Did you see the judge's face? Once we get that..."

"Hey bud, just drop it." Montana's tone was light, but he wasn't laughing anymore.

After about five seconds, Aubrey ventured, "You want to talk about it later, okay, I get that. You've had a pretty tough week. We can—"

"No, Aubrey, drop the lawsuit. However you do it, just do it. I've paid you over $50k in fees, they owe me $80k in repair costs. At this point, I'm out nearly $150 grand."

"Precisely why we have to stick with it. These people have robbed you. You fixed their building for them. You can't drop this and let them walk away. That would be like..."

"Criminal?" Montana lip raised into a smirk. "Obviously it is. Remember, in the eyes of the U.S. legal system, I am a criminal. I ran a stop sign." The lawyer laughed, but it was obviously forced. He was seeing another fifteen to thirty thousand dollars in fees slipping away.

"Montana, take a couple days and think this over. You're angry."

"No, Aubrey, I'm not angry, I'm mathematically literate. All this money is a sunk cost. Your fees are a sunk cost. I'll never get them back."

"Not necessarily true," the lawyer interjected.

Montana leveled a caustic eye at him, and the lawyer shut up. Recovering legal fees was dangerous ground upon which many lawyers had beached their proverbial boats[8].

"I'm not about to spend more money to chase less. I don't need to think about it. I'm done. Kill it. Email me a bill for whatever is left."

"Okay, but I'm going to wait a few days."

"No, now. As in today. File the papers to drop the suit. I'm sure you have a template that can be filled out in thirty seconds. I'm all done with this."

After his attorney left, Montana called the airlines. He booked a one-way ticket to Nicaragua. Because he had residency, he didn't need a round trip ticket, and he was damn sure not coming back. He also didn't care about hiding his escape. After five years in Nicaragua, he was certain that no one from the U.S. could find him down there if he didn't want them to.

He had been back in the States for three weeks. He had been sued twice, probably had some weird bullying lawsuit coming his way, and had been tossed in jail for running a stop sign.

The system was out of control, and it wasn't changing until the entire non-lawyer population was out of money. The government couldn't help. Montana read that it had only been open for 51% of the time over the last twelve months. Bad roads, bad schools, a crooked legal system, a broken government…Montana could get all that in Central America for an eighth of the price.

This wasn't a legal system. This was a get-rich-quick scam founded by lawyers and reinforced by judges.

---

8   Recovering legal fees from an adjudicated case is referred to as "fee shifting". Another option is to try and recover fees through a malicious prosecution lawsuit. Both options are *sold* to clients early in a lawsuit to help reduce the anxiety of paying large legal fees, the theory being that you would get your money back at the end of a successful prosecution or defense. Since 98.3% of cases settled prior to trial, most legal cases are never technically adjudicated, so neither a lawsuit or fee shifting apply. Settlements create a grey area as to who 'won' a case, one side could not claim to have been unfairly victimized by the lawsuit. The bar for proving malicious prosecution cases is so high that while they can be filed, as a practical matter, they are virtually never successful. The spin given to clients, after billing them to near bankruptcy, is that fee recovery stifles the ability of the common person to prevail against financially secure corporate interests. Thus, by blocking fee shifting, the legal system positioned itself as protecting its society, rather than bankrupting it. An estimated 2.7 trillion dollars in legal fees (up from 2.3 the previous year) bought the political cover necessary to ensure no meaningful reform.

As he exited the courthouse, a frail looking attorney handed him a flyer. On the back, the paper announced the conclusion of a class action suit against Colgate-Palmolive for $1.2 Billion dollars. If a client could prove they purchased a medium/soft toothbrush from 1980-2001, they stood to receive a settlement of up to seven dollars. Colgate-Palmolive accepted no fault that the toothbrushes were in fact determined to be medium/hard.

Montana smiled, *adios, 1ˢᵗ World.*

30

Alan Dunaway sat across from Teri for the second time in a week. Whining. Teri seriously considered stabbing him. The office was soundproofed, and his murder might calm down the ex-wife. The *accountant* ex-wife. The *accountant* ex-wife with access to The Bradshaw Group's financial records. It would certainly save the woman a hundred thousand in legal fees. Would she be grateful and leave Teri alone?

Probably not. She dropped the letter opener she had been fingering.

Rather than showing her concerns to the sniveling lawyer, Teri acted like it didn't really matter. She needed to end this meeting and make some calls. Alan indicated he was going to stay in Seattle for a while since he had no real need to return to Charlotte just then. Teri didn't care either way. His pending divorce had clearly wrong-footed him. He'd been watery-eyed and unfocused the entire lunch. Her indifference would make the anchorless lawyer work even harder for her approval. That was the only thing she needed from him just now.

She pulled out her chair to end the meeting when he made an offhand comment.

"Before we go, Teri, I just want to reemphasize that I'd really like to be more involved with the VC's parent organization. I've done a lot of advising, sort of off the books you could say."

He never got to finish. Teri saw this blackmail attempt coming the minute he walked into the office. It pissed her off, but since she might still need him, she needed to push him in another direction.

"Look, Alan, if you're so distraught with the divorce, just sue her for something. You're the one who told me that all you have to do is file a lawsuit and it will bury her. Doesn't even matter what the suit says. You said all you have to do is file and you win."

"Normally, yeah." He sniffed. "But I'd be the one paying both sides of it. The legal system doesn't work *for* you if you use your own money. That's why I advised you to file a lawsuit against Artie Goldstein before his employment contract was even terminated. Once he's on the defensive, he's done…unless he has millions tucked away somewhere that we couldn't find in our audit."

So frustrating. He kept circling back to try and insinuate himself into The Bradshaw Group's business. "Well, you need to figure it out. You're not useful to anyone moping around in tears. I agreed to let Dylan hire you because you had the reputation of a shark, not a goldfish. Quit whining that the legal system, which you represent by the way, doesn't work. That's not news to anyone. You're a goddamn insider. If you can't bend the system to your advantage, I shouldn't have hired you in the first place."

"Let me at least buy you lunch someday this week," he attempted meagerly.

Fuck, enough!

She rounded on him. "Why, you'd just bill it to my client file so I can pay it later while you and your buddies laugh that I thanked you for a lunch I paid for! Get to work, I'm busy." The fire in her eyes wasn't feigned. She was pissed. These damn leeches wanted respectability then pulled tricks like this? Alan must have sensed the rage. He nearly ran out the door.

With the lawyer out of the way, Teri contemplated what to do about the ex-wife. Or, the future ex-wife. She would have to be located, right damn now. There was no way a part-time accountant could grasp the full picture, but she could connect enough dots to make serious trouble. That woman needed to be suffocated under an avalanche of legal documents. She needed to intervene and manage Alan's divorce, too. Just to be sure. Emotionally, the guy hung by a thread, and once he figured out Teri had no further use for him, he'd collapse.

Her first call was to her own divorce lawyer, now much more successful and expensive. He was initially perplexed that she was going to be a repeat client, despite not being married. A $50,000 retainer later, he seemed much more understanding of the situation. Teri issued him orders, and he marched off to inform Alan Dunaway that his divorce was now handled.

Her second call went to her private security contractor. They connected her to a former-FBI agent out of Chicago. The guy now worked as a bounty hunter for hire. Her new bounty hunter booked the next flight to Charlotte that very afternoon. Teri didn't bother checking up on the guy. She was in a hurry. The Bradshaw Group's lawyers would email him the necessary info in-flight. He'd need a full dossier on both Dunaways, half a dozen types of non-disclosures, and anti-disparagement agreements for the ex-wife to sign. The agent wasn't worried. The target was basically a housewife. If she wasn't at home, he could track her down. Teri put limitless resources at his command. The guy estimated that he would be back in Chicago for dinner. Teri wired him ten thousand to start and offered fifty more when he got signatures.

That problem managed, she turned to the goddamned Wonderwheel. Early revenue reports were inconclusive. That wasn't good. "Inconclusive" was to accountants what "unacceptable" was to attorneys, a way to position defeat. Teri had Alice book her on a flight to Los Angeles. She wanted to see one of these sites for herself.

31

CHRISTIAN RAMÍREZ
Present Day
North of Bluefields, Nicaragua

Chris stretched out next to Juan and Gordo by the main bug fire. They all planned to catch an hour break while Brayan worked. Just digging up the treasure exhausted them. Cleaning, weighing, stacking, and hauling it up to the cave wiped them out. Gold weighed a lot. Now that both of Chris's eyes could open, he had just started to close them when Brayan yelped from the middle of the river.

All three of them jumped up at the noise. Out here, alone, it was impossible to know what had caused his panic. It could be a snake bite. It could be a monkey attack. There was no telling. Brayan's right arm was up to the shoulder in the river, and his face had a determined set to it. He obviously wasn't injured, but his face was stretched and straining. After a few more seconds of rotating his arm, he pulled it out of the water. A gob of mud the size of a microwave sat in his hand. He dipped it back in the water several times, splashed water on it, and looked up at his coworkers on the riverbank, then back at the thing in his hands. Chris couldn't quite make out what it was. Brayan started across the river towards them, holding out the object like a religious artifact.

When he was close enough, he rotated it in his palm. It looked like a...pineapple? Chris grabbed a water bottle off the ground, and slowly rubbed the mud off the object with clean water. It was a dang pineapple. A golden pineapple. All four of them exchanged excited looks. Gordo spoke first.

"*Madre de Díos*, who in Nicaragua has ever been rich enough to forge a golden pineapple?"

"Nobody." Chris confirmed, though he wasn't sure. "Nobody Gordo. Whatever this is, it comes from far away."

The rest of the day, the four of them worked. While they still pulled coins out of the river, other artifacts began to emerge as well. There were golden plates, broken pieces of jewelry, vases, and religious artifacts, all made of or mounted in gold. Chris's mind kept coming back to the conclusion that this wasn't a Nicaraguan treasure. Nowhere in any history he had ever read, did Nicaraguans eat off golden plates.

At the end of the workday, he dispatched Gordo up to the small cave to try and make some sense out of the haul. He instructed the man to separate the coins, as best he could, by metal. Then he wanted the items separated from the coins. Juan set about building crates to house the categorized inventory. It was time to take stock and see exactly what they were dealing with.

After a hours in the cave, Gordo came down and informed Juan, in a dour voice, "We're gonna need a half dozen more crates, at least."

By the following morning, it was clear that they were also going to need more donkeys to haul this out of the jungle, and they were still hauling artifacts out of the mud.

Christian typed out a text to Montana: *Get down here, fast.*

32

MONTANA AINSLEY
Present Day
Nashville, Tennessee

Montana received Chris's text the morning after he dropped his lawsuit against the laundromat's landlords. He needed to end the circus up here and get back down south, pronto.

In the back of a taxi, he took a call from lawyer number one. Langenholt informed him that the landlords now planned to file a suit against him for breach of the lease. Since his own lawsuit had been dropped, they were free to sue him. The landlords now claimed that by keeping the laundromat closed, Montana violated the occupancy rule. According to Langenholt, the lease would fetch nearly nine times more in the current market. They wanted him out.

He chided Montana again about dropping the lawsuit and cautioned him about being on the defensive side of a suit. Aubrey told Montana that the opposing lawyer said his clients would hold off on the suit if Montana agreed to tear up the lease and leave everything to them (including the roughly $100,000 of laundry equipment). Montana said he would think about it and call back.

First, he had a meeting with Savannah, his wife, and her new fiancé. While their divorce attorneys argued over rules for a potential conference between the parties, Montana tried calling her one last time. By luck, she picked up. Calling her directly was a clear violation of the legal rules, but Montana wanted to see if they could sort the divorce faster without lawyers. They agreed to meet without notifying respective counsel. She sounded as tired as he did. They met for salads at an out-of-the way local haunt called The Yellow Porch in Berry Hill. The restaurant was next door to Montana's bank, and he had an appointment there right after.

When he arrived, the estranged husband and wife hugged. Montana could feel the relief in his wife's hug, and he figured she could sense the same emanating from him. Montana shook hands with her fiancé, Jeff.

"I want to congratulate you guys. I hope you will both be happy. I really mean that." He turned to the fiancé. "Jeff, she's been through a lot. I obviously didn't handle this all that well, but there's a lot more to why I left than I can really explain. I heard you guys were engaged, and I came back to close out our divorce, so you could move on."

Savannah, laughed a little. "Yeah, I didn't really buy that whole missing person bit, but it did finally put a stop to that sucking sound in my bank account, so I didn't contest it. Besides, you were going to be declared legally dead in a few months anyway."

After a few minutes of conversation, Savannah's fiancé, Jeff, spoke up. "Montana, I actually do get where you're coming from. My family owns a trucking business. We're fighting off three separate lawsuits right now. It's a big company, so we have inside counsel deal with that stuff. But if we were a small outfit? I can see how all this crap can drive you off the rails a bit."

"Thanks, Jeff. I appreciate it. It's funny, we should be at each other's throats, technically, but I guess we're all on the run from the legal system together."

They all nodded. There was no disputing the point.

"So, this brings me to something I wanted to propose to you two. I'm currently trying to sell my parent's old house here, but I've been sued by some real estate developer out of Memphis who claims I promised him the house for, like, fifty-grand. They slapped a lien on the house under some pretext. Or, not a lien, but a Lis something? I can't remember what it's called."

Savannah frowned. "Your parents' place? Oh Montana, I'm so sorry. Jeez, you can't get a break. You haven't even been here for five years, and you're being sued again? I don't even understand how that's possible? Do you know the people?"

Before Montana could answer that he was actually facing up to four new lawsuits, her fiancé cut in. "It's called a Lis Pendens. I might…" Jeff stopped talking, considered his words, then carried on. "Yeah, sure, why not. I might know a way around that, Montana. Something kind of similar happened to my brother."

Savannah looked at her fiancé. "How is that even possible?"

"Because it isn't rare," Montana answered sourly.

Jeff continued, "I don't know the specifics of your case, Montana, but tell your lawyer to look into a little-used thing called "slander of title." In it, you'll be shocked to know that it's pretty easy to crush the Lis Pendens. Not only that, but this is the one and virtually only area of Tennessee law that specifically outlines that you can recover legal fees. Once they see that, they'll run away. I can get you the name of the lawyer my brother used if you want."

"Heck yeah," he agreed.

Savannah piped up. "It's a bit disheartening that your lawyer didn't come up with it." More laughter from all three. For the next half hour, Montana and his future-ex-wife's fiancé swapped legal horror stories. Between the two of them, they had faced down over a dozen types of lawsuits as business owners.

"Well, like you said, we're all on the run from the lawyers," Jeff concluded.

Montana changed the subject back to the matter at hand.

"Right. So…here is what I was thinking." He looked at Savannah. "Technically, we're still married. Would you be willing to sell the house for me? I'll split the proceeds fifty-fifty with you, kind of payback for dragging this all out so long…and a lot of other stuff. I can quit claim the title to you as my wife, sign off on the divorce, then you just agree to split the proceeds with me down the line. That would more than double any existing claims left in the divorce. It would cost you a lot to fight the lawsuit, but you'd make about twenty times that when it sells. I don't know about you, but I haven't got a whole lot of money left. Most of it has been bled out into the legal system."

This had been the sticky point of their divorce. His businesses predated their marriage and thus her interest in them was debatable. The marital home had been sold, long ago, and the assets put in legal trust as a guarantee against the divorce tax and legal fees. The problem was that, if the courts said she did have an interest in the businesses, Montana no longer had the money to buy her out. He would have to sell the businesses. That would take at least a year, and all the while, the legal fees would mount. That was why both lawyers had perpetuated the divorce with countless filings and mediation attempts. Neither client had much cash left, but the business sale would guarantee that all the legal bills got paid.

The three of them discussed the idea for a few more minutes before Savannah finally said, "Yeah, they've bled me dry, too. Are you really sure you want to do this?" She seemed genuinely concerned for him. "I mean, that was your parents' home. I never really was all that interested in the businesses in the first place. I'm not even sure how we got here."

She shook her head in a gesture of sadness and regret. Then she put her hand over his on the table. "I never meant this to be so nasty. Or so damn expensive. I just…I honestly don't even know what happened. It's like I just looked up one day and everything was a total wreck."

"Thanks, Savannah. Really. And yeah, I feel the same way. I have for a long time." He put his other hand on top of hers, patted it, then removed his hand. "So, what do you guys say?" he asked, lightening the mood. "Jeff, you think you can torpedo these pricks for a few grand and free up the house for sale? Call it Savannah's dowry?"

After lunch, they walked next door to the bank where Gena notarized the quit claim agreement. They faxed a copy to the real estate attorney, along with a letter cancelling his services. They all laughed talking about the reaction of the real estate lawyer when he learned he'd been fired. Montana smiled inwardly, *just wait till he finds out I'm not paying the bill.*

Afterwards, Gena post-dated the divorce agreement that Montana had filled out online the night before. It was dated for tomorrow. That was going to set off a holy hell with the divorce lawyers.

When the happy couple had gone, Gena and Diana turned to Montana. "So, what's left for you now?"

"Now, I'm going to sell the restaurant to Joanna, rid myself of some lawsuits, and exit stage left before I blow through a red light and wind up on death row."

The three of them discussed banking arrangements for the future incoming wires. Another of Montana's long relationships was coming to a close. They all hugged and parted ways. As they parted ways, Gena commented that his eyes seemed a bit brighter.

33

ELAINE DUNAWAY
Present Day
Augusto Sandino International Airport
Managua, Nicaragua

Elaine's Spirit Airways flight landed in the Nicaraguan capital at two in the morning. The flight was mostly full and appeared to be the only flight landing at that ungodly hour. Her travel experience outside of the U.S. had been limited to Caribbean Islands. With their organized structure, tourist friendly signage, and pastel dressed greeters, she had fond memories of travel.

At two in the morning, with armed guards everywhere, everything in Spanish, and all eyes lock on her, Managua was not that.

The airport appeared deserted, apart from armed police. On her way to customs, she passed a couple of white-coated Nicaraguans who looked her up and down and wrote something on a clipboard. That made her nervous. She passed some type of scanner that projected her outline and body heat concentration onto a screen mounted on the wall. She had never seen anything like that in an airport. Was there a disease outbreak here? She hadn't even bothered to check.

To her bleary eyes, everyone looked tense. Most of the police officers rested their palms on the butts of their holstered pistols or carried menacing-looking short barrel shotguns. Maybe this trip wasn't such a good idea.

With zero command of the local language, she followed a small group of surfer types who appeared to know how to navigate the airport. The intensity of the customs officer didn't help matters. He appeared none too pleased she spoke no Spanish. She eventually exited the arrival hall into a wave of humidity and a hailstorm of taxi drivers. She actually took a step back toward the airport. The heat shocked her. She instantly started sweating into her jeans and blouse. Elaine had grown up in the deep south. The very deep south. Her mother made Scarlet O'Hara sound positively Bostonian. She knew humidity. Managua was on a totally different scale. When she breathed in, she actually felt moisture going down her throat. She stopped outside the doors to take in the surroundings. Big mistake.

There were no barriers to separate her from a legion of Nicaraguans waiting outside the doors. They descended on her like vultures. Dozens of short brown men charged toward her shouting "taxi" and what sounded like "*chela*". When she stopped walking, they closed in from all sides and started jostling her like a pinball. She clutched her carryon bag tightly to her chest. The men all pawed at her, gesturing for her to follow them. One actually grabbed her by the arm and tried to pull her away. She was close to panicking.

At the last second, she spotted her name on a small sign and broke free of the man holding her arm. She fought through the crowd and gasped out her name and pointed to herself. The man led her a few feet away from the crowd and whistled. A car, and not a very nice one, pulled up to the curb in front of her. The driver and the sign guy exchanged words in Spanish, and he ushered her toward the back seat.

The thirty-year-old Russian Lada had no air conditioning. The interior was old, dirty, and torn to shreds. The door didn't even open from the outside. The driver, all of about fifteen, had to lean over and open it for her. He appeared young, wiry, and possessed shifty eyes. Elaine's senses went on high alert.

She knew the hotel was just a half mile away to the left, so when the kid turned right out of the airport, she started protesting loudly and, hidden from his view, pressed her car keys in between the knuckles of right hand. Through a series of gestures and Spanish, the kid seemed to be indicating that something was wrong with the road to the left. He patted the air a few times in a calming gesture and repeated the name of her hotel. He then drew a circle in the air. Lainey got it. They would be taking the long way around. Her anxiety level had never been this high. She was in an actual dangerous situation for the first time in her life, alone, and completely off anyone's radar. She briefly thought of Alan, but he would be useless unless her kidnappers wanted to buy a franchise. She almost laughed at that, but the chatter of firecrackers somewhere behind her distracted her attention. *Those were firecrackers, right?*

They drove through empty streets for the better part of twenty minutes. Lainey sweated through her clothes as the car rattled along cobbled side streets. She tried to follow the trip on her GPS, but the signal dropped in and out. It might cost a fortune in data, but she didn't give a damn what that bill would look like, she wanted to live long enough to see it. This wasn't a fight between parents at a stupid PTA meeting. This mattered.

Most of the streets they passed were dark, dirty, and unpaved. Down one dirt alley, she saw dozens of plastic garbage bags ripped open and trash strewn across the road. Dogs fought amongst themselves over the scraps. Plastic bags clung to power lines and wrapped around tree limbs. They whipped in the breeze looking like ghosts against the darkness of the alley. She smelled the stench of old garbage as they passed an open sewer, and she saw the outline of half a dozen figures smoking cigarettes and pissing into the sewer. She looked at her driver. He looked tense. He constantly scanned up and down the streets as he drove. They passed very few cars and virtually no more people. There were a few stoplights, but the driver ignored them. The city felt abandoned. Elaine felt the cold finger of fear creep down her spine.

After nearly half an hour, they emerged back onto the paved airport road from the other direction. There were lights and gas stations. Her anxiety level dropped below redline. They turned onto a side road blocked by a metal gate. One honk from the horn, and the gate opened and quickly slammed shut behind them. Past the gate, a whole neighborhood stretched out before them, completely surrounded by a ten foot concrete wall topped with concertina wire. Lainey let out a deep sigh of relief when the taxi pulled up outside the open-air lobby of her hotel.

The woman behind the metal check-in desk welcomed Elaine in thick Caribbean English. Elaine hugged her-she couldn't help herself. When Elaine told her about the weird detour, the woman explained the situation in her singsong voice. Five hundred yards to the left of the airport, half a dozen teenagers had dug up the cobbled paving stones and erected a three-foot tall roadblock, or *tranque* in Nicaraguan Spanish. The *tranque* would stop government pickup trucks from passing unmolested through neighborhoods.

She cautioned her new guest that the loud bangs she might hear during the night were from the *morteros* that the teenagers used to warn the neighborhood that government troops were approaching. Seeing the obvious panic in Elaine's face, she offered that the *morteros* weren't guns, they were mortar-like tubes that fired a baseball sized wad of gunpowder into the air and popped like a loud firecracker. In offensive terms, the boys didn't carry guns. She tried to relax her nervous American guest by assuring her the government troops wouldn't enter the neighborhood. They were hunting the teenagers in the streets.

"Government troops are hunting teenagers? Hunting them? What the hell is going on?" To this point in Lainey's life, sentences like that only came out in movies.

The woman looked at her strangely and responded, "You ain't hear nothing up there before you come down?"

"No," she admitted. "Basically, in the U.S. there is a media blackout of all non-U.S. political news."

"Well, we are at the start of major problems. Managua not the safest place to be just now." The two women talked a bit more before Elaine went off in search of her room. She had just lived through the first real danger of her life, and the adrenaline was wearing off. Just before she fell asleep, a thought strange crossed her mind; *apparently, those hadn't been firecrackers.*

While Elaine Dunaway slept, the sparsely populated country slid further and further toward the brink of complete collapse.

34

MONTANA AINSLEY

Present Day

Ft. Lauderdale International Airport

Montana sat in an executive lounge in the Ft. Lauderdale airport. He paid the fifty-dollar fee just so the airport auctioneer didn't deafen him every ten seconds. He had about four hours until the Spirit redeye connected down to Central America. He'd been working his email and phone for a couple of hours, wrapping up the last of his affairs.

He'd had a very busy twenty-four hours. Last night, he forever crushed the lawsuit hanging over the restaurant. The encounter with the cowardly young lawyer had clarified how to deal with that lawsuit. Based on the customers' reactions, Montana had come to several conclusions. First, there was indeed a faction of the population who no longer had use for the more bellicose generations that preceded it. But second, his bellicose generation still had a lot of members, and those people, most of whom actually had the money to dine out, detested having to live in fear of that faction.

So last night, he logged onto the world's biggest review site and found the girl's nasty review. He created an account, listed himself as the owner of the restaurant, and went through the verification steps. The original review read:

Reviewer: FoodieQueen2004-elite reviewer
Review: of The Pickled Parrot Restaurant-5 days ago
Rating: 1 star

"I SOOO wanted to like this place because I live close by, but its wayyyy expensive relative to everything else. But I took my boyfriend for our 3-month anniversary the other night. Special occasion-blow the bank, right? HUGE MISTAKE. First of all, the vibe totally creeped us out. I mean, it wasn't like dirty, but it wasn't clean either-it totally reminded me of like, a Hollywood set for a slasher film where the guy is trying to put up a "normal" front, but everything was just a bit off? You with me? After literally checking for dead bodies in the bathrooms, we were seated at a dusty table only to wait for an hour for our waters (forgot the lemons, shocker!!!!!). Then both our waters had to go back because they had PLASTIC STRAWS oozing PABA everywhere. Not a good sign, right? We should have left, but this is a neighborhood place, and we totally support local, so we decided to stick it out. The menu was ridiculously short, like, I get to choose from 7 entrees-end of story! I guess they lack the talent to do much else. Forebode much? The place was totally slammed, so it took our server forever to finally take our orders. Maybe staff appropriately for a busy night? You'd think they'd have figured this out by now. Maybe if they paid a LIVING WAGE, people would be more willing to work there? It doesn't take a master's degree in sociology to figure that out!! (trust me on that one). When our entrees finally did come out, my asparagus was cold, not, like, it had cooled off after being under a heat lamp; I mean their were literally ICE CRYSTALS on it!!! Obviously, by the time the server brought it back we were done with our food (meh), because it doesn't take us 2 hours to eat, right? Guess what? STILL frozen solid. For real. Like drop it and you'll break the plate. I was totally over it by this point and when I informed the server I wasn't paying for frozen food, he goes and gets a like nine-month pregnant manager to come over.

I literally thought she was going to go into labor on the spot. You know, on a side note, I don't really care if you choose to have kids, but is it really my responsibility to put up with your hormonal issues? Yeah, no. I mean, like, I'm the customer, right? I'm the one that caught you serving frozen food! Think these people care? Think again. I informed her and her child that I wouldn't be paying and got up to leave. She had the nerve to threaten me with calling the COPS! That's right, my 3-month anniversary dinner nearly ended with me getting arrested for being served frozen food. Yeah, that's not stressful at all. Sooo, how many stars do I give a "restaurant" that tries to poison and jail me?"

The review went on, but Montana couldn't suffer anymore. He'd stopped reading reviews years before. Want your business to fail? Spend your time focused on reviews. Instead, he banged out a response and posted it without thinking twice.

Owner's Response:

"Dear Delores Wilk, I founded this restaurant many years ago. While your hideously punctuated novella might be distressing for your alma mater, we found your harrowing story of survival uplifting. This was your most challenging ordeal since deciding to leave home at twenty-nine. We know, we checked. Every minute of your dull life is documented online. Your bravery is stuff of legend. I tried you at 615-555-1212, but you didn't pick up.

Once we failed to poison you with straw-based PABA, the kitchen assured us the Spanish Flu asparagus would work. Like your sociology master's degree (from Vanderbilt, where both your parents are tenured professors at $350k/year), that mistake cost us. Heads will roll.

Sadly, we have a policy that your parents have to pay for the food you eat, even if you don't like it. I know, that's like, so unfair. We mailed a free asparagus gift card to the half million dollar house your parents purchased for you at 212 Inglewood Trace Cir. We look forward to another shot.

We love that you love to support local by filing a $1.5 million expectation lawsuit against us. Would half of that be enough justice dollars to satisfy?

I encourage everyone to ask Delores, or her un-fire-able tenured parents exactly how much of our employees' money it takes to offset the trauma of a cold side dish."

At the end of the review, he listed every contact point he had for Delores Wilk. He had several, including all her social media links. The NADS database proved worth every penny.

Montana had a rough understanding what it meant to "doxx" someone. He also knew that like private phone records or attorney-client privilege, the law served more like a guideline these days. In the end, he just didn't care. The final lesson to the new owners, that a mob is a collection of people without money or a job, seemed much more important than any lawsuit-which he would ignore anyway.

Financially, a collection of people who couldn't afford to eat at his restaurant wouldn't be eating there anyway, regardless of how outraged they were. Those people were totally irrelevant. People with money worked; they didn't spend all their time getting outraged online. People who worked had a sense of humor, and if they bothered to read his response at all, they would probably find it funny. At worst, they'd eat at the restaurant two extra times. That was what Montana saw in the faces of his customers when he stood up to the bullying of the young lawyer. Pent-up frustration.

By the time he met with Joanna's family early this morning, his response had exploded locally. The review had been shared across media sites over 100,000 times and been viewed twice that much. Photos of his response were re-posted and shared in anticipation of his response being removed by the site. Delores Wilk and her social media sites had been overwhelmed with death threats and hate mail. Her employer had given her the week off to ensure the social media hatred didn't turn their way.

Even her university was being publicly shamed for granting a master's degree to someone whose writing skills were at an eighth-grade level. Questions were being raised about whether her parents had used undue influence to gain her admittance at Vanderbilt.

Before Montana and Joanna's father had even signed the contract, Nell called from the restaurant to inform them that a sheepish young man had come by and left a copy of some paperwork: the restaurant had been non-suited. The use of a non-suit was designed to prevent a defendant from suing for legal fees. It meant that: *no, the defendant isn't a clear-cut winner, the plaintiff is merely walking away.* Had Montana hired a lawyer, he would have been out that money.

While Joanna's parents found his actions hilarious and helpful, Joanna was a bit more nervous. "How did you know it would play out like that?"

He explained his mob theory to her, then continued, "More than anything, the parents. Parents who drop that much cash on a house for their kid are helicopter parents and nervous wrecks. Any amount of pressure gets applied to them and they fold. They have cushy, government teaching jobs. They're not going to risk that over a cold side dish."

"So, you just gave the mob a more compelling storyline: she was trying to get rich quick, well, richer, and she has rich parents."

"Yup. Mobs are like crabs in a bucket: if one tries to climb out by getting rich, they pull 'em back in and eat them. The important thing to remember is that social media doesn't matter. People who can afford to eat out, people who are busy having jobs, those people understand. They'll give us a mulligan because they are adult enough to remember that they've made mistakes, too. But her mob? Not a chance. One slip up and you're devoured. Being rich is a big slip up."

She laughed. "Man, I'm gonna miss you…the last man standing. And the doxxing? That's a serious thing. Did you know that? I think it's a crime. And the social media people frown on it, hardcore."

"No they don't, Joanna, look at the response. They just like to say they frown on it. Did they really care that I doxxed her? They love it. It gives them direct access to their prey. I just used the mob to pressure her parents into making her drop the suit. They can make doxxing as illegal as they want, but you just can't control the mob. Everything I put up was public, anyway, you just have to pay a database called NADS $1,000 bucks to subscribe. They give you the data on virtually everyone. I learned about it when they arrested me. It's one of the tracking databases. Besides, I signed my name to it so that you can disavow it, and me, if it comes down to it. I no longer own the place. By the time the dust clears, she can sue me all she wants. Good luck serving me with papers."

By the time everything was signed and sealed, Nell called back to let Joanna know there was a line of supporters three hundred long waiting for them to open.

Montana endured another heartfelt goodbye. They hugged and thanked each other for a thousand kindnesses over the years. He shook hands with her parents and wished them all fame, fortune, and happiness. He wouldn't see the inside of the U.S. again. The young lawyer's comments, that he no longer belonged in his home country, weren't wrong. As they parted ways, Joanna said, "You know what, sad as I am, you look really happy. I can see it. Your eyes have color again."

He caught a taxi to the airport, a short hop to FLL, and here he sat.

Two days earlier, he had paid two thousand dollars to the lawyer to handle his arrest. The lawyer assured him that he wouldn't even need to show up to court. Sure enough, the guy had made one phone call to the DA's office and cleared the charge. Finally, Montana had his bankers wire the guy an additional $500 to get his public record expunged. All told, running a stop sign had cost him nearly $3,000, a couple of fractured ribs, and a night in jail.

All in all, Montana thought, *well worth the price of exit.*

Savannah had called about the house. Her fiancé had been as good as his word. His lawyer had filed a title slander suit, and the lien had been removed within hours. She was meeting a local developer later in the day. The guy had already made an offer. The bad news, according to Savannah, was that the out-of-town developers planned to refile the complaint against Montana personally, hoping to capture the proceeds of the sale they could no longer block. Montana thanked her profusely and told her not to worry.

He had a foolproof way to defeat U.S. lawsuits.

The real estate lawyer, Roger, was less pleased about the outcome. He received Montana's fax and called early the following day. He left a two-minute message ending in the word *unacceptable.* Montana called him from the lounge. The lawyer was dubious about the legality of the strategy Montana was pursuing. He was equally distrustful of a plan involving cooperation with his ex-wife. The lawyer demanded that he be allowed to draw up a contract between Montana and Savannah to ensure she held up her end. Montana gleefully accepted the offer.

The lawyer, relieved he now had a new hook in a client who'd fired him, reminded Montana that they could just subtract the cost of drawing up the contract from the retainer, once Montana paid the original retainer. Montana assured him it was on the way. Without a PA system blaring announcements, the lawyer had no way to know where Montana sat. Another benefit of the lounge pass.

His next call had been to Sandy Sandberg, his divorce attorney. The normally unflappable lawyer was not pleased to have been cut out of finalizing Montana's divorce. He, too, found the situation *unacceptable*. When Montana pointed out that a sizeable portion of the real estate sale (which Sandy had his eyes on) would have gone to the real estate attorney anyway, Sandy's complaints dried up.

Lawyers know that they're the only collusion game in town. By billing hourly for everything and pricing nothing, the public can't price-shop legal services. This allows their hourly rates to inflate faster than college tuition. Although it is a brilliant financial strategy, clever clients who don't owe money represent a risk. Most attorneys are taught to cut ties with clients over whom they hold no power. Through his comment, Montana had signaled to Sandy that he knew the older lawyer had ripped him off, that he was okay with it, but Sandy better not push it.

Sandy didn't push it.

He did warn Montana that Savannah's lawyer was incensed and planned on investigating grounds upon which to sue Montana for circumventing the legal process.

Lawyer and client said their formal goodbyes. Lawyers, regardless of how well you got along with them, are paid friends. Once your money stopped flowing into their accounts, the friendships end.

His final phone call had been to his old business partner and former restauranteur. When he got voicemail, he left a brief goodbye.

"Hey bud, I'm gone. I just wanted to leave you with something in case things flare back up. It's called the Jack Welch Defense, Savannah's new fiancé told me about it. It's an actual legal precedent. If you can prove that you're following professional techniques from a certified management book, you bear no responsibility for the outcome. It's the reason those things sell so well. Best of luck, buddy. Oh, and if our old lawyer contacts you, let him know that I'm not paying him shit."

Montana started to put the finishing touches on the resolution to his final lawsuit. It was 4:30pm, it had to be done before 4:59pm. *It* took the form of an email, addressed to the current law firm representing the landlord of his laundromat business. His lawyer, Aubrey Langeholt III, was copied. It read:

To whichever of the twelve lawyers on the masthead represents Joe and Dee Baker, owners of the property at 1327 Meridian Street.

My name is Montana Ainsley, and I am the owner of the laundromat at 1327 Meridian Street. I am currently not represented by counsel, so all future correspondence should be with me directly. I don't know to whom to address this letter specifically because you are the fifth attorney of record. I wonder if the previous attorneys got paid? Regardless, your clients indicated a desire to file suit against me for violating the lease. They indicated I must now reopen the laundromat within twenty-four hours, or I will be in violation of the "occupancy" clause of my lease. I take this to mean that I am in violation because nobody is there.

Great news. As of this morning, I reopened the laundromat focusing on corporate accounts. I already have one restaurant client who has agreed to pay a monthly fee of $200. The restaurant will be utilizing my self-service laundromat services rather than outsourcing their tablecloth and napkin cleaning services to a more expensive vendor. I have arranged for this corporate client to mail the check directly to your client; my landlord. I know my landlords will be thrilled to know that I will be fulfilling the entirety of the fifteen-year lease that we agreed upon (a copy of which is attached) at our prearranged monthly rent of $200 per month...for the next eight years. Although the laundromat is no longer open to general public use, you will find this type of arrangement well within the purview of our agreed-upon lease.

I wish you luck recovering legal fees from your client. I look forward to reading the "legally required notification" of any lawsuit you may file.

-Montana Ainsley

Montana hit send. It was 4:55 p.m. He clicked on the profile button of his email account, a popular, encrypted, and untraceable email service out of Switzerland. He clicked *delete email account,* then, *yes, I'm sure,* then, *totally positive,* and finally, *okay.* The site logged him out. On the screen, a message warned him that his email address was now lost to him forever and could be utilized by a new party, but that all records of his ownership had been destroyed at 4:57 p.m.

He closed his computer, opened his U.S. phone, removed the battery, and tossed both pieces into a trash bin as he exited the lounge toward his boarding gate.

At 10:00 p.m., Montana boarded a half empty plane bound for Managua, Nicaragua.

The following morning, three emails pinged off his closed email account. Two legal bills, totaling over $26,000 would go unpaid forever. The third email, a threatening letter accompanied with a notice for electronic document freeze, also spun back a 'return to sender' notification. Two of those lawyers attempted to call the phone number they had for Montana Ainsley. The number was no longer assigned to a valid subscriber.

Within minutes, paralegals at three different offices searched frantically for a physical address or digital footprint upon which they could serve various lawsuits. Since Montana's divorce went final the week before, his ex-wife could not be considered a family member. His parents' home, which she now owned, had a contract pending. Montana had no registered address upon which papers could be served. His phone and email accounts were shut down. He had no social media presence. The United States legal system, the most vast, systematized, and complex structure in the Milky Way galaxy, completely folded if you didn't have an address.

35

TERI BRADSHAW
Present Day
Los Angeles International Airport
Los Angeles, California

Teri Bradshaw's head rested on the steering wheel of her rental car.

Wheel. There was that goddamn word again.

An hour earlier, she stood in front of the open gates of the Los Angeles franchise of The Wheel of Wonder. The site had two entrance kiosks. Above the left kiosk, a sign read "Admission". There were a dozen people in line holding leashed children.

Kids on fucking leashes, the thought made Teri laugh.

The opposite kiosk's sign read, "Collaborative Admission." That line stretched halfway around the block.

Collaborative Admission…Dylan-speak for 'free'. That thought didn't make Teri laugh.

She stood in the full priced line. When she got to the window, she asked the disengaged youngster behind the glass what the other window was for. He looked up from his phone.

"Oh, sorry." He put the phone down. "So, like, a collaborated admission is for, like, people of influence in the digital world. You know, social media influencers, bloggers, vloggers, elite reviewers…that kind of thing. They basically trade their services, pictures, or reviews for a discounted rate, right. The discount, like, depends on the number of followers and likes and shares and stuff. They gotta look up each person's thing, right, and apply a metric to it, so it takes a few minutes to figure out how much each person pays." He looked up at her, took in her middle-aged-ness, and recalibrated. "Does that make sense to you? It's like an advertising thing."

"Yeah, I got it." Her tone was the South Pole.

She paid for a full price ticket and entered the park. To her left, a franchised coffee shop was filled with twenty-somethings, banging away on keyboards and wearing massive earphones covering half their heads. Teri assumed they were listening to deep space communications. Each of them had a single cup of coffee in front of them. She followed a paved pathway toward the beginning of the exhibits.

As she cleared the first bend, an enormous, snow-capped mountain came into full view. It towered above her. It must have been seven stories high. It was covered with artificial rubber snow and ice pellets. About twenty feet up, a group of *hikers*, in full climbing gear, posed for a group selfie. A camera mounted on wires zipped around taking photos from angles designed to make that group appear to be ascending the *mountain*. Off camera, a machine blew rubber snow pellets at them. The sign at the base of the mountain spelled it all out: "Everest." The line extended forever.

The next *ride* she approached appeared to be Dylan's fucking Machu Picchu mock-up. The line led up a long set of stairs to a grass-covered viewing platform that looked down on a mocked-up version of the famous South American site. Long line.

Next, she came to a cross-sectioned boat floating in a man-made river mocked up to look like the Amazon. There was dense vegetation on the opposite side of the abbreviated brown *river*. The front end of the boat had been cut away so that people could board more easily, and the selfies and photos were taken at the back of the boat. A Latino looking guy stood in front of the boat's motor. Each visitor was handed a panama hat, a wet scarf (to put around their necks, it appeared), and got misted with water from a spray bottle to simulate sweating. There were even jungle sounds emanating from the opposite bank. Tiny drones disguised as all manner of birds floated in the background. Behind her, a vendor sold South American woven bags, trinkets, and all manner of Amazon-related paraphernalia.

The Pyramids at Giza were next, followed by a small alleyway featuring the white-washed buildings of Santorini, Greece.

Stonehenge.

The Eiffel Tower.

Saint Basil's cathedral in Moscow.

A staircase covered in graffiti.

A beat-up alleyway shaded by hundreds of umbrellas.

A small beach where yogis posed, framing inbound aircraft in the palms of their hands.

The rides went on and on. The loop was over three miles in length. You could even rent a golf cart for four dollars.

Only four fucking dollars!

The scenes were spectacular. The details were perfect, right down to the bird-shaped drones flying in and out of the Amazonian vegetation. The place made Las Vegas look like Legoland. Then again, half a billion dollars. It was, Teri had to admit, a modern wonder of the wonders of the world.

And it's basically free of fucking charge!

All the rides had long lines. It really was Six Flags for selfies.

Teri had seen enough. She spent four dollars to rent a golf cart to return her to the front. She purchased a coffee at the entrance cafe and sat among the digital nomads to take stock. The five-dollar coffee was actually less expensive than what she paid at this same franchise location by her house. Cheap coffee, cheap golf cart rentals, free admission. Dylan had designed this place to be cool, not profitable. It made her head hurt. Cool didn't make money. Apparently, Dylan assumed that Teri could subsidize the cost of changing the world. She was pretty sure The Bradshaw Group didn't have the budget.

Once the initial shock wore off, she started working the math in her head. *Each ride had half a dozen employees, and there were at least three dozen helpers walking around the park. Roughly one in thirty people were paying full price. The food and drink were discounted. The costumes were free. Even the damn golf cart was reasonably priced. The park was probably making...no, wrong word. The park was probably losing, how much? Times three corporately owned franchises?*

This was a problem she couldn't solve. The math she could do. But uninventing Wonderwheel? That, not even Teri could do. The sheer perfection of it all. The user-friendly setup with vendors and charging stations everywhere. The overall splendor. It must have cost half a billion dollars just to construct. Times three parks!

This was a firm ender. Clearly, Dylan had fudged the numbers. Once the final numbers were in, no franchisee would touch it. Governments couldn't afford this. The TSA would have to start repossessing children to offset this financial colossus. She didn't have any contacts in that universe? How would that even work?

Teri zoned out, just staring into space. This was done. She was done. Wonderwheel had undone her...and Richard Pryor.

A light-hearted argument at the next table caught her brain's attention. Three techies had removed their space headgear and started arguing over some product they were working on. Teri thought maybe listening-in would take her mind off her problem.

One of them held forth that their new ride-hailing app would be successful, in the face of much larger competition, because it focused strictly on riders with special needs. Her two counterparts argued that the differentiation from the industry's biggest players was too far marginal for any real product differentiation to exist. Calmly, the girl brought up the proliferation of prepared meal services.

Not a bad point, Teri thought.

Finally, the girl told the other two that this was her vision, and if they wanted to be naysayers, she would change the world without them. They could just go back to being corporate slaves for thirty years while she lived her best version of herself. Teri got goosebumps hearing the familiar refrain. The reminder of Dylan disgusted her, and she was about to get up when one of the web designers made a comment that got her attention.

"You know, it really doesn't matter whether the business makes money. We're thinking about this all wrong. We're using a classical definition of success. Think back to your common core classes. It's the process that matters, not the outcome. All we need is a hundred-thousand-person database of client data. That's Google's threshold for buyouts. Once we get that, we could sell the thing and retire as millionaires. I mean, that's what we're talking about here, right? Let someone else work out how to make the money. We need to create a process that gets us to thousands of users, not one that gets us to a profitable business, right?"

She finished her discount coffee and walked back to her car.

She weighed the kid's words while her head rested on the wheel. That kid in there was obviously an idiot, but did he have a point? Was this whole debacle designed to just get users and then get sold? Had that been Dylan's vision? A text message buzzed her phone. She looked down at it. It was from her ex-FBI bounty hunter:

Target not in Charlotte. Purchased a report. Subject in Nicaragua. Flight leaves in two hours.

Damn it, thought Teri. *Nicaragua? How the hell had a part-time accountant put that together? If she knew about Nicaragua, then she knew more about The Bradshaw Group's operations than anyone else on the Earth except Teri herself. If she could piece the Nicaragua operations back to The Bradshaw Group's cashflow. Damn it. I knew I should have offed the husband last week.*

Could she be bribed? Probably not. And certainly not by her husband's bed-mate. Surely the woman couldn't find the ops-center down in Nicaragua. Teri had visited the place twice, and even she couldn't have given anyone directions as to its location. There was no way Elaine Dunaway would be able to find it. Was there? Her sorting facility was at least thirty miles past the middle of nowhere. Nothing in Nicaragua was marked. There were probably seven road signs in the whole country. There was no internet presence for non-tourist businesses. Nicaragua was in the stone age. Her on-the-ground accountant was filing their monthly taxes BY HAND, for God's sake. If you didn't speak

Spanish, you couldn't find anything.

Wait. Did the ex-wife speak Spanish?

The woman had gotten this far. Shit. She needed to know just how hard-core her ex-FBI agent really was.

She typed, **what's on the table to force signatures?**

He replied, **?**

She typed, **enhanced tactics to gain signature?**

He replied, **not sure I follow.**

She typed, **forget it-good luck.**

Okay. She he had found his limit. She'd cross that bridge if she came to it. Now she had to get back to Seattle. Teri had a lot of work to do. She looked back up at the amusement park and thought, *a lot of work.*

PART II

THE ESCAPE

36

ELAINE DUNAWAY
Present Day
San Juan Del Sur, Nicaragua

Elaine Sawyer Dunaway, now Lainey to everyone she met in Nicaragua, sat in a plastic chair facing the rolling waves of the Pacific Ocean. A Toña brand beer sweated the last of its chill onto the uneven wooden table in front of her. Palm trees waved in the light breeze on both sides of the restaurant's sand-covered deck. It was an idyllic scene. The town, Nicaragua's premier tourist destination, felt a thousand miles away from the chaos in Managua.

Lainey fled the capital days earlier as it descended into violence. The staff at her Managua hotel arranged a taxi to take her around town searching for the office of The Bradshaw Group. The search proved fruitless. Worse, the excursions got more dangerous by the hour. She gave up the day a paramilitary force stopped her taxi in front of one of the roadblocks they had retaken from the protestors. Lainey saw blood and bullet casings on the ground.

The group surrounded her car. They wore motorcycle helmets and mismatched dark clothes. Each carried a menacing automatic rifle. They poked the barrels of their rifles through the windows of the taxi and demanded money. She remembered thinking, *these aren't cops, they're bandits.*

Her shaking hands dropped a twenty in the driver's lap, and his shaking hands held it out the window. After that, they drove straight back to the hotel. She got her bag, and the young driver took her to the bus station. The hotel staff assured her that the tourist town, San Juan Del Sur, would be safe from the violence. The ride down took four hours on a beat-up old school bus that was painted in a variety of outlandish colors. Inside the packed bus, passengers watched forgotten '80s music videos on a dusty television mounted up front. Lainey recognized the channel. Just under the white script naming the song, band, and album, she saw an old, MTV logo.

She couldn't imagine how they were picking up a forty-year-old satellite signal. Hearing the old songs soothed her tense nerves as the bus put Managua further behind. The bus, she had since learned, was called a chicken bus. It did indeed haul chickens, and tubs of live frogs, and a leaky carboard box full of raw fish. Vendors got on every few stops and offered bagged drinks. The passengers ranged from well-to-do looking Nicaraguans to farmers hauling massive bags of rice. Lots of people, it appeared, had the same idea. The bus constantly stopped to pick up or drop off passengers. Each time, people had to battle their way on or off through the crowd packing the aisle before the bus took off again. When they stopped, the wind quit blowing through the open windows and the ambient temperature in the metal tube skyrocketed. She sweated profusely. Lainey had never been completely wet for such a long time. She eventually switched to a non-air-conditioned taxi in a dusty hamlet called Rivas. The bus driver himself had helpfully guided her off the bus and into one of the several empty taxis for the thirty-minute drive to San Juan Del Sur. By the time she got out of the taxi, she could see white salt lines crisscrossing her blue tank top. Hot, filthy, tired, and nervous, Lainey finally started to relax when she heard ocean waves and not automatic gunfire.

The little beachside oasis looked nearly empty. For eighteen dollars a night, she secured a room across from the beach, with air conditioning. She bought several new climate-ready wardrobes from the little shops lining the town and gave her heavy U.S. cotton clothes to the girl at the front desk. After an air-conditioned nap and a couple of sunset beers, her stress level finally started to drop.

Two days later, after she had a few surf lessons, and her surf instructor (repeatedly), Lainey Dunaway relaxed into life along the coast. Vacation mode. She felt zero guilt over the instructor. To the contrary, she surprised herself at the pride she took in bagging someone nearly half her age...she beat Alan by nearly ten years. In between sessions, she alternated between reading *Spanish for Beginners* and watching her surf instructor catch the last waves in the dying light. The beach was a good place to think, and she was thinking hard about what she was going to do now. She pulled out her phone and dialed a number in rural Alabama.

A deeply thick, Alabama accent answered, "This is the Sawyer residence."

"Hi Mom, it's me."

37

MONTANA AINSLEY
Present Day
Managua, Nicaragua

ontana and a half-full plane of passengers breezed through late night customs in Managua. He hitched a backpack over his shoulder and rolled his checked bag past the mob scene of *taxistas* and out of the airport. At the main road, he hung a left into the humid Central American night. A quarter mile down the street, he saw a fire burning in the middle of the road. A few feet on, he could tell that the road was blocked off by a combination of felled trees and stacked cobblestones. Strange. Now that he thought about it, he hadn't passed any traffic. That was strange, too. It was also strange that his flight was only half full. Now that he thought about it, there weren't any Nicaraguans on the plane.

That thought stopped him in his tracks. Something was wrong. Something was really, really wrong. Not wrong in the *we don't have Wi-Fi and my coffee is cold* sense. Something was wrong in the BBC World Service sense. The far off popping he heard? Those weren't fireworks.

He approached the roadblock tentatively, and as he got close, several teenagers materialized from behind the cobblestone wall and approached him. They had tied shirts across their faces like underfunded highwaymen. Although the bandit look was a bit scary in the partial light, none of the kids appeared armed nor displayed a threatening demeanor. They came up and asked him for a couple dollars to buy water. When he responded in Spanish, they got excited and shook his hand. When he asked them what was going on, they looked surprised.

Then they answered and he looked surprised. They filled him in on the same story Lainey Dunaway had received a few days earlier. By now, the citizens were in an unarmed state of open war with the government.

He hadn't heard any of this on the news commercials back in the States. When he left Nicaragua three weeks ago, everything was completely normal. According to the students at the roadblock, the entire country was rising up against government oppression. They had put up hundreds of roadblocks all over the country to strangle commerce and force the government out of power. Based on the haphazard state of this *tranque* and the fear in their faces, Montana guessed the government was fighting back. Fighting back and winning.

Except for some of the old Contra rebels in the north, most Nicaraguans didn't own guns. Now, it was probably impossible to get them. Just how did these kids think they could defeat a heavily armed military?

Social media, they answered. They planned to shut down the country by mobilizing everyone, and the pressure would force the president to resign. Montana didn't say so, but he harbored serious doubts about their plan. He thought of an old Emerson quotation, something like: if you're going to strike a king, you better kill him. The internet, to his knowledge, wasn't armed.

They let him pass through the roadblock after he promised to return with some water. He walked about fifty feet beyond the roadblock, bought half a dozen bottles, and returned. Over cold cups of water, the kids spilled out the story on the current situation. Both the country's major roads were blocked in the north. The protesters, students mostly, allowed local traffic and buses through, but barred commercial trucking. Backups stretched for miles all over the country. In Managua, the government placed snipers on various rooftops throughout the city, and they shot people at random to sow fear. Police commandeered all the TV stations and broadcast that the protesters were doing the killing. Across the country, Sandinista Youth Groups, known as *Las Turbas*, rode around the city, wearing masks and beating protestors with lead pipes. Initially, the protesters used social media to coordinate.

It turned out, the *turbas* had Facebook accounts, too.

They used the site to identify vocal critics of the government, and then hunted them down in their barrios. Thousands had been arrested. Two of the kids had family members who had been captured in joint police/*turba* raids. The kids had been hauled off to the dungeons of *El Chipote*. Nobody discussed their fate. Everybody knew. The students had been slow to catch on to how they were being targeted. By the time they figured it out, a lot of damage had been done. Thousands had their lives altered forever. All the kids had removed their photos from the internet. The country's Vice President, wife of the dictator, went on television nightly to read her poetry and accuse the protesters of being vampires.

You couldn't make it up if you tried.

One kid told Montana they were encouraged because the United Nations had taken their side and promised to monitor the situation. The students were lobbying for UN Peacekeepers to be deployed. Montana bid them good luck, deeply saddened at the horror visited upon these innocent children. As he walked away, he wondered how many people across the globe had died waiting on the United Nations to do anything beyond issuing statements. Just like the American legal system, if someone opted not to play along with the UN, the UN was powerless to do anything beyond issue statements and confer with itself. These poor kids were very likely surrendering their lives to buy time for a saving force that was never going to arrive.

Montana slipped his Nicaraguan sim card into his phone. He scrolled to Christian's number and hit send. Why the hell hadn't the kid called him about any of this? He got a message telling him that the subscriber number wasn't valid.

Shit.

This was a common occurrence in Nicaragua. Someone ran out of money to buy minutes and had to buy more when they got the cash. The problem was that new SIM cards came with new numbers, so he had no way to contact Chris. It sounded like the roads out to the east of the country were going to be impassable. He could fly to the Caribbean coastal town of Bluefields, but there was no way to locate Chris's mining camp up in the jungle.

Absentmindedly, he walked to his hotel while chewing over his options. As he walked into the open-air lobby, he noted how empty the place looked. There were TV's lining the walls at ceiling level, and the center of the lobby was crowded with empty tables and chairs. To his right, a couple of employees sat in front of a closed down kitchen grill. They were staring into their phones. In front of him, the woman behind the metal card table got up and gave him a fierce hug. Her name was Esmerelda, and it was her hotel. Her whole clan was from Corn Island, a small speck of land forty miles off the Caribbean coast of Nicaragua. As a part-time resident of the island himself, Montana knew the family. Like all Corn Islanders, Esmerelda grew up speaking a combination of Spanish, English, and Creole.

In her singsong Creole accent, she lit into him for his carefree appearance.

"You ain't you got the sense God gave a lizard. Why did ya not stay in the States where it safe?"

Montana gave a sarcastic laugh. "It wasn't any safer there, Esmerelda, trust me. How are things on the island? What does your family say?"

"Awww, the island fine. This a mainland problem. The government never care what goes on in the Caribbean. Mostly care about the money here, the tourism in San Juan, and the students in Leon."

Leon was Nicaragua's second largest city. Although the city of Masaya fought the government the hardest, Leon housed the busiest university in the country. As a result, it contained a lot of young people. The revolution that brought the current dictator to power had started there. If social unrest was brewing, the town of Leon would play a part. More importantly, Christian's family lived there. Montana smacked his head. *Of course.*

"Leon! Oh, Esmerelda, you beauty. I'm sorry to say, but I'm not going to be staying the night. I've gotta get up to Leon."

"Leon, he says?" And she mocked indignation to an empty hotel lobby. "Is not possible, Montana. That road closed down for days. Notin' getting up there. People say they got over tree hundred *tranques*. The whole city blocked up. Them *turbas* burning everything. They even burn the University. It a mess, Montana. You can't go there."

Montana deflated. "Well, crap. Now what am I gonna do? I can't reach my friend's family. They all live in Leon. Well, except his uncle. I think he lives in San Juan Del Sur."

Esmerlda pushed him lightly in the chest. "That's where you need to go. That's a safe place. Get the bus down to San Juan. Them roads to the south ain't blocked up yet. Get down to San Juan and wait this out. I send a *chela* tourist to there just the other day. Like you, she walk right into the middle of all this without knowing a ting about it. What's wrong with all you people in the U.S.? You ain't got no news?"

Montana waved his hand in a so-so motion. "No Ezzi, not really. But I can tell you that the President's son is being investigated for potentially receiving inflated grades from his pre-school." She looked at him quizzically. "Forget it, it would take too long to explain." He thought for a minute. "I guess I'll take that room after all and head down to San Juan in the morning. Maybe I can find the uncle."

"That's the right move, now you're making sense. I need guests anyway. A revolution is bad for business."

"Thanks, Ezzie. I'm sorry all this is happening." He paid her in U.S. dollars.

"Thanks, Montana." She paused. Montana thought she was weighing whether to ask one more question. He waved her to proceed. "Montana, you think your country come down here and help us?"

Montana paused for a long minute in thought. For Nicaraguans to ask the U.S. for aid, things must be much worse than he knew. "No, Ezzie, I'm so sorry to say, but they won't."

The answer clearly deflated her. "Cause we ain't got oil?"

"That's part of it. The U.S. also has a bad history with Nicaragua. It was one of half a dozen brush fire conflicts we bungled at the end of the last century. I'm afraid our foreign policy has been pretty...wobbly."

She laughed at his word choice. "Wobbly? Too funny, Montana. What is *wobbly?*"

"Well, it's complicated. It means our politicians do what is popular, not what's right. The problem is that what's popular changes and isn't always right. So, the policies shift constantly. Invade one day, leave the next. It makes it hard to be friends with us because you don't know if we'll be there or not. So…it's wobbly."

She shook her head. "That don't make no sense. You got the most educated people in the world. Just do right, right?"

Montana struggled for how to explain it more thoroughly, couldn't, and just summed up the scenario. "They're educated, Ezzie, but most of them are lawyers. Being courageous or doing the right thing doesn't enter into it. It's a mess. There's a reason I'm choosing a war zone."

She thought for a minute. "Well, that just don't make no sense to me, but you being in San Juan is right. I check with my family and see if planes still be flying to the island."

"Thanks, Ezzie, Thanks a lot." Montana hated explaining the U.S. system to outsiders. It always made him look stupid.

* * *

An hour later, Montana sat in the lobby with a cold Toña beer and thought over his next moves. Normally, the lobby was jammed at this late hour. This hotel, *the hotel at the end of the universe*, as Douglas Adams might call it, catered to the crowds who used the off-hour international flights in and out of Managua. As a result, the lobby was usually jammed with people around 11:00 p.m., then again around one and three in the morning. Tonight, he saw only one couple who stared into their phones. Around two, he heard popping noises in the distance.

He looked over at Esmerelda's daughter who had relieved her mother and sat behind the check-in table. She stared wide-eyed into her phone, flipping back and forth on the screen with her finger. Transfixed. The other couple got up and left to go to their room. Barely any light separated their bodies. Montana walked out to the dirt road that ran in front of the hotel. Luis, the hotel's taxi driver and Esmerelda's nephew, slept behind the wheel of his ancient Russian Lada. He popped awake as Montana's shoes crunched the dusty road. Luis spoke no English, so they exchanged greetings in Spanish, and Luis confirmed that the popping wasn't fireworks.

"It's far off. There was a rally tonight outside MetroCentro. What you're hearing is probably the police shooting up the place, but it's still pretty far off."

Montana went back to the lobby for another Toña. The morning couldn't get here soon enough. The gunfire was getting closer, and now and again loud explosions punctuated the quiet. Montana remembered the kids at the *tranque* and their *morteros*. They said they used the things to warn people that the *turbas* were approaching. He looked out at Luis. Luis was wide awake now, eyes to phone. Montana finally went to bed around 4 a.m., to the sound of semi-automatic weapons fire. Whatever was going on outside, he hoped the kids at the *tranque* were safe. The *mortero* blasts were getting awfully loud.

At 5:00 a.m., Luis drove him to the bus stop. They passed by the *tranque* Montana saw the night before. What he saw in the daylight sickened him; bullet casings and shattered glass all over the ground. The trees had been cleared away, and one entire half of the cobblestone barrier had been removed. The kids were nowhere to be seen. They passed a half a dozen more *tranques* on the way to the bus stop. Each time, Luis either negotiated their way through with bottles of water or took side streets around the barricades. Luis explained that the soldiers weren't up this early, so all the *tranques* were safely occupied by students or other young protesters. By early afternoon, he said, you had to head indoors.

Montana eventually made it to the bus and on towards San Juan Del Sur. On the road, the bus passed hundreds of eighteen-wheeler trucks, all abandoned on the side of the road. They lined the northbound side for the first hour of the trip. He also noticed roadblocks being built the whole way south. He had to find Chris's uncle in San Juan and get a hold of his young friend before the whole country shut down.

38

TERI BRADSHAW
Present Day
Seattle, Washington

Teri wasted no time once she was back in Seattle. She spent most of the flight home researching the kid's comments about database size and tech buyouts. The *mauldy* guy sitting beside her in first class wasted her first half hour trying to engage her in conversation. When he nodded off, Teri wrote "not if you were the last fucking person on earth" on a napkin, stabbed her drink sword through it, and left it on his tray table. When he awoke and saw the note, he kept to himself.

Her now uninterrupted research led her to believe that while the techie kid based the claim on rumor, there was some evidence of an informal structure in place. Most of the buyouts were done by big public companies, so that information had to be public. Teri had waded through available income statements and annual call transcripts. It was like reading Dylan's memoirs; paragraphs of words that, when added together, meant nothing. That said, an awful lot of small companies had been bought up far before they reached, or even planned to reach, profitability.

Companies Teri had never heard of got snapped up before their products or services reached even regional launches. She could extrapolate, based on the limited info she could find, that most of the acquired firms were quickly rising up the ranks in user terms.

In summary, while the kid was precisely wrong, he might have been directionally correct. She may yet turn this around. She'd have to loop in that weak-kneed lawyer, Dunaway. He might be a lot of things, but well connected was definitely one of them. He was a franchise lawyer. Franchises were owned by big money. Teri was gonna need big money for what she had planned.

* * *

Within a week, Teri had her plan implemented. Her sole job now entailed monitoring The Wheel of Wonder. The park attendance numbers were climbing. Dunaway had sent feelers out to his biggest franchise investors, and there was interest. Teri conducted a round of initial meetings-there was interest. She bribed every magazine and online outlet she could think of to write about the park. Or the wheel, or whatever she was supposed to call it. Bloggers were easy. They'd never seen a three-thousand-dollar payment, so she had four dozen of them on the payroll. Everything was in the works.

She would raise the park's profile through the media; the pictures themselves would be stunning enough to interest reporters. Once she hit about a million users, she'd aggressively pitch her new big-tech contacts. Even selling at a small loss would be fine. Anything to unload this financial Hindenburg.

Earlier in the morning, she'd approved payments to a dozen bloggers, and she was in the middle of reading their reviews when her phone rang. It was the bounty hunter chasing Elaine Dunaway. *Where was he? Costa Rica?*

She hit the speaker button and continued reading.

"Teri Bradshaw."

"Good morning, Miss Bradshaw. Do you know who this is?"

His cloak-and-dagger stuff nauseated Teri. "Yeah, Columbo, you have news?" She asked in a flat tone.

One blogger referred to the Wheel of Wonder as "our first Wonder of the Modern World." Teri liked it. That idea would get attention.

"Not good news, I'm afraid, ma'am. I tracked the target to Central America based on credit card spending. I have a contact with the bureau." He paused so she would be impressed. She wasn't. "So anyway, I proceeded to follow the target here, but there's a problem."

"Can't find her?"

"Well, yes ma'am. That's part of it. The other part is, well, the country is in the midst of a revolution."

Teri shook her head and scrunched her face. Did that one blogger actually compare his experience at the park to the moon landing? *Jesus, now that was overselling it to the point of absurdity. Why not just admit you are a paid shill?*

Distractedly, she called into the speaker phone, "Come again?"

"Yes ma'am. A revolution."

"You have to be kidding. Like bullets and bombs revolution, or like whining in the street, social media revolution?"

"No, ma'am. I'm not kidding. Most of the roads are barricaded, and there is automatic weapons fire on a pretty consistent basis. I can rent a motorcycle to dodge the roadblocks, but I'm afraid I am having trouble accessing a weapon. Quite frankly, I'm not at all comfortable being in this situation unarmed. My reading of the target's file suggests she wouldn't be inclined to remain in an unstable environment such as this. My plan is to stake the airport for two more days. If she doesn't show, I will get an update from the credit bureau and take my search further afield."

"Okay, makes sense to me. Keep me informed."

"Yes, ma'am. Out."

Teri hit the hang-up button.

Out? Please.

Her phone buzzed again. It was Alice. "Ms. Bradshaw, just an update that the Atlanta park has hit one hundred thousand registered guests."

Teri thanked her and got her mind back into the game. Her bounty hunter would handle his job. He was former FBI, after all. She was so consumed by the Wonderwheel attendance numbers that it didn't even register in her head what the former agent had told her. Nicaragua was coming apart. Her Nicaragua. The Bradshaw Group's operational headquarters Nicaragua. Distracted, Teri failed to connect the dots.

39

MONTANA AINSLEY
Present Day
San Juan Del Sur, Nicaragua

It took Montana two hours to find Christian's uncle. Nicaraguan society centered around social interaction, and San Juan Del Sur was a small town. With virtually no tourists left, the locals gathered together to drink beers and listen to radio updates about the current situation. At the first gathering Montana tried, he met a guy who knew everybody, and that guy knew a guy from Leon. That guy wasn't Chris's uncle, but he knew the entire Leonese society in San Juan Del Sur. Turned out, Chris's uncle owned a small restaurant in town featuring typical Nicaraguan dishes for three bucks a head. Montana found it without trouble. It looked deserted.

Three bucks a head, and the place was empty? Not a good sign.

Two guys played dice at a front table and listened to the radio. When Montana approached, they looked up and asked, in English, if he wanted something to eat. He explained, in Spanish, who he was and how he was trying to get a hold of his friend's uncle.

"*Dios Mío*, you're the *chele* Chris is always talking about." One of the players got up and hugged him. "That's for saving my niece. I'm so glad you're here. He needs your help. He got attacked up by the *turbas* in Managua."

The uncle explained what had happened in the Capital, and that Chris left and went into hiding. Together, they called the boy's family in Leon. The entire family was relieved that Montana had arrived. They didn't know where Chris had hidden, but they had a phone number.

Within minutes, he was dialing the number.

"*Hola*?"

"Chris, it's me, Montana." They both breathed out a huge sigh of relief. "Are you okay? Where are you?"

* * *

After hanging up, Montana took a stroll on the crescent shaped beach of San Juan Del Sur. Chris had hightailed it back to the Caribbean, and he was holed up at his jungle campsite. Montana got directions and told Chris to hang tight while he worked on a plan to get out there.

Out on the beach, Montana saw only a dozen people milling about in the water. A far cry from the thousands that normally populated the emerald coast beaches.

How to get from San Juan Del Sur, in the very southwest of Nicaragua, to Blue-fields, at the very eastern edge?

In between the two locations, the situation on the ground had become deadly. The government had killed another two dozen of the protestors the previous night. In response, roadblocks had gone up everywhere, and people had stopped going to work. Schools and all non-governmental offices closed indefinitely. A national strike had been called for. They scheduled it to last for days.

As Montana walked through the surf, he racked his brain for ideas on crossing the country. A motorcycle would be too dangerous. It would take days, and the likelihood of being robbed by the *turbas* was too high. The buses, if they were even running, couldn't make it past the roadblocks in under a week. Up ahead, he saw the old fishing trawler that had been blown into the shoreline by the last hurricane. The old boat was half buried, nose first, into the sand. Nicaragua suffered a hurricane about every ten years, and the most recent one wreaked havoc on San Juan Del Sur. Unable to unbury what mother nature had seen fit to bury, some enterprising local converted the landmark into a bar. A lone customer sat amidst a dozen empty tables. A deep tan. Blonde hair. Bikini top. A beer and a book. *Tourist.*

Montana approached and said, "Hope I'm not crowding you. All the other tables are reserved." She laughed politely and waved her hand for him to sit.

"Do I detect a southern accent," she asked. "And how did you know I speak English?"

"Indeed, ma'am." He thickened the accent. "Tennessee by way of Auburn."

"Oh wow, my mother lives in Alabama. Lower Alabama, as they say down there, so she's on your side of the great divide. I'm from North Carolina."

"No kidding. Great place. Super clean…Charlotte, that is, not lower Alabama." He paused while she laughed, then asked, "So you're a tourist who picked the wrong time?"

"Maybe, what makes you assume I'm a tourist? Maybe I retired down here?"

Montana sensed the prickle in her voice. It made him weary. If they were in the U.S., he would have gotten up and left. But this was his turf and pointless outrage had no place here. She could either take a joke, or she'd be on the first flight out.

"Yeah, maybe, but there's a tag sticking out of the back of your bikini top."

She reached behind herself and felt the tag, then ripped it off. She looked at the torn tag, chuckled to herself, then stared out at the ocean.

"You got me. I arrived a couple days ago, and to tell you the truth, if it weren't for what was going on, I'm not sure I'd leave."

Montana filled out her profile instantly. The far-away look, the dreamy tone of her voice. She was on the run from a bad personal situation. San Juan Del Sur drew them by the truckload. She was either trying to start her life over or trying to match someone else's betrayal. Nicaragua's beautiful beaches and cheap prices made an excellent pre- or post-divorce getaway.

"Yeah, this place does that to a lot of people. I'm Montana." She finally turned her attention toward him.

"Hi, Montana, I'm Lainey." They raised beers in a toast. "Montana? Were your parents archeologists?"

It was his turn to laugh.

"Wrong state, but no, I was born there. My folks weren't the creative types."
She laughed politely. "So how long you going to stay, now that everything has
gone ass over teakettle?"

"Wow, you did live in the south. My mother says that." The comment made
him feel very old. "I'm not sure," she said, glancing back toward the water. "I
was going to leave, but I don't really have too much to go back to, so I think I'll
see how things play out with the political mess."

"No kidding." He was genuinely surprised. "Most of you guys get a couple
weeks, decide you miss home delivery, and head back. Add a war to that, and
I'm impressed you're still here."

"Most of us?" she eyed him warily. Montana sensed the outrage bubbling up
again, but pressed ahead, trying to see how long it would take her to call his
comments unacceptable.

"Yeah, divorcees. It's pretty common for them, both men and women, to
come down here on the cheap to forget about life for a while, as Billy Joel might
say. Spend a few weeks draining beers, whoring a tad, and then heading back
to overpriced coffee and stress. It's kind of a *thing*." Montana barely contained
his laughter as he prepared for the inevitable word.

To his surprise, she smiled at him, raised her beer, and said, "Is trying to piss
off women your pickup thing?"

"Me, nah, I'm not trying to pick you up. I'm just chatting. You're a gringa,
not my thing." That, Montana thought, had to drive her over the edge.

The woman looked skyward in thought, then surprised Montana by laughing.
Really laughing, then saying, "Makes sense to me. A month ago, I bet I'd have
been pissed. Now, down here in bullet-riddled paradise, I guess I'm realizing
what's worth being offended about and what isn't. Besides, I'm outside the U.S.
so I can admit when I'm wrong. That, and I've got guilt over the whoring thing."

Montana nearly spit out his beer laughing. Not the response he expected.

As if on cue, a hot-bodied local guy approached, slammed a wet surfboard
into the ground, and draped his arm around the woman as he sat. The gesture
of a young wolf protecting its turf. Lainey eyes perked up at Montana as if to
say, *see, told ya*. She out-aged the kid by a good fifteen years.

The kid stuck out his chin and asked Montana if he surfed.

Montana thought about messing with him. He really wasn't there to pick up on Lainey, or to tease her. He was just bored and killing time while he figured out a solution to his travel problem.

"Relax." Montana said in Spanish. "I'm not here to try and steal your girl. We are just talking." In English he said, "I do surf, and probably better than you."

The kid took a minute to process his statement. "Let's see it, old man."

"Tell you what," Montana said, "you go first, and I'll use your board when you come in. I don't have my board with me, and it wouldn't be fair for me to use a cheap, unwaxed one." The kid thought about it. Montana figured he was weighing whether to leave his girl alone versus win a bet. A kid that age couldn't let go of a challenge, especially one he would obviously win.

"Fifty bucks," Montana taunted, sensing the kid wavering. In this political climate, fifty bucks went a long way.

The kid smiled. The girl lost.

He jumped up, grabbed his board, and headed back to the surf at a half jog.

Lainey let out a sarcastic laugh. Then she narrowed her eyes at Montana and let out an actual laugh. "You have no intention of going out there, do you?"

"Not a bit," he said, smiling. "The advantage of being an old man. We're smarter, and we can part with fifty bucks."

"That's cruel. And you're not that old. Cruel, but not that old."

"Thanks. New boyfriend?"

She looked embarrassed. "He was teaching me to surf and…" She trailed off, shook her head, and facepalmed. "God, I'm a horrible person. He's just a kid, isn't he?"

"Relax. He is an adult. First rule down here, all the taboos from the States don't pass through customs. Foreign guys date younger women, foreign women date younger guys. Everybody has fun, everyone is an adult, nobody cares. It's kind of a *thing*."

40

LAINEY (FORMERLY ELAINE) DUNAWAY
Present Day
San Juan Del Sur, Nicaragua

The guy, Montana, surprised Lainey with his openness on the subject of sex with a younger man. Still embarrassed, she turned her face away to marshal her pride.

Six months ago, she couldn't differentiate a Monday in June from a Thursday in September. Every day had a pathetic sameness to it. Her husband had been sleeping with a client for nearly a year. She spent her life staring at numbers or following her daughter's college experience on social media. She ate polite lunches with her friends and attended client dinners when Alan needed her as a prop.

A few weeks ago, her life focus changed to tracking the corruption of Teri Bradshaw; wrecker of homes. She hopped a flight to Nicaragua with nothing but the clothes on her back. Less than a week ago, a taxi ride felt like it would end in Lainey being sold as a sex slave. Shortly after, she got robbed staring down the barrel of an AK-47. Now she sat in a beachfront bar, having a beer with a decent looking, albeit, kind of rough guy. The other guy, who was roughly her daughter's age, and who she'd spent the last three nights screwing, bobbed on a surfboard out in the bay. She was surrounded by ocean, sand, and the smell of coconut oil. How in the world had she wound up here?

"Twenty years younger than me." The guy, Montana, had been talking and Lainey's mind just heard the last comment.

"Huh? Sorry, I spaced out for a second there."

"I said, the first girl I dated here was twenty years younger than me."

"Twenty years!"

"Hey, she taught me how to use a smartphone."

The comment made her laugh and eased some of her tension. "Okay, okay," she admitted between cackles. "I admit it. Shame on me. My daughter is about his age. What can I say? I'm a cliché. I'm getting divorced, and somehow, sleeping with a younger man…I dunno, it made me feel…" She took a gulp of beer to cover the blank spot where her tongue had abandoned her.

"Younger," he suggested.

"Yeah. Maybe. I know, that sounds melodramatic. I guess I just needed it. I suppose I'm a statistic now, huh?"

"Hey, being in a bad marriage is a statistic, too. Look at it this way, you're officially a cougar with one trophy. Down here, some people are after us for our money, and we're after them for their youth. It's a social contract. Think of it like an MBA for real life. They don't want to go through their twenties or thirties being broke, so they're skipping that stage by hanging around us. If you've really got a problem sleeping with younger guys, you came to the wrong rodeo."

Lainey remembered her own reason for marrying Alan all those years ago. Was her life really moving in reverse? The thought was strangely encouraging.

She looked at the guy with his crooked smirk. "I mean, my mind gets it, but my body…wait, no, that's backwards. My body gets it." That made them both laugh again.

"It's my mind that can't wrap around the concept. I guess it's just so backwards from the norm. We're kinda wired differently."

"Like I said, check it all at customs."

"Do you really believe that or is that just the guy rationale?" She eyed him skeptically, but in the back of her mind, she hoped he could make a good argument and assuage her lingering guilt.

"I don't know, but I've seen enough marriages down here to think there is at least something to it. Think of it this way: if you "married well" among your friends it probably meant you got a BMW while they got minivans. To marry well down here? That means the first kid to go to college. It means your parents get to live longer because they have real healthcare. It means never wondering if there is gonna be dinner. The practice probably wasn't so strange in the U.S. a while back. Look around, you see a lot of other ways for some of the locals to change their family's trajectory? Maybe that's just a rationalization, but it makes sense to me, and it isn't just a guy thing, obviously." He locked eyes with her and raised his eyebrows.

She got the message. *Damn,* she thought, *I don't want to tell you this buddy, but it makes an awful lot of sense in my mind, too.*

"I don't know, Lainey, you tell me. What was your happiness meter pegged at in the States?"

His smirk reappeared-like he already knew he was right. But it wasn't a lawyer's self-satisfied smirk. He had the look of genuine confidence.

"Okay, okay. Ugh. Fair point," she admitted, then buried her face in her hands, miming misery. Talking into her palms she said, "Okay, so what about you? I've been embarrassed enough today, thanks. What about you, Montana. Did you come down here to wife shop?"

"No, uh, not exactly." He went on to outline, in general terms, his situation. He'd just come back from closing out affairs in the states. He had to meet this friend of his on the Caribbean side but couldn't figure out how to get there.

"So, wait," she said, stopping him. "You live here? Where?"

"Caribbean side."

They talked and laughed for another couple rounds of beers. There was something about this guy that Lainey really liked. She tried to zero in on it, but her surfer returned and slammed the board into the sand. "Beat that."

Montana handed him fifty dollars. "You win."

There was a tense minute before all three burst out laughing. The kid dropped back into the chair and replaced a wet, clammy arm over Lainey's shoulders. It felt a bit weird now. Not just him being so young, but with Montana sitting there. There was something about the new guy's presence that unsettled her a little. She suddenly didn't feel like letting this younger guy claim her as a possession.

She saw the kid trying to glare at Montana, and she wanted to intervene, but he spoke first.

"Relax man, I don't date gringas. They're too pushy. Besides, she is just using you."

That brought another round of laughter and wiped the remaining tension. The three of them talked and laughed as the sun faded to orange over the sea.

Lainey hadn't felt this good in decades. She sat here drinking with two guys, one half her age, and they were lightly sparring over her. She had spent her nights clawing at the rock-hard body of her surf instructor, and her days surfing and drinking. This was not how Elaine Dunaway behaved. But maybe Lainey Dunaway did.

This new guy wasn't bad looking. His green eyes had an amazing sparkle in them. But that wasn't it. That wasn't his...power. He had this weird confidence. Everything that came out of his mouth sounded so final, like it had been debated and settled a hundred years earlier. And he spoke with a total lack of bullshit. She hadn't heard plain English in years.

Now that she considered it, Lainey had grown tired of the pains her friends took to avoid speaking in direct terms. Everyone was afraid every little word would bother someone. This guy, Montana, just threw it out there. Fewest words possible with the most truth available. Like there was just no doubt in him at all. Was that what it was about him? Confidence? No, that wasn't it. Well, yes, but that wasn't what made him appealing. Relaxed. That was part of it. He was so relaxed. And he *completely* ignored all the social norms she had grown up with. It was like he was...liberated. That was it. He was liberated like she wanted to be.

She tuned back into the conversation the boys were having.

"So, I'm not sure what to do, man. Do you have any ideas? How the hell do I get across Nicaragua?" She recalled him telling her about his travel problem.

"No, *prix*, there is no travel right now. There is no nothing. My family lives in Managua, and nobody is going to work. Nicaragua is closed for business right now."

"What's Corn Island like?" Lainey asked. "I read about it. It's supposed to be stunning."

Her surf instructor answered, "It's beautiful. It's the most beautiful place in Nicaragua. Clear water, white sand...it's paradise. Except that you can't really surf that side."

"I wanna see it."

"Me, too," Montana said with a frown, "I live there."

"You live there!" Lainey and her instructor said in unison.

"Yeah, and I need to get back. Well, close enough."

They all sat there, staring at the table for a minute.

"Wait a sec," Lainey said, breaking the trance. "Isn't there an airport up in Playa Colorado? Esmerelda or something?"

Montana stared at her open-mouthed. Her surf instructor pulled his head back and looked at her quizzically.

"Yeah, y'all, there is an airport up there. I know it. I looked at renting a place up there, and I could have flown straight in there. Can we get up to Playa Colorado? Where is that?"

"It's..." Montana started slowly, "it's outside of Tola. Yeah" He looked at her like she just cured cancer. The he repeated, "It's just outside of Tola. I totally forgot about it. Lainey, you're a genius. And yeah. Yeah, I can get there." His tone sped up, locking in on a plan. "The roadblocks are all on the main roads, right?" He looked at her surf instructor but didn't wait for a reply. "I can cut right out in front of Rivas and double back. I'd need to...I'd need to rent a car."

"We," she said, just a hint of booze at the edges of her voice, "we're gonna need four-wheel drive in case the roads are washed out." Lainey turned to her instructor. "Who rents trucks in town?" He just stared at her. She snapped her fingers in front of his face twice. "Hello? Trucks?"

"Oh. Um, Vladimir. Over close to the Freedom Hostel. But you gotta pay cash. Are you serious? You're going with him? You are going to leave me?"

"Oh, please." Lainey pointed at the silhouettes of two girls walking in the surf. "Go teach them how to surf. Maybe I'll be back in a few days, and we can pick it back up." She gave him a peck on the lips. "You're a great guy." She turned to Montana. "Ready?"

He had a crooked smile on his face and squinted through those sparkling green eyes. "You're just a tad crazy, aren't you?"

She laughed. "Maybe. But you know what? Life is short."

As her instructor walked off toward the two girls, Montana touched her on the arm. "Hey, you don't have to do this. I mean, thanks a million for…"

"Save it." She smiled. "This is the only way I'm going to be able to get to see the Caribbean side. Besides, you're going to owe me huge. I haven't told you yet, but I'm actually in Nicaragua to find something, and you're going to help me find it."

He processed her comment for a second. "Should I be worried?"

She was about to give him an honest answer, but she hadn't flirted in years, and she was drunk with the pleasure of the feeling. She tossed her hair over her shoulder and patted his bicep.

"I won't torture you too badly."

They agreed to meet in an hour in front of her hotel. As they parted company, Lainey thought, *I'm not sure where exactly you went, Elaine Dunaway, but I'm not so sure I'm going to need you for this.*

41

TERI BRADSHAW
Present Day
Seattle, Washington

Teri had been on the phone with Alan Dunaway for nearly twenty minutes. She felt like she needed a shower. The haughtiness. That ingratiating tone. She should have stabbed him a week ago. He'd tried to whine about his divorce, but Teri cut that off at the pass and informed him they couldn't sleep together anymore. Queue the water works.

Just when exactly had men become so whiney?

And she'd slept with this guy? *Ugh*. She ended the call by reassuring him their professional relationship remained intact. Lawyers could stomach personal disappointment as long as cash kept flowing in. That kept the lawyer connected by one last string. When she snipped that, she figured he'd end it himself, so there was really no need to stab him. A purely mathematical decision.

He had secured meetings with three of the biggest franchise-owning venture capital funds in the U.S. and Saudi Arabia. The Saudis were interested because they could transfer employees into the U.S. under the renewed HB-1 Visa program. Teri wasn't entirely comfortable with that, but money was money. The country could fend for itself. She wasn't DHS.

The American firms drooled over the projected size of the client database. In just over a week, the three locations had logged nearly five hundred thousand visitors. The Atlanta location was really exceeding…no, that was the wrong word, Teri thought. The Atlanta location was sucking less than the others.

They were on pace to blow past Six Flags attendance figures, but that was where the comparison stopped. The financials were abysmal. The parks averaged less than twenty bucks a head in revenue. Sure, the pure revenue number looked good, but she had a bad feeling it was one-time revenue that wouldn't repeat. After all, how many times could you take a selfie climbing Everest? Worse still, when you evaluated it like a real business and subtracted expenses…she didn't even want to remember the one time she'd done that.

To the potential investors, Teri had positioned *that* little poison pill as a one-time cost of client acquisition. Her pitch was that it was Disneyworld for Millennials, and that they were flocking to it in droves. After all, rollercoasters weren't photogenic. Rollercoasters were old. Roller coasters were dangerous. Teri didn't mention that rollercoasters didn't operate on an inverted net income curve.

So far, nobody seemed interested beyond the pure revenue figures. The notion brought her mind back to the market crash of 2000. She remembered Nortel Networks putting up a white flag, and everyone ignoring it. She remembered the headlines about how only revenue mattered. *Idiots.* Then she remembered that awful market crash in 2008. A part of her wondered if they were headed off that same cliff. If so, it was past time to get off this ride.

The Saudi firm hadn't even asked about her franchisee commitments. It didn't seem to matter to anyone that this entire venture was a complete money pit. The more guests that piled in, the more money the parks lost since Dylan had priced all the ancillary services at a loss, and over half the guests weren't even paying entrance fees. The buzz, which she had paid for, was really all that mattered to her potential investors. She was going to be able to dump this giant disaster. She could just feel it.

Then her phone buzzed. "Yes, Alice?"

"Ms. Bradshaw, I've got a conference call from The Board holding on line two."

The Board? The TSA Lottery Board? Why would they be calling her? Why would they even be meeting?

"Okay, put them through." Click. Click. "Hello, this is Teri."

"Good afternoon, Ms. Bradshaw."

They went through brief salutations and identified who was on the call.

"Teri, we're calling to get your position on the developments in Nicaragua."

Her head jerked back. Nicaragua? Why were they asking about Nicaragua? Had she just heard something about Nicaragua? Her investigator? Didn't he say…the penny dropped.

Oh shit.

When she didn't respond, one of the voices on the phone prodded her by saying, "We had a supply backup at one of the warehouses, and while looking into it, we found some seriously concerning news. If you were not aware, there is civil unrest throughout the country, and a national strike has begun. Since Nicaragua is a vital interest to all of us, we wanted to reach out and see what you had in mind to deal with the situation. We have been unable to contact anyone down there, and product shipments have been cancelled both into and out of the country. We're calling to get your thoughts on contingency planning and how we proceed."

My thought, Teri mused, *is that we're fucked. Totally and completely fucked.*

"Gentlemen, I've been closely monitoring the situation on the ground. I'm negotiating alternative arrangements as we speak, but as you might imagine, that is taking a bit longer than I had hoped. Nicaragua was, shall we say, unique in its antiquated business reporting methods. Finding a suitable alternative has been a challenge, but I believe I am close to re-directing our efforts so that we can re-establish business as usual."

That was all they wanted to hear. The call was over in five minutes, but the problem sure as shit wasn't. They'd caught her totally flat-footed.

You'd think the goddamn news would report civil unrest inside our own goddamn hemisphere. Jesus, Central America ended with the fucking word America… maybe it was worth talking about!

She hadn't been in contact with anyone in Central America for months. Teri spent the next half hour trying to contact anyone she could in Nicaragua. Nothing. All cellular communication was down, even the Wi-Fi calls went nowhere. Her employees' social media accounts were erased. She was just staring into space when inspiration finally hit. She reached out to the head of airport ground personnel at Miami International. Tammy had dozens of Nicaraguan vendors working for her. Surely, Tammy could give her a heads up. When she got Tammy on the phone, the news got worse.

All Tammy's people were in an uproar. Half of them couldn't get through to their families, and the other half relayed horrible news. According to Tammy, the government had gone on a five-day shooting spree, and the citizens had responded by blocking off all the roads. The ports closed to commercial traffic because the employees wouldn't go out on the streets after noon. U.S. based air-carriers were cancelling flights, and the situation deteriorated by the hour.

Teri couldn't find anything on the U.S. news sites, so she logged into Al-Jazeera to get some actual news. The pictures looked awful. Burning tires, people in masks, people with guns. No way her operation, hidden in the outskirts of the port city of Corinto, was online. Her just-in-time shipping methods meant that thousands of orders were going to go unfilled. It also meant that re-filled water bottles weren't going to be headed back to the U.S.. This meant her vendors would have nothing to sell. Worse, all the items collected by the TSA teams were apparently standing around in plain sight, just waiting to get seen by some diligent cop or customs agent. A mountain of stolen goods, growing higher and higher by the day. All her shipping containers were either stranded off the coasts or being sent back to their point of embarkation.

Disaster didn't even begin to describe this. This made Wonderwheel look like a dispute with a fucking vending machine. The TSA lottery might mean jail.

42

THE ROBINSON HOUSEHOLD
Present Day
Matthews, North Carolina

Brian and Jane Robinson sat on the old couch in their living room, holding on to each other like teenagers about to leave for different colleges. The sun would be up in an hour. Neither had slept. Their faces were puffy and red from crying. They had just suffered through the worst night of their marriage. Their two girls were upstairs asleep, having cried themselves to sleep hours earlier. It seemed like the whole family had been crying ever since they purchased a Mother's Little Helper franchise for their youngest daughter, Maize.

The family had come home earlier to find the latest settlement offer from the franchisor, Mother's Little Helper. They put the kids to bed, then read the offer. They made a quick call to their attorney and hung up. The fight broke out in minutes. Blame, bankruptcy, divorce, the children, in-laws…they'd fought over it all. They weaponized every marital slight from the past fifteen years. Most married couples have some version of this fight. The Robinsons' was epic.

The girls, seven and four years of age, came to the foot of the stairs and instantly burst into tears at the sight of their parents fighting, again. Then Melly attacked Maize for causing her to have to leave her school. Both kids melted into heaving sobs. It took hours to get them back to sleep. The joint effort brought the two adults back to the diaper days and the forgotten nights of trading-off a few hours of sleep.

Team effort. Misery forgotten.

For just an instant.

The offer sat on the coffee table like a malignant cancer. It was signed by Alan Dunaway, attorney for the plaintiff. The offer was fourteen pages long, but it boiled down to three things: Pay $12,000 in restitution. Pay $140,000 in legal fees. Pay it now. The offer expired in thirty-six hours.

They owed $45,000 to their own attorney. All their credit was maxed. If they sold the house, they could pay their lawyer and keep less than five hundred dollars. Now that real estate prices were softening, even that window appeared to be closing. Their attorney advised them that if they couldn't pay, the court would submit wage garnishment notifications to their employers, and those orders would follow them from employer to employer until the amount was paid off. Their own attorney, so confident at the beginning, appeared eager to settle now. It was no mystery to the Robinsons why he had lost heart.

Brian was an untenured high school history teacher. A wage garnishment would be the end of that job. Janie's freelance work wasn't consistent enough to support them.

So, they fought until they battled in a complete circle; from love to blame, from blame to anger, to loathing, to divorce, and finally back to love. They had wrecked their lives, and now they were all they had. That was clear. But they had also wrecked the lives of the children they were put on earth to protect. They considered giving the children to Janie's parents to raise.

All this...over a goddamned lemonade stand.

They just stared at the TV, sound off, tears rolling down their cheeks, acid roiling in their stomachs, praying that a new day wouldn't dawn. When, as a parent, you've considered giving up your children, hope is a word without meaning.

Jane's phone vibrated. She glanced down without interest. Private caller. She ignored it, went back to staring at nothing. It vibrated again. Private caller.

"Just answer it, baby. I need to get up and clean up for work anyway. Maybe it's a new contract job for you. Those calls usually come at weird hours. We could use some good news." Brian let out a long sigh. "God. What a horrible,

horrible night." He kissed the top of his wife's head. "I love you so much." Fresh tears started rolling down his cheeks as he said it.

"I know, baby, I love you, too. And I don't know how, but we're going to find a way through this."

In Brian's mind, there was no way out. Jane's head was on his chest as she answered her phone. His hand covered his eyes to try and blot out the reality of their lives. It was 6:00 a.m.

"Hello, this is Jane."

"Mrs. Jane Robinson?" Jane didn't recognize the voice. She had never heard a southern accent so thick.

"This is Jane."

"Hello Jane, you don't know me. My name is Paige Ellen Sawyer." Every word had at least two syllables. "For quite some time, Alan Dunaway had been a member of my family…through marriage, fortunately. Happily, I am no longer constrained by familial commitment of support."

Did she say supp-awat.

Jane was so surprised it took her mind a second to engage. "Um…okay. This is a bit weird. My husband is right here. Can I put you on speaker?" She pulled away from Brian and pushed the speaker button on her phone, holding it between them. Brian mouthed, *what the hell?*

To Brian's surprise, a near perfect replica of Scarlett O'Hara's came through the tinny speaker. "Of course. Of course. I'm terribly sorry. I've forgotten your husband's name?"

Brian mouthed, *yaw-ah?* Jane actually smiled and pinched him to stop.

"Brian, this is Brian. And who is this?"

"Hi Brian, this is Paige Ellen Sawyer. I'm the former mother-in-law of Alan Dunaway. I assume you are both acquainted with my less than scrupulous former son-in-law."

"We are" the Robinsons said in unison, still stifling giggles.

"Wonderful, thank you for taking my call. I have to warn you both, I am calling from a cellular telephone in Alabama." The words were so spaced out it was almost a question. "That's why the connection might be a bit poor." Jane mouthed to Brian, *poo-wah?*

239

"I am calling because my daughter used to work as an accountant at the Dunaway firm, so she is very familiar with your case. She has sent me a letter, through the email, if you can believe such, and she asked that I call and inform you both before she sent it herself. The letter begins, Dear Jane and Brian, as you both probably know, the case against you all is a pile… of horse manure."

The woman paused for a second, then said, "Pardon my French, but my daughter made expanded use of a vocabulary word of which I do not approve. It appears I have failed in several respects as a mother."

Both the Robinsons laughed, as Jane said, "It's okay, Mrs. Sawyer, please continue."

"Of course," she said, making a three-syllable word out of *course*. "The long and short of the letter is that the franchise knew they broke your contract, did so intentionally, and figured they would use the legal system to bankrupt you if you tried to fight them. There are several additional documents attached to this letter. Lainey tells me they're from her ex-husband's law firm proving this. Apparently, it is standard practice to hide evidence since so few cases see trial nowadays."

Tears rolled down Jane Robinson's cheeks as she started laughing. Hearing someone say those words, even some crazy lady who sounded like Mark Twain's wife…it couldn't be real.

"The letter goes on at some length about your business insurance. Lainey seems to believe that y'all are covered under the false advertising provision and that you can reclaim your fees, but I assume she explains all that in more detail in her letter."

The woman on the phone went silent to let that sink in.

"Wait, Ms. Sawyer, are you serious? Are you sure? I mean…really?" Jane asked. Her desperation obvious.

In a haughty, prideful tone, the woman responded, "My dear Mrs. Robinson, if my daughter uttered the words, you can assume it as a lost gospel verse. Now, can one of you dear children please walk me through how to forward an email."

The three of them spoke for a few more minutes before the Robinsons exhausted themselves thanking the woman. Then Jane pressed end and dropped the phone. It pinged again indicating that she had just received an email.

"Babe, we're never making fun of a southern accent again," Brian said, speaking in a monotone and still staring at the phone.

They hugged tighter than they ever had, sobbing tears of joy.

43

LAINEY DUNAWAY
Present Day
Bluefields, Nicaragua

To Lainey, the Bluefields airport didn't appear open, or whatever you called an airport. Really, you couldn't call it an airport, anyway. It was more of a dilapidated airstrip connected to a low-slung building by a walkway covered by a blue awning. Lainey and Montana had exchanged stories for the entire two-hour flight. They'd touched down in Managua, picked up zero passengers, and then taken off again within fifteen minutes. As they talked on the plane, Lainey explained her mission in Nicaragua. She admitted that she had flailed away in Managua looking for the local office of The Bradshaw Group before heading for the safety of San Juan Del Sur when the situation got too dangerous.

Montana had been a bit more vague. He explained that his young Nicaraguan business partner had gotten himself into some trouble up in the jungle north of Bluefields and needed Montana to create an escape plan for the team up there. The whole thing sounded mysterious to Lainey, and it was obvious Montana was leaving something out. She couldn't blame him. They barely knew each other, but the incredible circumstances did allow them quite a bit more honesty than was typical for people who had just met. They met under pressure. Pressure changes relationships.

Lainey felt more comfortable with him as each kilometer passed under their feet. He had offered her the use of his house on Corn Island if she decided she didn't want any part of his crazy adventure, but she had declined. She preferred the adventure. Elaine Dunaway had spent a lifetime being bored. Lainey Dunaway wasn't wasting another minute. By the time they touched down, they were old friends.

Their plane stopped at the end of the runway. It was done taxiing. As the engines wound down, Montana and Lainey got up to leave. As they did, the pilot came out of the cockpit, and he and Montana had a conversation in Spanish. Montana then reached in his pocket, withdrew a slip of paper, and wrote a string of numbers on it. The two men shook hands, and all three exited the plane.

"What was that all about?" she asked him.

"Oh, he was hoping we'd want to keep going to Big Corn Island. He has a girl on the island. I told him we weren't, but that we might after the weekend. I offered him the use of the house for the weekend if he wanted. I just gave him my number, directions, and the code to give to the housekeeper. Never hurts to bank a favor with a pilot."

"But…he works for the airline, Las Costeña or whatever, doesn't he? How can he just take the plane? Isn't there…I don't know. Aren't there rules?"

"Yeahhh, about that, Lainey. You gotta get into the flow a bit down here." He laughed. "Things just don't always follow a set pattern of rules here. My guess is that the plane was going to develop a mechanical problem once he landed on Big Corn."

They were both laughing as they breezed through the tiny airport. Montana's guy, Christian, was standing in front of an old truck waiting for them. He and Montana hugged. He looked about fourteen years old.

Montana introduced Lainey, and the little Nicaraguan kid didn't blink for next twenty seconds. When he snapped to, his cheeks flushed, and he stuck out his hand. Lainey grabbed him by the shoulders and kissed him on both cheeks. His knees wobbled. He regrouped and handed the keys to Montana, opened the back door for Lainey, and hopped into the passenger seat.

"You aren't driving?" she asked.

"No, I don't know how. I had a friend drive me to the airport to pick you up. He took a taxi back to town."

On the bumpy ride through town, Lainey could see Christian whispering to Montana. The truck didn't have air conditioning, so the windows were rolled down, and Lainey couldn't hear a thing. She guessed that he was nervous about the new outsider. Montana just kept smiling and nodding. He was probably trying to reassure the kid. It didn't bother Lainey. She was fascinated by the fact that she wasn't sweating for the first time in two weeks.

The landscape amazed her. It was totally untouched by corporate construction. As they passed out of the dusty town of Bluefields, the roads worsened. The houses they passed were all simple affairs—nothing over a single story. Families either worked the land around the house or sat outside in plastic chairs. They passed into farmlands. Horses and livestock roamed freely, which caused the truck to come to a screeching halt more than once. The farms and pot-holed roads eventually gave way to a dirt road and untouched forests that loomed in on either side. She could see birds and monkeys flittering about in the trees. They passed into a tiny town and stopped for an early dinner of chicken and Nicaragua's famed rice and beans mix; *gallo pinto.*

Everyone in the little *pueblito* stared at them as they walked from the truck to the tiny restaurant. Christian explained to her that they rarely saw *gringos* this far north on the Caribbean side, and a *rubia,* a blonde, was bound to draw attention. After dinner, he directed them to a tiny ramshackle house where they were spending the night. Chris told them that the family were long lost relatives of his, and they would be striking out for the camp at dawn. The little *casita* was hot and uncomfortable, but the family was very sweet to her. Their daughter, who had only peered at her from doorways, eventually overcame her shyness and came out to touch Lainey's blonde hair. Christian translated so the mothers could exchange child-rearing stories. To Lainey's surprise, she and the young mom had a lot in common despite the language and age differences. Kids were kids and moms were moms the world over. Languages might be different, and governments might be at war, but the regular people were often a lot alike. When night came on and the heat broke, Christian and Montana covered themselves in bug-repellant and slept in hammocks on the front porch.

Lainey slept inside on an old mattress in the main room. She dropped off like a rock within minutes.

She awoke to Christian shaking her shoulder gently. The weak, pre-dawn light provided just enough illumination for her to take in her surroundings. She was on a mattress in the main room of the tiny two-room house. The little Nicaraguan girl was curled up beside her, gently snoring. It reminded Lainey so much of her daughter Ana at that age, she nearly started crying. Montana's head poked through the doorway and snapped her out of the memory. He nodded for her to follow him. Wearing last night's clothes, she followed him to a water pump out back. Everyone commenced their morning rituals, then they walked over to where three horses were tied up and saddled. Lainey stared at Chris, half in shock, half in jest.

"You're kidding, right? I haven't ridden a horse since I was a teenager."

"Sorry, Miss Lainey, but it's the only way up to where we're going. There are no roads."

Before she could protest, Montana looped his sturdy arm under her shoulders and heaved her up onto the horse. Even in the calm morning air, he smelled like the outdoors, like straw and grass. And bug-spray. In his worn-out cargo pants, hiking boots, and faded t-shirt, he really fit the part of an *adventurer*. He had a worn face, a confident air, and a sense of calm purpose to him. Lainey couldn't see any way in the world this guy could live happily in the States.

Christian came over to give her a few pointers on riding. He told her not to worry, the horses were old and knew what they were doing. They'd follow his lead horse. He was cute, this little Nicaraguan. Montana had told her that Chris was twenty-four-years-old, but she just couldn't get over how young he looked. He was obviously uncomfortable around women and it made her smile to watch him stumble over his words and feet each time they interacted. But the goofiness contrasted deeply with his eyes. Chris had the deepest black eyes she had ever seen. When she looked straight at him, it looked like his eyes sucked in the light around his face. Lainey had never seen anything like it. It was almost scary.

Montana nodded to them both, and Chris's horse trotted onto a path that led into the dense jungle. So far, very few words had been spoken. Excitement seeped through every pore in Lainey's body. She had never done something this bold in her whole life. She couldn't help but smile at Montana when she looked back to check on him. He smiled back and tipped his panama hat. She could tell he understood. He must have been at this point once in his life, too.

On their long ride through the jungle, Christian dropped back and peppered Lainey with questions. She filled him in on the basics of her situation and how she wound up in Nicaragua.

"I don't understand, Lainey." It had taken over an hour to get him to drop the *señora*. "How did you not know you were flying into a warzone? You guys invented TV. You invented CNN. Don't you watch the news at all?"

"Well, things aren't the same up there as they are down here, Chris. You guys have CNN International in Spanish. In the U.S., we don't even have a CNN channel anymore. When I say CNN, I really mean all the news channels. Ever since cable TV was de-regulated, people got to choose what channels they have access to. Since the news channels only covered D.C. politics—something nobody outside of D.C. cared about—everyone dropped them the second they had the choice. Suddenly, operating their own channel produced huge financial losses. The roles basically got reversed. Now news companies pay popular networks for thirty second or one-minute news slots. Things haven't really changed much, either. Instead of attacking each other for hours at a time, now the biggest news networks can only attack each other in thirty-second increments. Or, they run dumb stories about dog owners suing each other because one dog got the other pregnant, and that dog was a show-dog, and now its earning power was reduced...just typical stuff." Lainey didn't notice that Chris's horse had stopped. When she did notice, she was a few feet ahead, and looked back to see what was up.

Chris had stopped his horse.

"What?" she asked, genuinely perplexed at the look of confusion on his face. She glanced over at Montana for help.

He raised his hands in supplication. "Don't look at me, girl. I get the same look every time I try to explain *American normal.*"

Lainey looked from one to the other, put her palms to her eyes, and burst out laughing. She tried to talk, but just laughed harder. The other two caught the bug, and all three of them sat on horseback laughing until Lainey got herself under control.

"I…oh my God, I thought that was normal. I never looked at it from…" She looked at Montana through tears of laughter and saw the smirk. Then she shifted her eyes over to Chris.

He was smiling at her, but said very earnestly, "It doesn't matter now, Lainey. Now you're a Nica."

She felt the blood rush to her face and neck.

This. All of this.

They rode for nearly two hours into the dense jungle. Along the way, Chris explained what his great grandmother had told him about the family secret and about how personal this find really was to him. It answered some unasked questions about what Montana hadn't told her. She understood now. This was Chris's secret to share or not share.

Finally, Montana said, "Well, buddy, we're going to do our best to see that legacy come true. *Bisabuela* is pretty smart; things look pretty bad in Nicaragua just now. Whatever it is, we're gonna get it, hide it, then use it to get you guys outta here if you want."

Lainey smiled back at him. There it was again. Complete confidence.

After a few hours, Lainey's butt started to hurt. She forgot how hard horseback riding could be. She considered asking for a break when Christian reined up his horse and dismounted. She and Montana slipped off their horses and led them to a line to tie them up. Lainey's legs should have been sore, but her adrenaline kept pumping. At Montana's behest, she reapplied bug-spray, and Chris led them down a mostly-created path into the jungle.

Lainey couldn't believe she was doing this. On one hand, it was exciting beyond belief. On the other, she was in a jungle in the middle of nowhere with two guys she barely knew. What had happened to Ana's mother Elaine?

44

MONTANA AINSLEY
Present Day
North of Bluefields, Nicaragua

The three of them exited the jungle at the edge of the small camp. Montana saw one guy in the river with a traditional gold-sifting pan, while two more splashed water into a newly-built rocker box on the shore.

Old school, Montana thought.

In the American west, before automated mining, gold miners used three primary tools. Often, the speculators would first pan for gold. This involved taking an old pan, scooping up some riverbed, and slowly washing out the lighter particles, then sifting through what was left. The pans eventually gave way to sifting pans. This was basically a pan with a fine grate in place of a bottom. If the panhandlers found gold, they built a rocker box; basically a console television-sized version of a sifting pan.

A rocker box was a box the size of a large moving box, with a series of screens built at different levels. The concept involved dumping a large scoop of river-bed on the top screen and pouring water onto it. The smaller rocks and silt would wash down to the second screen, where gold particles could be found more easily. Beneath the box, a trough, approximately three to four feet long, extended out to carry away the water. Along the trough, small wooden slats, like speed bumps, were installed to catch smaller particles (gold being heavier than silt and small rocks) as the water rolled down the trough. The apparatus had a hand crank which would shake the box to help separate the particles. For larger finds, more advanced versions, called sluice boxes, were constructed. These were essentially giant versions of rocker boxes, but the construction involved damming up a portion of the river to speed the flow of water.

Montana saw that the team had only built a rocker. So, whatever they had found, it wasn't on an industrial scale. His plan to fly their gold find out of Bluefields would still work. By bribing the pilot with a free weekend at his house on Corn Island, he was pretty sure they could get a "no questions asked" flight anywhere in the country.

"I smell marijuana," Lainey commented as she came up beside them.

"Yeah, it does smell like that, but it isn't. The grass they burn to ward off the mosquitoes has that odor. At least…I hope that's what we're smelling."

When Chris's team noticed them, they stopped working and everyone gathered around one of the smoldering grass fires. Christian made introductions.

One of the Nicaraguans, a skinny, younger guy named Juan, asked Chris in Spanish, "Do the *gringos* know how to pan for gold?" His young buddy laughed.

Montana responded in Spanish. "No, we're here to help you sell it so that your wife doesn't run off with a rich gringo."

The other two group members pointed at Juan and broke out in laughter. In their experience, North Americans don't speak Spanish, let alone have a sense of humor. Montana translated for Lainey. Then Christian explained that Montana was "the *chele*" and had paid for much of the equipment they were using. Now that he was established as the *jefe*, all questions were directed toward Montana. Lainey didn't speak Spanish, but Montana could tell she caught the gist of the conversation. He also figured that the Nicaraguans would assume she was his *chica*, which would hopefully spare her the usual *machismo* nonsense. They'd probably think twice anyway, since Lainey had about five inches and ten pounds on the two younger ones.

The one she didn't outweigh, the hugely overweight digger named Gordo, approached her. In Spanish, he asked Montana a question about Lainey, and Montana translated the question to her. "He says, he wants to give you a proper

Nicaraguan hello because you're going to make him rich and ruin his life. He's just going to kiss you on the cheeks. He says he's never seen such a pretty woman."

Lainey arched an eyebrow at Montana then nodded to Gordo. The big man bear-hugged her and laid a pair of wet smooches on her cheeks. Everyone cheered. As he turned around, he spread his arms wide in a gesture of triumph. Montana wasn't sure how Lainey would take this. She'd shown glimpses of the patented U.S. *nervous outrage*, but she hadn't yet gone full tilt.

To his surprise, and everyone's delight, she smacked old Gordo on the butt, squeezed a handful of his ample cheek, and barked out *"buen culo!"* This brought raucous laughter from everyone. If the Nicaraguans had a question about her, grabbing Gordo's "nice ass" appeared to be the right answer.

Once the introductions were done, Lainey wandered around the campsite, inspecting the metal scales and the smelting oven. She wandered over to a dozen pack mules tied up by the small river. The Spanish speakers all gathered around Montana as he filled them in on the situation in Managua and un-packed the equipment he had brought from the States.

"It's not good, guys. The paramilitaries are shooting and burning everything in sight. The cops are running cover for them, but so far, the military is of-ficially sitting this out. Although, I have my doubts that the snipers all over Managua are ordinary cops." The conversation proceeded along these lines for a few minutes. Following the custom of every culture but the American one, everyone wanted to get caught up socially before they discussed business.

"That damn *Chayo*, we'll never be rid of her," Gordo said.

"She's worse than a cockroach," another agreed. "And now she is running the country."

"You know she's a *bruja*, right," Brayan, one of the diggers asked Montana.

Montana laughed. He knew how superstitious Latin Americans were, but a witch? "Yeah, you know, she is kind of an unnatural shade of grey."

"Ah, *si, jefe*. And do you see how many rings she wears? There are no rings left in all of Nicaragua, she wears them all."

This got laughter out of everyone. Juan called her *Sauron*, the evil Lord of the Rings. That got more laughter out of everyone.

"Well, guys, either way, it doesn't look like this is going to end soon. The protesters won't use weapons, so there is only so much they can accomplish. My original plan was to get this out through Corinto, on the Pacific side, but now I'm not sure I want to try and risk carrying this across the whole country." Saying the port's name out loud clicked something in Montana's mind. He made a mental note to check into Corinto for another reason.

"We could try and fly it over the top of the trouble, but I'm not sure where we could land over there. That basically leaves the Islands, but I'm open to ideas."

"*Jefe*, only the farmers from the north can challenge him. They kept all their weapons from the Sandinista Wars. That's why that cockroach won't dare send his people up north. Maybe we can take it that way?" Gordo added.

"North? Through Honduras? I don't know, Gordo. Honduras is in pretty bad shape. Gangs. Gangs and gold? Bad combination." They all nodded, knowing that their northern neighbor had been battling gang violence for decades, and as of now, the gangs were way ahead.

"Well, guys," Montana said, "that's just another reason we have to finish mining this river. We've gotta get whatever you've found outta here, so we can convert it to cash. I think I've got an airplane standing by in Bluefields, depending on how fa…" Montana stopped. The three diggers were staring at him, shaking their heads to indicate *no*.

"What?" Montana asked.

"*Jefe*, I don't think an airplane is going to work. At least, not an airplane that flies."

Montana tilted his head and looked at them. "I don't get the joke guys, fill me in."

They all turned to Christian. In a small voice, he addressed Montana. "So… did you hear me when I said I thought this was over our heads?"

"I did."

"Well, I think you need to come with me to really understand what 'over our heads' means in Nicaragua."

Montana whistled Lainey over and filled her in as the six of them started walking down a path that led into the jungle. They followed it for about two minutes before they came to a rock outcropping. There was a small cave entrance at the base of the outcropping. On the ground next to the entrance sat an ancient Styrofoam cooler full of flashlights, bags of water, and bug spray. Everyone grabbed a flashlight, and Gordo led them into the small cave. The opening was only about five feet high, and they had to duck to enter. Once inside, the cave was more like a small, roughly-cut room. After about six steps in, the outside light faded, and they clicked on the flashlights. Montana panned his light around. He figured the cave dimensions at about eight feet high and about twenty feet deep.

A few feet further in, they all stopped. They stood shoulder-to-shoulder facing the back of the cave. All six flashlights pointed at the dozen wooden crates on the floor. The crates appeared rectangular, about two feet wide by about four feet long; like little two-foot tall coffins. The wood was filthy and rough, and the crates had obviously been constructed in haste. Muddy water leaked from the corners. None of them had tops, and the contents nearly spilled over the tops.

Out of the corner of his eye, Montana saw Lainey's flashlight drop from her outstretched hand. It made a soft splat in the wet ground. She didn't try to pick it up. She didn't move at all.

After about twenty seconds of silence, Montana broke the trance. "We're in deep shit."

"Yeah," Chris said and looked up at him, "unless you got a space shuttle in Bluefields, we're not flying this anywhere."

45

TOM NICKERSON
Present Day
Augusto Sandino Airport
Managua, Nicaragua

Tom Nickerson, private bounty hunter for Teri Bradshaw, was getting pissed. Two days ago, his contact at the credit bureau told him that Elaine Dunaway had used her credit card in a town called San Juan Del Sur. He'd driven four-and-a-half-hours on a rented motorbike and passed through dozens of roadblocks, each with a different bribe. By the time he got to the town, he'd figured out the system. The guys with masks and guns wanted money. The kids with shirts tied over their faces wanted water bottles. He'd eventually stopped the bike and stocked up on both, but by that point he had passed them all.

He spent the night and half of the next day combing the deserted little beach town trying to find someone who had seen the blonde tourist. Although he spoke no Spanish, most of the locals appeared to know a few words of English. The place was so empty he couldn't believe no one could remember her. He was about to give up, when a Nicaraguan surfer approached him eating a late lunch on the beach. The kid tried to sell him surfing lessons. He had never heard of a woman named Elaine, so Nickerson waved him away.

The surfer walked a few feet away, then turned and said, in English, "Don't you know how this works?"

Nickerson felt embarrassed. He should have thought of that. Outside of politics, the U.S. had been off the direct bribe system for decades. Fifty bucks later, the kid admitted he gave lessons to an older blonde woman named Lainey. For another hundred, he told Nickerson she had bolted, with some older *gringo*, for the Caribbean town of Bluefields.

Frustrated beyond belief, Nickerson rode the motorcycle back through the roadblocks to Managua. The ride back, in the dark, had been twice as dangerous as the ride down. His lack of Spanish made it much worse. At night, paramilitaries overran all the roadblocks and they demanded cash bribes at gunpoint. Most of them were drinking, and more than once, a drunk paramilitary stuck a shotgun in Nickerson's face.

If it hadn't been for his GPS, he probably would have been dead on the side of the road somewhere. He'd maneuvered around two very one-sided gun battles on his way to the airport. When he checked back into the hotel across from the airport at midnight, the power was out. He spent a sleepless night listening to explosions and automatic rifle fire all around the city. At 7:00 a.m., exhausted and more than a little rattled, he walked across the street to the domestic *terminal*, what was little more than an afterthought attached to the real airport. The airport staff appeared a bit more casual about their start time. They staggered in over an hour later. Nickerson was good and pissed by then.

The more he raved at the woman behind the ticket counter, in English, the more she stared into space. Sensing a complete impasse, he went outside to find a cab driver who could translate. It took that guy half an hour to park the cab and come inside to help. Apparently, he had to catch up with some old friends he hadn't seen since pulling out of the empty pickup lane. Nickerson looked at his watch, 10 a.m. *Unbelievable.* Thirty minutes of negotiation led to the determination that: *the one*, yes one, flight between Bluefields and Managua was stuck somewhere because of a maintenance problem.

He exited the building, shaking with anger. From what he saw on his phone's internet, Bluefields was a shoebox of a town. He was sure Dunaway had stopped there on her way to Corn Island. As far as he could tell, that was the only thing worth seeing on the Caribbean side. On an island, he could find her in no time. But how the hell was he going to get to Bluefields? Driving his bike would take over seven hours, not including all the damn roadblocks. He just didn't have the energy for it. He started back across the street to his hotel when his translating taxi driver walked up.

"I can drive you to Rama. Four hours, four hundred U.S. dollars. We can go right now."

"Yeah, buddy, I'm not interested in Rama. I wanna go to Bluefields."

The cab driver laughed. "There is no road to Bluefields. You go to Rama. At Rama, you take a boat to Bluefields."

"What? Yeah, sure buddy." He waited for the cab driver to laugh. He didn't.

"Seriously? How can you have a town without a road?" Before the driver could respond, he held up a finger in a wait gesture and pulled out his phone. He typed in Managua to Bluefields.

After scrolling for a few minutes, "Holy shit, there isn't a road." To the cab driver he said, "You gotta be kidding me. I gotta take a river panga? Like a goddamn Vietnam War river panga? This can't be real." He touched two more websites on his screen. It was real. "What kind of backwards ass…" He trailed off and turned to the taxi driver, who was patiently smiling. "Okay chief, but one thing. I want air conditioning, and I'm only paying three hundred. We agree?"

"*Si*, okay, we agree. Four hundred."

"No, I said three hundred," Nickerson countered. Like he was gonna be swindled by this clown.

"Okay, I will take you to the bus station for twenty dollars. The bus to Rama takes ten hours."

Nickerson folded immediately. He had no other options. The stupid smile on the cabbie's face didn't improve his mood. Had he read just a bit further down on the website, he would have seen that cabs to Rama went for about fifty dollars.

After a miserable five-hour drive—without air conditioning—the taxi drove through the tiny town of Rama and straight onto the boat ramp. Nickerson had tried to sleep on the ride, but the constant roadblocks getting out of Managua had kept him awake. Every time he nodded off the cab jerked to a halt. If the student protesters were manning the *tranque*, they passed through without incident. But if government troops were, they would stick a rifle into the backseat until Nickerson produced ten dollars' worth of bribes. Two hours outside of Managua, the trip settled down, and he finally fell asleep.

He awoke as the taxi pulled to a stop, right in front of a an incredibly unsteady-looking river barge. Nickerson looked around and took in his surroundings. Dusty, wooden shacks lined the boat launch. The river water was a light brown, and he smelled rotting meat. Plastic bags, tangled in tree branches, flapped in the wind. He'd swatted at least five mosquitoes in the minute that he had been awake. By any American definition, this was a shithole. His driver got out and walked down to the boat and back. "Is all good. You pay them 150 *Cordoba*s, in a few hours, you at Bluefields."

What could Nickerson say? This was why he lived in the U.S.

The boat ride itself was pretty smooth. The panga was basically a flat-bottomed tourist boat with a small outboard engine. They cruised the river at a speed fast enough to keep the mosquitoes off, and he started to relax a bit. According to the internet, he could catch a ferry to Corn Island from Bluefields. Since the country's sole airplane appeared broken, he didn't have much choice. All in all, the boat ride was more comfortable than the taxi ride. Nickerson looked down at his once pale legs. He had two dozen mosquito bites, but they were hard to differentiate from the glowing red of the sunburn.

He had been totally unprepared for this trip. No sunscreen, no bug-spray, zero research on Nicaragua. He figured he'd just be able to locate her using the credit card search and be done with it. He didn't speak Spanish, but hell, most of the world spoke some degree of English now.

What Nickerson hadn't told Teri Bradshaw, nor any other client, was just exactly what he did for the FBI in his former life. Tom Nickerson spent three months as an analyst trainee in the Financial Crimes division. He made the final cut to become part of the agency but got so drunk at the celebration party that he overslept his first day. He was fired at 8:17 a.m., seventeen minutes after he was officially hired. Technically, he'd been an FBI agent.

Most civilians never ask. Even if they did, they had no real way of verifying what he told them. This was the beauty of his business. Everyone heard 'former

FBI agent', and they thought they were hiring Elliot Ness. He used language he got from books and TV shows, deepened his voice, and looked very stern at client meetings. That was all it took.

He took this job because it was an easy fifty grand. He had no idea the language barrier would be an actual barrier.

Outside of San Juan Del Sur and his taxi driver, not even the hotel clerk at the American hotel chain understood him. He also hadn't anticipated that the Nicaraguan economy was basically all cash. Throw in a goddamned revolution, and this job was going down the tubes, fast.

As Bluefields' boat dock came into view, his phone beeped. He hadn't had service for most of the day because of the remoteness of his travel. He lifted the phone to his ear and listened.

"Hey Nicky, it's Paul at Equifax. Hey, your subject just purchased a one-way ticket from Managua to Cartagena, Colombia. The airline won't give me the date, but judging by the price, and the fact that she bought it at the Managua airport, I'd guess the travel date isn't far away. It definitely looks like a last second fare. Good hunting buddy."

If Nickerson had possessed the physical strength of a former field agent, he would have crushed the phone in his palm.

46

TERI BRADSHAW
Present Day
Seattle, Washington

Try as she might, Teri couldn't figure a way out of the Central American mess. Nicaragua had been the find of the century. A stable Central American country priced like Honduras? No way could she duplicate that. The country's collapse just hadn't been on her radar. She didn't berate herself over it. If Teri hadn't seen it coming, no one else would have either. Blame wasn't important. What was important was that there was no way to restart operations in another country. Nicaragua had been the gold standard for cheap stability for a decade. All their northern neighbors were still losing the battle against gang and drug violence.

To the south, Costa Rica had basically become the fifty-first United State. Anything marginally illegal coming out of Costa Rica would be picked up by regulators in no time. No. It was Nicaragua, or it was nowhere. Teri had come to the dark conclusion that it might well be nowhere. Even if she could find another location, it would take months to re-create everything, and all that time the merchandise would just keep piling up, waiting to get discovered.

Without the TSA lottery money, the stupid fucking Wonderwheel was going to sink the Earth Ventures Fund by year-end. Dylan had screwed her good.

Even if she was able to offload the theme park, there was no way she could get a fraction of what had been spent. Without the lottery cash coming in, Earth Ventures and, by extension, The Bradshaw Group, had a financial black hole that could swallow her whole ecosystem. Teri stared into space shaking her head. Her phone buzzed.

"Ms. Bradshaw, I have Alan Dunaway holding." Maybe, Teri thought, the lawyer could come up with an idea. Painful as he was, he'd proven a clever and conniving business mind before.

"Okay, put him through," she sighed.

"Hi, Alan, thanks again for setting up those meetings. Preliminary talks have been very—" She stopped mid-sentence. Did he just sob into the phone? Was he crying? Now! When she actually needed his advice!

"Alan? Are you there? What's wrong?" Her tone was completely flat. She didn't care what was wrong, but whatever it was, they'd have to get past it to get to her issues.

"My...my partners removed me from the law firm. I don't know what to say. I've never done..." He blew his nose at the other end of the line.

Teri's thoughts shifted to all the documents that had been shared with his law firm. She envisioned the letterhead of Alan's law firm. There must be twenty names on it. How many lawyers had access? A dozen? More.

Jesus, could this day get worse.

"Alan, take a breath. Tell me what's going on."

"The..." He paused for a second, sniffed, then restarted. "The lemonade lawsuit. It's because of the stupid lemonade lawsuit." Teri didn't know what the hell he was talking about.

"The defendants' lawyer had proof I suppressed exculpatory documents."

"Alan, remember, I'm not a lawyer. What does that mean?" Getting him talking about legal matters would focus his mind. Was it really her fate to spend her whole life surrounded by adult children?

"It means," he sniffed, "it means that I had documents that proved my clients were lying. Technically, I have a legal obligation to turn that stuff over, but nobody really does that anymore. Nobody does. It's standard practice to hide that stuff because we never go to trial. I mean, I haven't been in an actual trial in years. We all do it. It's how we keep the lawsuits going."

"Okay, so what does that mean for…for you, for us?" Whew, she almost blew that comment, she thought.

"It means I'm screwed, Teri. It means my own firm, the firm I founded, is going to push to have me disbarred. It means I'm probably gonna get sued personally. It means the end of my career. This is all I know how to do. I've been doing this my whole life."

Typical lawyer, thought Teri, folds at the first real sign of trouble. No wonder the wife abandoned him; she was probably looking for someone with a spine. His being disbarred was something else entirely. Would that free him from the attorney-client privilege subterfuge? Alan didn't actually know anything critical, so she wouldn't have to worry about him talking. But the files? Clearly there was enough evidence in them that the ex-wife chased off to Nicaragua.

"Teri? Are you even listening?"

"Yeah, Alan, I am. I'm not sure what you want me to do here?"

"Do? I don't want you to *do* anything. I could use some support. You're a part of this, a part of my life and what's happened."

Oh, here we go, thought Teri, *here comes the passive-aggressive pitch.* She raised her finger and put it above the disconnect button.

"I'm in serious trouble, Teri. I don't know where to turn. I mean, I've lost my job and my wife in less than a week. You refuse to see me outside of work. I don't know what to do. I mean, it's not like I can run for office."

The words hit Teri like an electrical shock. Her finger nearly hit the disconnect button of its own accord. "Alan, listen, I've got an emergency here. I need you to calm down, and I want you to call me after you've had a chance to think and settle down. Can you do that for me?"

Alan started to whine, but Teri hung up while he was still talking.

"Alice, please connect me to Dunaway's former firm."

That his old firm had her files wouldn't work. Dunaway could go down like the Titanic, but he wasn't going to take her with him.

While she waited for the call to connect, she wanted to slap herself. It was so simple. The answer had been in front of her the whole time. Within a minute, she was on the phone with George Bernstein, he of the first name at Bernstein,

Alaways, Sinclair, Goldstein, Rogerson, Whitman, Milstone, & Dunaway, attorneys at law.

She established that Alan had been fired. Then she terminated her contract with the firm over Mr. Bernstein's objections.

"There's one last thing, George. I need all the files your firm has on The Bradshaw Group and every other entity we have."

"Sure, of course, Teri, we always send the originals back to the clients when the relationship has reached its zenith."

Reached its zenith? What the hell had happened to people?

"Originals? Does that mean you have copies? That's not gonna work, George. I'm going to need all copies, all electronic records, everything."

"Well, Teri, that's highly unusual, and totally unnecessary. Even after we're no longer associated, you're still protected under attorney-client privilege. Standard legal practice is…"

She interrupted him. "George, I don't give a shit about standard legal practice, and nobody has believed in attorney-client privilege in years. We all know it takes a flimsy subpoena and you guys will spill. Hell, you're already selling client data illegally."

"Now wait just a sec, Teri, there is nothing illegal about marketing aggregated client data. We don't sell individual client information. Anything that leaves our office is aggregated to hide specific individual privacy. It's perfectly legal."

"George, I don't have time to dance. Your firm provided me an underhanded sleaze, for whom we paid over $400,000 in fees over the past couple years. We can do this the hard way, or you can box up everything, put it on zip drives, and Fed-Ex it to me within twenty-four hours. I also want a letter acknowledging that you have sent every single ounce of client data, that we have been removed from your database, and that, as a result, future documents that may surface cannot be verified by your firm as belonging to me. Got it? I want this relationship terminated completely. If I hear anything other than 'yes ma'am', we can discuss the practice of document suppression and see just how firm-wide your problem really is. And don't give me the airtight crap. The fact that I already knew about document suppression should worry you."

Silence from the other end of the phone.

"You wanna discuss attorney-client privilege, now George? I'll yank your entire goddamn firm out of this cash re-distribution racket. Are we clear?"

"Yes ma'am."

* * *

Teri spent the rest of the day on the phone with Earth Ventures' biggest local investors. Investors who lost their shirts tended to sue. Rather than tie everyone up in legal battles, she planned to upsell them on a different idea, an idea that could double their corporate profits in six years. After all, if they sued, she would just be spending their invested money to defend herself. Surely, none of the investors were stupid enough to pay for both sides of a lawsuit.

Out-of-town investors didn't matter. Teri didn't care if they got screwed when the VC fund went under. Although she didn't have the legal obligation to pay back anyone, she needed to make sure she didn't have any enemies *locally*. She needed to start cutting deals with the Washington State based people right now. She had to convince them to take forty cents on the dollar for their investment. It was all she could afford to pay them out. It would be a huge loss, but then again, Earth Ventures had paid out handsomely thus far. Besides, the real payoff for the clients would be that by accepting the lower payback now, they would be putting her in a position to benefit them ten times over.

One of the biggest local investors also happened to be one of the tech-giants courting her to purchase the rights to the Wonderwheel.

Fuck. The Wheel of Wonder…I've gotta get that right.

"Wow, that's a big ask, Teri," said the British-accented voice on the other end of the phone. "Patty Williams has never indicated that she wants to retire."

"Of course not. She's only eighty-two." Both Teri and the man on the phone laughed. "That's why it's a big ask, Sonjay. But think about it from a corporate perspective. Who do you think is more likely to support your interests? Who has a background in business, and who's been all over magazine covers for the past two years? I've got star power, Sonjay, and I wanna cash it in on your behalf. Besides, I owe you, not the other way around. That means I'm working for your shop for free. That means I can never be accused of selling out, and you can't be accused of buying. There is no money exchange, Sonjay. Consider the 60% loss a down payment on the greatest invisible investment you could possibly make for your firm. Plus, there is absolutely no story for the press. My firm screwed your firm. There is no way we're in bed together."

"Yeah, I gotta admit, I'm liking what I'm hearing more and more. But it's a two-part problem, Teri. How do you get the other relevant party to play ball?"

"I've got that part covered, Sonjay. It's probably better that I keep everything compartmentalized to protect all parties."

"Okay, but I'm still thinking. I can't just call Patty up and tell her to retire."

"Sonjay, Patty has forty-year-old kids, right? And those kids have kids? She's gotta have at least a dozen kids and grandkids. I'm sure their entire lives are documented on the internet. Maybe they've documented some not-so-smart parts of their lives? Maybe Patty needs to focus on her family for a little while. She herself may have even…well, you guys run the largest text and email platforms on this planet, right? Sooo…"

He interrupted her quickly. "Whoooaaa, there Teri. That's dangerous ground you're walking on. I get where you're going, but it's an unacceptable business practice. We don't cross that line here. It's totally unacceptable."

She smiled when she heard the magic word.

"I get that, Sonjay, I really do. But you're a public company CEO. Tell me this, knowing that I'm a better supporter for your business, can you honestly say that you're discharging your duties to the stakeholders by keeping me out and Patty in? Clearly, I'm the optimal outcome. And Congress is breathing down your neck, right? They are talking about breaking you guys up. Aren't they going to level another multibillion-dollar fine against you? Who do you think is going take the fall if that happens, Sonjay? You don't win CEO of the year honors if the firm crumbles under your feet. You'll wind up the Chief Information guy at some retail chain in Cleveland, or an Insurance company in Hartford, Connecticut. Have you ever even been to Connecticut, Sonjay?"

Sonjay was silent on the other end. Teri hoped he was envisioning winter in Hartford. Her 'nice guys finish last' speech always worked.

"Let me just repeat for the record, Teri, that certain business practices here are unacceptable." He paused for a second. "That said, let's have lunch on

Thursday. I'd like to make a few inquiries."

Teri made two similar phone calls to big individual investors who lived in the Seattle and Olympia areas. Same basic outcomes.

And just like that, Teri Bradshaw started to close up shop. Her run at the helm of The Bradshaw Group was at an end. The Bradshaw Group, and by extension The Earth Ventures fund, had seen their last days. She'd banked nearly a hundred million dollars, and now it was onward and upward. All that remained was to bury every trace of The Bradshaw Group's dealings. She had secured large separation packages for most of her employees. She wanted them shouting from Mt. Rainier that Teri had been the perfect employer.

She knew the TSA lottery folks wouldn't be happy, but what could they really do? They had been breaking the law long before Teri met them. They were big boys. They could take care of themselves. It was every woman for herself now, and there was only one place where Teri would be immune from future investigations. She planned to hide in plain sight. Teri Bradshaw would get the governor to appoint her to the U.S. Senate.

47

MONTANA AINSLEY
Present Day
North of Bluefields, Nicaragua

Montana disentangled himself from the mosquito netting hanging over his hammock and checked the ground underneath for snakes. He stepped out to follow the smell of coffee wafting in from the middle of the camp. Along the way, he brushed his teeth with the last of his bottled water.

At the campfire, he found six people sipping coffee from plastic mini-cups, five men and Lainey Dunaway. Normally, the sight wouldn't have registered with him. He would have sat down, had a cup of coffee, and discussed the upcoming day. Except, when he had gone to bed the night before, there were four men and Lainey Dunaway. That made five people who should be having coffee, not six.

Chris and Lainey both looked up as Montana approached. He saw it on their grim faces. The problem list had increased by one. Nobody said a word. Montana had a sense of the problem, but he didn't want to address it until he had coffee. He grabbed the pot with a towel, poured himself a plastic cup full, and sat in the dirt facing the men.

It was Juan who spoke up first. He started, then stopped.

So, this is our rat, thought Montana.

"*Jefe*, this is my fiancé's...my girlfriend's...my friend's brother." Montana didn't respond, and the silence grew heavy. "*Jefe*, I'm so sorry. I...I told this girl, and she...well, she..."

"Talked," Montana finished.

"*Jefe*, I didn't..."

"Save it, Juan."

Now that it was out there, the other two diggers waded in angrily.

"She's not even his girlfriend, just some girl who has blown him off for years."

"He sold us out for sex."

A few more comments were tossed in, and when it became clear Montana wasn't responding to any of it, the group shut up and let the silence and grass-smoke re-fill the air.

Montana looked Juan and said, in a neutral tone, "You tried to impress a girl to get sex, and you told her about what you found up here to seal the deal."

Juan didn't speak, but nodded in defeat.

Montana switched to English so only Chris and Lainey would know what he was saying. "And by now, half of Bluefields knows about it. In twenty-four hours, they're going to descend on this place like a swarm of locusts."

The others looked confused. They didn't understand what he said. They understood that he was pissed, and they understood the name Bluefields. The implications sunk in when he repeated it in Spanish. Not even Christian met his eye. The crowd around the morning campfire grew increasingly uneasy as they thought through the problem. Several pairs of eyes narrowed and shifted over from Juan to the stranger.

Finally, Old Gordo braved the tension. "So, *jefe*, what are we gonna do? This is bad. Our lives are in danger up here." That opened the conversational flood gates. Everyone started in.

He let the small crowd spin up their panic level while he thought of an answer. Then, he held up his hand for quiet and looked at the newcomer. "The first question I have is, who is this guy, and why is he here?"

The outsider, who, to his credit, had remained silent, finally spoke up.

"*Señor*, my name is Diego José Vedana Auxilliadora. Maria", he nodded at Juan, "is my sister. She is not Juan's fiancé. We all live in the same house, and

I overheard Juan trying to woo her into bed with his story of found treasure. What Juan did not realize is that my sister is a die-hard Sandinista party member. The morning he left, she called Managua. She has always wanted a chance to get out of Bluefields, and she thinks this is her ticket. There is a good chance they ignore her. But there is a chance that they...well, I think everyone knows what's going on in this country right now. The economy is in tatters. No money is coming in. Ortega needs money for his war. And well, this would be money, no?"

"Okay," Montana said evenly. His mind incorporated the new data. This was actually worse than he thought. If the government's people came up here, there would be no way out. They might be able to barter with the locals, but government troops? They'd all wind up airlifted to *El Chipote*. He glanced at Chris and saw fear. Clearly the kid already arrived at the same conclusion.

Now that it was laid out in Spanish, the arguments started back up. Once Montana detected that their anger was turning to fear, he spoke. Once they were scared, they would be easier to manage.

"We have a saying in English; 'water under the bridge'. That means, there is nothing we can do about what he has done. What we do now is move fast. Diego, what exactly can you do? You do realize that by being up here, you're in as much danger as we are now."

"Si, *señor*. I worked in mining in Honduras for five years. I was born up North, if you understand my meaning. I'm no friend of the government. I can help carry stuff. Plus, I was a metallurgist. I know many people in the mining business who can help..."

"I mean," Montana cut in, "how do we know you aren't a Sandinista?"

There was a long pause.

"Maria is my half-sister, *don* Montana. We have different fathers. My father was a contra rebel. He was killed in the fighting. When we were forced to leave our homes, my mother remarried a party member in order to protect me. That man is Maria's father."

Gordo spoke up in the youngster's defense. "*Jefe*, I can vouch for that. I know their family."

Montana thought about that. Interesting career in the circumstances. "A metallurgist, huh?"

"Yes, *señor*. If you want to try to sell it, I have many contacts."

At this, a thought struck Montana. He ruminated for a couple minutes while the entire group stared at him. "No, we aren't going to sell it, Diego. Can we melt it down?"

The whole group just kept blinking at him. It was Christian who spoke first. "Montana, that's crazy. Why would we…it would take," he shot a look at Diego, "how long?"

"I am not sure, but if what Juan said to my sister about the amount is true, probably months, maybe even a year."

"Right," Chris said, re-addressing Montana. "A year. We can't stay here, and we can't move it across the country."

Then Lainey put in, "We don't even know what this stuff is. It might be some famous, long-lost treasure. It might have real historical value."

"And *don* Montana," Juan put in sheepishly, "we don't have a lot of time if Diego is right."

Montana looked at the whole group. "That's why we're going to move it to Corn Island. All of it. Starting right now."

The silence that followed lasted nearly a full minute.

Finally, Diego spoke up. "Don Montana, my cousin is the captain of the Corn Island ferryboat."

48

LAINEY DUNAWAY
Present Day
Cartagena, Colombia

ainey awoke to the ding of the plane's fasten seatbelt light. She had slept like a rock, and her mind felt groggy. The previous days had taken a toll. She had arrived in Nicaragua during the middle of a civil war, been threatened at gunpoint, fled across the country, traveled back across the same country, then up into the jungle where she witnessed a treasure find of fictional proportion. Now she might be marked for death by the Nicaraguan government. Busy week.

But Montana came up with a plan, and the two departed the jungle camp a day later. They made their way back to Bluefields and Montana's pilot proved as good as his word. The plane sat on the tarmac waiting for them. Lainey and Montana talked over the plan the entire flight back to Managua. He thought the plan their best available option.

Lainey wasn't so sure. She wanted to check out an idea that had swirled in her head since the shock of seeing that much gold wore off. That idea necessitated a trip to Cartagena, Colombia... alone. That thought would panic *Elaine* Dunaway.

Good thing she's long gone.

The two said farewell at the Managua airport, and she watched him stroll, unconcerned, out of the airport and into the eerily deserted city. She had to hand it to the guy. He didn't say much, but it sure took a lot to rattle him. She didn't like Montana's plan, but she didn't want to say anything until she could lay her suspicions to rest.

That meant a flight to Bogotá, Colombia, then onto the coastal city of Cartagena.

She hadn't wanted to admit it, but she was put off by his attitude towards the treasure find. He was so nonchalant at the concept of melting down a clearly historical find. She understood the need to get it out of there. The situation in Nicaragua was deteriorating. Obviously, a horde of armed government troops sounded scary. Part of her still couldn't believe this was happening. Movie characters dealt with problems like this. The need to move the gold was one thing, but the find itself absolutely had to be historically significant. Montana wanted to smuggle it to Corn Island and melt it down. You just didn't do things like that to history. Did you?

The find hadn't looked anything like Lainey had envisioned treasure would look like. Most of the coins were dirty and misshapen, but there was no mistaking the gold and silver glint that had pinged back from their flashlights. They'd tested the metals; it was gold alright. And the jewels certainly appeared real, though muddy and dulled by time. She'd sifted through oddly shaped rings, bracelets made of pure silver, and even a pair of earrings. It wasn't until she came across a few well-preserved coins that something in her memory sparked. There was something about the design she remembered, and the answer sat in Cartagena, Colombia.

About half a year ago, Alan forced Lainey to fly up to Seattle and sit in on a business dinner.

Teri must have been busy that night, she thought caustically.

Earth Ventures, Alan's new client, was entertaining a Seattle-based firm searching for investors in some mega-lawsuit they hatched. The firm claimed to be a part of a search team that located the holy grail of shipwrecks, just off the coast of Cartagena, Colombia. The guys said that the ship, the *San José* treasure galleon, went down hundreds of years ago off the coast of Cartagena; carrying almost four tons of gold coins, silver, and assorted jewelry. The ship went gone down fast and in complete darkness, so nobody had known exactly where, until now.

The gold had been collected from across Central and South America and had been earmarked for the Spanish Crown's war of succession. The Seattle guys had photos of the coins that were supposed to be on the ship, and they wanted investors to fund the lawsuit against the entire country of Colombia. Somehow, and Lainey hadn't remembered all the legal jargon, the Colombians had blocked the Americans out of the discovery. Earth Ventures decided not to invest in the lawsuit, but the story had fascinated Lainey and she'd looked into the old legend. It was the imprints on the Nicaragua coins. She was sure she'd seen those images before.

Something about Chris's family history and that old treasure galleon had been circling around in her mind since the minute she had laid eyes on those crates. The minute that old chubby Nicaraguan had said the word treasure, everything locked into place. She wasn't going to say anything until she could be sure, but the timelines matched.

The last thing the guys needed was her muddying the water with some crazy conspiracy. She told Montana she just wanted to get out of Nicaragua and clear her head for a couple days. He looked skeptical, like he didn't think she'd be back. She didn't blame him. *Elaine Dunaway* would have fled at the idea of being chased by an angry mob, or a government attack force, while escaping through donkey trails to protect a hidden treasure they'd unearthed in a remote river in the jungles of Nicaragua. But that was just a Thursday to *Lainey Dunaway*. Heck, she hadn't had a gun pointed at her in nearly a week.

She knew they were headed to Corn Island, and she'd planned to show back up there once she had a chance to do some research of her own.

Montana had given her a very rosy overview of Colombia. He even claimed Cartagena would "amaze" her, and that the best comparison was a *clean,* Spanish version of New Orleans…with beaches. He was sure her lack of language skills wouldn't be a hindrance, a lot of people on the coast spoke some degree of English.

"Worst case," he said and flipped one of the ancient gold coins at her, "bribe somebody."

"I intend to," she had replied. She absolutely loved the confused look that crossed his face.

When the plane came to a complete stop, she deplaned onto a mobile staircase and into the remains of a muggy day. The Cartagena airport was tiny, and it reminded her of those little Caribbean Island airports on St. Thomas and Jamaica. Although it was hot, a seriously strong wind blew off the ocean and kept the heat from becoming debilitating. Either that, or the Nicaraguan heat had made a professional out of her.

She followed the covered path into the little airport, and efficiently processed through customs in minutes. A quick and inexpensive taxi whisked her along the two-mile beach road and into the walled fortress they called The Old City. She walked a couple blocks to her quaint little hotel. It was a converted house with an open-air pool and garden in the courtyard. She checked in, dropped her bag, and set out exploring.

Montana hadn't been wrong. It did feel like a cleaner and more beautiful New Orleans. One with a with a four-hundred-year-old, twenty-foot stone wall around it. The narrow streets of the old city were lined with two-story houses, all joined together and painted in pastel colors. Bougainvillea bushes crawled up the sides of the houses, and their red, white, and pink blossoms hung over the streets high above her. Hibiscus plants tumbled down from shiny mahogany balconies. Between the flowers and the brightly painted buildings, it was picture-postcard cute. She wandered from shop to shop, taking in the sights and sounds of the bustling tourist town. Women in multi-colored dresses balanced baskets of fruit on their heads and posed for photos with tourists.

She window-shopped for an hour among open-air restaurants, plazas, and fruit vendors. As the heat of the day broke and the sea breeze picked up, she grabbed a coffee from a glassed-in cafe with Juan Valdeź painted across its deep red awnings. She smiled, remembering the old coffee ads from her childhood. She was glad something of those old memories remained.

Lainey eventually wound up atop the stone wall that encircled the old city. She was sipping a mojito at a massive outdoor restaurant and watching the sun set across the calm Caribbean waters. The view was staggering. Endless miles of ocean in front of her. To her left, she had a perfect view of the main beach area of Bocagrande with its rows of gleaming high-rise condos.

The wind had picked up, so she bought a straw hat and a beautiful knit shawl from one of the vendors wandering through the rows of tables. She must have been getting used to the climate down here. She had to hand it to Montana. She could see the appeal of living down here. He'd also been right about Cartagena-it was almost too good to be true. In a million years, she never would have dreamed that Colombia looked like this.

49

TOM NICKERSON
Present Day
Bogotá, Colombia

Nickerson had to overnight in Bogotá. He wasn't thrilled about it, but it beat being in Nicaragua. That place was a madhouse. He had been in Bogotá for a couple of hours, waiting on a connection to Cartagena, when a massive thunderstorm rolled in and flights got grounded. For once, he didn't complain about the flight delay. The late afternoon storm turned the sky nearly black. More disconcerting, the sky didn't look very far away. The clouds seemed to be inside the city itself. Colombia's capital city of Bogotá was nearly twice the altitude of Denver, Colorado. A massive, sprawling mess perched at nearly 9,000 feet in the Andes Mountains, thunderstorms didn't pass over Bogotá, they passed through it.

Standing in the taxi line outside the airport, Nickerson recoiled as a bolt a lighting, at least a foot thick, ripped across the sky. Simultaneously, thunderclaps rocked the entire airport structure just behind him. His first thought was that a bomb had gone off, and he instinctively dove to the ground. The laughing taxi manager had pointed at the sky and said, in English, "is thunder."

With his eyes and ears still powering back up, he dove into his taxi.

He found a U.S.-based hotel chain close to the airport, and now munched potato chips as he watched the heavens unload an ocean of rain into Bogotá.

When the storm finally ebbed, the temperature, which had been a mild seventy degrees when he landed, plunged down to forty. Nickerson didn't have any cold weather gear. He had anticipated the coastal heat. So, he was stuck in the hotel, eating potato chips and drinking beer. With nothing else to do, he logged on to his office server. Now that he was in a country with a stable power grid, he could bring the full resources of his employer to bear.

He'd been underestimating Elaine Dunaway for a week now. Time to pull rank. Because his firm, Circle Security, paid into the NADS database, he was able to gain access to her social media GPS tracking data. He wanted to make sure she stayed put in Cartagena. When NADS indicated she hadn't logged into a single social media site in over a month, he loaded in her daughter's name.

There wasn't much there, either. At least, until he called up phone records. She'd been placing internet-based calls, through a subsidiary of a major social media site, down to Central America for the past week. Although the encryption didn't allow him access to the actual text of voice records, it did show him that data packets had been sent and received from an IP address in the States to various IP addresses all over Nicaragua. But the most recent ping was from smack dab in the center of Cartagena, Colombia.

* * *

The following morning, Nickerson caught an early flight out of Bogotá. He landed in Cartagena less than an hour later. He left the airport and took a room at the Hotel Caribe on Cartagena's Bocagrande peninsula. It was only a two-minute cab ride to the central tourist district, the Old City, where he knew Lainey Dunaway had a room reserved at some cutesy boutique hotel.

Nickerson preferred U.S.-based chains, but the walled city didn't contain any. In fact, the only room he could find with a high star-rating was The Caribe, a non-U.S.-based hotel. Luckily, the place turned out to be five-star luxury. The entire staff addressed him in English, a welcome change from his Nicaraguan experience.

There were pools and palm trees everywhere throughout the massive interior courtyard. Dozens of scantily clad guests already sipped umbrella drinks, despite the early hour. And his room was perfect. Besides air conditioning, the room had hot water, something Nicaragua was sorely lacking. There was a luxurious, king-sized bed, and his room even had a small balcony that overlooked a crowded stretch of beach. There was even a western style Juan Valdez coffee shop just up the street. Civilization, at long last.

The main drag of Bocagrande reminded Nickerson a little bit of South Beach in Miami, with sky-high condo complexes lining both sides of the peninsula. The main drag bustled with normalcy; restaurants, clothing shops, a Fed-Ex office, and every standard convenience of modern life. Tom Nickerson felt a long way from the frustrations of Nicaragua. Mostly, because the power worked.

He decided right then, staring out at the beach, that he wasn't going back to Nicaragua for any amount of money. Twice in the past three days, teenagers with bloodshot eyes pointed guns at him. To risk losing his life, in some Central American backwater, to some eighteen-year-old kid who'd had too much booze and pressure applied to him at three in the morning…it just wasn't worth it. Teri Bradshaw could cancel his contract if it came to that.

He decided to take a morning walk along the beach before he went after the elusive Mrs. Dunaway. The beach was packed with people, but mostly Nickerson noticed the women. It was like Latin *Baywatch,* just without all the fabric.

Most of the women looked Latina and were already drinking, laughing, singing, and constantly dancing. Everywhere he looked, groups of them clustered for photos of themselves in provocative dance poses. He couldn't help but stare.

South Beach, eat your heart out.

Either this was a secret plastic surgeon retirement community, or Colombian women were just built differently than their American counterparts. Nickerson could barely keep his eyes in their sockets and it wasn't even 10 a.m. As he walked through the surf and fended off an endless barrage of vendors, he had to admit, this was not what his mind conjured when he thought of Colombia.

He headed back to the room, took a hot shower, which he desperately needed, and got back to work. He wanted to wrap this job up fast. He needed some down time here. His credit card people had come through. They'd traced Dunaway to a specific hotel in the old city, so the job transitioned from a chase to a stakeout. He dropped a message to Teri Bradshaw updating her on his status and caught a cab down to the old city. As quaint as the place looked, he made a beeline for her hotel. He wasn't here for tourism just yet. When this was over, he would take a couple months and enjoy his surroundings. There was a Juan Valdez just down the block from Dunaway's hotel. Perfect. Elaine Dunaway was an American. That was a coffee shop. No way she didn't go there at least twice a day.

He opened his computer and logged back into the NADS system. Once in, he ordered the algorithms to flood her social media sites and text messages with location-based suggestions focusing on coffee shops, like the very Juan Valdez café in which he sat. He closed down the system and struggled through ordering a plain black coffee (which the Colombians called *tinto* for some reason). All he had to do now was wait on the miracle of suggestive marketing do its work for him.

50

MONTANA AINSLEY
Present Day
Managua, Nicaragua

Montana couldn't blame Lainey for bugging out. Nicaragua had become seriously dangerous, and though he liked having her around-she was awfully intuitive-the odds of them having to dodge gunfire went up by the minute. Although she seemed pretty tough, he didn't know her all that well. Currently, Managua was not a place to test one's mental toughness. The wrong move here could prove fatal. That, and her lack of Spanish would have been a big hindrance in Nicaragua just now.

Montana sat in the open-air lobby of his favorite airport hotel again, waiting on the metallurgist Diego recommended to call him back. He needed some supplies from the man, and since everyone was afraid to open their stores, he was trying to convince the guy to sell him what he needed over the phone. Montana promised he would take a taxi directly to the guy's house to pick it up.

In the meantime, he'd placed a call to Christian's family up in Leon. He was hoping to get Chris's father to trek up to the city of Chinandega and to the port town of Corinto and poke around for The Bradshaw Group's operation. He owed Lainey that easy favor. He had forgotten to tell her that Corinto was Nicaragua's biggest (and only) commercial port. If the Bradshaw Group was shipping anything in or out of Nicaragua, they were probably based up there. She'd been looking in the wrong place.

The industrial town of Chinandega was all massive warehouses. It would be easy to hide up there. The Department of Chinandega, even by Nicaraguan standards, was the wild west in organizational terms. You could open up a nuclear power plant and nobody would notice. Even if they did, a couple c-notes would keep it quiet. He was hoping to get some information for her to serve as a pretext to staying in touch. He sensed that she was on the verge of throwing in the towel on her U.S. life, and he knew the feeling. She was going to need some support to make that call.

His phone rang. The metallurgist agreed to sell him the equipment, but he'd need at least a day to gather it all. That meant the soonest he could meet would be the following day before 2:00 p.m. Nobody, the man informed him, went out in the afternoon.

Montana passed the evening alone in the outdoor lobby listening to sporadic gunfire and occasional *mortero* blasts. He could see the reflection of buildings on fire shimmering off the low-lying clouds. The following morning, he walked from his hotel to the airport and arranged to purchase all the seats on the late flight to Bluefields the following day. The agent thought he was crazy, but he laid out the six hundred in cash and said he needed the space for supplies. She nodded thoughtfully and approved the purchase. She must have figured he was bringing food and water to the Coast. The roads weren't safe, so flying supplies made more sense. He made sure his equipment would be under the plane's weight limit and exited the terminal.

As he walked away from the curb, he saw a short, chubby, white guy walking out of the Best Western across the street, bag in hand. The guy was red-faced with anger, and his legs were horribly sunburned and covered with mosquito bites. He figured the guy was about the last tourist out of the country. By now, most U.S. carriers had halted flights into Nicaragua. Montana stopped at a roadside stand for an empanada and some gossip with the weary vendor. Normally, there were a dozen empanada vendors outside the airport. Today, just one. When he finished, he started walking back to the hotel, but decided to detour downtown. After waiting for half an hour, a taxi finally appeared and dropped him just south of the Metro-Centro mall.

He couldn't explain why, but like a moth to a flame, he wanted to get a sense of just how dangerous the area had become. He walked around for an hour, sweat soaking through his clothes. He was just winding his way back towards a main road to catch a taxi when a fleet of police-issue Toyota Hiluxes buzzed by at nearly 50mph. They came screeching to a halt just two blocks down from him. Cops poured out of the trucks and created a perimeter around a huge three-story house. Montana's blood turned cold. All the cops were carrying gleaming metal shotguns. Three-story houses were rare in Managua, so a house that big stood out.

If the protesters were hiding in there and the government goons had found out, things were going to get very ugly, very fast. He scanned the roads for a taxi or any car he could pay to get out of there. Instead of a taxi, three dirty Hiluxes slowly rolled past him. Each truck had a half dozen paramilitaries in the truck bed, fully armed and wearing black balaclavas. Those trucks parked behind the police trucks, and almost two dozen men, armed with AR-15s and AK-47s spread out to surround the house. Once the paramilitaries were in position, the cops turned their backs to the house.

Jesus, they aren't guarding the house, they're guarding paramilitaries.

One of the cops waved a gun at Montana and yelled out to him to clear out of the area. From two blocks away, the warning was clear. The day was over, and the crazy was starting. Montana saw three flaming orbs arc from the para-militaries toward the house.

Holy shit, those were those Molotov cocktails!

It was past time to leave. As Montana jogged away, he heard screams behind him. He briefly wondered if he could help, then remembered the three dozen armed government troops.

From four blocks away, he heard automatic rifles open up. A block later, he turned around to see black smoke billowing up into the sky. A civilian fire truck raced past him, and seconds later he heard rapid gunfire and the sound of tearing metal.

It took him forever to find a car that was willing to take him back to his hotel. By then, it was early evening. He nodded to Esmerelda behind the counter. He didn't want to engage her in conversation. He felt sick, and she certainly didn't need to hear about what was happening to her country. He stopped when he noticed that she was staring into her phone with tears streaming down her cheeks.

She looked up at him, misery pasted all over swollen cheeks. "They just kill a family downtown. Burn the house to the ground. No reason. Those people don't do nothin. They burn the house and shoot the kids trying to escape. That family, they just make beds. One was just…just…" She dissolved, sobbing, into his arms.

Montana's stomach dropped. He had just seen that live and in person. The wheels had officially come off the cart here. It was time to get out. He told her he would be on his way to the Island shortly, and that she should probably follow suit. The Island would be safe. Eastern Nicaragua was basically a separate country, and Corn Island had an ocean separating it from this madness.

51

TERI BRADSHAW
Present Day
Seattle, Washington

Teri arranged to sell Wonderwheel to her Saudi Arabian buyers. Her domestic suitors actually offered more money, since they could sell the user data to government security agencies, but the Saudis didn't have to report to U.S. agencies, and they agreed to destroy all pre-sale records. The terms weren't too hard to swallow, but they'd negotiated hard. With everything said and done, she planned to pay out about thirty-five cents on the dollar to her most important investors, and about half that to the rest. She finished the taxes for both companies and had prepared all the records for a "server" accident.

It was surprisingly easy to wipe any trace of The Bradshaw Group off the digital planet. She employed a skilled hacker for the digital work, and her senate position would provide any future immunity she might need. She handled the tax filings and investor K-1 documents herself. No outsiders. The war in Nicaragua had proved a blessing in disguise. She could easily bury the non-profit's records in the *fog of war*. There was still no U.S- based news on the subject, so she could make up any story she wanted. She was certain that U.S. tax bureaucrats would just write it off as another failed third-world state and dismiss her need to file anything.

Sonjay came through, and Senator Patty Williams scheduled a retirement announcement for the end of the week. Teri had no idea what kind of pressure he brought to bear, but she bet he'd been ruthless after she put a bug in his ear about being blamed for the breakup of his inherited tech giant. Her individual investors spoke with the governor, who was ready to announce Teri Bradshaw as the interim senator when the time came. Her re-election would be a shoe-in. Western Washington had been a one-party state for decades.

Once she was in power, she could quash any lawsuits that might get filed by investors from the sudden shutdown of The Earth Ventures Fund. She was taking Alice and a couple of key employees with her to D.C. Everything was set, except for one thing. Her bounty hunter still hadn't tracked down Elaine Dunaway.

She briefly considered including Alan Dunaway in her plans. Statewide polling had shown that having a dependent male spouse increased her popularity. However, polling also showed that having an attorney, disgraced or not, cancelled the advantage. She wouldn't see Alan again.

Teri informed him, in a final phone call, that she would not be retaining him in any capacity, personally or professionally. At first, he thought she was kidding. When she realized she wasn't, he attempted to guilt her into keeping him around. He had started off his passive-aggressive pitch by claiming that Teri had been the reason his wife had left him. When she stonewalled him with silence, he tried to bring up her relationship with Dylan.

Teri had simply hung up on him. She had no use for him any longer, and she didn't really care what happened to him. After his third call, Alice reported his harassing behavior to the police. It was quick thinking by Alice. Teri could score some political gender points out of being "harassed" if Alan surfaced to try and sully her reputation. She could just point to the police report and skewer him in the media.

All in all, the week shaped up nicely. Maybe Dylan had it right. Maybe if you just believed hard enough, everything worked out.

Nah, that idiot wouldn't be right if he claimed Monday followed Sunday.

Things worked out because she prepared for every eventuality.

She dialed her investigator down in Central America…or South America, or wherever. That dipshit hadn't reported any progress in over a week.

52

TOM NICKERSON
Present Day
Cartagena, Colombia

It had not been a good day. Elaine Dunaway had indeed come into the coffee shop as planned. The pretty blonde sat by herself, got a coffee, and commenced reading half a dozen brochures. He snapped some photos of her, then decided it was time to close out this case. That's when the plan went to hell. As he approached with the stack of non-competes, she turned bright red and shoved back from the table with such ferocity that her chair caught on something and tipped her over backwards.

The entire coffee shop came to a screeching halt. She got up and backed away like he was a pit viper. To this point, Tom hadn't said a word, and before he could, the goddamn blonde started shouting like a Spanish banshee. Whatever she said, a pair of menacing Latinos stepped in front of Tom. He reached for a fake badge, but one guy knocked his papers out of his hands, while the other started threatening him in rapid-fire Spanish.

The Latinos scarred the shit out of him. Had the staff not intervened, he might well have wound up in a Colombian hospital. By the time he collected his papers and everyone had cooled off, the damn Dunaway woman had evaporated. It was a total disaster.

He had just showered off the failure when his room phone rang.

He took the call, and before he could even say hello, Teri Bradshaw's voice exploded through the receiver. "Why am I not looking at signed documents?"

Nickerson sighed. He wasn't ready for this. "Look, I found her, but I couldn't approach her. She was sitting with half a dozen of her Latino boyfriends, and I figured the last thing you wanted was for me to make headlines by hospitalizing a bunch of people just to get a signature. I didn't want to scare her off. Besides, I know where she is. Now I just have to get her alone."

"Can't you just stick a damn gun in her face?"

"Are you kidding? Where would I even get one? And no, you aren't paying me for wet work." He figured the colloquial term, oft used by Hollywood, would help rebuild his diminished reputation.

"You're in Colombia now, right? Okay, plant a pound of cocaine on her, call the cops, and let's just send her to a Colombian clink. It's the same to me, either way. She won't be giving any interviews from a cell in some Colombian shithole."

The investigator paused for a minute, then responded, "Uh, and where exactly am I supposed to get a pound of cocaine?"

"Seriously?" the voice thundered. "You're in fucking Colombia. Knock on Pablo Escobar's fucking door. That's like asking Eskimos where you can find snow! It's narco-central. How the hell can you even avoid it is the question!"

She was pissed. He'd heard these volcanic explosions from her before. Nickerson thought about explaining to his client how far off her perceptions of Colombia were; that Escobar had been dead for nearly thirty years, and that Colombia was high-rises, coffee shops, and BMWs now. He decided against it. If he made Colombia sound easy, she would get even more pissed. Instead, he promised he would have something within a couple days. Her mood would soften soon enough.

"Tomorrow by close of business, my time, not whatever goddamn calendar you're on down there. Got that? It's tomorrow or you can kiss the fee goodbye. I'm not paying you to vacation with the bitch." Click.

Nickerson went straight to the hotel's rooftop bar. This was way beyond what he had signed on for. He'd almost been shot in a war-torn Nicaragua and now nearly beaten to death in Colombia. Fifty grand or no fifty grand, he was just about done with this assignment. He settled in the bar and started drinking. He was on his third beer and just starting to relax, soaking in the tropical music and the gorgeous scenery, when a part of that scenery took a seat next to him. Very next to him.

His nose registered the faint smell of flowers, and his eyes caught a flash of golden flesh. He turned his head, and the girl introduced herself as Pilar. Nickerson was too dumbstruck speak. He wasn't even sure how she could be talking...*to him*. Even in a sea of Colombian beauty, this girl took his breath away. Long, lustrous black hair fell all the way to her tiny waistline. The edges of her dark mane disappeared against the black of her tight leather miniskirt. Her skin was a brownish-golden color, and tiny spots of glitter dusted her shoulders and sparkled as she moved in the fading light. She had deep brown eyes and a soft thin face that smiled at him. Her lips were fire- engine red against beautiful, white teeth, and she had the faintest cleft in her chin. He had never seen beauty like this. Not in real life, anyway. And it wasn't just her face or her body. It was everything; from the inviting smile to the perfume and the clothes...even the accent.

All his senses crossed wires. His mouth went dry and his eyes watered. He felt a tingle in his ears. His eyes couldn't blink or stop staring at her breasts, pressed hard against a skin-tight, black leather halter top. He tasted her perfume in his nose. His peripheral vision scrambled to process the perfect shape of her crossed legs and the smooth color transition of black leather on golden-brown skin. He very nearly dropped his beer bottle. When she touched his arm and asked his name for the second time, his skin exploded into ten thousand goosebumps.

She giggled at him coquettishly, and he finally mumbled out his name. She repeated it in thickly accented English. "Neekirson." Tom, he corrected her, his name was Tom. She pronounced it "tomb."

"Buy *cerveza* for me, Tomb, *por favor*?" Nickerson would have bought her a Ferrari if he'd had the scratch.

Instead, he waived at the bartender and held up two fingers. Fresh beer in hand, Nickerson's composure limped back into his brain. He tried to engage her in conversation, but her English was limited to just the very basics. He told her where he was from. Yes, he was a tourist. Yes, it was his first time in Colombia. That exchange exhausted her English vocabulary. He cursed his lack of Spanish. Their brief interlude was dying out. He was trying to form one last hail-Mary question when she leaned into him and asked for another beer. At the same time, she placed her hand on his thigh. Very high up on his thigh.

A shock of electricity traveled directly from her hand to Nickerson's brain, then down to his feet, then up to his smaller brain. He was, in a very real sense of the word, paralyzed. His beer bottle slid through numb fingers and landed on the bar top a half-inch below. Tom Nickerson had never been this close to someone this attractive. He couldn't quite believe what was happening. After the drastic emotional swings of the past week, his mind felt woozy. He wondered if he'd been drugged. She was like a piece of art, and he was scared that the museum curator, or more likely, some six-foot Colombian guy, was about to come by and snatch her away.

The bartender deposited the two new beers on the countertop and winked at Pilar. When the bartender walked off, Pilar raised herself up and whispered into Nickerson's ear.

With her chest pressed against his shoulder, her hand on his thigh, and her lips brushing his ear, it really didn't matter what she had asked. The answer was going to be yes.

53

MONTANA AINSLEY
Present Day
North of Bluefields, Nicaragua

Just before Juan finally let loose his sneeze, Montana's hand landed on the back of his head like an anvil. He shoved Juan's face, earlobe deep, into the soft muck. Juan's sneeze exploded silently into the Earth, and half an inch of mud splattered into his eyes. In virtually the same motion, Montana's hands closed around Juan's hair, and he pulled the kid's face out of the mud, just as Juan took an involuntary post-sneeze inhale. Juan was about to protest, but the older man's green eyes burned a hole all the way through his soul. Juan kept quiet. He had caused enough trouble for the group, and that sneeze could have cost them all.

The two of them lay prone in the mixed ground cover of trees, tall grass, and bugs, one of which had crawled up Juan's nose and caused the sneeze. The third member of the team, Brayan, hid behind a tree to their left with the last two donkeys and the cart. Brayan had coaxed the donkeys to the ground and was slowly feeding and petting the beasts to keep them from making any noise. They were half a day's travel southeast out of their original campsite by the river. Fifty meters away, several figures clad in military uniforms hacked their way out of the jungle and into plain view. They were headed in the general direction of the campsite.

Montana had only spotted them by chance. He'd seen a flash in his peripheral vision, and with the benefit of binoculars, saw a lone military figure carrying a silver shotgun slung over his shoulder. The scout. The sun had flashed off the metal and given him away. Instantly, Montana ordered a halt to their march out of the jungle. Within thirty minutes, figures started appearing in the distance where the jungle gave way to a flat, muddy plain. He didn't need to tell the guys what to do. They knew instinctively to take cover and stay silent.

When the last military figure crossed the plain and disappeared back into the jungle, the small group waited another fifteen minutes before getting up. Nobody said a word. They all knew exactly what they had just seen, and exactly what it meant. As quickly and quietly as they could, they continued on their path out of the jungle. The donkeys were slowed by the cart, which held the last third-of-a-crate of treasure they had pulled out of the river. The crates had weighed so much that the group had been forced to split them into thirds.

It had taken them days of twelve-hour labor to haul all the treasure out of the jungle. Once they got a full crate worth of treasure out, Montana drove it to a warehouse he'd rented in Bluefields. Each crate weighed so much, so he had to drive back and forth nearly a two dozen times. Chris guarded the warehouse in Bluefields, and Gordo guarded the crates behind Chris's relatives' house. Once Montana took off with a load, Diego took Montana's place, leading the donkey trains.

After Montana's last trip, it was obvious that the village suspected something. A small crowd had gathered at the corner *tienda*, and they were drinking beers and pointing at Montana's truck as he drove past. They were running out of time. Juan had suggested that they try to bribe the villagers, but Gordo shot the idea down instantly. Once they initiated greed into the village, they had no way to control it. The just had to hurry and hope.

When Montana's team emerged from the jungle path into the backyard of Chris's relatives, they loaded the last third and everyone got into the truck. Montana met with the father, and the two had a long conversation in Spanish. Montana left him the four donkeys, two carts, and a promise of something more once the excitement of their visit died down. The two shook hands, and

Montana drove Gordo, the two others, and the last of the treasure to the rented warehouse in Bluefields.

"What did he say, *jefe?*" Gordo shouted above the wind whistling through the open windows.

"He said two dozen villagers had split into two parties and headed into the woods to find out what we were pulling out of the jungle," Montana answered, his eyes staring straight ahead. The Nicaraguans locked eyes with each other. They might have made it out of there just in time but returning was not an option for anyone.

Montana felt relieved. The first part of his plan had worked. But getting the gold from Bluefields to Corn Island was going to be tricky. They had to rely on Diego's help. So far, the newcomer had proven useful, but they didn't really know the guy. If he had set up a trap, now would be the time to spring it.

54

NICARAGUAN ARMY LIEUTENANT
VIKTOR MONTOYA

Present Day

North of Bluefields, Nicaragua

The day after he unwittingly passed within sight of Montana and his small party of treasure hunters, Lieutenant Viktor Germuto Díaz Montoya led his company of eight men deeper into the Nicaraguan jungle. Germo, as he was known, preferred this assignment to his last, no matter how pointless it may be. His detachment had been among the three hundred troops guarding the President's empty Managua compound for the past week. It wasn't just that the guard duty was boring; none of the men relished the idea of having to fire on their countrymen over the recent protests.

Most of the students were only a couple of years younger than Germo's men, and something about it just felt wrong. It felt wrong that they had to wear police uniforms instead of their military uniforms, and it felt wrong to gun-down unarmed kids their own ages. That they had to lie so the government could claim the military wasn't involved felt even worse. Every lie the government told made the military men feel like they were on the wrong side.

Now he was out on a wild goose chase, following up on a crazy story called in by a low-level party member out in the podunk town of Bluefields. Most of his bosses thought the story was crazy, but since there was a chance to recover money, and the government was so desperate for cash, the brass figured they could spare half a dozen guys to check it out. They didn't trust the locals in Bluefields, so Germo and his squad got tapped.

They first met the girl in Bluefields to get the full story. Germo thought the whole thing was a hoax, right up until the girl mentioned the American. She said a *chele*, Nicaraguan slang for a *gringo*, had flown in twice on a La Costeña plane. The first time he had a blonde woman with him. The second time, and this was what caught Germo's attention, he flew in on an empty plane with tons of crates full of equipment. For years, Germo's government preached that the American CIA had been arming guerilla's in the Nicaraguan hinterlands. Could the stories actually be true?

They'd followed the river she had indicated, but they were basically flying blind. She didn't have any specifics on where the camp was, and after three days of finding nothing, the heat was sapping his enthusiasm. His guys were even less sanguine. The break from Managua meant a break from its tight rules, which meant Flor de Caña rum could flow in the evenings, but the heat and the bugs were taking their toll. The hangovers were starting to catch up with everybody, too.

Germo thought about calling it quits until their point man radioed that he had found what looked like a heavily used mule trail a couple of kilometers ahead. As the patrol gathered to move ahead, they saw a farmer eyeing them from a small ridge upriver. As they hacked their way upstream towards the man, he ducked down behind the rise and out of sight.

Twenty minutes later, Germo's company made their way through the underbrush and up to the clearing where the man had stood. The whole company bunched up as they came to the clearing. It was about thirty feet in diameter, completely cleared of undergrowth, and about ten feet above the jungle floor. Obviously, this had been cleared out as an overnight camp. Before Germo could decide what to do next, they heard rustling from the woods all around them. A man materialized out of the dense jungle and walked up the small rise toward them.

Germo wasn't entirely sure what to do. At twenty-three years old, he was the elder statesman and ranking officer, but he didn't know much about this part of

Nicaragua. He knew that contra rebels, who fought against the current government decades ago, mostly lived in the mountains to the north. So it probably wasn't that. He also knew his men were the only Nicaraguans still armed, so he wasn't too worried about that either. But as the man approached, the fact that he didn't seem hesitant worried the young officer. Eastern Nicaragua had always been something of a puzzle. Germo started forward and the man stopped.

"What are government assassins doing out here in our farmland?" the stranger asked. The comment brought Germo up short.

Not a good start, he thought.

The man was short but powerfully built. He looked like a farmer with his muscular arms, bad teeth, and ragged clothes. Germo needed to be careful. He wasn't sure how things were playing out back at the capital. For all he knew, Ortega had been thrown out of power, and the military was in hot water with the new government.

"Good afternoon. We aren't assassins, we are just out here looking for a lost comrade." It was a good lie, smooth and uncomplicated.

"There is no one out here for you. Go back to your masters in Managua and tell them there was no one here worth killing and no farmland worth taking."

That was all he said before turning around and walking back down the small hill.

"Wait a minute, *señor*. We are Nicaraguan military. You don't threaten us." Germo thought his voice sounded commanding, but the man ignored him and disappeared into the trees. Germo started after him but froze as a pair of rifle barrels rose up out of the bushes.

The foliage was so dense, he couldn't see the men holding the guns, but he certainly knew a rifle barrel when he saw one. Behind him, Germo heard his men start moving to unsling their rifles. Before anyone could get to their weapons, a dozen barrels protruded from the bushes all around them. Bunched together in the clearing, his men were sitting ducks.

Everyone froze. All Germo could hear was the sound of howler monkeys chattering in the trees above him. He turned in a very slow circle, taking in the situation. He'd led his men into an obvious trap. The clearing, despite being the high ground, was completely indefensible. Even if they had time to draw their weapons, they'd be cut down in seconds. Germo raised his hands above his head and ordered his own men not to move a muscle.

"We are not here for trouble, and we are not scouting for farms," he called out towards the jungle.

"Well, you aren't here looking for a lost soldier either," a voice called back from the cover of the jungle. Germo had trouble hearing the man. The monkeys above had started screaming as if they sensed trouble. He heard the guy call him a liar, then something about the government stealing land. The message didn't surprise him, but the tone did.

There was a poison in it that scared Germo. The Nicaragua he had grown up in was a poor but happy country. People were kind to each other. The voice from the jungle had none of that in it. It was the voice of bitterness tinged with rage. His mind started to panic. He thought he caught the faint whiff of beer. If these guys were drinking? There was nothing out here. No help. These simple farmers could bury their bodies and no one, except a crazy bar maid, would even know where to start looking. With all the trouble in Managua, would anyone even notice they were gone?

Germo hadn't joined the military out of bravery or a desire to kill. He joined because there wasn't much work to be had in his hometown of Masaya. He was an average student and knew he couldn't compete with the smarter kids for a better job, so he joined the military. In no time at all, he was a lieutenant. Suddenly, he didn't care about his status as a lieutenant. He wasn't ashamed that he'd walked his men into a trap. He didn't even feel like a soldier right now. He was just a kid who didn't want to die. All he could think of now was how to get out of this alive.

"Okay, we will leave. But I have one man on point, a scout, out ahead of us. I have to radio him to come back."

For no reason at all, the monkeys above went silent.

Germo heard a voice whisper in the bushes. "They're going to report us. They're murdering people all over the country."

Germo's stomach clenched, and he felt his arms go limp with fear. His mind flashed back to the scenes he had witnessed in Managua. Innocent kids dead in the streets. He had a little sister, she had ten years. If he wasn't around, what would happen to her? Their father was long gone. Could his mother to stop a squad of paramilitary goons? Jesus, he was on the wrong side of this.

Germo called out in panic, youth shattering his vocal chords, "No, *señores*, no, I promise, we…"

Before Germo could finish the sentence, the radio at his hip squawked. It was his point man. "On my way to you, sir. I think I found something." Germo felt the blood leave his face as he processed how that would sound to the men in the bushes. He tried to speak, but his panic had such a tight grip no words came out.

"You see! I told you," he heard from the bushes.

The click of a bolt action rifle cocking, and his bladder released. He was so scared he couldn't even beg for his life.

55

TOM NICKERSON
Present Day
Cartagena, Colombia

Nickerson sat in bed, watching the ceiling fan circle overhead and rationalizing the previous night. After his first, relatively short, session with the girl, he held out a few hundred dollars-worth of Colombian pesos. He couldn't understand the Spanish explanation of her rate, so he hoped she would just take what she needed. When she took her fee from the proffered bills, he was floored. With the leftover, he paid Pilar three times her rate to stay overnight. Now he sat in bed dividing her rate into his fifty-thousand dollar take from The Bradshaw job, minus a sandwich here or there...and the hotel bill. The numbers encouraged him.

Guys like Nickerson didn't bed girls like Pilar. So what if he'd paid for it. A girl like that wasn't going to bed with a guy like him unless there was an exchange of money. What the hell were trophy wives, anyway? They were just dishonest versions of this. That thought finally cut through the rope securing the bag of guilt-bricks he'd been hauling around since his first Catholic communion. With that out of the way, he chewed over how to get his money out of Teri Bradshaw so that he could stay here, with Pilar.

Around three in the morning, he slid out of bed. Pilar was out cold. He'd had room service send up a full spread along with two bottles of wine. In between sessions, she would down a couple glasses and dance wildly to the Latin music pouring out of her phone. Nickerson himself had gotten pretty carried away. Now, in the half light, the room looked like Van Halen had stayed here in the '80s. Bottles and half-eaten food covered every surface. Even one of the sofas had been tipped over.

He opened his laptop and pulled up a picture of Elaine Dunaway that he'd snapped at the coffee shop. He opened it in his Photoshop application and made some alterations. He didn't change anything about Dunaway herself, that would be too easy to spot. Instead, he made a slight alteration to the document that she was writing on.

When he was finished, he opened up the digital file Teri Bradshaw had provided. There were copies of the Dunaway's marriage certificate, home mortgage, insurance papers…everything he needed. He cut out her signature from half a dozen documents and copied it onto a Bureau software application that he used as a trainee. For years, the Bureau used *SignMeUp* to help attain warrants and tie up loose-ends on insider trading cases. He matched the Dunaway woman's signature to all the non-disclosures from The Bradshaw Group and clicked "make real". He watched her signature appear on the electronic agreements. Then he printed out a dozen copies and carefully traced over her signature until he got it just right. It took him ten tries. Then he re-scanned signed versions back onto his computer.

He moved the photos and docs onto a zip drive, so he could have them professionally printed in the morning. First, he would send electronic images through email to Teri in the morning. Then he would Fed-Ex the document "originals" to Teri. The email versions would expedite his fee. Separately, he prepared an email to his firm demanding two months off. Nickerson crawled into bed with the sunrise and dropped off to sleep. When he awoke at ten, Pilar was gone. He found a napkin with a lipstick kiss on it. She had written her number in between the red lip stains.

56

LAINEY DUNAWAY
Present Day
Cartagena, Colombia

Seeing the lawyer hadn't panicked Lainey nearly as much she made out. She noticed him the second he walked in. It was the clothes. When he didn't stop staring at her, warning lights flashed. Under normal circumstances, she would have written him off as a creep. But this was in Colombia. He had a lot of other options for his viewing pleasure. A lot. When she noticed him snapping discreet photos of her, she made a plan.

The guy dressed as a tourist, carried a briefcase, and snapped photos of her. *Lawyer. Fucking Alan.*

That bastard had sent someone down here to serve her with papers. The second he approached, she intentionally overreacted and spilled her chair over backwards, smacking her head by accident in the process. Her guidebook taught her the phrase "help me", and she yelled it a dozen times. She couldn't believe it had come in handy. The blood on her scalp probably helped, too. Lainey got the Latino machismo she hoped for. It worked to perfection. She slipped out just as one of the Latinos shoved the guy.

She bolted back to the hotel, threw her stuff into her backpack, and checked out. She told the desk clerk to tell anyone asking that she was still staying here, but had gone to the mud volcano for the day.

As she passed under the clocktower and out the main entrance of the Old City, a smile spread across her face. For the first time in decades, Lainey Dunaway felt proud of herself. In her old life, people like Alan talked tough sipping ten dollar drinks. In her new life, Lainey lived tough. Alan and his cronies would melt at the sight of an AK-47 in their faces.

Her strides lengthened as she walked. She felt bulletproof, not because of some slogan or internet post, but because she kept facing trouble and finding a way through it. She had always compared herself to Alan or the other men in her life, but that comparison was false. The toughest moment in Alan's life was probably the bar exam. Being strong didn't mean acting like a man or a female superhero. Being strong meant never quitting on raising her child. Being strong meant navigating through a warzone in Nicaragua. Being strong meant seeing danger and not panicking. Alan's lackey didn't scare her. She wasn't leaving Cartagena until she finished what she came here to do. If she saw that lawyer again, she'd just punch him. But to do that, she needed to be able to see him first.

That meant she needed to reorganize. She had seen enough TV to realize that they'd tracked her credit cards. She swung by an ATM, withdrew the limit three times, and walked across the main square into the funky tangled streets of the Getsemaní neighborhood. Among the hippie and backpacker sets, she bought a prepaid flip phone with a Colombian number and took the battery out of her U.S. smartphone. Tonight, she'd go back to the old city, power it up, and copy the contacts from her old phone. In a cute, back alleyway shaded by a thousand umbrellas, she found a hostel full of young backpackers and booked a fifteen-dollar room.

No a/c, no hot water, no problem. She dropped her bag, fired up her computer, and sent off a short email to her lawyer in the States. If Alan wanted to reject her generous offer, fine. The system could bankrupt them both. In a year, a pair of lawyers would have all their money. After seeing how Alan had ruined peoples' lives to get it, she didn't want it anyway.

She got her hair cut and dyed black (over the objections of the Colombian stylist-who couldn't believe someone didn't *want* blonde hair). She bought a wide sunhat, a new bag, and half a dozen woven bracelets. Her new sundress felt so thin it was almost sheer. No wonder the locals could handle the heat. Some new perfume, blood-red lipstick, and she barely resembled the woman who left the U.S. a few weeks before. When a couple locals whistled at her walking by, she figured the outfit was complete.

Now she wouldn't have to worry about Alan's lawyer. She knew lawyers. All it took was a few cosmetic changes, and Alan himself wouldn't recognize her. Thirty minutes after the siesta hour, a brand-new Lainey Dunaway navigated her way along the winding streets of Old Town Cartagena and walked into the Museum of Naval History. Boldly, she asked to speak with the curator.

* * *

Just as boldly, the woman at the front asked her to wait. The woman didn't pick up the phone to call anyone. So, with nothing else to do, she wandered through the museum exhibits. Cartagena had a rich history of naval and pirate warfare. It brought her mind back to the coin burning a hole in her bag. She stopped when she came to the museum's main attraction; the history of the *San José*'s sinking, its discovery, and eventually its planned place of honor here in Cartagena. She wandered upstairs to the more densely populated modern section. She saw a door marked "staff only". Elaine Dunaway would stop right here. Lainey didn't hesitate. She walked through hoping to catch the curator off guard. Again, bureaucracy stymied her. The curator's assistant said that if she didn't have an appointment, or even a reason for one, the curator was off limits.

The woman behind the desk went back to her phone, and Lainey was left standing in the empty outer office. She pulled off her hat, fanned her face, and wondered what to do next. She jumped when a pair of female hands gently grabbed her shoulders from behind.

From behind her, a woman cried out, "*Dios mío, Lina, que linda, me encanta tu vestido.*" The mystery woman kissed both Lainey's ears from behind, then spun her around while jabbering in happy Spanish. The woman moved in for a hug, but pulled up short, shocked, when she saw Lainey's face. In heavily accented English, she said, "Oh, my God, I am so sorry. I am so embarrassed. I thought you were my sister. You look…you look exactly like her from behind."

Her face flushed at the embarrassment. Stalling for time to stay in the office, Lainey touched her forearm and said, "Anyone who smells that divine can do whatever they want with me."

The younger woman laughed and retouched her forearm. "You are too sweet. I am Julia Chávez, assistant curator. What brings you all the way to our office? The excitement is out there in the museum."

* * *

The two women sat in an open-air café just across from the museum drinking coconut-lemonade and sharing at a fruit plate. Julia, the assistant curator, was about ten years younger than Lainey, but unlike most Colombian women, she wore her black hair in a chin-length cut similar to what Lainey now sported. Lainey wondered if the uniqueness of the hairstyle wasn't half the reason Julia had agreed to talk to her. Every other Colombian woman seemed to favor waist-length locks.

Of course, Julia was absurdly beautiful. What was it about this place? Lainey was going to get a complex if she stayed here much longer. Julia had a sculpted oval face, high cheek bones, completely and amazingly perfect lips, and dark almond eyes. Her skin tone and slightly slanted eyes made her appear almost Egyptian. She had a beauty mark on one cheek and wore the multi-colored earrings that Lainey had seen all over the city. Her white mini-skirt dress laced up on both sides, and she accented the look with three-inch black heels, a decorative belt of thick gold rings, and about a dozen gold bracelets on her wrists. A thin golden band looped twice around her right upper bicep. To Lainey, she looked somewhere between professional and, well, *a professional*. She carried off the duality with a practiced ease that made Lainey jealous.

Julia was from Bogotá and had a pair of degrees in Marine Biology and Marketing. She had been transferred to Cartagena to help the museum with its expansion plans for the coming *San José* exhibit. The find would become the city's centerpiece attraction once it got raised from the ocean floor. Both women wore sunhats and sunglasses, and they leaned toward the center of the table speaking English in hushed voices. To anyone passing by, they looked like chic tourists from Medellin gossiping over a late lunch.

"Well, if you managed to get out of Nicaragua to here, the least I can do is share a drink with you. That poor place. It's really beautiful. Sad what's happening now," Julia sympathized.

Lainey had given her some of the backstory that led her to Cartagena. For her part, Julia was more than happy to speak with the American. Colombia, she informed Lainey, wasn't yet very big on the U.S. tourist scene, so Colombians were always interested when they came across one.

"It really is sad, Julia. You've been there? Do you get to travel much?" Lainey asked, trying to build rapport before her big pitch.

"I do. My family is in government service, so we've been travelling around since we were little. But tell me, why did you come to Cartagena, and why do you want to see the curator?" She paused and lowered her sunglasses to the tip of her nose. He dark eyes twinkled with innuendo when she asked, "Do you... *know* him?"

My goodness, an echo of Elaine Dunaway thought, *the Latino culture was certainly more overtly sexual than in the States.*

"No, no, nothing like that," she smiled back.

"Oiy, this is sad. He needs to find a new girl. I noticed you have no ring, and Alvaro is divorced. Colombians don't like to see single people. We think everyone is happier in a relationship." She faked pout. "Well, if not that, why do you want to see him?"

Why. The question Lainey hadn't thought through when she first went into the museum. Why in the world had she expected to just get a meeting with the curator. On the walk to the café, she decided that she would have to come clean, sort of, and hope to pique Julia's interest.

"Well, I wanted to get some information about the shipwreck. I mean, more than just that it's gold and treasure." She laughed nervously. "I was curious as to what exactly they expected to find. What the actual treasure supposed to look like?"

Julia cocked her head slightly. "Why do you ask?"

Lainey detected a bit of suspicion.

This was the hard part, and she really didn't have a good answer. "Well, it's virtually impossible to get any information online, and I saw a thick book at the museum, but it's in Spanish and I...I just," she sputtered. He mind went blank trying to form a lie.

Julia leaned back and stared at her for a couple seconds. She pushed her sunglasses back up to cover her eyes and re-crossed her legs. It was a cold gesture.

"Well, the thing is, Lainey, much of the information that you're seeking is, how would you say it...a class secret?"

"Classified?"

"Yes, that's it. Classified. In fact, we are being sued by some Americans who want to take control of the wreck and claim the treasure for themselves." She stopped speaking and let the comment dangle in the air.

Lainey sighed. "Typical," she mumbled, trying to sound shocked at the revelation. She could feel the door closing because of, yet again, a lawyer.

"Wait," Lainey straightened up. "You don't think I'm...oh, no. No, no, no, Julia, I've got nothing to do with that. Honestly."

The Colombian woman didn't change her posture but reached out her hand and patted Lainey's as if to indicate, *it's okay, you don't have to keep lying.* Lainey had to give it to the Colombians. Even when they stonewalled you, they were so sweet about it.

"I'm sorry, Lainey, but there just isn't more information I can divulge."

Lainey was rifling through her mind now. This was it. Her one and only shot. How could she get this woman to understand? Damn it, why was it always lawsuits? Was there a soul on Earth some damn American lawyer wasn't suing? What had Montana told her? Bribe somebody? This woman didn't look like the bribable type. Then a thought hit her. Maybe she could bribe her curiosity.

"Wait," Lainey said. "Just give me a sec." She dove into her new purse. Her coin pocket was littered with junk pesos from Colombia and Nicaragua. She frantically rummaged through coins before she spotted it. The coin Montana had so casually flipped to her. She paused for a second before pulling it out. She could protect how she found the coin, at least for a bit, but she needed some way in with this woman. She pulled out the old gold coin and carefully placed it on the table between them.

"I found this on my travels. I don't want to say where, but I'm curious if this is something like what you expect to find."

Julia removed her sunglasses and furrowed her brown eyes at the coin. Then she tilted her head at Lainey. She reached down and picked the coin off the table. She studied both sides of it, then took a very thick pair of glasses out of her bag to get a better look. Her eyes went from the coin up to Lainey.

To preempt her objections, Lainey added. "Julia, I know you're gonna want to test it. I wouldn't try to pawn off some kind of fake. Believe me, it's real. Or at least, I'll pay you a year's salary if it turns out to be fake. I just want to know where, or even when, it came from."

Julia looked at the coin again, then she eyed Lainey up and down. Then she looked back at the gold coin. Her expression opened up just a little.

Lainey realized that the woman wanted to change her mind, but she needed a slight shove. She added, "If it's fake, I'll take your boss to dinner."

Julia's features relaxed and she smiled broadly. "Now you are negotiating." She grabbed Lainey's hand in a friendly gesture. "But you have it the other way around. If the coin is real, you have a date tonight."

57

LAINEY DUNAWAY
Present Day
Cartagena, Colombia

The gold coin turned out to be real, and the curator, Alvaro, turned out to be very handsome. She met him at the museum after closing. They were about the same height, and he was several years younger than Lainey.

Score one, Julia.

He wore a bright linen suit with a pastel collared shirt underneath. He had the piercing hazel eyes of a cat and a full mop of dark hair so fine it looked almost feminine. He wore it a bit too long, so he repeatedly had to brush the long bangs out of his eyes. If it hadn't been for the accent, Lainey would have taken him for a European. When he kissed her cheeks, she detected a faint whisper of chocolate.

The good looks gave way to boyish clumsiness at the beginning of their date. He kept dropping his reading glasses each time he removed them. Then his fork, then his spoon. The combination of nervousness and good looks charmed her. Alvaro had *academic* written all over him, but his Colombian accented English was so seductive she didn't care. She could listen to him talk all night. He told her he'd been single for a year, after a quick two-month divorce.

Lainey missed his next three sentences. Her mind kept repeating: *two-month divorce? You can't settle a traffic ticket in two months in the States.*

A couple glasses of wine seemed to take the edge off him, and his personality settled in by the time their entrées had arrived. They talked very openly of their lives through a romantic two-hour rooftop dinner overlooking the harbor. Afterwards, Alvaro took her dancing at a tiny salsa club on the outskirts of Getsemaní.

It took Lainey less than a minute to determine that dancing in Colombia had no comparative action in the United States. Alvaro, along with the rest of the men at the club, not only danced, they moved like liquid mercury across the floor. Weirder still, all of them danced. The club's tables sat empty. Somehow, the women outclassed the men. She had never seen women move like the women from Cartagena…the *Costeñas*. Every part of their bodies moved with the music, but each action was independent and perfectly timed with the rhythm. And the guys were right there with them, step for step, perfectly choreographed. Lainey couldn't dance like that. Nobody could.

She tried her best for two hours, and the salsa music seeped into her soul as the night wore on. Every twenty minutes or so, they'd take a break and split a mini-shot of rum, then it was back to dancing. By the time her date walked her back to her hostel and pecked her on both cheeks, they were both sweaty and a little smitten. As Lainey fell asleep, she wondered, like a teenager, if the cute boy would call her the next day.

Sure enough, her phone rang early.

Not Alvaro.

"*Hola Chica*," Julia said, laughing into the phone. "You must have had a fun night. I haven't seen Alvaro so light on his feet since I moved down here."

Lainey laughed and sat up in bed. She tried to tuck wild strands of hair behind her ear, but realized they had all been chopped off the previous day. "Oh, it's not what you think, Julia. My gosh, you've got a dirty mind."

She heard the Colombian woman smile into the phone. "Well, I think there is some spark there. But this is not my purpose. We need to talk about your coin."

That woke Lainey all the way up. "Oh, okay, really? That's great. Should I meet you at your office?"

"No, I think we should meet outside of here. Unlike you, I did not party all the night away. I spent the night on the phone and in front of a computer. I need coffee. Your coin in interesting, but it is also a very...*delicado*. I want to know a little more about the origin, and I'm willing to trade information with you. We both have to be careful, Lainey. Latino culture is not the United States. This is a male culture. We are women, so if we are wrong, we get dismissed. We need all our facts straight. Then we can plan how to manipulate the men."

"Ah, the famous *machismo*, right?"

"Yes and no. Men are in power, but women are not without power. As I hope you will see with Alvaro, we control the bedroom, which means we control the men who control the power." Lainey laughed. Even Julia's conversations hovered somewhere between professional and well, *professional.*

Julia went on, "I think it is easier to control power from behind the curtain. There is less stress." She paused for a couple seconds before continuing. "Lainey, what you found, maybe, is going to need careful manipulating. If I am right, this isn't something that can be a secret. But we have to be right. Completely right. I have a feeling there is *mucho* you aren't telling me, but I think I understand why. As I said, I can trade some information, but can you tell me this one thing...this isn't the only coin you found, is it?"

Lainey paused before answering. This was it. She was right and she knew it. She knew it because she felt it. This woman wanted to help because she felt it, too, and that bonded them. Then she thought of Montana. How would he play this? He wouldn't sugarcoat it at all. He'd tell the truth, and he would do so with so much airy confidence that it would win people over. "No, Julia, it isn't," she paused. "Not by a long shot."

"I thought not. Let's meet in an hour."

* * *

Lainey sat sipping a café *tinto* in a Juan Valdéz off a side street close to her hostel. Like all Juan Valdéz cafés, the front was glassed in so that the patrons could look out over the sun-baked city. This one afforded her a view of the towering Castillo San Felipe.

She watched groups of tourists labor up the stone parapets in the mid-morning sun. She didn't see the door open, but when every male eye widened in astonishment, she knew Julia had arrived.

One glance explained the looks on the guys' faces. Julia wore a sheer sundress with calf-length suede boots and a belt of woven gold. Her dark hair blew loosely in the wind of the closing door. The fact that you could make out the black bra and panties underneath accounted for the stares.

Every moment a fashion show.

Julia indicated a coffee to the woman behind the counter and joined Lainey after a hug and cheek kiss. As they sat, she maintained a friendly grip on Lainey's hands.

"You have to tell me about your date. Tell me everything."

Lainey didn't know how to react. Julia appeared to think their friendship spanned decades. Once again, was she Lainey or Elaine.

She made her choice, then described the entire night, concluding that she definitely wanted to see Alvaro again. She felt like a teenager swapping boy gossip. Deep down, she had to admit she kind of liked it. Julia seemed concerned that Alvaro hadn't been more aggressive. She announced that she would have a talk with him, then switched conversational gears like a race-car driver.

"There is some history you may not know about the *San José*. Originally, there were three treasure galleons in the fleet. The captain of the *San José*, José de Santillán, was the captain of the entire fleet. He was a bigshot back in Seville called the Count Alegre."

The waitress set down coffee and Julia thanked her.

"That doesn't matter. What does matter is that one of the other ships, the *Santa Cruz*, was led by a man named de La Rosa. De La Rosa owed his career to de Santillán because of family connections back in Spain."

Lainey was totally focused. She fed off the energy emanating from Julia.

"The British sunk the *San José* by accident. They were trying to capture it, but one of the cannonballs must have struck a magazine, and the whole thing went up in a fireball. That's why nobody knows exactly what's down there."

Laine nodded. "Okay, but what's so urgent and secret?"

"Well, I've been working on a theory for a few years now. The *San José* had a sister ship in the same battle, the *San Joaquín*. The *San Joaquín* made it out of the fight and safely back to Cartagena harbor around four that morning. That was captained by a man named Villanueva. The third ship, The *Santa Cruz*, the one captained by the friend of de Santillán? It was captured by the British hours after they blew up the *San José*. And guess what?"

Lainey's head was swimming with all the names. "Wait, Julia. So, they blew one boat, the *San José*, then they caught his family friend's boat, the *Santa Cruz*. Right?"

"*Exactamente*. You wanna know what the British found in the hold of the *Santa Cruz*?"

The penny dropped in Lainey's head. "Oh. My. God."

Julia nodded her head in celebration. "Yup. *Nada*. The hold was completely empty of treasure. Now, I spent all night going back through the digital logs in the archives back in Seville. There is an entry from de La Rosa's log about following 'José's example'. Historians have always assumed de La Rosa meant 'the *José*', as in *the San José*. As in he wanted to go down with his ship like de Santillán did with '*The San José*'. But remember, de Santillán's first name was also José. I think De La Rosa was talking about José the man, not José the ship. I think de Santillán offloaded the treasure, and de La Rosa followed suit."

Julia took a sip of coffee, looked past Lainey, and raised her middle finger in the universal sign to f-off. Lainey wanted to ask, but Julia waved the question away. Whatever it was, it appeared so standard that Julia didn't even break conversational stride.

"Villanueva, the guy that got away, his log mentioned a fisherman, pressed into service 'from the land north of Portobelo.' Present day, that would be Costa Rica or Nicaragua. The log goes on to mention that the fisherman had dark skin and…well, this doesn't translate, but the log said he had 'tricky' eyes. Villanueva didn't trust him. He wrote that de Santillán, 'made a mistake letting the suspicious little man go'…on the day of the battle."

"Wait, Julia…"

Julia held up a finger indicating she wasn't done. "So here is what we have. According to Villanueva's logs, when the fleet left Portobelo with the treasure, they got attacked by pirates. They beat off the pirates and captured one of their corsair ships to take with them to Cartagena. Nothing of this shows up in the other two Captain's logs. The thing is, there is no record of that corsair ship in any of the histories of Wager's Action."

Lainey looked surprised. "Wager's Action?"

"Oh, sorry. Yes, that's what the battle was called, Wager's Action. Wager was the British commander. So, from Villanueva's log, we have a guy with suspicious eyes from somewhere north of Panama. He disappears the day of the battle, and we have a ship that's unaccounted for. Then we have the *Santa Cruz*, who's holds are empty because they 'followed José's example'."

Julia took another sip of coffee, then leaned back. "And then we have your coin…from somewhere north of Portobelo," she winked at Lainey, "which happens to be an exact match for some of the coins printed at that time."

Lainey wanted to say something, but she wanted Julia to say it first.

"Lainey, I don't think there is a single gold peso out there in the Caribbean. I think your coin is the first clue anyone has ever found to that treasure."

58

TERI BRADSHAW
Present Day
Seattle, Washington

Teri heard a knock on her home-office doorframe. She looked up as Alice walked in carrying a Fed-Ex envelope.

"Madam Senator-Elect, here is the Fed-Ex from South America you wanted."

Now that her old businesses had been tied off, Teri moved her new operations north of Seattle to a converted law office in Greenlake. They were getting organized while they awaited the confirmation and special election process. Alice and a couple of staffers worked out of the front room, while the rest of the staff worked remotely until they had senate office space. Teri had been waiting on this Fed-Ex envelope since she received the electronic version a couple of weeks earlier. This closed the loop on The Bradshaw Group. The contents would go into a safe deposit box. A box she never wanted to reopen. Whatever skeletons she had to keep, she kept them in that box.

"Great, thanks, Alice. Will you authorize the remainder of the payment to the guy, whatever his name was? And what does the rest of the week look like?"

"I'll take care of final payment, ma'am. You have donor lunches every day, because we have to pay. You also have lobbyist dinners every night, because they pay. Your two magazine spreads are all set for release on Monday following the governor's announcement. The Wall Street Journal wants an interview. I scheduled it, tentatively, for after you're sworn in. The reporter is a friendly. He profiled you a couple of years ago for the Earth Ventures launch. I indicated that all questions had to be focused on your future goals within government. Nothing about the past businesses. He didn't like it, but he agreed. I think he wanted to tie in the female entrepreneur thing, but you said you only wanted to highlight that if you were attacked in the press. Your calendar is up to date."

"Very efficient as always. Anything else?"

"Well, Sonjay Vikram called before you came in. He'd like a call back."

With that, Alice departed the office and Teri called the tech giant's CEO.

"Madame Senator-Elect," Sonjay's smooth voice came over the line, "how nice to hear from you. I trust you are all prepared for the transition?"

"I am, thanks, Sonjay. What can I do for you? You know, I'm not technically sworn in quite yet."

"That's just a formality at this point. I am calling regarding a slate of upcoming legislative proposals that we anticipate being pushed onto news commercials in the upcoming weeks. I would also like your feedback, as a seasoned accountant, on how we might synergize with the Senate to open up some markets currently thought of as, shall we say, less than politically ideal. Then there is the issue of patrolling speech across a variety of platforms. I have assembled a small circle of technology advisors from Silicon Valley. They'd like to fly in next week and have a sit down to ideate with the Senate's newest member. There is mixed consensus that we could forward a proposal for a new governmental agency tasked with speech advocacy and control."

A mixed consensus? So, when we're scheming, it's in English. When he wants to circumvent the first amendment, it's back to Dylan-speak.

"Of course, Sonjay. Just have your people schedule through Alice. I welcome any suggestions your forward-thinking community can offer to strengthen our democracy by controlling any speech that might subvert it."

A mouthful of crap. Was she really back to this?

If he sensed any irony in her words, he didn't say it. The comment was a test, and Sonjay passed with flying colors. She already had her sights set on a higher office, but she needed one of these child billionaires as arm candy. Sonjay wasn't bad looking. Like most of these empty-suited CEOs, she assumed he lacked the background to have real conviction about anything except acquiring more users. His head seemed empty of anything that wasn't related to the word *growth*.

That was a big advantage for Teri. The emptier the head, the easier she could fill it with whatever she needed. All she had to do was play girlfriend to one of these screen slaves and he would do whatever she needed.

Masters of code and adolescents in life.

Sonjay had just made her short-list, and Alice had lunches set up with a dozen more.

59

MONTANA AINSLEY
Present Day
Big Corn Island, Nicaragua

Montana couldn't keep the lopsided grin off his face when he saw Lainey step off the little airplane. She jumped out of the tiny de Havilland Dash-8 and ran across the cracked Corn Island tarmac for a hug. Good thing she did, Montana didn't recognize her with the new look. They exchanged a huge hug and left the airport in one of the island's three taxis.

"Boy, have I got some interesting news for you," she said once they settled into the back seat. A beautiful line of white sand and turquoise water stretched out to their left.

"Well, I've got some news myself, including some things you might find interesting about that group you were looking for."

"What group?" She paused for a beat. "The Bradshaw Group?"

"Yeah, that's the one."

"Oh. Uh, what did you find?"

"Not interested anymore?"

"No, no, I am. I just...I just sort of forgot about it."

"Well, Chris's dad went to the port city of Corinto to dig around a bit. I forgot to mention to you that Corinto is probably where any kind of shipping outfit would be located. Gustavo, that's his dad, didn't come up empty-handed."

"Oh, wow! Seriously? What did he find? And in the middle of all this? How?"

"Well, that's the good and bad news. I've got info for you for days, but the operation itself is shut down. Once the protests started, it was one of the first businesses to close. Because the owners are foreigners and not on the ground in Nicaragua, nobody was home to threaten them if they didn't show up. As for how he found out, well, now that this has been going on a few weeks, everything has settled into a rhythm. You can travel at certain times, go to certain places, that kind of thing. Another informal rule is that you can't go out after 2. It's a weird kind of normal. Even in a warzone life goes on, I guess."

"Ah. That makes a kind of bizarre sense."

The taxi pulled to a stop in front of a cute, little pink house, just across the street from the beach.

"Wow, that was quick. Wait, you live in a pink house?"

Montana laughed. "No. For the time being, you do. I rented it for you for the next couple weeks. We can extend if you want. The owners live in Canada, and they're deathly afraid of coming back. We told them that the government is targeting foreigners. Since no news makes it up there, they bought it lock, stock, and barrel. Hell, if you like it, they'd probably sell it. I'd let you stay at my place, but I've got a few unexpected people crashing there."

"That's cruel. Funny, but cruel. So the whole team is at your place?"

"Yup. One big, happy family. We put some basics in your fridge, the house already has towels, soap, what have you. There is a scooter out back, so you can get around."

"A scooter? It's safe out back? Just outside?"

"Lainey, the island is about an inch long and currently houses about a thousand people." He smiled at her. "Let's just say it would be easy to find if it went missing."

"Okay, but by that same token, aren't, uh…" She glanced at the taxi driver. "Is it safe…you know, to…"

"Corn Island the safest place in Nicaragua," the driver burst out in Creole-flavored English.

"Oh! You speak English," Lainey responded nervously.

He laughed. "Whole island speak English, Miss America. Spanish the second language here."

Laughing, they exited the taxi, and Montana walked her to the door.

"Whoops, I almost blew that. Good thing the guy interrupted me."

"Yeah," Montana said, "sorry about that. I'm not a very good tour guide. I forgot to mention that part."

"But, since the island is so small, you think it's safe to hide, you know, *it*... here?"

"We'll talk about it tonight, but we've got a plan in place for now. As for the outfit you were asking about, yeah, Lainey, I've got a good bit of info on it. I'm not sure what it all means. I actually had to take notes, so I can't really remember it off the top of my head. It sounds like they had a lot going on up there. I left directions for how to get to my house from here. If you get lost, just spend another seven minutes and circle the island again." He laughed, but Lainey didn't share the joke. She was just staring into space and nodding.

With nothing else to say, he grabbed her hand and dropped keys into it. "Full briefing tonight over lobster at eight. Be on time if you want, but this is the Caribbean. This neighborhood is called Sally Peachy. The north end of the Island is called the North End. It's the place with those amazing beaches we passed. I live on the windward side of the island, in an area called the Long Bay. Sally Peachy is in between the two. Look at the map and it should make sense pretty quick."

Lainey just nodded and looked at the keys in her hand.

Montana left her alone to get settled. Her sudden lack of responses once they were alone had unnerved him a bit. As he walked back to the taxi, he couldn't quite figure out why she'd come back. It was good to see her, but if she was thinking that they...the two of them...nah, surely not. But he would need to iron this out before it became a sitcom. He liked Lainey, liked her a lot. But after five years in Latin America, the thought of something emotionally serious with a North American woman made goosebumps pop out on his flesh, and not in a good way.

60

LAINEY DUNAWAY
Present Day
Big Corn Island, Nicaragua

The little pink house was small but well appointed. Two bedrooms, two bathrooms, a cute little backyard garden. A porch wrapped around the whole house. The two bedrooms had air-conditioning window units, but she didn't need it. The air blowing through the place made it feel like a giant, covered porch.

Lainey picked a bedroom, tossed her bag on her bed, and pulled a pineapple juice out of the refrigerator. Montana's revelation about The Bradshaw Group had seriously thrown her. She hadn't thought about them in weeks. Once he'd brought it up, her mind went blank to everything else he said. The Bradshaw Group. Teri Bradshaw. The woman whose affair with her husband had started all this. For weeks, she hadn't thought about anything else. All her rage. All that sadness. But as she thought about Bradshaw now, it was hard to summon the anger that had burned so brightly just a few weeks ago. She had been so busy living her new life she had forgotten about the old one. Ever since she met Montana and started this crazy adventure, the anger just didn't seem to matter so much. She remembered something about an island map and found it underneath a sand-filled vase.

She unpacked her meager belongings and took a cold shower. She was on the scooter in fifteen minutes, ready to check out the island before dinner.

For the next two hours, Lainey cruised the island's road and took in all the sights. About every quarter mile, she wound up stopping to investigate a different shop, business, or beach spot. The road was so close to the sand she stopped a couple times just to walk in the surf. The place was beautiful. Corn Island was completely undeveloped from a tourist perspective. When people talked about "nothing but palm trees and sand," Corn Island is what they meant.

There were a couple of bungalow-type rental complexes, but most accommodations were just rooms in people's homes. The main port on the western side was the busiest part of the island. In the north end, she saw a small group in the beachfront restaurant-just taking life slowly. She passed the same taxi three times. She saw a few houses here or there, a pizza place, a bar, but not much else. She had a leisurely margarita with the scuba set at Dive Shop's bar in the North End. Together, they watched sun set in between her island and Little Corn island across the water. The dive shop's owner told her that business had dried up since the trouble started. Lainey promised to come back for dive lessons and headed off looking for Montana's house.

Close to 9 p.m., she finally found it at the end of a dirt road on a hill overlooking the ocean. There were three houses on the road. All of them were blocked off by heavy, steel, rolling gates with looping concertina wire across the top. She recognized Montana's because of the Auburn sticker attached to the gate. The dive shop owner, a graduate of the same school, had told Lainey to keep an eye out for it. A security light clicked on when she approached the gate, but Montana had told her it would be unlocked, and she could just roll it open, enter, and lock it when she got in. She did.

Inside, she saw beat-up cars spread all over the dusty driveway. They all had their hoods propped open. It looked like a junkyard, and for a minute, she wondered if Montana had been lying this whole time. Was he running a chop shop and smuggling parts off the island? Was he just a beach bum? To call the front of the house *run-down* was generous. It was pastel blue stucco with a small porch, a couple of dark windows, and dying plants everywhere. The front of the house was so dark she needed the moonlight to showed her where to go.

She picked her way across the auto boneyard to the front door. This wasn't a good sign. She really didn't know this guy that well. Weren't con artists good at this kind of thing?

The door opened as she approached the door, and the interior light outlined Christian's small frame. Light reggaeton music poured out of the doorway. She relaxed.

They did the cheek kiss, and he ushered her into the house. The front door opened into the main room which was filled with wicker furniture all facing in a circle. There was no TV or any electronics. There were no photos or knick-knacks hanging from the walls. Empty Toña cans and well-used scuba equipment were strewn all over the floor, along with various ocean-based detritus: paddles, life jackets, and even the remains of an old, outboard motor. Guy clutter.

The place looked more like a giant dorm room than an adult's house. A dark hallway led off to the left of the main room. In front of her, in the lighted kitchen, the original digging team raised beers in greeting.

Chris led her through the kitchen, where bags of ice melted in the sink. The guys were obviously preparing a meal, chopping vegetables and boiling water. Beyond the kitchen, the entire back end of the house was glass. A pair of glass doors stood wide open to the backyard. As she stepped outside, it became obvious why the front of the house got ignored; the back yard looked like paradise.

A long, covered porch ran length of the house. Directly in front of her, surrounded by grass and flowers, a well-lit swimming pool had been dug into the ground. Hammocks were strung in between tall palm trees. She saw a pair of small, stone picnic tables and matching benches. Lime and banana trees dotted the well-watered grass.

She laughed to herself thinking about the difference between the front and back of the house. Beyond the palm trees, the backyard ended at a cliff overlooking the ocean. Although there were lights strung everywhere, only the pool light was on, and the night sky shone brightly overhead. At the edge of the yard, she saw the top of a ladder that looked like it descended the cliff face. The whole thing looked like a commercial for Corona beer.

Turning her attention back to Chris, who's face had mostly healed, she sat him down at one of the stone tables and made small talk for a few minutes. She finally summoned the courage to ask him about his run-in back in Managua. His usual nervousness around her abated as he related the tale. She couldn't believe the story. The trauma itself would be enough to send the average American adult to therapy for years. Yet here was this kid, nearly healed and completely over it.

Just as he finished the story, a mesh nylon bag came flying over the top of the ladder that descended the cliff. Lainey and Chris both jumped and turned their heads to see Diego, the new addition to the team, heaving himself over the last step of the ladder and into view. He was wearing a wet suit and had a scuba buoyancy vest and air-tank slung over one shoulder. He was soaked. He waved once he cleared the ladder.

The bag he tossed over rolled once on the ground, then came to a stop. Then it rolled again. Lainey was halfway through asking, "what the hell," when Montana popped over the ladder wearing the same outfit and similarly soaked.

"Who's hungry?" He snatched up the writhing bag and shook it. "We're go for lobsters."

"You're kidding me, right? You didn't just go freaking diving for lobster?"

"Not at all. I keep a secret lobster trap a few hundred feet offshore. They were just sitting there waiting. Sorry we're running late, but this *is* the Caribbean. Hungry?"

She shook her head at him and smiled. "I gotta admit, I'm somehow not totally surprised."

Chris interjected. "Don't be too impressed, Lainey, he couldn't catch a fish if he had a bucket of dynamite."

Montana laughed. "Very true. That's why I keep a spear gun."

"You have a spear gun? Is that even legal?"

She didn't bother pursuing the question. His smirk said it all.

* * *

While Chris and Bryon went into the kitchen to help prepare dinner, Montana cleaned up and took Chris's vacated seat at the table next to Lainey. He had a notepad in his hands and read off what Chris's father had found up in Corinto. He'd located a former employee at The Bradshaw Group's warehouse, and that guy explained what went on. The former employee said there were three main sets of employees, and they received two to three massive shipping containers from the U.S. about every two weeks. His group handled the water bottles. Their job was to sort, sanitize, and strip off the labels. They refilled them with purified water, then resealed them by slightly melting the caps to the plastic collars using hot needles. Then they glued labels onto the bottles and crated them up for shipment. The guy had a sister up in the States, and she and her crew eventually received the bottles and resold them on airport tarmacs.

Lainey was shaking her head as Montana finished reading the first page of notes. "Wow, what a total scam. Unbelievable. No, I take that back. Totally believable. What an awful person." She looked up at Montana. "That woman is actually worse than I thought."

Montana nodded to her. "Hey, it gets worse. But yeah. I've actually seen this. When I flew into Fort Lauderdale, I saw a woman selling water for like ten bucks a bottle. I didn't think anything of it at the time. I just don't understand where all the bottles come from. Do they own a recycling plant or something?"

Lainey thought back through her Bradshaw Group files. "No...no, they don't. At least, not one I ever saw on their books."

"Hang on, Lainey, there is more. A lot more. According to the former employee, the second crew was much bigger and received thousands of items out of the containers. Everything from pocketknives to fancy corkscrews, bottles of expensive lotion, bottles of alcohol, you name it. All those got separated, logged, and photographed. Everything got an ID number and was warehoused in bins on site. The third group was a bit smaller, but they received the smallest part of the shipments. Those contents were never shared publicly with the rest of the warehouse staff, but it was an open secret that the contents were much more expensive: electronics, jewelry, expensive booze, cigars, that type of thing."

He stopped and looked up at her, she figured, to gauge her shock. Nothing about Teri Bradshaw surprised Lainey at this point.

"This stuff also got photographed, numbered, and warehoused, but they took an extra step to match the stuff to a shipping invoice. I assume to ensure nothing got stolen. I guess losing a pair of nail clippers here or there wasn't too big a deal, but a bottle of Havana Club goes missing? Somebody's ass gets whacked. So, the third group had a crew that lived on computers. The guy wasn't too sure what they did, but you could fill in the blanks."

"Yeah," Lainey said in disgust, "she's running a black-market Amazon out of Nicaragua." She exhaled some hate. "I bet that bitch even had pickers going from bin to bin. Probably had them on timers, too. Jesus."

"Well," Montana said evenly, obviously trying to cool her down, "he didn't know where the stuff came *from*, but they were definitely shipping it out. The guy said they sent big trucks full of shipping boxes to Managua twice a day. The third group was completely compartmentalized and didn't really interact with the rest of the employees."

Lainey mulled it all over. "So basically, The Bradshaw Group is a white-collar fencing operation masquerading as a venture capital fund and consulting group? The question is where does the stuff come from?"

Montana shook his head. "Beats me. I mean, I get it in broad strokes, but I've kinda had my hands full."

"Yeah," Lainey said softly. She stared out over the cliff toward the Caribbean, wondering if she even cared. Absentmindedly she asked, "where do you even get weird knickknacks like that?"

* * *

Montana watched her. Her jaw was set, and she looked like she was fighting down rage. This was obviously the point where she would decide if she wanted to stick around with them or head back to the States and raise holy hell. Lainey had told him the story of her husband sleeping with the woman from The Bradshaw Group. He knew it must be a tough pill to swallow. Her husband had destroyed their lives over a woman, and a pretty slimy sounding one at that. Montana knew they were operating out of Nicaragua because there was virtually no oversight, and if someone did come looking, the bribe was small potatoes. He wasn't entirely sure what all this information meant, but he knew

Lainey had come down here to find it. Her original plan had been to use it to even the score with the woman who had wrecked her marriage. That would be a strong incentive to go back to the U.S., guns blazing.

After a minute, she looked over at him. The anger was gone, and there were tears in her eyes. "I just don't know what I should do. I mean, I don't know if I have the energy to go back there and…"

He put both his hands flat on the table. "Lainey, let me just say this if I can." He paused, making sure his voice came out even. "I haven't known you long, but for the past few weeks you've been a pretty happy person. You've been laughing, smiling, and enjoying life. And surf instructors." The corners of her mouth turned up at the joke.

"The only time I've seen anything less than excitement from you is just now, when we talked about life north of the border. I'm not gonna even try to tell you what I think, or what you should do. Obviously, that's on you. What I can tell you is this: if you decide to go back and re-engage up there, whether it's the divorce or the Bradshaw people, you'll get pulled back into the system. The Bradshaw people are going to sue you the day you land. Their lawyers will know exactly how much money you have, and it will be a race to see whether they can drain your accounts before the divorce lawyers do."

"Sue me?" She looked at him quizzically. "What could they possibly sue me for?"

"It isn't…" He started then stopped. "Are you sure you want to hear this? It's like that red pill. Or the blue pill, whichever. You can't unhear this."

Her quizzical look didn't change, but she nodded.

"Okay. But don't say I didn't warn you." He took another deep breath. "They don't need an actual reason to launch a lawsuit. They just can. And they'll wipe you out. Say you're a business that pays an insurance premium. You get sued. First, you pay a lawyer out of panic, so you're out that money. Then you file with the insurance company telling them you got sued."

Lainey interrupted. "I know all this. Really well, actually. I told the lemonade people."

"Huh?"

"Sorry," she said, "go on."

"Well, you may not realize it, but your insurance carrier decides whether to cover you or not. If they do cover you, they raise your monthly premium. That way, even though they are paying the money now, you will eventually pay them back in the form of increased premiums forever. The insurance company is basically just loaning you the legal bribe, knowing that you'll be paying them back, plus interest." He paused and realized he was trying to keep himself from getting wound up.

"If you're covered by insurance, everything is all basically lawyer to lawyer contact. You're removed. The money now flows from the insurance company to your lawyer. Once everyone has made enough money, the case will settle, and everyone signs a piece of paper that ensures the truth of the lawsuit is never revealed so that it can't be scrutinized. The money will then flow from your insurance carrier to the other lawyer, with some making it to the actual plaintiff who brought the suit. And that's *if* you're covered. Basically, all the lawsuit did was ensure that you can't say a word once the suit is over. Well, that and cost you a bunch of money in inflated premiums. It's not just a racket for the lawyers to get rich, it's a way of hiding the truth. People in the U.S. are so loathe to admit someone is wrong, this non-disclosure stuff got invented to ensure nobody can prove they were right or wrong."

Lainey put a finger over her mouth and nodded slowly. "Yeah, I can see that."

Montana continued. "If your insurance company doesn't cover you, then it's basically like being sued as an individual. You'll have to mortgage the business, or your house, to fight off the suit. If you don't have enough money, the business goes under and the employees are on the street, or you'll have to sell the house. If you have money, the lawsuit will grind on for a year with depositions, letters, calls, motions, and a variety of other delaying tactics that are designed to draw down your account to the point where a lowball 'settlement' gets made."

She interrupted, "Yeah, this part I know. I was married to one of them, remember."

"Okay, so you know. A lawsuit isn't filed to fulfill justice. Lawsuits get filed to move money from the private sector into the legal one in exchange for silence.

And now, there are virtually no barriers for entry because judges never really adjudicate lawsuits."

"What do you mean?" She looked confused. "Sorry, the divorce is my first real foray into the legal system, but surely there has to be some basis for bringing a lawsuit?"

Montana just smiled. "Nope, none at all. That's why I just left all mine outstanding."

Her jaw hung open. "You mean you just walked away? From active lawsuits?"

"It was either that or the pyrrhic victory of giving four-fifths of my money to the legal system so that no one could ever discuss why the case was brought in the first place."

"You have no interest in proving you're right?"

"That's the whole point. Nobody gets to prove they were right. It's all wrapped up in non-disclosures. You know how Americans all claim some portion of being right? They call it their own 'truth' nowadays? That's what the lawyers have done to the culture. They removed accountability. There isn't any truth because there are no final outcomes. If you try to say, 'I'm right, here is my evidence', you'll get prosecuted for violating your non-disclosure. And can you really call it a victory if you become destitute proving you didn't do something that you didn't do?"

"I don't know, Montana. I mean, take my divorce. Sure, Alan cheated and all that, but you could argue that our diminished sex life pushed him into it. I mean, I take some responsibility there."

Montana laughed. "That's because you're a product of the system, Lainey. The decision to cheat was his and his alone. Black and white. Everything else is a diversion to keep everyone from looking at the real thieves. What's up there isn't a real system anymore. It's just a reverse ATM. You'll spend two years fighting off allegations, or trying to prove them, only to wind up settling on neutral-ish ground. In the end, you'll get wrapped in a document that says you can't discuss it. If everyone shares responsibility, then no one is actually wrong. If no one is fully wrong, all sides of a lawsuits have merit, so money well spent, right?

She looked curiously at him. "I have seen news commercials about actual cases being resolved."

"Yeah, actual legal outcomes are pretty just, but who has the cash to get there. The system isn't really about that. They made lawsuits readily accessible to get rich, and the system grew out of their control. They can't put the toothpaste back in the tube."

"I don't understand, what do you mean?"

"Lainey, lawsuits are an investment strategy, like buying gold or bonds. There isn't anything about the law left. Let's say your stocks aren't performing, so you decide to sue me. You pay a five thousand dollar retainer and sue, claiming I promised to give you my retirement fund. You're basically done. You've dropped five-grand."

"Okay," she said with a slight smile.

"Now, I have to pay a fortune and waste weeks of time disproving every allegation you made. I have to file motions to try and get it thrown out early. I have to pay my lawyer eight hundred dollars an hour to draft those motions. We go to court, at eight hundred an hour. You delay by saying you need depositions to 'investigate'. I pay eight hundred an hour to get deposed. Then I pay eight hundred for my lawyer to acquire everything you subpoenaed: my text messages, emails, on and on and on. Every conversation I have with my lawyer, every email, every court hearing: eight hundred an hour. Conversations between lawyers..."

"Okay, I get it." She interrupted. "I get that part. Jesus, I lived with one of them. But I don't get the investment strategy part. That sounds a bit nuts," she smiled.

"Okay, hang on. So, as we get close to a trial, you add my family to the lawsuit, claiming they were in on it. Then we have to do the deposition and email thing again. Just by filing your lawsuit, I'll lose thirty-grand in legal fees alone. Wouldn't it just be easier to give you twenty, accept the fact that I can't call you a liar because of the non-disclosures, and move on with my life?" Montana paused to let her think about that.

Lainey's smile turned upside down and her face took on a disgusted look. "Oh my God, that actually makes sense. That's horrifying. But, okay, what if you have a bunch of money and keep on fighting. Eventually it would get to court, and..."

"Simple," he interrupted. "You drop the suit, which is called 'voluntarily non-suiting'. I can't sue you back because malicious prosecution lawsuits are virtually impossible to win if you voluntarily non-suit me. That would lead to a "loser pays" system which would reduce lawsuits."

Her mouth formed a perfect O shape as she breathed out, "Ohhh."

"But back to the investment angle. You sued me, you invested five-grand in the suit, right? I decide to pay you twenty, rather than pay my lawyer forty-grand in fees and drag this out for a year. Your five-grand fee is covered, and you get to keep the fifteen thousand left over. You just tripled your money. Mathematically, you're better off suing someone than buying stock."

Lainey looked at him skeptically. "No way. People would be talking about this."

"Would they, Lainey? Remember the non-disclosure discussion?"

The muscles in her face went slack and her hand covered her mouth. She looked like she had just witnessed a car-crash.

"Meanwhile," he continued, "the legal system cleared somewhere between ten and forty-grand between the two lawyers. Nothing ever went to trial, so you never have to admit you lied, and my kids now go to public school."

Lainey looked like wanted to throw up.

"Yeah, sorry to be the bearer of bad news. It's a pyramid scheme and we're all at the bottom. It's a big reason why I live here. You can't sue me if you can't serve me."

"You mean, you chose Nicaragua because they can't find you?"

He laughed. "Yeah, started out that way. Grew to love the place. But look, I'm not unique and special. If I'm here, I'm probably not alone." Montana stopped talking for a minute while Lainey absorbed his words. He didn't bother to mention that with the new regulations on speech and action, he probably couldn't go back to the U.S. at all.

"That's a lot to think about, but I can honestly say I don't disagree with any of it. I actually think I knew all this, I just never connected the dots. It's really hard. I mean, to just walk away. It feels so…irresponsible. Or liberating. Jesus, you weren't kidding about that whole red pill thing."

Before they could talk more, dinner was ready. The small group devoured the lobster, rice, and salad that had been prepared. By the time dinner was over, it was past midnight. They all said goodnight. As she drove her scooter along the nearly deserted island road back to her house, she thought about Montana's take on the legal system.

She didn't want to believe him. But in the back of her mind, she kept thinking about what Alan had done to the poor Robinson family. The thought nearly brought tears to her eyes. Then she remembered Seattle firm, shopping for investors in their lawsuit. *Oh, Crap.* She almost wrecked the scooter smacking her forehead. *I forgot to tell Montana about the Cartagena trip.*

61

CASA DE NARIÑO
(OFFICE OF THE PRESIDENT)
Present Day
Bogotá, Colombia

Colombian President Alejandro Hernández sat in his office with his feet propped up on the corner of his mahogany desk. He had twenty minutes before his next meeting. Trouble brewed in Colombia's eastern neighbor, Venezuela. He wanted to settle his mind before the cabinet discussion. He had reports that a slow trickle of refugees now crossed the border because of worsening conditions in the socialist country. He had a full staff meeting scheduled after the siesta hour, which he never got to enjoy, to discuss Colombia's official position. Everyone seemed to agree that the trickle would become a flood in the coming months as Venezuela's bus-driver-turned-dictator continued to pile-drive the economy into the ground.

A bus driver president, he thought to himself. *How does that even happen?*

His presidency had moderate success so far, but the approval ratings started to drop a month ago. A series of major setbacks over the past few months tarnished his reputation as a man who got things done. His launch of Colombia's first stock exchange seemed hopelessly mired in technological delays, so the upper classes complained about him. The economy showed signs of slowing, so the middle classes fidgeted about job creation.

To complete the trifecta, his PR coup, announcing the discovery of the long sought-after *San José* treasure galleon, appeared hopelessly mired in lawsuits with the North Americans. He had boldly announced that the rumored billions in treasure would be leveraged for a variety of social programs for the poor and museums to help boost tourism. Within days, a dump-truck of legal paperwork landed on his desk. Nothing could move forward until the lawsuits got adjudicated. The delay of the social programs meant that the poorer classes and their massive informal economy lost patience by the day.

The president and his chief advisor both held Doctorate degrees from the same Ivy League university. They knew how the game worked when it came to the U.S. legal system. Once paper started flying, the legal mosquitoes from the States wouldn't stop until everyone's blood was sucked up. The *San José* project was dead.

He had just closed his eyes when he heard Lina striding into his office. Her ability to destroy his naps amazed him. Lina Florez was about as attractive a secretary as he could get away with and stay happily married. Luckily, his wife loved Lina. She loved Lina even more when she learned that Lina was a happily married mother of four. It wasn't surprising. Everyone either loved Lina or was in love with her. What had surprised the president, who was the mayor of Bogotá when he hired her seven years ago, was that Lina had a razor-sharp mind when it came to evaluating people, angles, and the squishier side of politics.

He opened his eyes to see her long, blond ponytail bouncing from side to side as she clicked down the hallway toward his office suite. He still couldn't get over the change in hairstyle. Fake hair clips had taken over Colombian fashion and the daily appearance changes threw him.

She was accompanied by his chief advisor and childhood friend, Javier Antony Rodríguez Gutiérrez. Lina smiled as they approached the desk. Javi had a thoughtful look on his craggy, pockmarked face.

"Señor Presidente," all three said in unison. It was an inside joke among them that, in reality, each one of them had a piece of power. Javier spoke first.

"Mr. President, something interesting has come up regarding the *San José*."

The president lifted an eyebrow. *Interesting* wasn't bad. *Interesting* could be good.

"Okay, what is it?"

Javier turned to Lina who started in. "Mr. President, as you know, we were coordinating with the museum down in Cartagena for expansion plans when… well, when things came to a halt."

The president rolled his eyes. "Do either of you think it's possible that there is someone, anyone, somewhere on this planet, who isn't being sued by an American lawyer?"

Lina continued as though the question was serious. "It's doubtful, Mr. President. But I think not all Americans are cut from the same cloth."

Perfect, Lina, thought the president, *a dead pan joke in the midst of a formal report.*

That comment made him pop his feet off the desk and give her his full attention. "Okay, *señora* Florez, you have my attention."

"Well, I just got off the phone with the assistant curator at the Cartagena museum and she…well, let's just say she had something interesting to discuss. I have her scheduled for a 6 p.m. conference call. I've arranged for our legal counsel to join the call, along with the juvenile chief of staff to my right. It seems that perhaps the raising of the *San José* isn't all we think it might be. Nothing is definite, but Javier and I have discussed it, and we think it's interesting enough to bring to your attention at this point."

"What do we know about her? The assistant curator, and why are we talking with her and not the curator?"

It was Javier's turn to jump in. "Well, Sir, it seems that, perhaps, the actual gold wasn't on the *San José* when she went down. I stress the word *perhaps.*"

"Noted," the president said. Despite the attempt to dampen his spirits, he could feel the excitement returning. He didn't even care that they dodged his question about the curator.

Javier continued, "An American woman came to Cartagena last week bearing a coin that she wanted the museum to evaluate. It's a dead match for what we believe was on the *San José.* If you recall, the *San José,* was picking up treasure and taxes from current-day Panama before shipping it all over to the Spanish Crown. What's interesting about this coin is that the coins on the *San José* were a very specific lot. We have a full inventory of what was on that ship. The coins on there were only in use in certain places. If this woman is to be believed, this coin has no business being where she says she found it."

The president deflated a bit. "Oh. So, it's just a coin." He preferred Lina's soft delivery of bad news to Javier's military-like reports.

Lina cut in. "Mr. President, that was my reaction as well. It was also the assistant curator's initial reaction. In fact, she asked the woman if the one coin was all she found, and the American responded, and I'm quoting her, '*Not by a long shot*'."

Lina let that sink in. "The point being, Mr. President, if there are a lot of those coins, coins that have no business being there..." she faded out and let him fill in the blanks.

The president mulled this over for a minute. There was no way he was this lucky. "Okay, I'm slightly interested. So, tell me why we aren't talking to the curator?"

Javier and Lina looked at each other, uncertain of who should speak. Eventually, Lina rolled her eyes at him and turned to the president. "Sir, it appears that her boss, the curator, has taken a romantic interest in the American woman, and the assistant curator is handling the business side of the relationship."

The President and his Chief of staff locked eyes. Slowly, the exact same smiles formed on their faces. The president started. "So, they were both handling various pieces of the busi..."

Lina let out an audible sigh. "You're both children."

The two men laughed. "Okay, Lina, what do we know about the assistant curator? Is she reliable?"

By way of an answer, Lina furrowed her perfectly plucked brow and tilted her head at the president. "Mr. President, I've never known my sister to be wrong about anything academic." She spun around, and the two men ogled her behind as she marched off. At the doorway she stopped and whipped her head around to catch them staring. "I can always take this perfectly formed ass to an employer who believes me," she called out as she closed the door behind her.

Both the president and chief of staff stuck their fists in their mouths and bit down. Javier looked at the president. "That head tilt...is there any way we can jail her husband on false charges?"

"They teach that in beauty school. As for jailing her husband, that might look bad." The president grinned. "But," he paused as if in thought, "we could have him transferred to the embassy in Venezuela." The both laughed out loud. "But seriously, what do you think about all this?"

"Well, Mr. President, if Lina's sister is half as sharp as Lina…"

62

MONTANA AINSLEY
Present Day
Big Corn Island, Nicaragua

ainey showed up at Montana's house on the Long Bay in much better spirits than when she left the night before. He couldn't blame her. She had a life in-flection point ahead. He'd been there. He meant to fill her in on the treasure plan the night before, but the conversation got sidetracked with the mention of The Bradshaw Group.

She arrived with pastries from a bakery in the Sally Peachy neighborhood. After everyone finished, Montana filled her in on what she missed.

"So, about the junkyard out front," he started.

Lainey laughed and said she wasn't going to ask.

"It took us a few days to mule the crates out of the jungle. We had to make trip after trip after trip. Gold is heavy. Really heavy. Once we got them to the truck, we made several trips down to Bluefields and stored them in a rented warehouse. I bought a few junk cars in Bluefields, and we stripped them down to shells and axles. Diego welded the crates under the hoods." He tipped his *Angels* baseball hat to the newcomer, Diego. Diego probably didn't understand, but he figured he was getting credit for something.

"Then we towed the suckers onto the ferry, two cars per day, and towed them up here. We had to go back and forth a few times, which got a little weird. We told the police we were starting a taxi service on the island after we fixed them up. The tragic beauty is that as things get worse on the mainland, it will dry up tourism here. Nobody is gonna ask why the taxi service never opens."

At this point, Lainey interrupted. "How in the world did that not raise suspicion? I would think towing cars back and forth would look REALLY weird."

"That," Montana said and nodded at Gordo, "was Gordo's idea. Once we brought the empties back to Bluefields for refilling, we repainted them. Told the ferry captain, Diego's relative, that we the originals had problems and we needed to swap them out. Thing is, this is Nicaragua. That happens all the time with high-ticket items. It's almost expected."

"Okayyy," Lainey said, "but that's going to leave a trail, obviously. How in the heck do you plan to get it off the Island? Or do you? Surely you can't want to keep it here. Like you said, a small island is bad place to hide."

Montana took a big breath and sighed it out. "That's where this gets less smooth than I'd like. The plan is to melt a portion of it into bars and the rest into smaller objects we can move back off the island." Lainey's posture stiffened at the word *melt*, but she didn't say anything.

"So, we're gonna start with melting down a batch and making a hollowed-out gold scuba tank. Paint it silver, and see if we can pass it off. A full dive tank is about thirty pounds. That's about 430 ounces of gold, which, amazingly, is the weight of a gold bar. Which is currently worth about $500,000 dollars."

Lainey's eyes did a slow blink.

"I know, the amounts are insane."

"Um," she started, then stopped. "Okay, first, how do you melt gold? Do you have actual metal melting stuff here?"

"We do. I picked it up in Managua and flew it back when we parted ways at the airport. You went off to Colombia, and I went shopping. How was that trip by the way?"

Lainey didn't answer him, which was curious.

"Lainey?"

She turned to Chris and asked him to translate to the team. He nodded.

"Okay guys," she started and turned to Montana, "when I first saw the writing on that coin, it sparked a memory of something I came across back in my old life."

She explained about the Seattle firm and their search for lawsuit investors. It didn't surprise Montana, but the concept of lawsuit investors was new. Then she gave them the story about the treasure galleon's sinking.

"The thing is, the Seattle guys had all these photos of the gold coins and stuff they expected to find. It was part of their pitch. That's what the coin reminded me of. I didn't just *go* to Cartagena, which is wonderful by the way," she patted Montana's arm while she said that part. "I went down there to dig around about the ship they had found, the *San José*. The Spanish Treasure Galleon." She paused to let that sink in for the whole group.

The Nicaraguans were wide-eyed. They already knew where this was headed.

"No way," Montana said before she could continue. "There is absolutely no way. The world doesn't work like that, it…it can't."

Chris' hand covered his mouth. "It might," he said, caught up in the enthusiasm. "The timeline fits with my family's sudden turnaround from fishermen to regional chiefs."

"Well," Lainey continued, "I met with the museum directors down there, and there was this one woman, Julia, who was just razor sharp. She did some research, and it turns out that there were actually three ships. One got away. The *San José* was sunk, but there was a third ship that got caught. When the British boarded it, it was empty. It turned out that the captain had offloaded his part of the treasure when he realized the British were closing in. But the money from the *San José*?" Lainey paused to breathe in.

Nobody in the room blinked.

"So, this woman, Julia, she spends all night on the phone to the archives in Spain. It turns out that the captain of this third ship, a guy named de La Rosa, made a passing reference about following José's lead. Everyone always figured it was just a reference to the *San José*, the ship, and that de La Rosa was thinking he was going to be sunk. But the captain of the *San José*? A guy named de Santillán? Guess what his first name was?"

"José," Montana said in a flat, unbelieving tone.

"Right. José has gotta be José de Santillán, the captain of the *San José* treasure galleon. And what example could he have set?"

"Offloading the treasure," this from Chris, who had a smile a mile wide on his face.

"Exactly," Lainey said while pointing at him. "Montana, Julia thinks that depending on how much we found, which I didn't tell her, nor did I tell her exactly where, we might be sitting on the most famous pile of Spanish treasure in the history of the world."

The room was silent for a full minute. Finally, Lainey said, in a small but whimsical voice,

"So. I'm in the *don't melt it* camp."

Gordo spoke up first, always the pragmatist and nay-sayer. "So now we have the Colombians after us. *Dios Mío.*" Everybody started laughing. Eventually, all eyes shifted to Lainey. Gordo's worry wasn't too farfetched.

"Not exactly," she smiled, slyly. "The thing is, while the Colombians have found the wreck, but they can't get at it. They're being sued by that Seattle firm who claims part of the treasure is theirs. The legal situation is murky, but the bottom line is that the Colombians can't go forward because no other bidders want to risk being sued by Americans."

"Seriously," Montana said, letting out a morose laugh. "They're being sued?"

"I don't get it," said Chris, a complete novice in the machinations of the U.S. legal system, "Colombia is a country. A sovereign country. How can a U.S. business sue a country? Colombia can just ignore them and hire out someone else? Right?"

His eyes shifted to Montana. "Chis, there is no place on earth that the U.S. legal system doesn't think it has sovereignty over." He turned to Lainey and was about to ask her a question when her phone rang.

She looked at the screen, then back up at Montana. "Guys," she said, "it's Colombia calling. I gotta take this."

63

TERI BRADSHAW
Present Day
Seattle, Washington

One of the first meetings freshly-minted Senator Bradshaw accepted was from a local Seattle business, Sea Solutions, LLC. Teri had been hesitant to take the meeting based on their name alone. She was so sick of the word *solutions*. Everything was a damn solution now. Just that morning, she'd seen a truck that said, *Roofing Solutions*. Why couldn't the idiots just say they sold roofs. Did you really want a Harvard-educated roofer? In her accountant's mind, solutions were either liquid mixtures or answers to math problems. Worse still, Alice had informed her that these guys had been making the rounds in Seattle for years looking for funding for their big lawsuit. The lack of takers indicated to Teri that this was going to be a waste of time. But local was local. She was a senator now and they were constituents.

The meeting eventually proved interesting. It seemed these guys were due a share of a massive hunk of buried treasure down in the Caribbean. Teri wasn't really interested, and her body language had made that pretty plain, even after they offered a campaign contribution. When they offered to use a portion of the recovered treasure to build a "Bradshaw" wing at the Puget Sound Naval Museum, Teri finally asked what they wanted her to do. It seemed that the

Colombian government was completely ignoring all the lawsuits that the U.S. firm had filed, claiming the treasure for themselves.

Could the senator believe it? Ignoring the U.S. legal system? It was completely un-American! If the Senator could, perhaps, use some influence in Washington to threaten to cut off aid funds to Colombia…

Teri told them that she would see what she could do, no promises.

64

LAINEY DUNAWAY
Present Day
San Andrés Island, Colombia

ainey and Montana stepped off the airplane and onto the tarmac at Gustavo Rojas Pinella airport on the tiny Caribbean island of San Andrés, Colombia. The island sat less than a hundred miles east-north-east from Montana's house on Big Corn, but because of political considerations, direct travel wasn't possible. They had to fly to Panama, then to mainland Colombia, and finally onto the island.

Lainey and Montana had agreed to meet with the two museum curators, and they all agreed it best to meet in person and avoid digital footprints of the conversation. They left the airport and walked along a well-organized beach promenade toward their hotel. Unlike the Nicaraguan Islands, San Andrés was full speed ahead for tourism. Shops lined one side of the brick promenade while beautiful beaches and dazzling turquoise water fronted the other. Everywhere they looked they saw packed beaches, families with strollers, or kids kicking soccer balls. Lainey imagined that Corn Island could look like this one day. Then she wondered if the residents, like Montana, really wanted that.

Off to her left, the water's color changed from turquoise to light blue, back to a different shade of turquoise, and back to yet a different blue as it approached the horizon. A few hundred yards out to sea, she saw several boats coming and going from a perfectly circular sandy cay with palm trees in the center.

Lainey elbowed Montana and informed him, "That's Johnny Cay. It's supposed to have fabulous beaches." Montana just nodded his head, and Lainey wondered if he was nervous about the meeting. She tried to reassure him. "Hey, what's wrong? Trust me, you'll like these two, and I think they're sincere about working out some kind of deal."

"I hope so," he said flatly. "I just can't get over what old Gordo said. I've been turning it over in my mind. What is to stop them from just arresting us right here and tossing us in a Colombian jail?"

She'd been a bit concerned about that, too, and hearing Montana voice the same concern didn't exactly fill her with confidence. "You're the one who said it wouldn't do them any good. How could we recover it for them if we're in jail? As far as they know, it's just the two of us. And it's not like they could invade Corn Island." She paused on the brink of laughter. "Could they?"

Finally, Montana laughed. "Well, it wouldn't exactly put them out much. A handful of guys could manage it."

They reached the hotel, a beautiful but humble three-story affair right in front of the main beach. At check-in, their rooms had been upgraded and paid for. The girl at the counter wouldn't say who had taken care of the bill, but it was pretty obvious. They shared late afternoon beers at a second-story hotel bar overlooking the promenade and the ocean. Palm trees waved at them from every direction. Montana had just ordered another round when Lainey spotted Alvaro and Julia walk in, looking like jet-set millionaires. Lainey jumped out of her chair and half-ran towards Julia, who made a similar dash toward Lainey.

After the two women had embarrassed themselves like school-girls, Lainey turned to Alvaro. He was wearing a white linen suit with a light blue dress shirt and a Panamanian hat. She could feel a bit of embarrassment fill her cheeks as they faced each other. She felt like she was at prom, waiting on her date to pin a corsage to her. He grabbed both of her hands, told her how wonderful it was to see her, and kissed both her cheeks. When she hugged him, he smelled like coconut oil. His outfit was so old-world sexy that it was almost more than she could bear.

She kissed him right there in the middle of the bar. He responded by putting both his hands on her face as he returned her kiss. The action was so intimate, Lainey's knees actually got weak. They broke after a couple of seconds to a loud catcall from Julia. She was staring at them with a radiant smile and raised eyebrows. Now, thoroughly embarrassed, Lainey led them to where Montana stood with his sardonic smile. She hoped that knowing the curator was basically her new boyfriend might ease the meeting tension.

It did.

By the time introductions were made and a round of drinks had been delivered, it didn't so much look like a business meeting as it did a double date. Lainey sat next to Alvaro on one side of the rectangular table with Montana and Julia on the other. She had sacrificed a little dignity by acting the smitten teenager, and it had paid off. Everyone was at ease, and Julia had already started working her charms on Montana. Lainey remembered the Colombian woman's comment about wielding power through the bedroom. She wondered if Montana stood a chance against the Latina beauty.

* * *

Montana's first thought was relief that he wouldn't have to have a relationship conversation with Lainey. His second was that the Colombians seemed like typical Colombians. The curator was exceptionally cordial, stylish, and organized. The assistant curator, Julia, was expertly dressed and had already displayed a shrewd sense in managing the men in her company. She'd made enough physical contact with Montana to be covertly suggestive without being overtly forward. The short haircut almost distracted him from the natural beauty that seemed to be a Colombian woman's birthright.

Almost, but not quite, he thought.

An obvious stunner at first glance, something about her kept gnawing at the back of his mind. A slight slant to those almond eyes, the small nose, and all that gold jewelry. She looked like an Egyptian princess. What she didn't have, Montana noticed, was a ring.

The foursome talked for the better part of an hour about what had led each of them to their current seats at the table. The curator was a typical academic who had studied all over the world. The assistant curator had been, not surprisingly, a model in her youth. She abandoned it when it became clear her older sister would win every pageant. For his own part, Montana gave them an overview of how the insanity of the U.S. legal system had driven him from his home, his businesses, and his country. Finally, Julia, the assistant curator, broached the real topic.

"Well, I believe we must address business matters, sadly. *Don* Alvaro, why don't you give our friends a sense of where Colombia stands on the matter."

"Yes," the curator straightened. "We have been in near daily contact since Lainey and I met in Cartagena." He touched Lainey on the arm and gave her a warm smile. "Since that meeting, we are agreeing that the coin Lainey presented is possibly part of the shipment that was supposed to be on the *San José*. However, a single coin is not much evidence. Without a sense of exactly what you found, we are holding our breath to learn more. We came here to discuss just this. I'm afraid that the only way to know if your find is from the *San José* would be...how do you say it in English, in pudding?"

The two Americans smirked and Montana said, "It's, *in the pudding*. But great reference."

Alvaro corrected himself, not the least shy, "Ah, in the pudding. Well señor Montana, how much is your pudding?" More laughter. Genuine laughter.

Montana really enjoyed talking with these two, but in his experience, Colombians were tricky. Behind the friendliness, they were shrewd negotiators. Before he gave away his cards, he wanted a bit more from them. "Before we get to the amount of pudding, what does your government have in mind? Are they expecting us to just hand it over? If we don't like the terms, are they going to make a big stink about it? Is this a media event or a secret? Basically, Alvaro, what might we be stepping into?"

Alvaro looked to Julia for help.

She touched Montana on the arm. "Yes, well, naturally, our government would like *confirmación* before making any decisions about how to move forward. But..." she looked at Alvaro, who nodded slightly. "I mentioned to Lainey that this would have to be *delicado*. While the government is interested in the find itself, *don* Alvaro and I are a bit more interested in the historical value of the find. We don't have a monetary…" She looked directly into his eyes, "A dog fight?"

"You are so cute," Lainey interjected and smiled at Julia.

For his part, Montana tried to avoid looking at the Colombian. Between her eyes and her accent, he was afraid of being hypnotized. Instead, he glanced at Lainey, just in time to see her give a covert wink to Julia.

He leaned back. *Son of a bitch. This whole thing had already been schemed out.*

"A dog in the fight," Montana responded, smirking sarcastically at Lainey.

"Yes," Julia perked up, her eyes shining up at him. "Exactly. We don't have a dog to fight. So, we are more interested in the find itself. And so," she looked to her boss. He nodded and stuffed a cucumber slice into his mouth. "We are prepared to step over the bounds that our government has given to us. We hope that will show our good faith." She grabbed his forearm lightly to emphasize the point.

Montana decided to have a little fun. He turned to her boss, Alvaro, and asked, in Spanish, "Do you think I'm this handsome, or is it the gold she's after?" Alvaro exploded into laughter. Julia's head snapped back and she pulled her hand away. Montana translated for Lainey, who smiled and kicked him under the table.

He turned his smirk on Julia. She furrowed her brow and tilted her head at him. She was trying to mock being mad, but her devious smile went all the way to the corners of those sexy eyes.

She arched an eyebrow. "So, the keeper of many secrets. Okay, so the true problem is that we are not in a position to salvage the *San José* because we are being sued by the Americans."

Montana interjected with a head shake and a sarcastic laugh. "I guess the answer is no, there is no one America isn't suing."

Alvaro nodded his agreement, halfway through swig of beer.

Julia continued as though he hadn't spoken, "We are prepared to move forward with a Scandinavian Recover joint effort. However, it seems the Americans have influenced a senator to pressure your government to intervene. We now have pressure both from your lawyers and your government. In truth, Bogotá is not sure how best to proceed. I have a contact in the government who is very close to this." The Colombian woman paused, looked at her boss, Lainey, and then back to Montana.

"She is sure that *if* you found what we all hope you found, the government would be willing to work with you somehow, in confidential." She winked at Lainey, who golf clapped at her nearly correct use of the word.

They all sat for a full minute. Finally, Montana cleared his throat and took a swig from his beer. "Okay, so the question is how do we verify it for you. And how much…uh…*confidential work* is Colombia willing to exchange?"

It was Alvaro who answered. "Considering the potential size of the pudding, I would suspect that if verified, much *confidential work*, but I would remind you, an overreach on your part would make this a much more difficult situation. Julia and I are risking our reputations. If everyone plays fair, this can work. Both sides, if we are all satisfied, want to reach a quick conclusion to this business, no?"

Everyone at the table locked eyes with everyone else.

This was the gamble, right here.

Montana fixed his gaze on Alvaro, then on Julia, before settling on Lainey. She nodded slightly, her eyes glittering brightly, a slight smile on her face. He drained the last quarter of his beer.

"Four tons," he mumbled.

The curator's hand froze in midair. The fork, with its piece of hummus-covered cucumber still attached, dropped from his hand, clanged off his plate, and spun to the white tiled floor. His mouth opened, then closed. He didn't even seem to care that he had hummus all over his suit. Montana didn't look at Julia, but he felt her slowly pull away on the bench seat, and sensed her gaze locked on his face.

"We found four tons of pudding," he repeated, just to press the point. "But there is probably a little more. We couldn't get at it because a military patrol was in the area, and we barely got out of there before we got discovered." A light breeze gusted through the open bar and the palm leaves banged together in the wind. Everyone took a long drink of what was in front of them. Montana and the curator's locked eyes and slightly nodded. The moment broke.

While Lainey laughed and wiped hummus off Alvaro's suit jacket, Montana pulled a stack of 5x7 photos out of his pants pocket and handed them to the assistant curator. She didn't utter a word as she flipped through them. They were pictures of the find from various angles.

Once they had both seen the photos, the Colombians retreated to the bar to talk alone. The conversation got animated, quickly. Judging by the back and forth, it looked like they would agree, but then one of them would say something, and they would start talking over each other again.

While the Colombians blasted away in rapid-fire Spanish, Lainey asked to Montana. "Are you mad?"

"Mad? Mad, like crazy? No, I just get the sense that..."

"No, not mad crazy," she stared at him like he was an idiot. "Mad as in angry. I mean, me and Alvaro. I mean about your plan. I know you had a plan on the island. I know you guys were gonna melt down the gold or whatever. I mean, I know I'm kind of butting into your profession."

"My profession?" Montana asked, a bit surprised.

"Yeah, treasure hunting. Speaking of, I've been meaning to ask you this since I met you. How did you wind up doing this? How does one go from restaurants and laundries to searching for treasure?"

"Holy crap that's a lot of questions. Lainey. You got it all wrong. I wasn't lying about building libraries. I've been a treasure hunter for as long as you have. And no, of course I'm not mad about you and the museum guy. I'm happy for you. He's older than the surfer," he deadpanned.

"Barely" She grinned back at him.

"This isn't a profession, Lainey. I don't *do* this at all." He shook his head. "Last year, I helped build a school up in Leon. The year before, we put together a library in a small town outside of Managua. I was actually about to get into hydroponic gardening on the island when Chris called me about this."

She looked confused. "So, wait, you're telling me this is your first cut at this? Seriously? But I thought, I mean, you seemed to have this all planned out. You're so damn calm about everything all the time." She paused. "Seriously? This whole time, I thought what you were planning was...I don't know, just sort of what you do with gold finds?"

He just smiled at her. "Lainey, Mike Tyson, the old boxer, once said, 'Everyone has a plan until I punch them in the face.' When I ran the restaurant, I learned that you make a plan based on what you've got, and when everything changes after two seconds, you change with it or you're sunk. No sense crying about it, you still have the same goals, just a different plan to get there."

She looked deep in thought about that. Then she smiled happily. "So, you've been making it all up. The key to getting what you want is to make stuff up and don't panic. Geez, I guess when you got it, you just got it, huh?"

His smile changed to a look of caution. "Well, your new gal pal just opened up her phone. I assume she is calling home base in Bogotá. So I guess we'll see whether I've *got it* or not."

"Hold on a sec," Lainey said. She got up and pulled a photo of her own out of her bag. She walked it over to the Colombians and handed it to Alvaro. Julia was going back and forth with someone on the phone. Alvaro glanced down at the image and completely stopped moving. Montana wasn't sure he was even breathing. Without a backward glance, Lainey walked back over and sat down with a Cheshire cat's grin on her face.

"Okay," Montana said, "I give up, what was that?"

"Well, I decided that you're right. Everyone has a plan. I had a plan for life, but I got punched in the face. The Colombian government had a plan, too, for dealing with us. A slow plan that would take months of bureaucracy. Julia and I just punched them in the face. It's kind of a *thing.*"

65

CASA DE NARIÑO (OFFICE OF THE PRESIDENT)
Present Day
Bogotá, Colombia

The Colombian president and his three top advisors had been sitting in his office sipping coconut lemonades for two hours, waiting on an inbound phone call. Lina put all other state business on hold. They had been joined by Manuel Calderón, the chief legal counsel for the president. They all waited on the president's phone to ring. When it finally did, Lina touched the speaker button and announced the room.

"Mr. President, senior members, good evening. I am sorry to call so late. I am going to put señor Alvaro Espinosa on the phone. He is the curator of the museum in Cartagena and the head negotiator." The members heard her harsh whispering, then the woman came back on the line. "I'm sorry, Mr. President, the curator is temporarily indisposed for the moment researching some notes. Based on the images we have seen and the amounts the Americans claim to have found, the odds are good that this is what we hoped."

Julia relayed the conversation they had with the Americans and reiterated that the curator shared her belief that it was very possible this was the *San José* treasure. She closed by suggesting that, pending a visual inspection at a location the Americans hadn't yet provided, she thought it prudent for Colombia to put forth some kind of proposal for an exchange.

"What," the president asked, "makes you so sure señorita Chávez? How can we be sure this isn't the indulgence of an academic fantasy?"

"I understand your concern, Mr. President. We've just seen pictures of the find, sir. The coins are minted with the eight shields and effigy of Felipe V. That news has never been made public Mr. President. One of the coins making its way north would be one thing, sir. But over four tons of them? Obviously, we would have to verify the 26.7 gram-per-coin weight. But if that checks out, sir…"

"Did you say four tons?" The president cut her off. When she confirmed, he looked around the room at his advisors. From their blank stares, he took it that this was his decision alone. He authorized a monetary offer. "You are further authorized to make arrangements for yourself and your boss, should he find it convenient, to verify the find. If it is what we hope it is, please coordinate with Lina."

When the phone call ended, the lawyer jumped in immediately. "Mr. President, you understand what a bizarre position this presents, I trust. Even if we assume that they're telling the truth, there is no real way to authenticate with one hundred percent certainty that this is the *San José* treasure. Legally speaking, we're on dangerous ground here. If we announce we've found the *San José* treasure, the Americans will just file more suits. We're talking about twenty billion dollars here. Even their government will probably want a cut. If we pay off these two Americans who found it, nothing would prevent them from threatening to go public and exhort more money in the future. If they did go public, we would have a lot of explaining to do, not to mention that the American firm in Seattle would file a fresh lawsuit. I just don't think—"

Javier cut him off. "Yes, Mr. Calderón, we understand that nothing in life comes without risk unless we create four thousand pages of legal documents. But since a non-disclosure means less in Colombia than attorney-client privilege now means in America, I think the legal system has cancelled itself out here. We're talking about whether we can trust these two individuals, not whether a legal system can insert itself. We're trying to figure out if they're honest, and honesty is the last thing a lawyer can decide."

The two advisors went back and forth for several minutes, speaking. Lina, obviously exasperated, addressed the president.

"Mr. President, our people on the ground say that they have a good sense of these two Americans."

"Really," said the president with a touch of sarcasm in his voice, "after a three-hour meeting?"

"Yes, well, the curators have been in contact with the Americans for a while now." She starred a laser at him, willing him to shut up. "We checked out her story through our investigation firm in Miami. She checked out. Accountant, housewife, mid-divorce. Nothing of note. We're looking into the other one, the man, but so far, all we can find is half a dozen law-suits filed against him, but no real outcomes. Most of the suits were either dropped or are just pending."

"Great," the lawyer broke off his skirmish with Javi and cut into Lina. "So this is a shakedown? He's broke and trying to scam us?" He had another comment loaded up, but Lina cut him off.

"No, Mr. Calderón. He isn't the one filing the lawsuits. He isn't what we would call rich, but he has some money. My point is that we aren't dealing with US lawyers. They're both middle-aged, one an entrepreneur, the other is a part-time accountant going through a divorce. They're just normal people. Julia also thinks that the curator and the American woman are becoming seriously involved."

"Oh, *Dios mío*," the lawyer opined dramatically. "So he's in on it. Who better to rob us of money than—" He stopped when he saw Lina's face. It was flush, pinched, and real fury boiled behind her eyes. Still staring death at the lawyer, she re-addressed the president.

"Mr. President, the assistant curator, texted me while these two were arguing. The woman, Lainey, wants a long-term Colombian visa as part of whatever deal we draw up."

That shut the room up. The implication was obvious. If you were going rob Colombia, you wouldn't seek to live there. Lina locked eyes with Javier and nodded imperceptibly. "That's all the information I can provide, sir. My last thought, however, is that if we had to take a big risk, I'd rather trust a people than lawyers." She mumbled a curse at Calderón as she left the office.

He followed a minute later, making sure she was long gone.

"Thoughts?" the president asked. Javier sank back in his chair.

"Well, I have three. The first is that I think Lina just cast a spell on your chief counsel." That got a laugh. "Second, the criticism that you are *Americanized* is off base. If that were true, you wouldn't have dismissed your lawyer before making a major decision."

That too, got a laugh out of the president.

"Javi, it was clever of Lina not to let on that the assistant curator was her sister. Calderón would just accuse her of being in on the plot. I wonder how she knew not to blow the lid off that one." He stared at the ceiling while he talked, but his old friend got the message.

Javier shifted uncomfortably. "My final thought is; what if we just ignore the lawsuits? We are basically doing that now, aren't we? Our U.S. lawyers seem to just meet with each other. Surely we can find someone willing to bring up the wreck?"

"Okay, that's easy. We just ignore it." the president said, warming to the idea. "But what about the treasure? How do we bring that into the open?"

"We could wait a few months and *find* the treasure somewhere else. If there is treasure onboard at the *San José* site, and the stuff from these Americans is something else entirely, who cares? We would have verified that it's real gold, paid a pittance for it, so we win either way."

"Well, we do need to do something. We can ignore the lawsuits, but the foreign salvage firms are petrified of pissing off the Americans," the president mused to himself. "Plus, the Senator raises a new issue."

"The Senator?" Javier raised an eyebrow at his boss.

"Yes, perhaps I forgot. Some new senator, Bradshaw is her name. She called personally and read off a prepared speech threatening to sanction us if we kept ignoring the U.S. legal system."

The president's advisor didn't seem surprised. "Mr. President, the Americans believe their legal system rules over the entire planet. They don't like the fact that we've been ignoring it, so naturally they're going to try to pressure us financially. Just remember this, America has virtually no allies in South America. If they press us, we can press back. All we have to do is make a call to China, and the U.S. come back begging. Their politicians are just a theatre act. Most of them couldn't even find Colombia on a map. But I don't think it comes to that. I don't think this senator has any power in D.C., or she wouldn't be calling herself."

"True. And the downside? Suppose we just take it from these two?"

"The downside is that they go public, and we risk losing control of the whole thing. I assume its hidden somewhere. We'll know which when our team goes and inspects it, but I don't exactly see how you can steal four tons of anything without someone noticing. If they are in Nicaragua, where we suspect, that country is already on a war footing with its own internal struggles. Their tin-pot dictator is in dire need of an enemy the country can focus on. He's also in dire need of cash. If he finds them first? The two Americans have this well-timed, whether by accident or planning. Besides, they seem to be playing in good faith."

As the two sat in silence thinking, Javier's phone vibrated. He pulled it out of his pocket and read the message. He was still staring at it when the president asked, "Anything interesting?"

"Yes. Message from Lina. The sister just called her and basically verified the find. Apparently, they were given a photo of, get this, a golden pineapple. Such a pineapple appears on the unpublished inventory from the *San José*."

The two men just stared at each other.

"How on Earth..." the president started.

Javier finished his thought, "would they know to take a photo of something so peculiar and yet clearly identifiable?"

A pause. Both men looked at the door Lina had exited a few minutes earlier, then back at each other.

The president's desk phone beeped, and he touched the speaker button.

"Lina, we were just admiring your work."

"Thank you, sir, Mr. President. What if we offered the Seattle firm fifty percent of the treasure we find at the *San José* site. They pay all costs to raise her and outfit the museum...up front. We pretty much know there is nothing under that wreck."

The two men stared at each other, smiles growing wider by the second. They both shook out their right hands like they had touched something hot. It was a gesture of excitement.

Javier spoke into the phone. "Lina, even by your standards, that's genius."

"Don't thank me, sir, the Americans came up with it. It seems they're adept at this game. They also warned that once the Americans find the site empty, we should be prepared for an *expectation* lawsuit."

Both men looked perplexed. Happy perplexed, but confused, nonetheless.

"Lina, what in God's name is an expectation lawsuit?"

EPILOGUE

Chicago, Illinois
One Month Later

Tom Nickerson lasted less than a month in Cartagena. He left the country with only four thousand dollars remaining. It was enough to cover an intensive 3-week antibiotic regimen, though he would never be fully cured. Circle Security viewed the job as a success, and Nickerson failed forward into management.

Phuket, Thailand
Two Months Later

"So literally, like, I had an existential crisis, right? Working three straight years? I mean, like, who does that, right?"

The interviewer nodded along.

"My energy was just bad. I felt I wasn't inspired. Worse, I felt like I wasn't inspiring others, so I just walked away."

355

"That takes a lot of bravery."

"Sure. But it's time for me to focus on lifestyle. I'm franchising my surf-hotel concept this year. That's literally my focus. People want to share experiences and to like, co-marinate their accomplishments. We provide that space. It's going to be challenging, but whenever people tell me it can't be done, that's when I know I'm on the right track."

"Well, that's it," the interviewer said, clicking off her recorder. She signaled the camera man and closed her notebook. "Great interview, I think your perspective is really going to make an eye-catching story."

"Thanks, Amy. I've read some of your other stuff in The Online Entrepreneur. You always have great articles. And I follow your blog, too."

"Oh, thanks. Blogging is such a thankless service. I'm glad to hear some positive feedback."

They both rose from reclaimed wooden chairs in the small, beachside hotel lobby. Palm trees rustled in the open windows. Waves lapped onto the shore. Paradise in Southeast Asia.

"So, where to now, Amy? Can I show you around? You know you guys are welcome to stay another night. Totally on me, I mean, the publicity is certainly worth a free night, right?"

"Oh gosh, I WISH I could. I'm not really an influencer, though. I've got to get back to New York." Her cameraman filed out of the hotel in front of her, grabbing their luggage from behind the wicker check-in counter and loading it into a waiting taxi.

"Well, thanks again, it was great learning your story, and I can't wait to share it with the world. This is a really special hotel, sorry, lodging solution, that you've created." She stuck out her hand just as he came in for a hug.

The guy pulled up short on his hug and shook her hand. "Right on, Amy, same to you. Safe travels. Call me if you ever need to share emotions."

"I sure will," she said, making eye contact with the two bikini clad girls whispering to each other in the corner. The young hotel owner followed her gaze. He hadn't noticed them before.

Once the reporter was gone, he grabbed a beer from the fridge behind the counter and contemplated the two girls. He couldn't make out what they were saying, but just caught a whiff of an Eastern European dialect. Obviously, the girls had seen him interviewed and wanted to know what it was about.

* * *

The girls *were* Eastern European and *had*, in fact, been talking about the handsome young American. Their names were Anna Szvetnova and Milina Kuryenko. Both were in their early-twenties, and both had the slightly Slavic features of their forefathers. One blonde, one dyed redhead. Both girls were pretty in the way of their young generation, which was to say that they were flashy and photogenic, tall with small busts and waists, prominent cheekbones, pouty lips, and shiny, skimpy clothes. If you could see through the flash, neither would be considered a classic beauty.

But like nearly everyone in their age bracket, they'd mastered the flash so you couldn't see through it. They used angles and facial expressions to distract and enhance their overall appearance. Unlike previous young women, these girls had the help of tens of thousands of self-portraits to dissect and fix every flaw.

Anna and Milina had worked as mafia hackers since they were fifteen. As the young American approached, Anna turned to her best friend.

"Oyyy, Kosha, here he comes. It's your turn to service him. I take the passwords. And don't give me any crap. I had to smoke half a pound of weed to do that last flabby tech dweeb."

"With pleasure, Koska. Thank Vladimir, this one is cute. Look at those stomach muscles."

"Da. But slow him down. I need more than three minutes to crack his banks codes." They both giggled at that private joke.

"I try, but I can't help it if I am too hot for him."

"Whore." They both giggled again. "You better cool him off. We blow this, and it is back to that Gulag in Yekaterinburg with Alexei drooling all over our tits."

As the young hotelier approached them, Milina giggled a final comment to her friend. "Okay slut, we're on. And fix your accent. You mumble worse than Stalin."

They both looked up at him with pouty lips. "Hi girls, I'm Dylan Largent. Welcome to my vision of paradise."

Washington, D.C.
Three Months Later

Teri Bradshaw entered her D.C. senate office in a good frame of mind. She had just returned from a $700/a head lunch, thrown in her honor, at *To the Bone* steakhouse on K street. The Plaintiffs Association had paid her to sign her name to a new bill. It limited how long a U.S. citizen could be outside the country before they had to "check back in" at any port of entry. From there, facial recognition software would submit everyone's information to the LICE database for legal examination.

"Senator," Alice looked up as Teri walked in. "I've got a Steve Largent holding."

6.4 ounces of filet mignon turned a circle in her stomach.

What the hell could that guy want?

"Sure, Alice, put him through."

"Steve. How are you." A statement, not a question.

"Quite well, Madam Senator. Retired, actually."

Typical, she thought, *he'd blown his advantage in the first sentence.*

"Well, that's good to hear." She refused to ask if she could help this nitwit.

"Senator, you remember my son, Dylan?"

For the second time in as many minutes, her stomach flipped. "Of course," she replied flatly. "A young man with big dreams."

"Yup, that's him. Well, the thing is, when he decided to re-deploy from your outfit, he struck out on his own. I was awful proud of him. It takes a lot of courage to set out on your own at that age. Young, not much experience, not much money. That's what I call courage."

Not much money, thought Teri? *We paid that little shit over $300,000 during his disastrous tenure with us.* If it hadn't been for Teri's sharp mind, they might all be in jail now.

"Well, Senator, Dylan ran into some trouble."

Good, Teri thought, *I hope he was traveling at a high rate of speed.*

"He set up an all-inclusive resort down in Southeast Asia and really maximized his potential marketing sphere. There's even an article in one of the entrepreneur magazines."

"Steve, please cut to the chase."

Chastened, the man did. "Well, he got hacked. They stole everything. His personal accounts, the business accounts, all of it."

The thought made Teri smile. Was this happiness? Was this how happiness felt?

"Well, Steve, I'm sure he had insurance for that sort of thing." *Please let the answer be 'no'.*

The line was silent for several seconds. *Yes! This is happiness.* Teri was happy!

"Senator Bradshaw," he paused. "Teri. I'm wondering if you could do me a favor. Like the old days."

She almost laughed in her happiness. "Steve, Steve. I can make some calls on his behalf." *Never.* "But I'm afraid a position on my staff would not only disappoint him mentally and financially. Besides, the decision isn't mine to make. The taxpayers have spoken on this. I have a very limited staff size."

"Well, Teri, the thing is, I'm not really asking, if you get my drift. Back when we worked together, I'm not sure if you realize this, but it was my job to monitor the daily goings on of the TSA," he paused. "All the goings on, Senator."

For the briefest of instances, Teri almost felt fear. Or an emotion that your average person would call fear. *God damn happiness! I knew it.*

She tried to think of a way out, but her mind drew a blank. "Let me see what I can do, Steve, I'm still feeling my way around. There might be a regulation I'm unaware of." He rung off, and Teri stared at the phone.

Alice, noticing the Senator's face, knocked on the door frame and asked what was wrong.

"That was Dylan Largent's father," she said despondently. "He wants me to hire his idiot son again."

Alice looked nonplussed. "Here? In an office full of women? He'll hit on everyone in the middle of the night, Ms. Bradshaw."

Teri's eyes slowly moved from the phone to Alice's face. A devious smile crossed her face.

"Alice, please make sure you get a recording of it when it happens."

"I certainly will, Senator."

Finally, Teri thought, *I can bury that family once and for all.*

Charlotte, North Carolina
Four Months Later

"Look, I'm sorry, Alan. We've filed half a dozen lawsuits against your wife, but we can't proceed with any of them. She seems to have completely disappeared. It's a real shame, too. I was looking forward to seeing if we could win a divorce case under the tort of failed marriage expectation."

Dunaway listened as he sat on the floor of his nearly empty apartment, a cheap rental north of town. The news from his divorce lawyer further depressed him. He stared out the window as his fellow residents scurried off to work. Half the complex's tenants appeared to be single men in the middle of divorce purgatory. He couldn't get a job while his disbarment proceedings ground toward conclusion. Teri had reported him to the police for harassment. Even his daughter wouldn't take his calls.

"So, Alan, there is one last thing. I'm sorry to be the bearer of bad news, or, well, worse news, but uh, my firm made me file a *lis pendens* against your house. The *lis pendens* filing used up the last of the retainer Ms. Bradshaw paid for. We had to take steps to ensure that our fees are covered for the coming divorce proceedings. It's standard stuff, you understand."

Cartagena, Colombia
Five Months Later

Lainey's smartphone pulled her out of a deep sleep. She rolled over, hoping that Alvaro would wrap his arm around her, but his side of the bed was empty and cool. He must have already left for work. She listened to the air conditioning hum for a few minutes while the phone stopped vibrating. She looked out the window at another of an endless procession of perfect days. Her phone vibrated again. She reached over and pulled it to her ear, still wrapped in the cool bed sheets.

"*Allo.*"

"*Hola, señora, como estas,*" a familiar male voice boomed back.

She sat up quickly and smiled into the phone.

"Montanaaaaa! I'm so glad to hear from you." She switched to Spanish. "How are things on the Island? How is Chris? Did he get his family moved? You have a thousand things to tell me about! I know Julia flew up there a few weeks ago, so you know I'm gonna need to hear about that, too."

Montana laughed. "My, my, look who went native. You're a quick study. Language and everything. Did you ever bother going back to the States?"

"No." Her tone got a bit more solemn. "No. I took your advice and just walked away. I'm glad I did, too. I don't think I've stopped smiling for four months. Or five…I'm not even sure how long I've been down here."

"Hah. I know that feeling. Well, that's great to hear, Lainey. Good choice. And the visa? They came through with it?"

"Oh, they came through with it and then some. Full dual citizenship. To go with my three million dollars, thank you very much. I haven't spent any yet, though. I'm waiting for the perfect buy." She laughed. "I do have to find something to do, though. This whole retiree thing just isn't my scene. I can't just sit on the beach every day. I mean, I can, but you know."

"As for the cash, you earned it. As for the boredom, I think I can help there."

Lainey's head leaned back onto the headboard and she closed her eyes. Whatever Montana was up to, she could just about guarantee it would be interesting. "Okay, lemme have it."

"Well, you remember that guy, Gordo, right? One of the diggers?"

"Oh, of course. The chubby guy whose ass I slapped. He was great. Mr. Dour Consequences."

"That's him. Right. Well, Gordo has a problem. I assume being in Colombia you're hip to the disaster that is going on in Venezuela?"

Lainey knew the situation over there was getting dire. Millions of refugees had poured out of the country searching for jobs, food, and even drinkable water. The economy had tanked and their currency was completely useless. "Yuk. Yeah, it's awful. Why?"

"Well, Gordo's wife isn't actually Nicaraguan. She's Venezuelan by birth. So, about three weeks ago, Gordo loaded up some of his loot and went down there in the hopes of buying his wife's family passage out of there."

"Oh God. No. Please don't tell me…"

"No, no, nothing like that. Well, sort of. Her family lives in some dusty, one-horse town up by the northern border with Colombia. The local cops got wind of some rich guy showing up in town and, well, long story short, they dropped our boy in a Venezuelan clink and stole the cash."

Lainey's heart sank. "God, Montana, that's so awful. That place is a black hole now. No real information is getting in or out."

"Yeah, we know. So, thing is...Chris and I are gonna go get him out." A pause. "You want in?"

"You mean, like, you're going to bribe his way out? Montana, I'm not sure..." She trailed off. "No. N-O. Montana, a bribe wouldn't work. They'd just do the same thing to whomever tried it. These aren't calm people playing a long con. These are desperate, corrupt cops with no oversight. They're stealing whatever they can to buy food, or more likely, booze. How exactly are you planning to get him out?" she asked.

Montana stayed silent on the other end of the line.

The silence told her everything. She put her hand over her forehead. "Jesus, how does this stuff find you?"

All she heard was the hiss of a bad connection.

"So, you want me to leave my totally gorgeous, younger boyfriend, my city by the sea where it never rains, and help you and Chris illegally cross the border into Venezuela, a country that has basically descended into medieval chaos, so that you can engineer a spaghetti-western-style jailbreak?"

"Well," he said finally, and she could hear that damn smile in his voice, "you said you were bored."

ACKNOWLEDGEMENTS

The Spanish treasure galleon *San José* is a real ship. She was sunk with 600 souls and, we think, 4 tons of gold off the coast of Cartagena in 1708. The site was discovered in 2014. I fictionalized my research of the events to fit the narrative of this story. There is more detailed historical fiction about these events available on my website at vicadams.com. Sadly, and perhaps not surprisingly, the lawsuits surrounding her discovery are real, too. The rest of them are mostly drawn from 1st or 2nd hand accounts of actual lawsuits. Somehow, I became a repository of legal horror stories for other business owners I know. To those of you who shared, I hope you get some closure knowing that at the very least, the stories are out there.

Operationally, I will be forever grateful to Antoinette Kuritz for being the first person to have some faith. Her crew brought this project out of the shadows. Gwyn Snider and Brian Sheehy were masterful bringing my limited creativity to life on the cover. Likewise, my editors were fantastic, and any errors in this book are the result of my tinkering.

Creatively, I owe much to my family, friends, former colleagues, and employees. I would love to thank my big brothers emotionally, but that just wouldn't be us. Without each other to lean on, we'd all be digging ditches. We'd laugh a lot and we'd be good at it, but mom and dad would be pissed. Thanks for a billion hours of comedic cynicism. And thanks for always picking up the phone.

No one has been luckier in their choice of friends, so a big thanks to the Auburn crew as well. Someone tell Dumb to lay off, a book has finally been written. Kate, stay strong. To Nancy, DeeAnna, Mark C, Jaylene, Hart, Donnie G, Melissa, Mary Nell, Holly, Z, Chris G (in exile), and everyone else who kept the ship together while I tried to crash it, thank you. Thank you more than I could ever say. To Josh and Reid-you're diamonds in a sea of filth.

I would also like to thank the people of Nicaragua. Not all of them, obviously. I could do without the people in power currently. The rest are the kindest, most welcoming, and darkly funny people I've met. Thanks for the shelter, friendship, and Band-Aids. I hope that one day, things will change. Special thanks also go to the many Colombians who have treated me just as well. I will forever be in awe of your country, your people, and your ability to dance. I tell everyone I know to visit Cartagena just once. I just hope you don't kick me out for spilling the secret.